The Northern Lights Lodge

Julie Caplin

A division of HarperCollins*Publishers*
www.harpercollins.co.uk

Harper*Impulse* an imprint of
HarperCollins*Publishers*
The News Building
1 London Bridge Street
London SE1 9GF

www.harpercollins.co.uk

This paperback edition 2019
3
First published in Great Britain in ebook format by
HarperCollins*Publishers* 2019

A catalogue record for this book
is available from the British Library

ISBN: 9780008323677

This novel is entirely a work of fiction.
The names, characters and incidents portrayed in it are
the work of the author's imagination. Any resemblance to
actual persons, living or dead, events or localities is
entirely coincidental.

Set in Birka by Palimpsest Book Production Limited,
Falkirk, Stirlingshire

Printed and bound in Great Britain by
CPI Group (UK) Ltd, Croydon CR0 4YY

For the original Viking Princess, my marvellous editor, Charlotte Ledger, who probably wouldn't have been a very good Viking, certainly not at the pillaging, because she's far too kind, warm-hearted and generous.

Chapter 1

Bath

'I'm afraid there's still nothing. Like I said last week and the week before. You have to understand it's a difficult time. The economy isn't great. People aren't moving around as much.' This was said with a mealy-mouthed, pseudo-sympathetic smile and shark-like small eyes that slid away from meeting Lucy's as if being unemployable was catching.

Difficult time? Hello! Lucy was currently writing the bloody book on it being a difficult time. She wanted to grab the recruitment consultant by the throat and shake her. Instead she shifted in her seat opposite the other woman in the brightly lit office, with its trendy furniture and state-of-the-art Apple Mac screen taking up most of the desk, trying to look serene instead of utterly panic stricken.

The other girl was now dubiously eying Lucy's lacklustre blonde hair, which hung in limp rats' tails, unable to hide an expression of horrified curiosity. Lucy swallowed and felt the ever-present tears start to well up. You try styling

1

hair that's been coming out in handfuls for the last three weeks, she thought. She didn't dare wash it more than once a week because seeing the plug hole full of blonde strands seemed even more terrifying than all the other crap going on in her life right now. Things must be bad when your own hair started jumping ship.

Lucy could feel her lip curl. Oh God, any minute she might snarl like a wild animal. It was increasingly tricky to try and behave like a normal human being these days and, at this moment, a particular challenge as she looked back across the desk at the girl sitting there in her cherry red, fitted power suit, with her perfect glossy bob and darling plum gel nails. The epitome of success. What someone looked like when they were going places. When their career was on the up rather than going down the swanny faster than a canoe going over the Niagara Falls.

With a sigh, Lucy swallowed hard and forced herself to calm down. For the last twenty minutes, she'd fought the temptation to grab Little Miss Professional by the lapels and plead, 'there must be a job somewhere for me'. She'd had to resort to sitting on her hands with her shoulders hunched up by her ears as she listened to the same spiel that she'd heard in the last ten other recruitment consultant offices; the market was down, people weren't recruiting, no one had a career for life these days. And *they* didn't need to bloody tell Lucy that, she'd discovered that inconvenient fact the hard way. *But*, whined the persistent voice in her head, she was looking for a job in hospitality, the whine became shriller and more insistent, *there were always jobs in hospitality*.

'Perhaps if you could...' The girl tried to give her an encouraging smile, which didn't disguise her raging curiosity, 'you know ... get some more recent references.'

Lucy shook her head feeling the familiar leaden lump of despair threaten to rise and choke her. The girl tried to look sympathetic, while taking a surreptitious glance of her watch. No doubt she had an infinitely more placeable candidate for her next appointment. Someone whose CV was dripping with recommendations from her last boss and hadn't had her shame shared among all in her professional world.

'There must be something.' Desperation chased the words out with the glee of naughty fairies escaping. 'I don't mind taking a step down. You've seen how much experience I've got.' She heard herself utter the fateful words, which she'd promised herself, no matter how bad things got, she wouldn't say. 'I'll take anything.'

The girl arched her eyebrow as if wanting her to elaborate on *anything*.

'Well, almost anything,' said Lucy, suddenly horribly aware that *anything* covered an awful lot of situations, vacant or otherwise and this woman's income was derived from placing people.

'W...ellll, there is one thing.' She gave an elegant shrug.

Now Lucy regretted the 'almost anything.' What was she opening herself up to? She didn't know this woman. How could she trust her?

'It's ... erm ... a big step down. A temporary to permanent contract. On a two-month trial. And out of the country.'

'I don't mind out of the country,' Lucy said, sitting upright. A two-month trial was good. Actually, out of the country would be bloody marvellous. Why the hell hadn't she thought of that before? A complete escape. An escape from the sly sniggers behind her back from her former colleagues, the *that's her, you know the one who* furtive looks, the *we know what you've done* secretive smiles and the occasional *I bet you would* knowing leer, which made her feel positively sick.

The girl stood up and strode several paces to the corner of her office to rummage in a small stack of blue files on the beech console table behind her. Even from here Lucy could tell that they were the barrel scrapings, those jobs that had been consigned to the 'we'll never fill these in a month of Sundays, Mondays, Tuesdays and the rest' category. With a tug, a dog-eared folder was pulled out from near the bottom of the pile. Lucy knew how that poor file felt. Overlooked and cast aside.

'Hmm.'

Lucy waited, sitting on the edge of her seat craning her neck slightly trying to read the words as the other girl trailed a glossy nail down the A4 page. 'Hmm. OK. Mmm.'

Lucy clenched her fingers, glad that they were jammed between her thighs and the chair.

With a half-concealed tut, the girl closed the file and looked worriedly at her. 'Well it's something. Anything.' Her expression faltered. 'You're very over-qualified. It's in...' and proceeded to say something that sounded rather like a sneeze.

'Sorry?'

'Hvolsvöllur,' she repeated. Lucy knew she'd looked the pronunciation up.

'Right,' Lucy nodded. 'And where exactly is...' she nodded at the file, guessing that it was from the sound of the word somewhere in Eastern Europe.

'Iceland.'

'Iceland!'

'Yes,' the other woman carried on hurriedly. 'It's a two-month post for a trial period in a small lodge in Hvolsvöllur, which is only an hour and half's drive out of Reykjavik. An immediate start. Shall I call them, send your details over?' Her words spilled out with sudden, unexpected commission bonus enthusiasm.

Iceland. Not somewhere she'd ever considered going. Wasn't it horribly cold there? And practically dark all the time. Her ideal climate was hot with tepid bathwater temperature seas. An hour and half's drive out of Reykjavik sounded ominous, the sub text being *in the middle of nowhere.* Lucy gnawed at her lip.

'I don't speak the language.'

'Oh you don't need to worry about that. They all speak English,' said the girl blithely before adding, 'of course, they might not want you ... you know.' Her smile dimmed in silent sympathy. 'I don't want to get your hopes up. But I will tell them what good previous experience you've had.

It's the ... er recent references might be a problem. You've got a bit of a gap.'

'Perhaps you could say I've been taking a sabbatical.' said Lucy, hurriedly.

The girl nodded, plastering her smile back on. 'Let me go and make the call.' She stood up from her desk looking a little awkward. Lucy suspected she usually made her calls from the phone on the desk but wanted some privacy to try and persuade the client to take someone on with a three-year gap on their CV.

For the last year, she'd been Assistant Manager for the flagship hotel of a big chain in Manchester having worked her way up through the company during the previous two, until said big chain sacked her for gross misconduct. Lucy gritted her teeth at the memory of the heartless HR storm trooper of a woman Head Office had sent up from leafy Surrey to deliver the killer blow. Of course, they hadn't sacked Chris.

For a minute, self-pity threatened to swamp her. Job application after job application, rejection after rejection. Not one single interview. Every time she got another rejection, the bleakness grew, like a shadow spreading in the setting sun. Her bank account was running on empty, she was rapidly running out of sofas to bunk on and, the end of the road, holing up in Mum and Dad's two up, two down terrace in Portsmouth, was looming large. And there was no way she could do that. Mum would want to know why. The truth would kill Dad. Lucy gnawed at her lip, opening up the ulcerous sore already there. For some reason, she'd taken to chewing the inside of her lip and it had become a horrible habit over the last few months that she couldn't seem to shake.

'It ... it is live in?' asked Lucy hurriedly as the girl was about to leave the room.

'Oh Lord yes, no one in their right mind would look at it without accommodation.' Her eyes suddenly widened as she realised she'd probably said far too much. 'I'll be right back.' Rather tellingly she'd scooped up the file to take it with her leaving Lucy alone in the office.

'Are you sure it's the right thing to do?' asked Lucy's best friend, Daisy, shaking her head, an expression of diffidence on her face, as she stared at her laptop screen. 'You're massively over-qualified for this. It's only got forty-four rooms,' she paused. 'And you hate snow.'

'I don't hate snow. It's not so nice in the city when it goes all slushy and black,' protested Lucy thinking of childhood snow. That first winter fall when it was clean and crisp and begging for virgin footsteps, snowball fights and snowmen.

'Hmm,' said Daisy, disbelieving. 'You'd only just acclimatized to Manchester. Iceland will be far worse. Although,' she wrinkled her forehead, 'it does look very nice.'

Lucy nodded, nice was an understatement. According to the gallery of photos on this website it looked gorgeous. The outside, with its turfed rooves and hotchpotch of buildings was dwarfed on one side by a snow-covered hillside strewn with the dark shadows of craggy outcrops and, on the other, a wild rocky coastline where foamy waves crashed onto a narrow shingle beach. The beautifully photographed interior showed stunning views from each of the lodge's windows, several huge fireplaces and cosily arranged nooks with furniture which invited you to curl up and doze in front of a warming hearth. It all looked fabulous. Which begged the question, why hadn't the job of General Manager been snapped up before? Her teeth caught at that damn sore on the inside of her lip and she winced.

Daisy mistaking her sudden intake of breath, gave her a stern look. 'You don't have to take it. You know you can stay here as long as you like.' Her eyes softened. 'I really don't mind. I love having you.'

Tempting as it would have been to stay in Daisy's cute one man flat in Bath, Lucy had to take this job. 'Dais, I can't sleep on your sofa forever and if I don't go for this job, it probably will be forever.'

A familiar gloom threatened to descend again, dragging her down. She swallowed, ignoring the panic beating like the wings of a bird inside her heart and glanced at Daisy. How did you admit that you no longer thought you were capable of doing a job? She was so trapped by indecision at every turn, constantly questioning her own judgement.

Should she go for this job? The brief Skype interview seemed a mere formality, a quick check to make sure that she didn't have two heads or anything, conducted by a woman who hadn't even bothered to introduce herself and didn't seem to care as to whether she could do the job.

Which was just as well because all of Lucy's stuffing had been well and truly knocked out of her, and if she'd had to sell herself she'd have withered on the spot.

Daisy put an arm on hers jolting her from her thoughts. 'Don't take it. Something else will come up. You can create your own—'

Lucy raised a hand to stop one of Daisy's characteristic pithy quotes and lifted a pertinent eyebrow and her best friend had the grace to smile weakly.

'Ok.' Daisy clenched her petite little hands into fists. 'But it's so f-fu flipping unfair. It wasn't your fault.'

'Daisy Jackson! Were you about to swear then?'

A dimple appeared in the other girl's cheek as she smiled like a naughty pixie. 'Might have been. But it makes me so mad. It's so...' She made a 'grrr' sound.

'You see, another reason I need to get out of here. You're making animal noises too. I'm a bad influence. And it was my fault. No one's fault but my own ... and Chris's for being a grade A shit.'

'It wasn't your fault! Stop saying that,' said Daisy, her voice shrill with indignation. 'You can't blame yourself. It's Chris's fault. Although I still can't believe he did it. Why?'

Lucy's jaw tightened, they'd been over this a thousand times over the course of the last sixty-two days and numerous glasses of prosecco, wine, gin and vodka. Rumination and alcohol hadn't provided any answers. It was her fault, for being so utterly, utterly stupid. She couldn't believe how badly she'd got it wrong. Four years. A flat together. Working for the same company. She thought she

9

knew Chris. One thing was for sure ... she would never trust another man as long as she lived.

'It doesn't matter "why" he did it. I need to move on and I need a job.' Lucy gritted her teeth. Going to Iceland was a terrible idea but she was all out of options.

Chapter 2

Paris

'Here you go.' Nina slid the coffee cup across the table towards Alex and handed him a plate with a gorgeous looking confection on it. 'On the house. I want your opinion, it's my latest idea. Raspberry Ripple Éclair. It might cheer you up,' she added with a smile that was underpinned with a smattering of sympathy.

Alex felt a touch of regret. Nina was lovely. His plans to get to know her better had been well and truly scuppered by a prior claim. Sadly, she'd been in love with his mate Sebastian forever and he had to admit as he looked at her now, requited love had put a gorgeous bloom on her cheeks. You couldn't begrudge anyone that shiny happiness. He took a bite of the éclair and groaned.

'Wow, that's good, Nina. Really good.'

'Excellent, now are you going to tell me what's wrong?'

He rolled his eyes, as she pulled up a chair and sat down ignoring the outraged glare from Marcel, the manager of the patisserie. Nina might officially run the place, but

Marcel definitely wore the trousers in this business partnership, ruling the roost with silent, stern officiousness.

'Who said anything was wrong? asked Alex, trying to sound blithe.

'I have brothers. I have a Sebastian. I know when the weight of the world is bowing those broad shoulders. You have a distinct droop about you,' she declared with a knowing grin.

He glanced left to right at both shoulders and she gave a peal of laughter.

'I'm a wee bit pissed off. The new hotel opening is delayed and the manager lined up to take over from me has already rocked up.' Alex was due to take over the running of a brand new, minimalist, uber trendy boutique hotel on the other side of Paris any day now, except during the renovations the builders had discovered bones in the cellars. Human bones. Thankfully they were at least two hundred years old but it had still caused a humungous delay.

'You can take a holiday then,' said Nina.

'You'd have thought so but my boss in his infinite wisdom has decided to give me a temporary posting.'

'You're not leaving Paris, are you?' Her pretty mouth pouted and Alex felt another one of those little pangs of regret. Nice guys did finish last. He'd well and truly missed the boat with her.

'Only for a couple of months. Quentin wants me to go and check out a hotel he's planning to buy. He wants me to assess the viability of the place and put together a report on my recommendations to turn it into one of our boutique hotels.'

'Where are you going?'

'Iceland.'

Nina's mouth dropped open into a little 'o'. 'I thought you meant somewhere else in France. Not another country. Well that doesn't sound so bad. Isn't Iceland supposed to be beautiful with all sorts of amazing natural wonders? Bubbling geysers, hot springs and glaciers? Being Scottish I'd have thought you'd like the idea.'

'No problem with going to Iceland. It's the job Quentin wants me to do, which isn't that great.'

'I thought you said you had to put together a report.'

'Yes, but it includes reporting on the current general manager and how the place is being run without telling them who I am. It doesn't sit right with me. The last thing I want to do is be a spy.'

'James Bond,' said Nina, sitting up straighter. 'You've got the Sean Connery accent.' She launched into a dreadful impersonation of his Edinburgh accent. 'Ah Moneypenny.'

'Well, that must mean I'm qualified,' Alex quipped, amused by Nina's enthusiasm, his spirits temporarily lifted.

He was still rattled by the meeting and the conversation with his boss when he'd raised a certain disquiet about not telling the manager why he was there. His boss's response to that had stung. 'Thing is Alex, nice guys finish last. This is business. Pure and simple. I need someone to report back, warts and all. Without anyone sugar coating it. It's far easier if the staff don't know who you are. I'm not hearing great things about the management of the place. The recent TripAdvisor reviews have been shockers. With you on the ground, I'll get a much better picture. You've got a good eye and you'll be able to tell me what needs doing to sort the place out, what the staff are like and whether I can keep them or fire their sorry arses.'

The 'nice guys finish last' bit kept going around in his head. What was wrong with being a nice guy? Besides, he could be tough when a situation needed it. Last week he'd thrown a customer out of the hotel's a la carte restaurant for pinching one of the waitress's bums, faced down a belligerent delivery driver, who reversed into the hotel gates leaving a hole big enough to drive a herd of cows through, and fired the pastry chef he'd caught hurling a frying pan at the young, barely out of school, bus boy.

'Alex is going to be James Bond,' announced Nina as Sebastian walked in and put his arm around her, placing a confident, lazy kiss on her lips, completely ignoring Alex.

'Hi gorgeous, mmm you taste of raspberries and deliciousness.' He went back for a second longer, lingering kiss, which had Alex rolling his eyes.

At last Sebastian drew back from Nina and turned to face him. Alex's mouth twitched, he'd got the message loud and clear.

'Bond, James Bond?' Sebastian lifted a perfect Roger Moore eyebrow.

'No, Nina's exaggerating my undercover credentials. I've been asked to do some recon work. Quentin Oliver is looking at buying a place in Iceland and as I'm between hotels at the moment, I've been asked to go and survey the place. On the ground as it were.' Sebastian would laugh his head off if he mentioned he was thinking of going under-cover as a barman!

'Sounds like a great idea,' said Sebastian with a sudden grin, which Alex could guess had a lot to do with how far away Iceland was. Although he needn't have been worried, Alex had backed right off when he realised that Nina had been in love with Sebastian since she was eighteen. For a second, he wondered what might have happened, if he'd put up more of a fight for her, if he'd really thought he had a chance. Had he bowed out because it made it easier on Nina?

As he thought about it, he gave Sebastian a broad smile. Maybe the best man had won. Nina adored Sebastian and she was good for him. Possibly too good. But Alex had never seen Sebastian so settled and happy.

'I have no problem with going to Iceland. Like Nina said, I'm used to a northern climate. It's the undercover element of it I'm not so keen on.'

'Why not?' Sebastian shrugged. 'You need to remember it's business. It's easy to be ruthless when something you really want is at stake.' Was there a knowing look in his eye as he stared at Alex?

And then he flashed Alex a warm, approving smile. 'There's no one else I'd rather have on the team, mate. I know why Quentin Oliver's asked you. Better that it's you. You've got integrity and you don't bullshit anyone. You don't suffer fools that's for sure. If the current manager is an idiot, are you seriously going to have a problem reporting back on that? You hate coasters and people who don't pull their weight. If this guy is any good, he's got nothing to worry about.'

Chapter 3

Iceland

Lucy's thoughts came back to haunt her as she stood outside the firmly closed front doors of The Northern Lights Lodge, in total darkness, her breath huffing out in a great cloud of white as the cold nipped at every last one of her extremities. This was a terrible idea. Why had she listened to a perky recruitment consultant with her eye on commission? Why hadn't she remained in Bath with Daisy?

She almost laughed out loud, mild hysteria threatening to take hold of her. *Because you were desperate. You knew it was a terrible idea and you were right. You should have trusted your own instinct.*

Blinking furiously, because bloody tears were not going to help, she hammered on the door for the third time, stupidly crossing her fingers, as if that would help, and praying that someone would answer. Why had she let the taxi driver drop her at the bottom of the path? She should have made him wait, but no the taxi had roared off, twin brake lights vanishing into the distance leaving her totally alone. On the journey here, she'd seen two cars. Two! Both going the other way.

Why hadn't she stayed the night in Reykjavik?

With a shiver, she glanced around into the total blackness, the only light from her phone. There was absolutely no sign of life, not human anyway. As she got out of the taxi, after a two-hour drive in the pouring rain – it hadn't stopped raining since the plane landed in Reykjavik three hours ago – there'd been a low growl to her left and the glow of yellow eyes when she swung the torch on her phone in that direction. Did they have wolves in Iceland? The pathetic beam of light caught the flash of a tail as something slunk away which made her extra wary as she'd traipsed up the path, picking her way over the stones, her suitcase complaining with each jolt and dip.

Now standing outside the wooden doors trying to peer through the side lights, she could see the place was in complete darkness. Above her she could hear the rustle of the grass on the roof, or was that more creatures lurking? There were far too many *Lord of the Rings* images dancing fancifully in her head. With a last burst of energy, she wrenched on the ornate iron scrolled door handle, with that fruitless bang-your-head-against-a-wall hope that she'd got it wrong and the door had been open all along, even though she'd tried it umpteen times already. So much for everyone leaving their doors open, which she was sure she'd read somewhere about the country. She banged her fist on the door, before looking at her phone and the rapidly dwindling battery. Sinking to the floor, she slipped off her gloves, which weren't going to cut it in this climate, and phoned the only contact number she had. Mr Pedersen, the hotel owner, currently in Finland, was the man who'd officially hired her, but he'd given her the number of one of the hotel employees. For the second time, her call went straight through to voicemail and this time she listened with growing despair to the message in a stream of what she assumed was Icelandic, a volley of harsh syllables and guttural sounds.

Taking a deep breath and hoping she didn't sound too panicky she spoke. 'Hi, this is Lucy Smart from the UK. It's eleven o'clock and I've arrived, but there doesn't seem to be anyone here.' She'd sent an email with her date of arrival and had received one back in confirmation from someone called Hekla Gunnesdóttir. Her hand shook, her grip so tight on the phone. 'I wonder if you could give me a call back,' she asked with restrained politeness when what she really wanted to say was, '*Where the fuck is everyone?*'

Of course, she was polite, she thought grimly, she was going to have to work with these people. Making a good impression was imperative. More than a good impression, she needed them to keep her on after the two months. She had to survive at least a year here to make her CV viable again. Besides, she had nowhere else to go.

Ten minutes, later after anxiously watching her phone as she paced up and down to keep warm, the battery died. The rain had stopped which was little consolation as she considered her options, all of which seemed in short supply. One; walk down the road and see if she could find any kind of settlement nearby despite the complete absence of any lights in the near vicinity, two; stay put and hope that someone had listened to her message or three; break in.

Scudding clouds streamed across the night sky, periodically revealing pockets of a star laden universe. The number of the pinprick lights was astonishing. No light pollution here. Lucy had never seen so many stars and in one brief break in the clouds thought she might have seen a shooting star, although she was so cold, she also might have been starting to hallucinate.

Now that her eyes had adjusted to the dark and the cold had numbed her fingers and toes, she decided to circle the building. Maybe she'd find an unlocked door. With a shiver she walked along the front of the building. How long did she wait before she picked up a stone and broke one of those amazing floor-to-ceiling windows?

As she rounded the corner of the hotel, the ground level started to fall away quite steeply and she stumbled as her ankles felt the sharpness of the sudden decline. She could, however, see a faint glow as if there was a light on around the next corner.

Carefully she began to pick her way down the steep slope, slipping and sliding on loose scree. Each crunch and skitter of stone echoed noisily, making her jumpy and disorientated. Every now and then she paused and thought she could hear water lapping but the sound bounced around in the darkness and she couldn't quite determine where it was coming from. Cocking her head to one side, she listened carefully and took another few steps forward. Ah, wood. She was on some sort of decking and then she stepped into thin air.

As she stumbled forward, arms flailing like spokes on a spinning bicycle wheel, she registered the glint of water and tensed for the cold as she pitched in face first.

If it weren't for the weight of her clothes and the unexpected shock of falling headfirst into shoulder deep water, the warm, no, piping hot, water, might have been quite pleasant, except for the rush of water up her nose and swallowing a great mouthful. Yeuch, Lucy shoved her head up to the surface spluttering and gagging. That was disgusting. Her head felt even colder in contrast to the cosy cocoon from the neck downwards. The heat flooded Lucy's fingers and ears with sharp pain, like pins and needles, as a flashlight came bobbing around the corner and tracked its way across the stony ground to land full on her face.

'No using the hot springs after nine p.m.,' called a deep voice, brimming with amusement as the light came closer and closer. Lucy muttered to herself, 'Kill me now,' feeling at a distinct disadvantage under the nearing dancing spotlight.

Her sodden parka had wrapped itself around her like a duvet weighted with rocks, her ankle boots were almost floating away with each step and her jeans had a stranglehold on her legs as she floundered towards the edge.

'Here, there are steps,' said a second singsong voice with a musical up and down inflection, using the torch to guide her along the wooden edge towards a set of steps that rose up out of the water.

Lucy put her shoulders back and waded through the water towards the wooden handrail with as much dignity as she could muster given she was close to tears.

Lights suddenly came on illuminating the whole area. She was in the equivalent of a small swimming-pool sized hot tub surrounded by wooden decking, with two sets of steps descending into the water. Above her on the side were two figures, wrapped up against the cold night air.

'Are you alright?' asked the taller of the two, crossing quickly and holding out a hand, stepping forward to grasp her arm and help her counter balance the weight of her ten-ton coat.

Kind eyes, thought Lucy as she caught a glimpse of concerned brown eyes above a tartan woollen scarf while she let him haul her up the steps.

'Let's get you inside quickly before you start to chill down. That heat isn't going to last long.' Kind voice too. The slight Scottish burr was soft and gentle, a rather wonderful contrast to his firm and decisive hold as he pulled her forward and steered her off the decking.

'Thank you,' she said, subtly shaking off his grasp, even though for some contrary reason she didn't want to. Kindness had been in short supply in her world for a while. 'I'm fine,' she added, with more of a sharp bite to her voice.

After everything she'd been through this year, she was never taking anything at face value again. Kind was as kind did or whatever the phrase was.

'I'm Alex.' The man's hand still hovered by her side as if ready to catch her. 'And this is Hekla. I'm so sorry there was no one to check you in. We weren't expecting any guests today.'

'No. It is most strange. Did you have a booking?' asked Hekla, in her glorious musical voice.

'I'm not a guest. I'm...' Lucy swallowed. No crying. Dripping from head to toe had put her at enough of a disadvantage as it was. 'I'm the new manager, Lucy Smart.' Automatically she lifted a business-like hand and then dropped it quickly as she realised how ridiculous it must look, with water dripping from her sleeves.

'Oh!' The girl's voice echoed with surprise. 'But you are not expected until next week.'

'Everything was confirmed by email,' said Lucy, her words quick and sharp with sudden panic, not wanting them to think she was disorganised or all over the place.

'But we had a phone call yesterday saying your plans had changed and you would be coming next week.'

'Well that wasn't me,' said Lucy.

'Must be the huldufólk making trouble,' said Hekla with a straight face, nodding. 'But you're here now and we'd better get you inside, quickly,' she paused and then added with a mischievous twinkle that once upon a time Lucy might have been charmed by, 'it is usually best to wait until daylight before using the hot springs.'

'I've been waiting to get inside for the last half hour,' muttered Lucy, wincing as her feet splish-sploshed on the wooden decking, the water squelching out of her favourite boots and great clouds of steam rising from her sodden clothing. Just bloody marvellous. These people were clearly her new colleagues. So much for making a good impression from the start.

'But the door is open,' said Hekla. 'It's always open.' Her stalwart, sure declaration made Lucy feel doubly stupid. The door had definitely been locked. Hadn't it? She was sure. She'd tried everything.

'Well it wasn't today,' snarled Lucy in a heartfelt undertone. 'Why else would I would be wandering around in the dark, trying to find my way in?' The door had definitely been locked. Her sharp rebuttal was ruined when she slipped on the decking. She pinched her lips and ducked her head as if concentrating on her footing feeling unaccountably tearful all of a sudden.

'Hey, let me give you a hand,' Alex's voice lowered, his tone gentle. She jerked her eyeline to meet his. Warmth and compassion lit those kind eyes as he took her elbow. For what seemed far too long they held hers with a serious steady gaze, as if he could see right through her to the constant shadow of misery that resided in her chest. When he gave her a reassuring smile, his eyes never leaving her face, she felt a funny salmon leap in her stomach.

Sense warred with self-preservation and much as she wanted to shake off the firm gentle support of his arm, that prickle of awareness had unnerved her. Lucy let him guide her back up the slope, trying hard not to like the feeling of letting someone else look after her for a change.

Slightly open-mouthed Lucy peeled off her soggy clothes, gazing around the cosy apartment room as she curled her toes into the soft fluff of one of the sheepskin rugs dotting the wide-planked honey-coloured wooden floor. This was some staff accommodation and the bathroom was to die for. Steam was already billowing from the huge walk in shower with its bucket head sprinkler.

Hekla, who with her flaxen hair clearly came from Viking Princess stock, had ushered Lucy through the hotel leaving her with an impression of wooden beams, airy, wide spaces and huge plate glass windows. Her new colleague was talking nineteen to the dozen disclosing a barrage of information, only some of which Lucy took in. Alex was the head barman. Hekla was the assistant manager. The hotel was half full, or was that half empty? The northern lights season was about to start. Other names, some of which sounded as if they were straight from Norse mythology, were mentioned; Brynja, Olafur, Gunnar, Erik, Kristjan, Elin, Freya.

Lucy padded into the bathroom that was, thankfully, beautifully warm. It had a distinct, luxury designer feel to it with its rustic wooden shelf holding a round sink, black floor tiles and a big square shower cubicle.

She stepped into the hot shower and let her head droop as the delicious hot water rained down on her wet hair. *Way to go Lucy. How to impress your new colleagues.* Why had they thought she was coming next week? They must think she was a complete flake. She couldn't have got the date wrong, could she? Admittedly she'd been all over the place recently and her once famed organisational skills had done a bunk in the last few months, but getting the date wrong? No, she couldn't have done. And the door had definitely, definitely been locked.

After the bliss of the shower, and a brisk rub with a towel that was perfectly fluffy and soft, Lucy felt a hell of a lot better, although it was still depressing to see another few handfuls of hair circling the plug hole of the shower.

Carefully she dried it, fearful of losing any more, and deliberately avoided looking at herself in the mirror, knowing only too well she'd see Morticia's second cousin staring back at her. Over the last few months, gaunt shadows had set in, shading her cheekbones, and dark circles had taken up residence, underscoring her eyes with purple black bruises, making her look part panda and part ghoul. Along with the hollowing of her features, a constant queasiness had settled in her stomach.

Her scooped out face seemed to reflect the complete shambles her life had become. Wincing, she put down the hairdryer and looked beyond her reflection through the doorway of the bathroom to the wonderful temptation of the double bed in the other room with its thick white cotton duvet and soft blue throw.

Before she gave into tiredness, she quickly explored the living space, her home for the next two months. Despite feeling trampled on, her spirits couldn't help but lift. The wooden-framed double bed faced a large open fireplace smack bang in the middle of a run of picture windows, which was an unusual but striking design feature that she'd never seen before. Maybe it was an Icelandic thing. The imposing hearth was built of rustic stone, with an internal chimney breast that rose the full height of the room to the triangular peak of the sloping wooden ceiling. It gave the space a lofty open feeling, but the honey-coloured wood on the walls and ceilings along with the soft rugs and the colourful woven fabric wall hangings saved the room from feeling cold.

Over to the right was a small lounge area with a neat two-man sofa, draped in the softest cashmere perfect-for-snuggling-in-on-a-cold-day throw, two armchairs facing the fire and beyond that a compact kitchen area with a breakfast bar and two stools.

With a tired smile she promised herself that on her first day off she'd be wrapping herself up in the throw, building a fire (something she'd need to learn how to do) and watch the flames.

She climbed into the cool sheets, immediately snuggling into the soft embrace of a thick mattress topper. As her head settled into the clutch of feather pillows, the duvet nestling around her, she let out a tiny sigh. Stop thinking brain, she told herself. As usual it refused to play ball and instead delighted in torturing her with an image of herself clambering out of the hot tub like a bedraggled drowned rat. What a first impression. She sighed again and curled on her side, succumbing to the delicious softness of the bed, feeling herself start to drift. What must Hekla and Alex have thought of their new boss? At worst they'd think she was a clumsy, flaky, klutz. They had no idea what she'd done ... at the moment. Under the covers, she crossed her fingers. Hopefully they never would. She swallowed back the stupid threatening tears that had suddenly sprung from nowhere. Would Alex's kind eyes hold the same expression if he ever saw that bloody video? Would Hekla's quick, easy smiles turn to sneers of disgust if she looked up Lucy Smart on the Internet? Lucy scrunched her eyes closed and burrowed deeper into the mattress, drifting off to sleep as she succumbed to the soft cocoon of the bed.

Something had woken Lucy and she lay confused as the weight of silence pressed in on her. It took her a slow processing couple of seconds to remember where she was. Iceland. In the middle of nowhere. With a frown, she pushed away the pale green duvet, the warmth now suffocating. Wait, the duvet was green? Blearily she looked around the room which was suffused with a soft unearthly light. It took another moment to register and she raised herself onto her elbows, sleepily squinting out of the windows. It had been so dark when she'd gone to bed, she hadn't bothered with the blinds.

Wow! Wide awake, she pushed herself up, cool air hitting her shoulders.

A silent symphony of pulsating green light lit up the dark sky, swirling in ethereal waves. Pushing back the covers, she grabbed the throw from the sofa wrapping it around her shoulders as she padded to the window. Mesmerised she placed a hand on the ice-cold window as if she might trace the path of the dancing lights. Her heart expanded in her chest, her eyes wide with wonder.

The eerie magical light revealed a shadowed landscape, the sea meeting the land in a seductive curve and bathing the rocky crags on the hillside in cool colours. Clutching the throw tighter she sank to the floor, enchanted by the serene, soundless spectacle unfolding before her with the grace of a gentle ballet.

Like silk flowing in the wind, the lights danced to a soundless tune, slow and slumberous. Goosebumps prickled her skin as she traced their progress. The sight filled her with a sense of awe and unexpected contentment. All the worries and fears of the last few months faded into insignificance, puny and irrelevant in the face of one of nature's constants. She wondered for how many thousands of years had the aurora borealis been appearing and what ancient races had made of them. Magic? The presence of a god? Did they see them as a sign? Lifting her head she stared up, suddenly feeling stronger, almost as if she were absorbing the cosmic energy. There was a whole universe out there and she was nothing but a tiny speck in the scheme of things. At this exact moment in time, she was nothing and everything, a part of the natural cycle. She clenched her fist in a silent promise. Forward. Look forward. Instead of seeing being in Iceland as a penance she would make the most of it. A second chance. She wouldn't be shaped by her mistakes. Fanciful as it was, this was a sign, she was sure of it. She would take this chance and use all her skills and experience to make sure that the people that came to The Northern Lights Lodge had a memorable stay.

Chapter 4

The next morning, having dressed with care, determined to make a better impression, Lucy followed her nose finding her way to the empty reception area. She could hear voices raised in argument, the harsh consonants of the unfamiliar language interspersed with some English. They came from the office beyond the reception desk. When Lucy entered the room, she could almost feel the tension thickening the air.

Hekla was standing behind one of two desks, the pen in her hand rattling on the surface of the desk as she faced two other women who wore uniforms. This morning there was no sign of the sunny smiles of the previous evening, instead Hekla's face was scrunched in mutinous resignation as she argued, although it appeared her heart wasn't really in it, with a trim girl of perfect proportions and the sort of make-up that made you wonder how on earth she'd perfected those uniform neat eyeliner flicks on both eyes. She looked as if she were about to go on an upmarket shopping trip rather than the task of cleaning bedrooms as her uniform suggested. She tossed her neat glossy brown bob and cast a quick look towards Lucy, her mouth closing sharply as if swallowing her next sentence. Hekla snapped her mouth shut and the awkward silence stretched out as all three of them, curiously, couldn't seem to meet each other's eyes.

'Good morning, can I help?' asked Lucy in polite but firm enquiry, stepping forward and standing still, determined to mark her authority from the get-go. It was only then that she realised that the head barman who'd fished her out of the hot tub last night was also there, leaning up against the wall, his arms folded and an expression of impatience on his face.

The taller blonde girl opposite Hekla raised her head and her long fluid arms dropped to her side. She looked uncertain and worried at the same time.

Hekla pursed her lips and cast an agonised look towards the two girls before she said, 'We have a slight problem with huldufólk.'

'Sorry?' Lucy thought she remembered hearing the word last night but wasn't sure she'd heard correctly as she tried to copy Hekla's rather cute accent, 'huldufólk?'

What the hell were they?

The two girls nodded vehemently.

Hekla sighed. 'They've left mices. Freya,' she indicated the dark-haired young woman, 'and Elin,' she nodded towards the second blonde woman, 'and the other staff who live in the staff quarters want to leave but then we will have no one to clean the rooms or to serve the breakfast this morning.'

Lucy gave a quick glance at her watch. It was eight o'clock, although it was still dark outside, surely breakfast service must be underway?

'Mices?' She was starting to feel completely stupid, echoing everything the other girl said.

'Yes, you know little furry mices.'

'Mice,' said Lucy, finally cottoning on. 'You have mice.' She glanced down at her feet and around the skirtings of the room. This she could handle. 'OK,' she gave the two women a smile, 'we can get some mousetraps. I'm sure that will solve the problem. No one needs to leave.' Now she understood the underlying panic on Hekla's face. Getting staff here on short notice would be difficult if not impossible. Yesterday's taxi ride had established they were in a remote location. The nearest town had been a good twenty minutes away. 'Humane traps.' Then she added for good measure. 'Or perhaps we can borrow a cat?' She'd always prided herself on finding solutions to problems. Even Chris had complimented her on her ability to think outside the box.

Alex, the barman, snorted and she shot him a quick snotty look of enquiry. He had a better way of getting rid of mice?

Hekla shifted from rubbing one foot down the back of her calf. 'Nrr.' She shook her head. 'It's not the mices, it's the huldufólk.'

Alex stepped forward, a look of exasperation on his face, his mouth tight. 'Hidden folk. Like Elves.'

'Elves?' Lucy repeated calmly. Alex nodded and she

caught him rolling his eyes. Unsure she hadn't misunderstood, she raised an eyebrow at him. 'You have elves?' His mouth crimped tighter in response.

'Ja, huldufólk,' said Freya, 'in our bedroom.'

Lucy frowned. 'You've seen them?'

Freya shuddered and looked horrified. 'No! It is very bad luck to see the huldufólk.'

'Riiight.' Lucy glanced at Alex who folded his arms, giving her a stern stare. 'So there are mice in the bedroom?'

Hekla did her stork impersonation again, the picture of awkwardness.

'Yes, on the pillows,' insisted Freya. 'Left by the huldufólk.' She bent to pick up the rucksack at her feet and hefted it onto her shoulders, with Elin following suit.

'Wait,' she said, trying to piece things together but it was rather like having all the straight bits of a jigsaw and none of the corner bits. 'You're leaving?'

The two girls nodded apologetically. 'It's ... well there is a bus going back to Reykjavik soon.'

'Wait a minute.' She looked at Hekla who didn't meet her eye.

'Most of the staff live in,' explained Alex in that lovely soft Scottish accent which made her think of David Tennant, as he rather unhelpfully pointed out, 'we're going to be short-staffed if they leave.'

Thanks Einstein, I hadn't worked that one out for myself.

'Ja, that's correct.' Hekla nodded, her blonde hair glinting under the soft light of the room.

Elves? Hidden folk? Seriously? Were they pulling the

34

newbie's leg? Alex's eyes held hers still with that expectant *so what are you going to do about it*. Until she got her head around this, she needed to tread carefully.

'And these huld ... hulder.'

'Huldufólk,' interjected Helka helpfully.

'They like to play tricks?'

'Sometimes,' said Elin, 'they move things. Make disruptions.'

Lucy nodded thoughtfully as she racked her brains. During her hospitality degree, there'd been a module on observing local customs. In South Korea, you shouldn't pour your own drink and there were several countries where blowing your nose in public was offensive, but she'd never come across an elf problem.

To her mind, dead mice on people's pillows sounded like someone playing a bit of practical joke, although not a particularly funny one. And this was her first day.

'So, what do we do about them?' asked Lucy.

Alex shot her an incredulous look as if to say, 'you're listening to this rubbish?'

And, what, did he have all the answers?

Hekla's eyes widened. 'There's nothing we can do.'

'OK,' said Lucy, wondering just where she'd come to, 'I'm not familiar with the hulder ... elf people but I'm sure there must be a way around this.'

If Alex rolled his eyes any harder they might pop out of his head.

Elin and Freya gave apologetic shrugs, shuffling on the spot. Lucy noticed that they hadn't actually made any move toward the door. In fact, she got the distinct impression that they were stalling, almost as if they were as keen as she was to find a solution.

'Wait,' she held up a hand, grateful that it was steady. She couldn't believe this was happening on her first flipping day. 'What if...' Come on brain. Think. 'What if we...' Elin, Freya and Hekla looked at her hopefully. 'What if we...' she stalled again and then inspiration made her words rush out in a flood, 'move the staff into guest rooms for the time being?'

Alex didn't look impressed. What was his problem?

'All of them?' Hekla creased her forehead in quick mental calculation and started ticking names off on her fingers. 'Olafur, Brynja, Gunnar, Olga, Freya, Elin, Dagur ... Magnus, Odin, Alex.' She pulled a mournful face. 'We have lots of guests arriving in the next few days.'

Lucy lifted her chin ignoring the balloon deflating sensation in her stomach. There had to be a solution. There had to be. It was quite odd, Freya and Elin seemed to want to stay, so it wasn't as if they were using the elf situation as an excuse to do a runner. Absently she rubbed at her neck, her fingers snagging on the chain of her necklace as she racked her brains. Dropping her hand, she tugged at the little charm Daisy had bought her to wish her luck, her fingers finding the tiny horn of the silver unicorn hidden under her shirt. She worried at the little point like a talisman.

'We need a unicorn,' she said, engendering her voice with absolute authority, pleased to see Alex's mouth drop open, although whether it was admiration or astonishment she wasn't sure. 'In my country elves and fairies have enormous respect for the unicorn. They wouldn't dare trespass on a unicorn's territory. Even the symbol of a unicorn is enough to make fairies and elves think twice about entering a place.'

Hekla nodded, clearly having no idea what she was talking about. Did unicorns even feature in Icelandic folklore? Alex's lips were pressed together, his hands now rammed in his pockets and he was taking great interest in the floor. However, she held both Freya and Elin's attention.

Lucy pulled out her necklace, undoing it and holding it up.

'Ah Einhyrningur,' said Hekla reaching a finger out to touch the necklace. 'There's a mountain called Einhyrningur about forty kilometres away from here. Unicorns.' She nodded, looking ridiculously relieved. 'That is interesting.'

'Yes, apparently their magic is stronger,' said Lucy, straightening up, 'they're known to...' To what? She knew bugger all about them because ... they didn't exist. But then neither did elves.

With a heavy sigh, Alex pushed himself away from the wall, gave Lucy a resigned, *I can't believe I'm doing this,* look and said, 'The huldufólk avoid them because it's reputed that they can steal their magic.' The seamless interjection was so smooth she almost believed it herself.

'Yes!' Hekla looked excited and clapped her hands together. 'If we take the unicorn into the staff quarters it will make the huldufólk leave.'

'And,' said Lucy, 'it's made of silver. You know in folklore that werewolves and vampires can't touch silver, is it the same with the huldufólk?'

'Of course,' said Elin thoughtfully and Lucy wondered how much Elin really believed in such things as hidden folk. Perhaps believing in a silver unicorn was a useful face-saving exercise.

'Wonderful,' said Hekla, with a broad smile, her blue eyes shining now that all was well with the world. Lucy wanted to hug her. Perhaps she should warn Hekla about trusting too easily. It could cost you. Instead she said, 'Hekla, why don't you, Elin and Freya,' she was pleased she'd remembered their names, 'take the unicorn back to the staff quarters and find a good place to hang it up? And then perhaps you can come back and show me around the hotel and introduce me to the rest of the staff?'

As soon as they'd gone, she turned to Alex, raising an eyebrow, waiting for him to speak first.

'Nice save,' he said, 'although you shouldn't have stood for any nonsense. You're storing up trouble.'

Straightening, she smoothed down the skirt of her black suit, the closest thing she had to armour. She'd just arrived, she'd been running on empty for months and he wanted her to come up with all the answers on day one. And wait, hello, he was the flipping barman!

'And what would you have done?' she asked coolly. 'You'd have been happy to pitch in making beds and cleaning bathrooms, would you?'

'You should have knocked the whole elf thing on its

head. It's going to be used every time some kind of leverage is needed.'

'Maybe I was being sensitive to local cultural beliefs.'

Alex snorted. 'They were trying it on. Your first day.'

'You don't know that for sure,' she said defensively.

'Er, hello. Elves? Seriously?' The stern expression on his face relaxed and she saw amusement dancing in his brown eyes.

'Well they seemed quite serious about the dead mice,' retorted Lucy.

'Mmm,' admitted Alex. 'Sounds like you might have a practical joker with a rather warped sense of humour on the staff.'

Lucy hoped not, she had enough on her plate without having to contend with that as well.

Chapter 5

'He's very cute,' observed Hekla, showing Lucy into the guest lounge she'd glimpsed briefly last night.

'Who?' asked Lucy, pretending she didn't know who was being referred to.

'Alex. The barman. Very cute.'

'Mmm,' responded Lucy, with a non-committal twist of her lips. 'I hadn't noticed. How long's he been here?'

Hekla gave her a startled look but Lucy lifted her chin with the regal tilt she was known for ... rewind ... had been known for. Once upon a time, her reputation for being a boss you wouldn't mess with preceded her.

'Only two weeks. I don't think he plans on staying long either. I think he's just passing through.'

Lucy had met plenty of people like Alex in her career. Always on the move, travelling around the world. The hospitality industry relied on people like him.

'Shame, because he's very popular with the guests,' said Hekla with a sly grin. 'Perhaps you could persuade him to stay longer.'

Lucy shot her a quelling look as if to say '*you've got the wrong person here*'.

OK, so you couldn't miss how cute Alex was. In fact he probably had the monopoly on cuteness with those warm brown eyes and the super cute crinkles around them. Lucy was driven not blind, but for the next two months her focus was going to be on being the very best manager The Northern Lights Lodge had ever had, so that Mr Pedersen would be begging her to stay and she was not going to be noticing anyone no matter how ... 'Oh, Oh, Oh!'

Her thoughts were brought to abrupt standstill by the spectacular view showcased by a run of floor-to-ceiling windows which took up one entire wall of the room.

'Wow,' she breathed, crossing to the window. 'This is...' Directly below was a steep drop and it felt as she were in mid-air. Some clever architect had designed the building to maximise the views and the contours of the hillside. Away to the right the rugged coastline snaked away, disappearing behind a slender spit of land that poked out like a snake's tongue, topped by a series of pillars of rocks that in this light looked like ancient rough-hewn chess pieces. To the left, folds of crag-topped hills filled the skyline, each getting bigger and bigger until they finished in a majestic snow-capped peak. No wonder people believed in elves and trolls and other mystical creatures. There was definitely a *Lord of the Rings* sense of sorcery about the landscape. It was easy to imagine cloaked horseback riders racing across the meadows down by the sea. *With that longish dark hair, Alex had a bit of the mysterious Aragorn about him.*

And where the heck had that thought popped up from? Focus, Lucy. Last night's northern light display had messed with her head, she decided.

'We will have snow this week,' said Hekla following Lucy to the window as they looked out at the heavy white clouds which were broken up by patches of blue that allowed sunbeams to dance across the sea making the waves glisten and sparkle.

Lucy turned back to survey the room, frowning slightly, her eyes scanning the polished wood floors and colourful rugs and the high beams criss-crossing the apex of the roof. The stylish sofas with their beech legs and deep teal-blue upholstery were the same ones she'd seen on the hotel's website, along with the numerous lamps casting a soft light in the room. But something was missing. It took her a second to work it out. Where were the cosy throws and inviting cushions? What had happened to the books and carved sea-birds arranged on the low open shelves? Perhaps the previous management had brought them in as window dressing for the photo shoot...

'I think we should get some throws and cushions to put in here,' she said, wishing she'd thought to grab a notepad and pen from the office. 'You know, more hygge?' Back in Bath, Daisy had been obsessed with the Danish way of keeping cosy and had a fine collection of soft furnishings as well as a special pottery mug for the expensive China tea she treated herself too.

Hekla's face brightened. 'We have huggulegt here in Iceland.' She turned a slow circle in the room. Then she frowned. 'There were some,' she rubbed her fingers together and then stroked the fabric on the sofa, 'very luxurious cushions.'

'Velvet,' suggested Lucy, remembering the jewel bright colours from the pictures.

'Ja, that's right. Lots of velvet cushions and colourful throws. I don't know what happened to them.'

'Oh, this is lovely,' said Lucy, distracted by the beautiful shine of the burnished chestnut wood of semi-circular bar in the next room. A young man glanced up from his task of putting away glasses on the shelves suspended above the bar. Behind him on the stone wall, stylish shelves of varying lengths were offset at different points and on each one bottles were arranged in attractive groups, interspersed with little pots of herbs in polished brass planters that glowed in the subdued lighting.

'This is Dagur. Dagur, this Lucy, our new manager.'

'Hi, welcome,' he said, a quick, easy smile lighting up his pale blue eyes as he gave her a brief salute, making her drop the hand she'd been about to offer. It seemed that things here were a lot more casual and less formal than she'd been used to in her previous hotels, not that that was a bad thing.

After a brief exchange, Hekla and Lucy moved on again, skirting through reception down to a cleverly designed glass corridor that linked the main hotel area to another building. Somehow the ultra-modern glass construction, bridging the separate buildings, could have been transplanted from a skyscraper in Manhattan and should have been totally out of place, but worked surprisingly well in the rural landscape.

'And this is the library,' said Hekla, coming to a halt in the centre of the room.

'A library,' said Lucy, turning a slow three hundred and sixty degrees, her neck tipped backwards as she looked up at the rather grand high-ceilinged room with a balcony all around the top housing shelf upon shelf of books. She looked again, her face breaking into a delighted smile.

'That is so cute,' she said to Hekla, pointing upwards. All the books had been arranged by the colour of their spines to create an eclectic rainbow with shades of red, running into oranges, yellows, greens, blues and purples.

'We Icelanders love our books,' said a voice from behind them. When Lucy turned a dark-haired, stocky woman uncurled herself from a button-backed armchair, a book in her hand.

'Hey Brynja,' said Hekla with warmth. 'This is Lucy, the new manager. Brynja is one of our receptionists. It's her day off today.'

'Hey,' said Brynja.

'I love that you have a proper library,' said Lucy, taking another look at the brimming bookshelves. 'And so many books.'

'Ah, it is a big tradition for us. You have heard of the jólabókaflód.'

Lucy shook her head.

'You would translate it as the Christmas Book Flood, jólabókaflód' explained Hekla as Brynja nodded.

Lucy grinned. 'A book flood? Now that sounds awesome.'

'Everyone gives books for Christmas,' explained Brynja, her sharp dark eyes flashing with enthusiasm. 'Lovely to meet you Lucy. If I can help in anyway, let me know.'

'Thank you. It's going to take me a little while to find my feet.'

As soon as she said it, both Brynja and Hekla in complete sync looked down at her shoes.

Lucy laughed, realising that despite Hekla's amazing command of English there were still language and culture differences between them. 'It's a figure of speech.'

Brynja nodded, her sharp eyes thoughtful as if she were carefully cataloguing the idiom and adding it to her own personal lexicon.

'So you weren't bothered by the huldufólk?' asked Lucy, thoughtfully realising that Brynja, despite her day off, had not been planning to leave.

Hekla looked awkward again as Brynja gave her an older sister sort of look.

'No,' said Brynja with alacrity. 'I might not believe but then,' she lifted her shoulders, 'things happen and then you think that perhaps they do exist and it would be bad to ignore them in case they do.'

'So,' Lucy was struggling to get her head around this. 'What you're saying is that people don't necessarily believe in huldufólk but they don't count out the possibility that they might exist.'

'Yes,' said Brynja. 'That is exactly right.'

* * *

45

Exhausted by handover and introductions overload, along with Hekla's boundless enthusiasm, Lucy snagged a quick sandwich from Erik, the hotel's chef. With his huge broad shoulders and brawny frame, he looked an unlikely figure in his whites as he grinned at her from behind a huge bushy beard. When her eyes widened at the size of the half loaf of rye bread stuffed with thinly sliced lamb that he handed her, he let out a belly laugh and a stream of Icelandic, which she guessed translated as she needed feeding up. He wasn't wrong there. Food had been low on her agenda for months.

Deciding she needed a break and some fresh air, she wrapped herself up in her newly purchased down coat, which Daisy had insisted she buy, and took the still warm sandwich wrapped in foil down to the shingle beach in front of the hotel. She ought to give her best friend a call.

Huddled into her coat, Lucy perched on one of the rocks. The bracing air around her seemed to sharpen her appetite and the delicious smoked lamb sandwich disappeared without touching the sides. It was probably the biggest meal she'd eaten in a long time, although she'd burned so much energy just thinking this morning.

'Hey Daisy.' Thankfully she could still tap into the hotel's WiFi and make a WhatsApp call.

'Lucy, how is it?'

'Stunning, interesting ... there's a lot of work to do, but I can do it.'

'Atta girl, that's the Lucy I remember. What's it like then? What are the people like?'

'So far, so good,' Lucy said, neutrally. 'I've got an assistant manager, Hekla. She's ... very enthusiastic with a real can-do attitude, which is...' Lucy refrained from her natural incli-nation to say irritating, Daisy wouldn't approve, 'kind of refreshing.'

'Ha!' Daisy laughed. 'I know you, Miss Organised and Practical. She's irritating the hell out of you.'

'Actually ... she isn't. She's so friendly, she's made me feel incredibly welcome already.'

'She sounds adorable.'

'Mm, not sure I'd go that far but bless her, she works really hard and I don't think there's been much in the way of direction over the last year.'

'Well, if anyone can offer that, it will be you.' Daisy's voice held laughter and sunshine but the words made Lucy pause. The quick observation wasn't a criticism, but it scratched at her. Predictable, organised, Lucy Smart, which could also be read as routinised, unimaginative, dull.

'I'll do my best.' She softened the clipped delivery with a sigh, looking back up at the striking architecture, the combi-nation of modern and traditional blending into the rugged landscape. 'The hotel is ... well gorgeous. It's got so much potential but it needs a lot of TLC.' She paused. 'You should see the guest rooms. You'd love them. So cosy. Honey-coloured wood and then every room has a proper stone fireplace or a wood burner. Loads of sheepskin rugs everywhere and these really pretty woven wall hangings with those Scandinavian love heart patterns picked out in white. I've even got a wood burner in my room'

'Hygge!' squealed Daisy. 'Oh I want to come. It sounds gorgeous.'

'And another reason for my call. Tell me more about the hygge thing.'

'Ha! I knew you'd come around one day!'

'Don't get too excited,' Lucy's voice was dry with sarcasm, 'it's a décor theme I'm thinking of.'

'Lucy, Lucy, Lucy. It's a not a décor thing, it's a mindset,' she chided and proceeded to give Lucy a good ten-minute lecture all about contentment, well-being and cosiness, which Lucy sucked up without interruption because she thought it would go down well with guests and Hekla. It still sounded like a load of old nonsense to her.

'I'll let you know how I get on,' said Lucy, after Daisy insisted on her sending pictures.

'Cool,' Daisy laughed, 'or hot if you've got a fireplace. Any nice men you could cosy up with on a sheepskin rug in front of the fire? Mmm. I might have to come over.'

Lucy groaned. 'Trust you. I'm steering clear of men for a while, you know that.'

'Lucy, Chris was a dick. Don't let him turn you into a dried-up old stick.'

'I'm not. But I've got too much work to do.' She thought of the mental list she was already compiling. Paintwork needed touching up, taking the staff in hand and the cleaning in many places was not up to Lucy's standards.

'Apparently there has been a succession of managers. I'm the eleventh in the last year. None of them stayed put for very long.'

'Until you arrived,' said Daisy staunchly.

'Yup, I think I can make a difference here.'

'Sounds like you might have landed on your feet.'

'Hmm, I'm not quite sure of that,' replied Lucy, thinking of her brief introduction to Eyrun, the housekeeper, a slightly scary but diminutive lady of indeterminate age, who'd chased them away when Hekla and she visited the laundry. Eyrun had met them with a stream of angry Icelandic that even Hekla was reluctant to translate. It seemed she ruled her hot, steamy kingdom like an angry troll managing the washing of all the sheets and towels and rarely venturing out of her lair, which wasn't terribly helpful for someone who was supposed to be responsible for the upkeep of the rooms.

'It is a bit chaotic. I can't figure out how the staff rotas have been done, so I'm going to have to sort that out.' It appeared no one person was responsible for the daily rotas and matching staffing levels with guests checking in or out. Hekla had revealed that often rooms weren't ready for new arrivals and that she and Brynja had to double up as chambermaids and waiting staff.

'And if anyone can do the job, it's you Lucy,' said Daisy, encouraging as ever.

Lucy sighed. This beautiful, but rough around the edges, lodge was a far cry from what she was used to. At the hotel in Manchester she'd had a chain of command and everything ran like a well-oiled machine. Although The Northern Lights Lodge was lovely, everything seemed to be limping along like a rusty old lawnmower. There was so much she could do with the place but could she achieve enough in two months to persuade the owners to make her contract permanent?

Chapter 6

Alex lunged against a craggy outcrop, resting a hand on his thigh and eyeing the phone in his other hand with all the enthusiasm of a man about to phone an irate boss. Today the brisk cold air, carrying a definite hint of snow, bit at his cheeks. It was good to be outside after yesterday's day of drizzle that had shrouded the lodge, although in the last two weeks he'd quickly learned that the weather in Iceland had the monopoly on changeable. One minute you could have driving rain and black clouds and then suddenly the wind whipped them away to bring in brilliant blue skies and sunshine. Seeing the break in the weather, he'd rushed to change to take advantage of the dry day and enjoy some down time. Although any enjoyment he found in being outdoors was about to be doused.

With a heavy sigh he looked out over the choppy sea, enjoying the crash of the rolling waves dashing against the rocks that lined the shore, wishing he could enjoy the clean fresh air a while longer, without having to pollute it with business talk and a conversation that would make him feel crap inside. He'd been wrestling with his conscience all morning and really it should have been quite a short tussle, but that bloody *nice* gene kept intervening. He studied the horizon where the sky met the water's edge and pressed the call button on the screen.

Sod's law the line to Paris was crackle free. 'Hey Alex, about time. I called you two hours ago.'

'Some of us are working, Quentin.'

'Working! What the hell are you doing? You're supposed to be working for me. You didn't say anything about that the last time we spoke.'

'That's because the new manager wasn't in place. What did you think I was going to do? Loll around a guest room for two months? Besides this way I have a better excuse for poking around a bit more and pulling together a proper report. I have access to all areas, which, if I was a guest, would be pretty difficult.'

'Dear God, please tell me you're not the bus boy.'

'No ... there isn't one. I'm the head barman and waiter.'

'Nun on a bicycle, Mclaughlin, what are you playing at? Couldn't you have been a writer or at least a ruddy orni- thologist?'

'Given I have no skills or knowledge of either, I think that would have been a mite difficult to pull off,' said Alex dryly. 'Besides I had to do something. I'd go out of my mind with nothing to do and it's not as if I mind getting my hands dirty. No one's keeping an eye on me. I pretty much do as I please.'

'You mean the new manager hasn't rocked up yet. Where the hell is he? Pederson told me they'd recruited someone.'

'He's a she and she's arrived. She's definitely arrived.' He thought of his first glimpse of Lucy Smart emerging like a bedraggled mermaid from the hot tub, her long hair slicked across her face and her stand-offishness when he'd tried to help. He still couldn't figure out why the hell she'd insisted the front door was locked, even when they'd returned to reception and it was clearly open.

'And?'

Alex scowled thinking of her and her unicorn charm as he took a pace away from the rock, starting to walk along the shore.

'She's got an unorthodox approach to problem solving that's for sure.'

'I don't do unorthodox,' grumbled Quentin, which was a bit rich coming from one who cornered the market on eccentric sometimes. 'Does she run a tight ship?'

'She arrived yesterday,' said Alex, hedging a little. If it had been him, he would have been a lot firmer with the staff. Surely she could see they were taking the piss with the whole elf thing. A decent manager would have shut that down immediately and made it clear that she wasn't taking any nonsense. She was storing up trouble there, although her spur of the moment solution had been pretty neat.

'I thought she wasn't due for another week.'

'Mix up with the dates.' Alex winced. That had been very odd. He'd been there when Hekla took the call. Why would someone phone and change the date? Lucy must have had a change of heart, got someone to phone on her behalf and then changed her mind again? What other explanation was there?

'Well that wouldn't fill me with confidence. Do you think she's any good? And I want an honest no bullshit answer.' Alex pursed his lips and kicked at a small stone in his path. It knock, knock, knocked over the other grey stones on the shingle beach. Quentin waited on the other end of the line, the silence stretching out for Alex to fill. He knew his boss's tactics well. Quentin hadn't got to be the multi-millionaire owner of The Oliver Group, running a string of boutique hotels, without being extremely shrewd. He wanted an honest report on the hotel's potential, what needed to be done to bring it up to Oliver Group standards and whether Lucy and the current staff were the right people to do that. At the moment, if he was entirely honest, he wasn't convinced.

There was something about her haunted appearance that worried him and last night she'd been brusque and sharp, extremely unwilling to accept help. He suspected she was a loner if her stand-offish attitude was anything to go by and she didn't look robust enough to cope with the rigors of the job. The hours were long and the role involved everything from marketing, budgeting, premises management through to managing the staff. Not to mention that a good manager was on show the whole time, making themselves accessible and approachable to guests and staff alike. Should he mention his quiet misgivings to his boss? He paused and scooped a stone and launched it skimming across the sea. It bounced three times, shall I, shan't I, shall I?

On the fourth bob the stone sank making his decision. *Nice guys finish last.*

'The jury's out,' he said, his words terse. It was the truth.

'Do you think she's got what it takes?' pressed Quentin.

No, was the word that came to mind but instead Alex wrinkled his nose, grateful Quentin couldn't see him. 'I don't know ... yet.'

'Come on,' groaned Quentin. 'Don't fob me off. You're a good judge of character. Quit pussy footing around. First impressions.'

Alex sighed, he owed Quentin so much. His boss had taken a risk, giving Alex his first big hotel to manage despite Alex being the youngest, most inexperienced candidate. And now these days they were practically, no they were family. He picked up another stone and chucked it across the surface of the sea. 'There are quite a few issues. I need to see how she tackles them.' Except, he thought to himself, Lucy had been holed up in the office going through paperwork for the last couple of days. If Alex was manager, he'd have prioritised making those small quick win changes that guests – the guys that paid their wages – actually noticed. Put more staff on at breakfast, so that guests could get out of the hotel more quickly in the mornings, make sure the bedrooms were serviced by lunchtime, have the fires in the communal areas lit by the time guests returned in the afternoons and offer one complimentary drink to guests on arrival to encourage them to visit the bar in the evenings.

'So if you were manager what would you do? Top line.'

Relieved by the change of tack, Alex screwed up his face in thought.

The wind caught his hair, whipping it into his eyes as he turned his head to survey the building sprawling across the top of the hill behind him. The place could be fabulous. 'Staffing is a problem. No one is managing the rotas. Everything is last minute. I'd sort that out. I'd also make an inventory of exactly what needs to be done in the hotel, because the place is looking very tired. And I'd have started on that list yesterday. I guess the bottom line is, the new manager isn't cutting it yet.'

'Have you seen the latest TripAdvisor reviews?' asked Quentin, changing the subject again as he was wont to do.

'No.' Alex didn't need to, he could gauge things from the guest's reactions. They weren't exactly raving about the place.

'Not great. Not awful but blah ... we don't do blah. At least if they were shite, you have something to work with. Mediocrity is worse. When do you think you can pull together a detailed report on the place? I'm beginning to regret buying it.'

'It's not a done deal yet, is it?'

'No but we're getting close. Pedersen is a tricky bastard and I can pull the deal but ... what do you think? It's got potential hasn't it? I thought Iceland would extend the portfolio in a new direction.'

'It's got great potential. It needs managing properly,' said Alex. 'Why don't you wait until I've done some more digging?' he suggested even though skulking about the hotel and poking into things when no one else was around was not something he enjoyed. He hated this undercover crap, but on this occasion it had to be done. He knew that directly asking questions often sent staff into defensive mode, covering things up, so you couldn't get a real picture and more importantly, if anyone found out that the Oliver Group were interested in buying the lodge, it would stimulate a lot of speculation among competitors, many of whom might want to get in on the action and no doubt push the price sky-high. 'I'll send my report over in the next couple of weeks. I still need to find out more about what goes on in housekeeping.'

'Not a lot judging from the reviews. I should have got you on the job,' said Quentin.

'That would have been difficult as you don't own the place yet and besides, I've got a nice five-star hotel waiting for me in Paris. How's it coming along? Any progress.'

'None, and that's giving me a shitting ulcer. Those wanking bureaucrats. Won't cut through the red tape. There's still some doubt about the age of the skeleton. All work has stopped. It's going to be at least four months before we can get the floor down there re-laid and dried out enough to open the hotel.'

'Well at least I'll get to see the northern lights while I'm here.'

'I'll want you back here to oversee things. Don't get too settled there.'

'I won't.'

'Good.' And with that Quentin terminated the call.

Alex stared back at the building perched on the edge of

the small cliff over the seashore. It hadn't occurred to him before, but maybe one day he could come to a place like this. It was outside his usual type of hotel but there was a certain rustic charm and otherworldly magic to the place that intrigued him. Although working in Paris had been a challenge and never a dull moment, he realised that the new hotel would be more of the same. Smooth sophistication. Nothing too unexpected. No adventure. It was a long way from where he'd started, as a barman in his family-owned hotel, a small but highly prestigious former castle on the outskirts of Edinburgh which one day would be his. When that day came it was his dream to create a hotel that would rival the famous Gleneagles. Until he took over from his mother, at a time considerably distant from now, he was garnering the best possible experience he could.

With a sudden start, as if the reminder came with a physical punch he realised that he'd missed the sharp, freshness of the open air, the wheeling cries of seagulls overhead, of being outdoors all hours of the day and through it all, whatever the hour, the scent of the sea air. Home, even after years in France, Switzerland and Italy, was still the Leith shore in Edinburgh, where his abiding memory was the sound of the waves whispering in his ear. Sitting here on a damp rock in Iceland, the familiar song of the sea brought back a sense of community and home. He'd missed this, the rhythm of the waves, the blustery wind and the wide expanse of sky. Being in a city, he'd missed the hills and the rocky crag behind him now was a welcome reminder of Arthur's Seat. It was surprising how much he didn't miss

Paris and how quickly this magnificent scenery and the rustic lodge was starting to feel more like home ... Which was all totally ridiculous because he had a great job waiting for him in one of the best cities of the world. Coming somewhere like this would be a backward step. Not something that he would ever consider.

Chapter 7

Hekla appeared in the office, carrying two mugs of coffee. Lucy, who had spent the last four days attempting to turn her desk from chaos into order and failing miserably, looked up gratefully.

'We need to get a coffee machine in here,' declared Lucy looking at the drips of coffee running down the mugs where it had slopped over the sides during the trip back from the kitchen on the other side of the hotel.

'Great idea,' said Hekla, almost bouncing on the spot. 'Why don't I take you to Hvolsvöllur, some time? We could get one of those machines that makes hot chocolate and tea too.'

She took a quick slurp of coffee and pulled a face. 'Hot coffee would be so much nicer, although Erik might not give me cookies.' She dug in her cardigan pocket and pulled out a napkin wrapped bundle. 'Loganberry and walnut. Still warm…' she wrinkled her nose. 'They were.' She looked around the office and winced.

'I know, I know, it's a mess,' said Lucy wearily, wanting to bash her head on the top of the desk at the sheer amount of neglected paperwork. The previous manager, who had lasted six weeks, had been a proponent of piling rather than filing and in the second pile under her desk (there were three piles under there as well as the four on top of the desk) she'd found a dozen overdue invoices.

'I could help,' offered Hekla, 'when I've finished room service.'

Lucy hesitated. 'You shouldn't have to do that. I need you in here.' But there had been no choice today because not enough staff had been scheduled to cope with the number of guests checking out.

'I need to speak to Eyrun about the room service rotas.' Maybe in her agitated, cross mood, now was the perfect time to beard the lion in her den.

Hekla exchanged a wry look with her.

'It's ridiculous,' snapped Lucy. 'The housekeeper should be responsible for them.'

'She ... won't do paperwork.'

'Well, she's going to have to,' Lucy said, with a determined jut of her chin. 'We can't go on like this. You have enough to do without stripping beds and cleaning bathrooms.'

'I don't mind,' said Hekla, with a gracious shrug. 'And she runs the laundry really well.'

'Well I do.' Lucy's firm voice made the blonde girl smile. 'Laundry or no laundry. I need you in here.'

'Thank you,' she replied before adding with a mischievous twinkle, 'are you going to tell her?'

They both laughed as Lucy shuddered. 'Is it ridiculous that I'm scared of her?'

'Nrr.' Hekla's vehement head shake and quick down turn of her mouth was the decider.

Lucy jumped up. 'It is ridiculous and I'm not standing for it. I'm going to go down there now. I could do with a break from blasted paperwork. Hold the fort. I'll be back.'

Eyrun's dark eyes flashed as she gave the sheaf of paper in Lucy's hand a contemptuous sneer.

'So,' said Lucy with a determinedly pleasant smile on her face. 'I'd like you to take over the organisation of the chambermaid's rosters. I've printed some templates that you can fill in and here are the bookings for the next week. We need a proper rota. Poor Hekla is spending too much time having to drop everything to help clean the rooms.' There was no response from Eyrun, she simply stared at Lucy with a steely gaze. 'And we're quiet.' That was an understatement, bookings were down by fifty percent, year on year.

'But,' Lucy lied valiantly, ignoring the fear crimping at her stomach, 'things will start to get busy soon.' They had to, she told herself digging her fingernails into her right palm. Hekla kept dangling the northern lights' carrot saying that things picked up later this month. Lucy wasn't convinced. Worryingly, there was no evidence of any kind of marketing in recent months, especially when she had two months, or rather one month and twenty-five days, to prove herself.

Eyrun sniffed and turned her back, reaching into the still warm dryer to pull out a handful of towels.

'Eyrun.' Lucy snapped, knowing she was venting her

frustration unfairly, but they needed to improve the TripAdvisor reviews, most of which said the lodge looked tired. 'The rooms need inspecting every day. This is your job.' Realising she was in danger of letting her temper get the better of her and forgetting all the management training she'd ever had, she took in a deep breath. Firmness. Consistency. Clear, plain speaking. You're the boss. Stay calm. 'I've compiled a check list for you.' Lucy put down the papers on the nearby shelf and pulled out the typed list that she'd put together this morning.

'Ok. I check the rooms,' said Eyrun, her mouth signalling her displeasure, edging away from the piece of paper. 'No list. Now go. I'm busy.' She indicated the soft cloud of towels in her arm.

'It will help.'

'Nrr.' Eyrun shook her head vehemently, backing away clutching her bundle like a shield.

'You will inspect the rooms each day?' Lucy pressed, realising that this was a minor victory even if the rotas were a lost cause.

Eyrun glowered but nodded.

'And let me know what needs fixing, repairing or changing. A lot of the bedspreads need cleaning or replacing. You do a great job with the laundry but some of them ... I think are even beyond your magic.'

Lucy almost smiled when Eyrun's head lifted with a touch of pride. The older woman's English was clearly better than she let on and like most people she wasn't immune to flattery.

'I've removed some,' in a whistle stop tour late yesterday afternoon, when she'd finally given up on the office for the day, 'but could you compile an inventory of what can be kept and how many new ones we need to order? You will know best. I'll follow your guidance on that.'

A flash of surprise flitted across Eyrun's beady eyes and she tilted her head like a suspicious blackbird.

Lucy held up the list. It was non-negotiable. There were tick boxes beside each of the items and a place for Eyrun to sign at the bottom to confirm everything had been done.

'I'll pin this one up on the noticeboard for you. And leave the spares here. When you run out, Hekla or Brynja can run more off for you.'

Eyrun looked boot faced as Lucy crossed to the felt pin board above the desk in the other room.

'That's your list,' she said, pinning a second drawing pin to the board to secure it.

Eyrun made a small *hmph* noise and marched back into the first room with the dryers, dumping her load on top of Lucy's papers and pulled out a towel, shaking it out before folding it with quick, neat precise moves.

Letting her go for a minute, Lucy stepped back and frowned, pricked by a sense of something not being right. She looked at the noticeboard. Shouldn't there be health and safety notices, emergency numbers, fire evacuation procedures, any number of basic notices? Glancing around the room, she realised that it was a blank canvas. It stirred a memory but she couldn't place it.

* * *

'Grr,' said Lucy returning to the office as Hekla looked up. 'That went well, not.'

'You're still in one piece then.' Lucy whirled around to see Alex with a teasing smile on his face. 'I hear you've been taming dragons.'

'Uh,' she said rather stupidly, taken aback by the unexpected friendly expression. Shit, he was cute.

'I'm not sure about taming,' she finally replied, smoothing down her skirt, as if that might make her feel more professional. 'I won one small battle but I don't hold out much hope on Eyrun arranging the rotas.'

'I could do them,' said Hekla.

'No,' said Lucy with a firmness that earned a small approving nod from Alex, although what it had to do with him, she didn't know. It earned him a scowl. 'I'll do them for the short term and I'm thinking about promoting one of the other girls and giving them the job. What do you think about Elin or Freya?'

Hekla grinned. 'Elin Jónsdóttir and Freya Flókisdóttir. Jón and Flóki are my dad's cousins.'

Lucy frowned, 'Jón and Flóki?'

'Their fathers. In Iceland we take the name of our father or mother for our surname. I am Hekla Gunnesdóttir. My father is Gunnar. Elin and Freya are my second cousins. You would have to choose between them. But I think either will be excellent.'

'So, Alex, how can I help you?' He had perched on the edge of her desk as if he had all the time in the world and he was completely at ease. And then at her question, all that ease vanished and, oddly, he seemed a little discon-certed.

'I ... er, I ... um ... wondered if you'd like me to do an inventory of the bar stock? And I was wondering how you were after your tumble in the pool. No ill effects? Must have been a bit of a shock,' he asked with sympathy, and seemingly back on smooth ground. 'I never asked if you hurt yourself.'

'Oh, no. Well, not badly.' Absently she rubbed her hip. 'A bruise or two.'

'And your boots?'

She closed her eyes, in sudden pain at the state of her favourite footwear. She'd abandoned them in the bathroom and done nothing with them. 'Not looking so good. They're still a bit damp inside.'

'You need to stuff them with paper, there's plenty in the office. Hekla,' he shot her a grin, 'has an ongoing vendetta with the printer, I've got shoe polish...' his voice trailed off lamely before suddenly laughing. 'Shoe polish! Super hero Alex to the rescue.'

'That's er...' Lucy smiled, charmed by his boyish chagrin. Charmed and something else that made a tiny frozen part of heart melt just a little.

'A bit boy scoutish,' laughed Alex. 'Prepared for every eventuality, that's me.'

Alex's unexpected kindness threw her and Lucy's face sagged. 'I ... I used to be,' she said in an almost whisper.

'The printer does not like me,' said Hekla with unex-pected petulance, looking up from her computer.

'No,' said Alex, laughing at Hekla's pouting face. Lucy could have kissed her for the timely interjection. Where had her sudden misery come from? She lifted her chin, quickly schooling her features to hide the brief lapse of her game face.

'Er, Lucy,' said Hekla with a worried expression, 'we have a booking arriving next week.'

'And?' They were a hotel after all, bookings were what they wanted.

'It was made directly with Mr Pedersen and I don't have any details. No names. Nothing. But it's a complimentary.'

She noticed Alex looking intrigued and again wondered why a barman was hanging around the office or taking such a keen interest in things.

'Ah, that is odd. Are they VIPs we need to impress? Relations of Mr Pedersen?'

'I don't know. It's for five rooms.'

'Five.' Her tongue flicked automatically to the sore on her lip. That was a lot of rooms to give away for free. What was going on?

'All it says on the original email is that they are media.' Hekla looked up, a happier expression on her face. 'I think they might be press or something.'

'Press?'

OK, she *could* handle that. Being so close to the BBC and ITV as well as two premier league football clubs in Manchester, she was used to dealing with journalists, celebrities and footballers on a regular basis.

'English press. A film crew.'

Oh shit! Automatically her hand went to her lip and she began to pick at it.

'You OK?' asked Alex, concern etching his eyes. Stepping toward Lucy, making her catch her breath, he briefly brushed his fingers over her wrist. 'Don't, you'll make it worse.'

She pulled her hand away, already tasting the tang of blood in her mouth. It was a bad habit she'd got into.

'You OK?' he asked again.

'Yes. Yes. I'm fine,' said Lucy, conscious that the blood had drained from her face and her heart rate had sky rocketed and everything about her was probably screaming NO!

She wasn't fine at all and at that precise moment, she couldn't have said whether that was the unexpected effect of Alex's gentle touch or the prospect of a film crew arriving.

She took a calming breath. She was being stupid. It wasn't as if the film crew would be filming the staff. They probably wouldn't pay any attention to them. No one was going to recognise her.

Chapter 8

When Lucy woke, anxiety immediately clutching at her thoughts, she lay staring out of the window at the cloud filled sky. Although it was still dark, there was an odd light to the sky. Maybe she'd stay here today, study the clouds and give into the heaviness of her body. Even though she'd been here for nearly two weeks now, it was taking her time to get up to speed. The frequent turnaround of previous managers meant that so much had been left undone. This morning just lifting the duvet seemed an effort. Minutes ticked by, turning into ten, then twenty. She squinted through the glass, was that a snowflake?

Was that why the clouds looked different today, they were full of snow? She tracked the progress of a few leisurely snowflakes, watching their gentle wayward descent. The familiar prick of childish excitement nudged at her, making her wince. Once upon a time the first magical sight of snow would have had her dragging her wellies on, wrapping up like a Sherpa, desperate to be out there, but the dark slush of city snow had cured her of that fantasy.

Sighing, she forced her stiff body to roll over, sliding her legs out of the bed and moving into a sitting position. She had to get up. She needed this job. She was being ridiculous. The film crew wouldn't be interested in her. They'd be filming the sights, using the hotel as a base. *She was being ridiculous*. Repeating the words over and over, like a litany, she dragged herself into the shower.

Once she was dressed, she left her room and as she crossed through the communal area of the staff quarters on her way to the office, a loud cry accosted her.

'Lucy, Lucy,' called Hekla, with her usual boundless enthusiasm.

'Morning,' she said stiffly, conscious of the other girl's glowing skin and shining eyes, contrasting with her own dull complexion and purpled shadowed bags.

'Come, come,' she said linking her arm through Lucy's. 'I want to show you my favourite thing. Well,' she amended, 'one of my favourite things.' Dragging her along like a rampant St Bernard on a rescue mission, Hekla led her from the staff area back to the main hotel.

Helpless to resist all that enthusiasm, Lucy allowed herself to be propelled along without complaint to the long glass corridor connecting the two buildings.

Hekla stopped dead, her head tipped back and her arms stretched out wide, almost touching the glass on either side of her. 'It feels like you're outside, but you're not.' She grinned at Lucy with child-like delight, her arms flapping up and down as if she were making snow angels. 'Look.'

Outside the snow which lit up the twilit sky, had started falling in earnest with huge flakes floating down like feathers settling on a gentle breeze. In a slow waltz, they danced and whirled, swirling around the glass structure like delicate ballerinas, almost hitting the glass and then at the last second spinning away as if teasing death before they escaped. Entranced, Lucy looked up through the glass ceiling, the sight almost dizzying, as the concentration of layer upon layer of flakes seemed to be coming down in never-ending torrent strings.

It was like being in an inside out snow globe, she thought, as those less fortunate flakes, doomed to an early eclipse, hit the glass with tiny pfft, pfft sounds, as the ice crystals splatted against the surface.

'I've never seen such huge snowflakes,' said Lucy in sheer wonderment, as she followed the path of one which she could have sworn was the same size as her hand.

'Hundslappadrifa,' beamed Hekla. 'We have a name for this type of snow. In translation it means dog's feet snow.'

Lucy clapped her hands in delight. It was the most perfect description. 'I love that. Although, I guess we won't be able to go to Hvolsvöllur this morning.' The snow had settled fast in the last half hour, a good inch already rounding off the edges of the fences and rooflines outside. She'd been looking forward to getting out of the hotel and seeing a bit of Iceland, even if it was only the nearest town twenty minutes away.

'Of course we will,' said Hekla. 'In Iceland, snow doesn't stop us. Petta reddast.'

'What does that mean?'

Hekla grinned. 'I'll tell you in the jeep on the way.'

* * *

Buckled in, cocooned in the warm fug of the car, they drove along the straight road towards the lights of the town glowing in the distance like a beacon.

'Will we be alright?' asked Lucy dubiously looking at the thickening layer of snow which was building quickly.

'Ja,' said Hekla, with blithe confidence patting the steering wheel. 'This baby will get us there and back with no problems.'

'At home, everything would have ground to halt already,' observed Lucy, thinking of last winter and the mass influx of snow-clad travellers turning up at the hotel in Manchester unable to get home.

'Ha, this is Iceland. We're made of strong stuff. Like I said before, petta reddast, it's a saying we have. Everything will be OK. Living here, we have a belief that we can do things. There is always something to face, the storms, floods, snowfall, ice and volcanoes. It is the land of heat and fire, but we Icelanders, we can do great things. We have self-belief. Remember our football team,' she turned with a sly smile haunting her mouth. 'We beat the English, a small team from a country of 340,000 people. Our manger was a part-time dentist.'

'I remember,' said Lucy dryly, thinking back to Chris's cocky pre-match dismissive attitude to the threat of the Icelandic team and his irate howls at the television during the match when Iceland scored two goals to England's one.

'It is a positive attitude,' she cast an arm towards the scene outside. 'It is hard living here, you have to survive.

The Vikings that came here from Europe had to carve out a life. It breeds a toughness but also a team spirit. Together we can make things happen. For example, Elin, believes that she will write and publish her book, Freya will be a great actress one day and Brynja trains for the marathon. All of them believe that they will succeed.'

'And what about you?' asked Lucy.

'One day I will travel. As a child I went to many places with my parents but I want to do what you've done, travel to a new country and work in a good hotel.' Hekla grinned. 'But I want to make The Northern Lights Lodge the best hotel before I leave. I've lived in many places but this is the place that feels like home. I want people who come here to see how wonderful my country is. I want them to remember their stay here forever.'

'You and me both,' said Lucy. 'I hope you don't plan to leave too soon.'

Hekla shrugged. 'It depends on the new owners.'

'New owners?' The words croaked out of Lucy's throat in sudden alarm. 'What do you mean?'

Hekla gave her a startled look. 'You know, the hotel is for sale.'

'For sale?' Panic clutched at Lucy, her stomach clenching in fear. A change of ownership often meant a change of management. 'What, now?'

'Ja, there is a prospective buyer. They are negotiating but Mr Pedersen said that it is likely that things will be signed in December.'

Lucy swallowed hard. December. Her contract was up

in December. At her sharp indrawn breath, Hekla looked at her.

'Don't worry. They will need a manager.'

'Yes but...' Not necessarily me. Now the short-term contract made perfect sense, she realised with a sinking heart. Not the probationary period she'd assumed because they were taking her without proper references but short term because they wouldn't need her.

'Petta reddast,' reminded Hekla gently. 'It will work out. I think already you have good ideas. You have good experience, ja?'

Lucy nodded. She did have bloody good experience. The best. She could make this work. Maybe she needed to believe in herself, she always had done before. Everything had been fine before that damned video had gone viral, until head office had fired her, before Chris had shafted her so well and truly.

Hvolsvöllur was even smaller than Lucy had expected, the town sitting in a flat vale with a few roads. Red rooved houses lined the roads as Hekla drove through, pointing out where her cousins had lived, an uncle, her school friend's mother's house. It seemed as if Hekla knew everyone in town. She knew exactly where to go to buy the coffee machine that had been their principal purpose and within half an hour they were done.

'Would you like to stop in the tourist shop, Una Local?' she asked. 'It has some nice things.'

'That would be nice,' said Lucy gloomily. 'I might have

to buy Christmas presents to take home with me.' Something for Daisy who'd been so good to her this past year and her Mum and Dad who thought this was a great adventure and had no idea what had driven her to make such a radical career change.

Hekla shook her head. 'Petta reddast. You are an Icelander now. A solution will come.'

'I hope so,' muttered Lucy, who until now deliberately hadn't thought beyond mid-December.

'It will,' said Hekla, with what Lucy now thought of as her Viking Princess resilience.

The shop wasn't the prettiest building. It looked more like a series of three airport hangers painted red, yellow and blue with a large puffin painted on the front door, but inside the white airy space was filled with well-displayed traditional Icelandic crafts and gifts on little wooden tables. Fairy lights were strung around the ceiling and Lucy did a double take at the sight of a bicycle suspended on its side and the various ornaments dangling from the spokes of the wheels. On the walls, hanging from hangers on hooks, there was a fine selection of the heavy wool jumpers she associated with Northern Europe, the necklines decorated with the familiar Scandinavian knitted patterns, along with woollen poncho style tops, scarves and hats. There were pretty watercolours of puffins, photographs of hardy Icelandic ponies, papier mâché trolls, printed cushions and colourful tea-towels. Everything, although eye-wateringly expensive, was beautifully made and Lucy could have spent a fortune. In one corner there was a Norse Viking figure made of sheepskin, with a knitted helmet around which a couple of tourists crowded taking selfies with lots of laughs and smiles. Even Lucy had to smile at the sight of the big shambling figure.

Hekla had already struck up a conversation with the sales lady as Lucy wandered around. She stopped again beside a display of puffin watercolour pictures. Simple but effective, she thought, they would look perfect in the guest lounge. She picked one up and carried it towards Hekla.

'You're going to buy a picture?' she asked.

Lucy shook her head. 'I'd really like to display a couple in the hotel, we could direct guests here to buy them, if,' she turned to the sales lady Hekla had been chatting to, 'you'd be interested.'

She was interested in the bite-your-hand-off sort of way that Lucy had hoped for and it didn't take long for them to sort out a mutually satisfying arrangement that had her humming to herself as they carried three paintings out to the car, with the promise of more to come which could be picked up in a couple of days.

'Nice work,' said Hekla, 'that is a good idea.'

'Yup,' said Lucy with a mischievous smile, feeling a sense of achievement. 'Free decorations for the walls. The guest lounge is lovely but it needs more. We never did ask Eyrun about what happened to the other things.'

'No, we didn't.' Hekla's airy response made Lucy giggle.

'You're scared of her too.'

Hekla tried and failed to keep an innocent face before giggling back at her and nodding.

'She terrifies me. That's why you're the boss. You have to ask her.' Hekla threw her a challenging glance. 'Two shots. Tomorrow night.'

'Sorry.'

'Tomorrow. We are playing card games in the staff lounge. Drinking games.' Hekla's face wreathed in mischief. 'Dares. If you don't ask Eyrun, you have to drink two shots.'

Lucy laughed. 'And what do you do, if I do?'

Hekla shrugged. 'I guess I have to drink two shots.'

'Does this happen often?' asked Lucy.

'The evenings are long and dark, we like to get together. The card games are Elin's idea. She and Brynja and Freya are all good fun. And Brynja's boyfriend, Dagur and Gunnar are so funny. Olafur can be a bit sulky sometimes but then he forgets and he's nice. And new Alex is fun too and very easy on the eye as they say.'

Back in the car on their way to the hotel, Hekla reminded her of their dare. Lucy shrugged. She'd never backed down from a challenge, even so she was going to have to steel herself for another run in with Eyrun.

'Eyrun?' Lucy called, cross with herself for being so timid. She was in charge here for heaven's sake. Despite the dull rhythmic thud of towels in the huge dryer, there was no sign of the Head of Housekeeping. Lucy let out a small sigh of relief

Was it any wonder Eyrun rarely left her little cave, there was something rather soothing about the somnolent thrum of the dryers? The warm dry air made her feel pleasantly dopey and relaxed and she closed her eyes for a few minutes, just letting herself be for a while. Hekla's positive attitude and talk of petta reddast this morning had given Lucy food for thought. She'd always been organised and successful through hard work and diligence but, before now, she'd never had to face much adversity.

All the angry bees that had been buzzing in her head for so long, keeping her awake at night with their *what ifs* and *if onlys,* had taken flight, leaving a welcome nothingness in her head. The cycle of constant recriminations and fear of doing everything wrong that had hamstrung and exhausted her the past year had dissipated for once, and with Hekla's words taking root, she was thinking about being more resilient. Not letting Chris win. She'd needed to take charge, assert her authority and not just with Eyrun.

When the dryer had finally finished its cycle, the quiet of the Lodge echoed in her ears, so silent and still she could almost hear the soft buzz of the dust and fibres settling.

For a second, she gave into the quiet atmosphere, slouching against a trolley, her head resting on the metal handle.

As she drooped over the trolley, she saw the sliver of light widen as the door opened very, very slowly.

Someone slipped in and with furtive intent looked around, overlooking her in the dark corner. The male figure moved forward towards the other room which housed the huge industrial washing machines and a couple of floor-to-ceiling storage cupboards. She watched as he carefully pushed the door too behind him, leaving it an inch open.

What on earth was he up to? And who was it? Lucy felt uncomfortable spying but as someone in the hotel had been playing unwelcome games, she felt justified even though there'd been no repeat of the dead mice or any other tricks recently. Was she about to catch the culprit in the act? She grabbed an armful of sheets from a nearby trolley to give her a reason for being here and creeping forward to the doorway of the stockroom, she peeped through the gap.

Alex! What on earth was he doing in here?

For a few seconds she watched him as he sifted through a pile of duvet covers, poked at the stack of pillowcases, opened a few cupboards and crouched down to take a closer look at the washing powders and cleaning fluids on the shelf.

Lucy pushed open the door making as much noise as she could.

He whirled round, his handsome face a picture.

Handsome. For God's sake, Lucy, he's nice looking, that's all. But there was a distinct flutter in her stomach.

For what felt like a second too long they stared at one another, with that momentary *now what* of a pair of gun slingers facing each other.

'Alex!' Her voice was an octave too high. 'Fancy seeing you here? Are you helping out with the laundry now?'

'No, I was...' he looked around as if hoping inspiration might jump up and slap him in the face.

'You looked as if you were looking for something?' she asked, tensing as she realised she was desperate for him to be honest about what he was doing.

'Er yes ... some cloths. For the ... er ... kitchen. Tea-towels.'

Lucy narrowed her gaze at him, before pointedly looking towards to the room behind them and the shelves by the door, neatly stacked with smaller cloths and tea-towels, used by the kitchen.

Alex flushed, following her gaze. 'Sorry. Not thinking. Completely forgot. You know what it's like when you've worked in lots of different places. You get a bit confused every now and then.' His gabbled speech was so unlike his usual cool, collected self, that Lucy almost felt sorry for him until he changed the subject quickly.

'And how are you finding things?' he asked in that cool, authoritative yet charming way as if he were the one that was in charge. 'I hear you've promoted Elin.'

'Yes,' she said stiffly, wondering what business it was of his. 'She's now Assistant Housekeeper. Doing a great job.'

'Good move.'

'Thank you,' she said with a touch of withering sarcasm. Had he forgotten who was in charge here?

He shrugged, with an anodyne smile that irritated her even more.

Why was it that he always managed to catch her at a disadvantage?

'Is there anything else you need in here?' she asked desperate to reassert her authority.

'No,' he looked at his watch, 'I must be off.' And with a

quick smile, he sauntered away as if he had all the time in the world.

'You forgot your tea-towels,' she called with a triumphant crow, but he'd already left the room. She scowled after him, so much for her taking charge.

Chapter 9

The following morning, Lucy heard the unwelcome words, 'Hi, I'm Clive Tenterden with See The World Productions.'

She bustled out of the office to join Brynja at the front desk.

'We have a booking for five.' He winked. 'Cribs for my crew.' He hoicked his thumb over his shoulder. 'Camera man, sound man, production assistant and grip.'

'Good morning, I'm Lucy Smart, General Manager. Welcome to The Northern Lights Lodge. I understand you're filming in the area and will be staying with us.'

'Hey Lucy. Nice to meet you. This is the crew, I'll introduce you all later. You're going to get to know us real well over the next few weeks.'

Behind, a group of men and one woman had gathered around a mountain of black boxes and were talking quietly to one another. Alex was helping one of the men with a few cases, doubling up as he was prone to do and helping out taking luggage to rooms.

Lucy nodded smiling even though her cheeks were

hurting with the effort. Few weeks? Where was the memo on that one? Was their stay complimentary? At least there was plenty of room. Bookings were still down despite the hideously expensive ads she'd signed off this week in a couple of international travel magazines.

'I hope you're going to have an enjoyable stay here. I've allocated you some lovely rooms and The Northern Lights Lodge is a great base for exploring the local area. If you'd all like to check in and get settled. Dinner, this evening, is between seven and nine in the dining room. Would you like me to book you a table?'

'That would be great. Perhaps you could join us for dinner and we can talk about what sort of thing we need from you and the sort of access we're going to want.'

Lucy stared at the man's smiley isn't-this-going-to-be-so-much fun face and tried to adjust hers into professional indifference, although inside she was starting to have the mild signs of a panic attack. *Access*. What did that mean?

'You look a bit uncertain, Lucy. Don't you worry about a thing, once you get used to the cameras, you really won't know we're here. You never know it might make you a star.'

Lucy froze. That was the absolute last thing on the planet she ever wanted to be.

'Cameras?'

'Well, just the one really but it'll be right there, in your face.'

'I'm sorry. I don't understand.'

Clive looked at her, a slightly worried frown on his face. 'You do know we're filming a fly on the wall travel documentary. Warts and all in an Iceland lodge chasing the magical aurora borealis. In between visiting the top tourist must-see sights, we'll be filming how a local lodge is run.'

No, she did not know that. The hotel wasn't anywhere near ready for that kind of spotlight. There was still so much to do. And ... it hit her. Fuck. Fuck. Fuck. It all came rushing back. Everyone looking at her. Sniggering behind her back. The lewd remarks. Suggestive stares. Talking about her. It would all start up again. For a minute she thought her legs might collapse beneath her. Her lungs felt tight in her chest and ... and she couldn't...

'E-excuse me,' she stammered, waving her hand at Brynja. 'I n-need to check the ... the ... C-can you...'

To her relief Brynja stepped forward and smoothly took over, sliding the registration forms towards the man.

She backed away. She needed to get to the office. Needed to breathe. Look normal. She caught sight of one face. One of the crew. Was she imagining it or was he staring at her with one of those don't-I-know-you expressions on his face? She ducked her head, backed up another step and mercifully felt the door behind her.

Safe in the office, she closed the door with a firm thunk behind her and put her hand on the door leaning over. The room went black and her chest constricted as she desperately tried to suck in air. It wouldn't come. She tried again. And again. Her head was about to explode.

'Lucy?' A voice sounded as if it were coming from a very long way away. 'Lucy. Are you OK?'

She forced herself to focus on Alex's voice. Forcing herself inch by inch up the black tunnel. Tight bands held her chest. She gasped, trying to take in another breath that did nothing and another and another.

Hands grabbed hers and led her to a chair, pushing gently, until she sat down.

'It's OK, Lucy. You're safe. You're fine. Listen to me. You're OK.'

She felt his hand come to rest on her stomach.

'Next time you try to breathe push out your stomach against my hand as you inhale and try to breathe in through your nose.'

He repeated the words and she tried to make sense of them. Breathe out. No inhale. Nose. She closed her eyes and listened to his voice.

'Inhale through your nose. Push against my hand. And again. Inhale, push. That's it. Inhale, push.'

His voice took on a gentle rhythmic monotony which was both soothing and reassuring.

'That's it. You're doing fine, Lucy. You're doing fine. You're going to be OK.'

Gradually she felt the panic subside and although her pulse thudded furiously, she felt herself start to settle. Alex's hand was still lying on her stomach, just above her diaphragm, and his other hand rubbing soothing circles on her back. She blinked up at him, trying to assimilate everything, grateful for his quiet presence. Through the door she could hear the busy reception, Brynja talking, people laughing and the sound of luggage being wheeled over the polished lava floor tiles.

'You OK?'

Feeling dazed, she nodded, tears pricking at her eyes as shock and embarrassment set in. Her mouth crumpled as she muttered, 'I'm sorry,' with a little hitch to her voice. She couldn't believe she'd made such a fool of herself. And in front of Alex of all people. The man who saw so much, there were times when she thought he should be running this place. He always seemed so together with that natural easy authority of his.

She sniffed and tried to turn away.

'Hey,' his voice resonated with something that made her heart ping in her chest. 'Don't cry.' With gentle hands he pulled her into a hug and, although she was not normally one for the damsel in distress routine, for once it was rather nice to bury her head against his chest. And when his arms closed around her, she sank into his warm hold and let the rest of the world and all its problems recede away. There was something rather wonderful about being held. No words, just another body, cocooning her and keeping her safe. Beneath her cheek, she could feel Alex's chest lift and fall in a steady, reassuring rhythm through the thin cotton of his shirt.

He smelled good, male and clean, with a hint of cedar and sandalwood. She closed her eyes realising this was the first time she'd been held for a very long time. After what had happened, she'd shied away from other people, even Daisy. She hadn't wanted comfort, she was too angry and humiliated for that. Too determined to put a brave face on things and show the world that she was OK, when inside she was dying of shame.

Breathing in Alex's scent, she was grateful for his quiet steadiness, the way that he didn't try and say anything. It demonstrated that gentle confidence he had and the unassuming authority he wore so well. Today he felt like an ancient harbour hewn of stone that had offered shelter in stormy seas countless times and would always be there to do it again. And when had she become so fanciful?

She pulled away and looked up at him. Those amber flecked eyes studied her, solemn and unblinking, radiating kindness and concern.

'Thank you.' She tried to summon up a tremulous smile but failed miserably. 'Weren't you helping with their luggage?'

'I saw you needed help.'

'I appreciate it.'

'Anytime.' His grave tone and simple response reassured her. No platitudes. No fuss. No false sympathy, just steadfast silent support as if he knew that was exactly what she needed.

'Sorry about that I...' she winced. The whole sordid escapade was still too raw and hideous. 'I-I...'

'Lucy,' he laid a finger to her lips. 'You don't have to explain anything.' He gave her arms a quick squeeze. 'Can I get you anything? A coffee? Something to eat?'

She took in a deep breath and exhaled, shaking her head.

'Have you eaten this morning?'

'No, Mum. I grabbed a coffee.' Thank goodness for the new coffee machine which had proved a big hit.

'Coffee?' Alex said and then tsked.

'I haven't had time,' she protested, horribly aware of her untidy desk directly in her eyeline. Every day there seemed to be more to do.

'Well there you go, you daft woman,' his Scottish accent deepened. 'You should've had your porridge.'

Now she did smile at him. 'Porridge, of course. So that's where I went wrong.'

'And you probably need a break from this place. Have you had a proper day off since you've been here?'

She shrugged.

'And when's your next day off.'

'Supposedly ... today,' she muttered, dropping her gaze.

With two fingers he lifted her chin as he lifted one arched eyebrow. 'It just so happens it's my day off too, today, and I'm off to see a waterfall which I've been assured by Hekla is one of "the" things to see. Gullfoss.'

Lucy smiled, he sounded rather proud that he could pronounce it. 'Excellent Icelandic accent,' she teased.

'To be honest, it is the only place that I can pronounce. Might as well start somewhere.' His face sobered and then he asked. 'So, why don't you come with me?'

A car pulled up in front of her, a tiny white Toyota Aygo and Alex waved from the driver's seat as the passenger window slid down.

'Hop in.'

'Sadly no porridge, but...' she held up two foil packages, 'I did blag some bacon butties for the journey,' she said, climbing in and fastening her seatbelt.

'Excellent and don't tell anyone but I don't miss porridge that much,' said Alex, with a crooked grin, 'not when bacon butties are on offer.'

'I'm not convinced the 3G en route is going to be that great. How's your navigation?' he asked with a cheery smile, handing her a map.

'So, so.' She unfurled the map to peer at it. 'But it's not as if there are a lot of roads here. It looks pretty straight-forward. I had a quick look on Google.'

'I should have known. You are a planner. Don't worry, we stay on the main coast road for most of the way and then we take a right, by which time it should be light. Hekla says it's well signposted. You can probably stand down as a navigator.'

'I wonder if it's going to snow again,' said Lucy looking up at the sky, which was the clearest it had been for a few days. The previous dump of snow had melted fast leaving the roads completely clear and it was a couple of degrees warmer. 'The forecast for today is quite good. Allegedly there will be sunshine.' She wasn't convinced but Brynja had insisted on checking three different weather pages once she'd heard where Lucy was going.

'Yeah, it's supposed to brighten up later. You have dressed for every eventuality, haven't you? The weather is very changeable.'

He slid the car into gear and swung out of the car park onto the road.

'So Hekla and Brynja keep telling me.' Lucy laughed and leaned back in her chair adjusting the seat back. It felt good to be out of the hotel. 'Hekla's been fussing around me like a mother hen. Three layers. You need three layers. You can take layers off. Put layers on.' She attempted to mimic Hekla's accent. 'And no jeans, they take too long to dry. Hence these rather attractive khaki numbers she forced Brynja to lend me.' Despite the fact that Brynja was several inches shorter and a size bigger. However, thick long woolly socks filled the missing inches above Lucy's walking boots and she'd pushed them around her ankles leg warmer style so that she didn't look completely ridiculous.

'She said the same to me,' said Alex, focusing on the road. 'And my fleece was given her personal seal of approval.'

'Well done, my waterproof wasn't. It was snatched out of my hands with a spiel of heavy-duty Icelandic disapproval before she went rifling through the lost property box in the office to find this.' Lucy held out the zipped edge of the sturdy navy Berghaus coat before wriggling out of it and stowing it at her feet. 'She gives the same lecture to the guests at least once a day. I think she might be an undercover operator for Mountain Warehouse.' Lucy looked down at her drab, sensible but practical clothing and remembered the recruitment consultant in her red suit. Home was a very long way away.

'Neat theory, although it could be she wants to make sure everyone enjoys their time here. I've noticed she's very passionate about her own country. There's nothing worse than being cold and miserable.'

Outside the car the heavy cloud cover made it difficult to believe the promised sunshine would materialise. It was still quite dark despite the sunrise at quarter to nine. The car's headlights carved a strong beam tracking along the ribbon of mostly single-track road.

'Tell me about it. It took me four years to get used to the weather in Manchester.'

'You'd be fine in Edinburgh then.'

'I've been a couple of times on business. I loved it. The company I wo… I went to a couple of conferences up there. The city is so dramatic, especially with the castle perched up high above the town.'

'And wet and cold in the winter,' said Alex. 'So where do you come from originally?'

'Portsmouth, although I can't imagine ever going back there. I like living in the north.'

'This far north?'

'Hmm not sure that I could live here forever.' Her spirits drooped. 'My plan was to stick it out here for at least a year, before I knew the place is up for sale. Unfortunately,' she held up a hand before he could comment on her stupidity, 'I'm on a temporary contract.' There was a silence when she thought he might have commented, so she carried on, 'I thought it was a probationary precaution, now I realise it paves the way for any new owners to bring in their own team of people. And yes, feel free to tell me that was a dumb thing to do.'

Alex didn't say anything, he seemed to be focusing hard on the road.

In the quiet of the car, with the engine humming, she brooded about the future. Reluctant to disturb Alex's concentration, she stared out of the window at the endless black tarmac road lit up by the golden beam of the head-lights.

She could see the grey ribbon of road stretching ahead for miles, weaving its way through the virtually uninhabited landscape. As they drove along, houses were few and far between, although the sheep were plentiful and quite a few strayed dangerously close to the road. As they followed the signs towards Reykjavik, Lucy reflected that it seemed a long time since she'd first driven this way, her heart sinking at how far the lodge was from any town of any size.

'I can't believe I've been here nearly two weeks already.'

'Time flies when you're enjoying yourself,' teased Alex.

'Or working double shifts,' she retorted. 'I'm glad that the staff are all more settled and there's been no more talk about flipping elves. Although I'm still wondering where the dead mice came from and what stopped them.'

'You mean it wasn't the magic unicorn?' he asked with a quick raise of his eyebrows.

'I never thanked you for that. I don't think I'll ever forget the "steals their magic". It was inspired,' she laughed.

Alex smirked. 'Not as inspired as the unicorn idea to start with.' His face softened and he turned to her. 'I owe you an apology actually. You handled it well. I'd have told them to stop with the nonsense if they wanted to be paid. I realise now that some people do take this elf stuff seriously.'

'Mm,' said Lucy, remembering his stern expression that morning and the disapproval he'd radiated. 'I think you'll find it was less inspiration and more desperation. My first day and I panicked. God knows what I'd have done if all the staff had walked out. Funny there hasn't been a repeat of the anything like the "mices". You haven't heard of anything?'

Alex shook his head. 'No, it's a bit of a mystery.'

'Mystery? That's a kind way of putting it. Pretty mean trick. Someone playing a joke that really wasn't very funny. Let's hope with the arrival of the film crew, they'll keep their tricks to themselves.'

They lapsed into thoughtful silence.

'Do you want any music on?' asked Alex, his hand straying to the radio.

'Hmm, not sure. Apart from Björk, I don't know any Icelandic music.'

'Don't worry, I've got a playlist on my phone.'

'Could be interesting,' said Lucy. 'What sort of playlist is it?'

Alex looked worried. 'It's just a playlist.'

'Not a driving playlist, then.'

'No,' he said warily. 'A playlist of tracks I like.'

She pulled out her phone. 'I have playlists for running, driving, cleaning.'

'Cleaning? You have a cleaning playlist.'

'Yes,' said Lucy. 'Doesn't everyone?'

'Clearly not,' said Alex. 'Although it's not something I think about that much. I do the bare minimum when I absolutely have to.'

'Typical man.'

'I prefer to call it an efficient time and motion approach.

So, what's on your driving playlist? Is it fit for human consumption?'

'Of course. Don't you trust me?'

'No, you might be a closet Metallica fan.'

Lucy pretended to think for a moment.

'I might be.'

'Are you?'

Lucy giggled and stopped. She was rusty in that department. It was a long time since she'd felt like giggling. 'I couldn't name a single one of their tracks.'

'No, you look more of a Take That type.'

'And what does that look like?' She lifted one dangerous eyebrow daring him to comment.

'Er ... you know ... normal.'

'I'll take normal. To be honest I'm not really that into music. I never had that much time to listen.'

'Give us your worst, put on your playlist.'

Luckily Alex didn't seem to mind her music and even commented a couple of times that he liked a track. He made her skip one but then she wasn't a huge Justin Bieber fan either.

'Look, the sun's coming out.' They'd been driving for forty minutes and the earlier thick black clouds had started to thin, like a ragged net, their edges tinged with pale pink and gold, and within the breaks Lucy could see pale blue sky.

'I think Hekla might have got the weather right, it is going to be a nice day.'

'Ah look, I think this is our turning. And yes, there's a sign post.' They followed the signs which were excellent, but then Lucy figured, you wouldn't want people getting lost out here, the landscape was pretty inhospitable and even quite eerie in some places, like an alien planet. On some stretches of road, there hadn't a been a single sign of human habitation for miles. She was glad that Alex was driving.

The road began to climb and before long they were pulling into the car park at Gullfoss.

'Oh goodness, you can hear it,' said Lucy, listening to the boom of water as they started walking up the footpath, passing early risers going the other way, drenched in their sodden waterproofs although managing cheery grins.

They stopped on the path as they caught their first glimpse of the torrent of water crashing down the craggy rocks. Fine sprays of water drifted through the air, rising up from the deep river bed billowing across the chasm like gossamer curtains floating on the breeze.

'Wow,' said Lucy, staring down at the roiling, foaming flow racing over the edge of the dark rocks like an unstoppable force.

'It's quite something.' For a moment the pair of them marvelled at the view.

'Do you want to go up there, out on the ledge?' asked Alex, pointing to the rocky ledge protruding almost into the heart of the waterfall. There were already a few people up there, standing like tiny ants against the backdrop of the white foam of the water. It frothed, boiling with movement before racing down in perpetual columns through the rocks to the edge where the wide river simply dropped away into a deep channel.

'Or up there?' he turned and pointed to the much safer vantage point on the hill above the waterfall.

Lucy lifted her face, welcoming the cold bite of the fine mist against her skin, and looked at the wooden fenced enclosure on the top of the hill and then back at the ledge around which the water churned and foamed like furious white horses. Down there the sound would be deafening, the air laden with water droplets and the proximity to the edge terrifying.

'The ledge,' she said feeling a punch of adrenaline, turning and grinning at Alex, the hair escaping from her hat already plastered to her face.

'OK,' said Alex grinning back, taking her hand as he picked up the pace and headed forwards with a purposeful stride. 'Let's do this.'

By the time they reached the rocky plateau, they were both slightly breathless, their faces covered in a fine sheen of water, with rivulets running from chins and noses. Alex stepped out first, gingerly side-stepping puddles and sharp rocks, and then waited, holding out his hand again to guide her through. She hesitated, a mix of fear and excitement scrambling her thoughts and then saw him nodding at her, encouragement shining in those warm brown eyes. With a tremulous smile she took his hand and followed him out onto the shelf of rock.

When they reached the centre of the ledge, surrounded on two sides by water, her hand gripping his, they stopped.

The roar of the water thudded through her body sending her pulse racing in tandem with the elemental thrill of the raw power of nature. She stood absorbing the sensation of sheer power and the feeling of being a hairsbreadth away from annihilation.

Alex caught her eye and she beamed at him. 'This is amazing,' she yelled above the noise of the water, unable to keep the emotion from her face. Exhilaration pumped through her along with the crash of the water. She'd never seen or heard anything quite like it. For a moment she was convinced she could conquer the world.

He grinned and pushed the water-soaked hair from his face, his skin coated in fine droplets. They caught in the faint stubble on his chin and sparkled like diamonds in the rising sun. When Lucy saw them, she smiled.

'What?' he asked loudly but she had to lip read to understand.

'You're sparkling,' she shouted.

'What?'

She lifted on to her toes and yelled again in his ear, 'Sparkling!' Raising a hand, she brushed at his jaw. He shifted his head, ducking his chin, laughing as if it tickled and her fingers accidentally grazed his lips.

For a brief second, something shimmered between them, as his eyes met hers. Hyper alert, every sense tuned in, she noticed the tiny amber flecks around his pupils, envied the thick dark lashes fringing the lower lid, felt the tiny prickle of stubble under her fingers and the dart of something hot and sharp in her chest.

The roar of the waterfall around them receded and it was just the two of them, holding each other's gaze like a lifeline between them. She didn't drop her hand like she should have done, instead for some crazy reason, her fingers explored that intriguing little indent in his lower lip. Hot breath caressed her skin and then his upper lip closed down in a barely-there kiss and … she felt the touch of his tongue. The shocking dart of heat between her legs made her drop her hand with a quick indrawn gasp.

The intensity of his gaze softened, replaced by the warmth and kindness she was used to, almost as he knew how unnerved she was by that sharp prick of desire.

'Who doesn't want to sparkle?' He grinned at her again, that friendly happy smile she'd become used to and to her relief the moment evaporated. 'Do you want to go nearer to the edge?'

'You bet,' she called back, surprising herself. This was what the old Lucy would have done. How long had it been since she had appeared?

Buffeted by the spray of water, they picked their way through the pitted surface of the rocks, by this time completely soaked and Lucy was extremely glad of the woolly hat and the super-efficient waterproof that Hekla had insisted she bring.

The thunderous roar of the torrents of water pounding over the rocks made it impossible to hear but Alex mouthed the words. 'You OK?'

She gave him a thumbs up even though she couldn't decide whether she was terrified or exhilarated. When she pulled her phone out of her pocket to take a few pictures, the screen was covered in water drops within seconds and she quickly decided it wasn't worth risking.

Out on the rock, so close to the water was like being in the eye of the storm. Water, thunder, fury. Pounding and cascading, torrents and torrents of water flooded down over the stepped rocks. She felt surrounded by sheer power, reverberating underfoot as the fine spray crept into the seams of her waterproof and coated her face. Awed, her pulse pumped hard and despite the moisture in the air, her mouth had dried up. Lucy kept well back from the edge where a single green rope was all that marked the end of the safe zone and the edge of the rock. If you went over, you'd be a goner. There'd be no coming back. It was easy to imagine you'd be swept into the depths of the earth. From here the waterfall dropped a good hundred foot to another ledge and then the water changed angle and there was another level below before the river cascaded into a deep rocky channel below to flow away to the sea.

She and Alex stood side by side, staring at the mighty show of raw power. He glanced at her and shook his head and mouthed *Whoa. Amazing.* She nodded back. Looking at this, her problems seemed puny and insignificant. The world, nature, so much larger than everything else. It was as if something loosened inside her, freeing her from the web of angst that had wrapped itself around her.

She lifted her head and took in a long deep breath, savouring the water on her face, the thunder in her ears. Alex caught her expression, concern shadowing his eyes.

She gave him a brilliant smile, her mouth curving involuntarily. 'I'm OK,' she mouthed, wanting to share with him the delicious sensation of a load lifted. 'I'm OK.' When he responded with a sweet smile, it hit her with an unexpected ache in her chest, stirring an acute longing, for quite what she wasn't sure. Whether it was the sense of the two of them being so small against the maelstrom of nature's power around them, a subtle solidarity in a unique shared experience, she didn't know but something shifted between them. He put an arm round her shoulders and pulled her to him and together they stood watching the sheer power of the water crashing around them.

Eventually the creeping cold working its way inside their layers drove them back to the path and they walked up to the vantage point, their hands still linked, saying little as if the power of the water had taken away the ability to think and talk.

Once at the top looking back down on where they'd been, Lucy felt as if she were coming back to earth.

'That was quite something,' she breathed as they leaned over the wooden rail watching the tiny figures of people standing where they'd been. 'I'm going to tell all the guests that they have to come here.'

Alex laughed. 'But it's the first place you've been to. You might say that about our next destination.'

'Seriously, if anything can beat this, I'll eat my...' she tugged at the woolly hat on her head. 'Well perhaps not literally. But come on ... how could anyone not be impressed by this? I had no idea it was going to be... Do you think the other places are as amazing?'

'This is what people come to Iceland for. The geological and natural wonders. I'm guessing a geyser that shoots boiling water 100 feet in the air every few minutes is fairly mind blowing.'

Lucy shivered. 'Boiling is starting to sound good. I'm getting cold.'

'Me too, shall we track down a coffee and something to eat at the visitor centre? Hekla says we have to try the meat broth.'

Lucy hid a wry smile. 'You're as bad as me. What Hekla says goes. She's very keen that we fall in love with Iceland.'

Having dried off and warmed up with coffee and a bowl of the very heart-warming lamb and vegetable soup, which was delicious, they got back in the car and headed off to see the geyser geothermal springs, which Lucy read up on from a leaflet she'd picked up at the visitor centre. Feeling that she'd been woefully under prepared in coming to Iceland, she read the leaflet from cover to cover before peppering Alex with facts as they drove. Whatever had happened to the queen of TripAdvisor and planning the shit out of everything, as Chris had accused her of doing? (And he wasn't being complimentary.)

'Did you know the last time–'

'Enough, enough,' teased Alex. 'Take a break Tour Guide Lucy. I know enough for the specialist subject round on Mastermind.'

'You'll be grateful, when we get there,' said Lucy primly, burying her nose in the leaflet again with mock indignation, before adding with a quick mischievous grin, 'did you know, they used to put soap in the geyser to make it erupt.'

'Really?' He shot her a disbelieving look.

'Honest.'

The weather had completely changed when they arrived at the carpark and they abandoned their waterproofs as they climbed out of the car.

'Phew, it's a lot quieter here,' said Lucy, stretching her arms out, welcoming the warmth of the sun's rays and the silence after the constant roar of water which had left a ringing in her ears for a while.

'And drier,' said Alex running his hand through his dishevelled hair.

'It's lovely to be outside,' observed Lucy, realising that since she'd arrived she'd stayed inside far too much. They crossed the main road to the site of the geothermal field, which needed no signage. The rolling clouds of steam were advertisement enough.

'Did you get out much when you were in Manchester? There's some nice scenery around there isn't there? Moorland. Not too far from the Lake District.'

'There speaks a Scot,' said Lucy. 'It's a good hour or two.'

'That's nae time at all,' he said, his accent broadening.

'I guess not,' said Lucy sadly. 'But I never seemed to have the time.'

They strolled along the path, Lucy tipping her head up to catch the sun on her face.

'Sounds like you worked pretty hard in Manchester. What made you move out here? Take on the Lodge? It's quite a radical change.' Somehow Alex had taken her hand again and it didn't feel odd or strange.

Despite feeling comfortable with him, the familiar lie slipped out easily, she couldn't bear to see disappointment on his face. 'I fancied a change of scene. I was a bit burnt out. Fed up with working for a big faceless corporation. I wanted to...' she gazed over to where a large crowd had gathered in a semi-circle. Everyone was watching a small crater in the centre of the pond, the water roiling and bubbling. She knew how that felt. When she thought about her old job, that same bubbling anger rose to the surface. She pulled her hand from his and shoved both hands into her pocket, forcing her face into a mask of calm serenity she certainly didn't feel.

'Wanted to?' prompted Alex as they veered towards the gathered people.

Diverted by the anticipation of the crowd, Lucy reconsidered what she'd been going to say. Ever since she'd come to Iceland, she'd had a glib rehearsed line about wanting to reconnect with the guests and get to know her colleagues. For a minute the words eluded her as if she couldn't bring herself to spoil the day with lies. She stared at the smooth film of water covering the dome in the centre of the circle of people. The surface began to move and there was a whisper of anticipation, the water seemed to breathe, taking in a breath, before exhaling and then with an almighty force there was a belch and Lucy jumped as a column of steaming water shot into the air, before drifting away soaking the people in its path.

'Wow, that surprised me, even though I was expecting it,' said Lucy, her hand over her chest, still a little shocked. 'The force of it is quite scary.' And quite cathartic, she realised. The angry roll and boil before the explosion and the serenity afterwards. Perhaps keeping everything inside wasn't such a good idea.

'Do you know, there's a lot to be said to downsizing,' she said, giving into the anger. 'I didn't come here by choice.' She turned to him, her face taut and teeth gritted. 'You might as well know.' She paused before giving the words the venom they were due. 'I was sacked.' The release of words, like the geyser, spurting out with raw honesty brought a burst of freedom.

Now she realised how mad she felt about it. Furious. Before she'd been too stunned and dazed by the decision and the overwhelming sense of powerlessness.

Alex looked genuinely shocked.

'And I don't want to talk about it,' she snarled. 'Iceland was last chance saloon.'

Alex being Alex didn't say anything, he was good at this stuff. Instead he let her rant.

'End of the road. Because I was shafted big time.' She lapsed into silence waiting for the geyser to erupt again. There was a hushed quiet among the gathered anticipatory crowd and a collective gasp when it came with an explosive shower.

'Can I ask you a question?' His words came as the geyser settled. The calm voice of reason.

Surprised that her brief burst of anger had made her feel better, she nodded.

'If this is end of the road, do you care about the Lodge? Or is it another job?'

His quiet question made her give careful consideration to her answer. Taking hold of the barrier in front of them, she weaved her fingers around the rope, watching the glassy surface of the waterhole in front of her. It took a while for her to think things through, the geyser erupted twice more and not once did Alex press her for a response or give up by starting a new subject of conversation. He exuded that quiet strength, standing next to her, not pushing or prompting.

At last she turned to him, feeling an unexpected sense of release. 'I think you must be some kind of magician or a mind reader.'

His eyes crinkled at the corners, making her heart bump a little as they shared a long look.

'Thanks for bringing me out today. I feel like I've reset myself. I feel a bit more like me again.'

'Glad to be of service.'

'That's what it's about isn't it? Service. Although "in service". That was sort of seen as a dirty word wasn't it? But I was always proud of my job.'

'In the old days it was about class and servitude,' said Alex. 'A lack of choice, I guess. These days there is more choice, for some people.'

She linked an arm through his and began walking purposefully away from the geyser and along the path. 'Yes, there's a career path, the hierarchical climb but there's a sense of satisfaction when a guest tells me how much they've enjoyed their stay or how good the service has been. There's something about the ability to remove them from their everyday lives, the chores, the washing, the ironing. Giving them a break. And every day is different, I like the mechanics of everything working together and interlinking like a jigsaw.'

They'd climbed a light incline passing other pools of bubbling water.

'I thought coming here was a downgrade. Beneath me. But I've realised that actually it's brought me back to the basics. It's making me more aware of things. More appreciative of what I've got. Sounds a bit pretentious, but much more in touch with my own capabilities.'

She squeezed his arm. 'Thinking about it, you've made me realise, I've not been here that long, but already I'm really enjoying working at the Lodge. I'm starting to get lots of ideas of how to make the experience even better for guests. When I was at the … the other hotel, I was so busy, I was going through the motions. I'd forgotten why I went into the hospitality industry.'

As they stopped by yet another lunar landscape, white steam puffing up from scattered bubbling pools, Alex looked thoughtful. 'Why did you?'

'Because, at its simplest level, I like looking after people.'

Alex nodded, his gaze following hers. 'I like that idea. It's really important when I … when I'm pouring drinks I want to make sure the customer is happy.' He shot her a quick smile and she looked away focusing on an azure-blue pool on the far side of the field, before asking, 'So you don't think I'm talking rubbish?'

She didn't need to see his face, the enthusiasm in his voice said it all. 'Not at all, I love working in the hospitality industry. I'm not sure if I could break it down and tell you why exactly. I've not really thought about it that much.'

'I have,' Lucy relaxed, continuing to walk up to the highest point on the gravelled path. 'Running a big hotel is like a well-oiled machine, all the component parts working in tandem to support each other. And when it all goes smoothly, there's nothing better.' She let out a little sigh. 'And I haven't felt like that about work for a long time. I lost sight of it ... and when it was taken away ... when I lost my job...' She pulled a face.

'Ah,' said Alex wincing. 'I'm sorry you lost your job.'

They'd come full circle and were now back at the first geyser where a new circle of people had gathered to watch the performance.

Once again Lucy took the rope in her hand. 'Don't be. It was my own fault.' Her lips curled in bitterness. 'Lost. It's a figure of speech. You don't lose a job, do you? It's taken away from you. Like a rug, pulled out and you end up flat on your back.'

'Is that what happened?' asked Alex, his voice matter of fact.

'Yes. You saw me that first night. I was pretty pathetic, but at the time it felt like the end of the world.' She stared thoughtfully at the calm dome. 'I'd never imagined myself working in a much smaller place,' she paused, gripping the rope as the surface began to belch and bubble again. She stepped back just as it erupted and threw her head up as the powerful jet of water shot upwards and she laughed. 'And now I realise I'm starting to love it.'

Chapter 10

'We'll need all the staff to sign these release papers to say they're happy to be filmed and for the content to be shown on television,' said Clive, swirling a double whisky around the bottom of a tumbler.

The day out had cleared Lucy's head and she'd felt much better equipped to meet with Clive.

Although Alex offered to join her and the director for dinner, Lucy had declined. She needed to handle this one on her own. Neither was she going to let the cocky director with his child-like enthusiasm and blithe disregard for reality, call all the shots. Refusing dinner, she'd arranged to meet him the bar at nine instead. It seemed more business-like.

It was now five past nine and she was already regretting sitting down with Clive. Before she'd left with Alex this morning, she'd emailed Mr Pedersen's PA asking for more details about the arrangement and on her return had received an email trail confirming the crew's visit. It was a watertight deal and it seemed there was no wiggling out of it.

Clive had insisted on them sitting in a little alcove away from everyone else as it would be quieter, particularly now that the rest of the crew were also in the bar and were getting louder with every drink. Clearly they were not footing the bill, but neither, Lucy noted grimly, was she. The emails had made it very clear, the stay included accommodation and food only.

Lucy took a sip of her vodka which was heavy on the tonic, she wanted a very clear head for this discussion.

'Mr Tenterden–'

'Call me Clive.'

Lucy flapped a hand as if to say whatever, she didn't care what she called him, she just wanted to get rid of him and unfortunately that didn't look like an immediate possibility. She also wanted to take control of the conversation. This was her hotel.

'I wasn't aware that you were coming and no one had told me anything about your documentary.'

'You don't have to sweat the details. Everything's hunky dory with Mr Pedersen,' Clive beamed at her, brushing at his thin wispy blonde baby hair on top of his head. He looked around the room. 'It's a banging place ... and not what I was expecting to be honest.'

'Oh?' Lucy tilted her head in enquiry, with a prickle of defensiveness.

'Yeah, I was thinking concrete blocks. Pared back Ikea without the primary colours. Dorms and cafeterias. You know all very functional. This is kinda nice. Got a cosy vibe going on.'

'Thank you,' said Lucy, wishing she'd found the throws and cushions she was on the hunt for.

'Yeah, the perfect spot to film a couple of fillers. Guests relaxing. Nice views. That will give the punters some tourist travel insider footage and great that we've got access all areas.'

'Pardon? You have?' Lucy shot him a horrified glance. The emails unfortunately hadn't been that specific.

'Oh yes indeedy. Back office, kitchen ... staff quarters. Access all areas.' He caught sight of her frozen expression.

'What exactly does that mean?'

'What it says on the tin! Anyone in this building is a fair target. It means anywhere in this building, if someone moves, we film it, you speak, we record it. Nice and raw. We don't rehearse anything. We've got a tight turn around to send the footage back to the UK for a weekly show. We edit the segments out here, send it back and out it goes the very next day, part of a new travel show on Channel Four.'

Lucy swallowed hard.

'Hey, you really don't need to worry. I promise you, you won't even know we're here.' Clive smiled, all twinkly and terribly reassuring. Lucy didn't feel the least bit reassured.

'What we want to do is a mini documentary on the tourists chasing the northern lights; the highs, the lows, the disappointments. And we thought there might be much more scope for human drama if we filmed the staff here as well. You know checking the weather forecasts for the guests, talking with them at breakfast.' He gave a conspiratorial wince. 'Basically, we need a story in the can, in case the aurora borealis doesn't play ball. We've got a few sights to see but hell, that's been done a gazillion times before. We want some human drama, so it was agreed that we'd do a fly on the wall documentary on a place with people trying to see the lights. Genius, right? And everyone wants to be on TV. We'll film the staff, the food and all the rooms. It will be great publicity for this place. It's going to put,' he held up his hands and Lucy schooled her face as he did showy jazz hands for effect, 'The Northern Lights Lodge. On. The. Map.'

Lucy swallowed and fidgeted in her seat at the two-edged promise of publicity. If she made too much fuss about not wanting the publicity, he might start to wonder why and do some digging and that was the last thing she wanted. And what if someone saw her and recognised her? On the other hand, the current bookings were down and if sales improved, it would help her position and that would make it harder for the new owners to get rid of her. She started to worry at the sore on her lip with her teeth and stopped herself with a slight smile. Alex would tell her off again.

'Seriously Luce, this is a potential PR dream,' Clive's face tightened, 'if you play your cards right.' In that brief moment she saw beneath the bonhomie and false charm, a whisper of implicit threat.

She looked around the room which now looked at its best, Elin and her team had worked hard in the last week. The lounge had a cosiness to it that had been sorely lacking before and despite the horrendously pricey bar, guests were drawn here in the evenings. Tonight, the bar was nicely busy, the embers of the log fire glowing as the wood snapped and crackled in the huge grate. A lovely convivial atmosphere prevailed. A new trio of English guests were chatting enthusiastically to two Norwegians about the cathedral and concert hall in Reykjavik, while a Danish couple were sharing snaps of a glacier field they'd visited with a younger couple from New Zealand, who looked like hardened hikers.

Damn it. The lodge deserved to have its moment in the sun. It wasn't about her. She hadn't been here that long but she'd already picked up from Hekla, Kristjan, Olafur and Brynja that they were fiercely proud of their country. Loathe as she was, she was going to have put up with the fly on the wall stuff, although she'd make sure she kept a very low profile.

'OK, Mr T–,'

'Clive, Luce. Clive.'

'It's Lucy,' she said trying to summon up a smile to take the irritation out of her voice, 'Clive.'

'Cool. So tomorrow, we'll film some general footage of the place, the views etcetera, etcetera, depending on the weather of course. And we'll need a pile of these release forms photocopied for guests and staff.'

'Can I see?' Lucy managed to get a finger on the corner of the sheet of paper he'd whipped out of a laptop bag.

'Ah, you don't need to worry over much. They're standard boiler plate. To be honest, we nicked them from the BBC. Industry standard.'

'I'd still like to see,' said Lucy, giving him an implacable stare.

He pushed the form over the table and she scanned it

quickly, one clause in particular making her take in a sharp breath.

...you agree that the production company may edit, adapt or translate our contributions and you waive irrevocably any 'moral rights' you may have.

What would happen if she refused to sign one, would they avoid including her in any filming?

'I need the staff and any guests we film to sign one. Can you organise that for me?'

'Yes, I'll get Hekla to do that for you.'

'Oh, is she the statuesque Viking blonde. She's going to look great on camera.'

'What, showing you how to use the photocopier?' asked Lucy.

'Nice one Luce, funny.' He drained his whisky glass and pushed it towards her. 'And I'd love a refill while we talk about northern light hunting. That's going to be a key part of the footage.'

Over in the corner the crew were getting louder with the occasional raucous shout. Lucy noticed Alex behind the bar shooting them a few thoughtful glances, keeping an eye on the situation and watching the other guests to make sure they weren't being irritated by the frankly unacceptable behaviour. She caught his eye and dipped her head in a subtle gesture. He gave a nod as if to say he had it all under control and then sent her the sort of look that said, *you can leave it to me.*

With a wry smile that he could read her so well, she turned back to Clive. 'While we're talking details, can I confirm my understanding that the lodge is providing accommodation and food, drinks are not included?'

'This is a business meeting, that you invited me to, as I seem to recall,' said Clive with, what she felt sure he thought, was a winsome grin.

'Fine,' said Lucy with a small, pleasant-enough smile, prepared to allow him that small victory. 'This one's on the house.' She looked over at the noisy group. 'I hope your colleagues are aware that the drinks are on the company's expense account and not the Lodge's. Alcohol is ferociously expensive here.'

Clive blanched as he looked at the drinks' menu on the table. 'I think I'll remind them.'

'Why don't I see if Olafur is available to talk to you while you speak to them?' said Lucy feeling she won a very small skirmish. 'He arranges the northern lights' tours. I'll see if Alex can spare him at the moment. And if you could ask them to keep the noise down a bit.'

Lucy went over to the bar taking the glass with her. Alex came to serve her. 'Another double?'

She rolled her eyes. 'No, he can ruddy well have a single, cheeky git.'

'What about you or would that be a dangerous thing to do? You look as if you might disembowel him at any second.'

'I'm channelling my inner Icelandic Viking. He's a pain,' said Lucy under her breath. 'Do you mind if Olafur comes over and talks about how he organises the aurora tours?'

'Not a problem. Are you happy for me to say anything

to the guys, they're getting a bit rowdy?'

Lucy glanced at them. 'I've asked Clive to get them to keep it down and remind them that the drinks are not on the house. I'm sure they're not paying for them, but they need to be aware that we aren't either. I've already let Clive know that.'

'There are no guarantees that we will see the lights,' explained Olafur, a little later. 'Seeing them is dependent on exactly the right combination of weather factors, which luckily we are uniquely placed in this area to provide. We need good darkness, the right cloud–'

'Cut the sales pitch Olaf,' said Clive. 'Do you think you'll get us footage of the lights this week?'

The heavily bearded Icelander looked fierce. 'It is dependent on the weather,' he repeated. 'A clear dark night, no cloud cover and the right solar activity, which we cannot predict more than a few days in advance.' He levelled a serious gaze at Clive. 'You cannot predict the lights. Sometimes you can see them here from the window, other times you have to drive to find breaks in the cloud, which is why we organise the jeep tours.'

'Is that a yes or a no?' asked Clive.

Olafur didn't budge, he stroked his beard and carried on looking at Clive with dark beady eyes. 'It is nature. Life in nature is not predictable. I have been doing the tours for many years and lived here nearly all of my life. There are no guarantees.'

Lucy wanted to cheer the dour Icelander.

'I get it ... so we could be going on a wild goose chase. Hell, I guess we can work up a bit of drama. Got any oldies staying?'

'Sorry?' Lucy asked.

'You know bucket list types. Last chance saloon to see the aurora borealis. I can hear it now – wonder if we can get Jo Lumley to do the voiceover – sixty-year-old Val, has brought her eighty-six-year-old mum, to fulfil one last wish ... to see the northern lights. This is their last night in Iceland... You know the sort of thing. Great TV.'

'Do you know who is booked to go on the tours this week?' asked Lucy.

Olafur looked at her. 'There is a list in the office,' he shrugged. 'We go tomorrow evening.'

'Great,' said Clive. 'Do you think you've got any people that would give us a good human-interest story?'

Lucy winced. 'I think that might be an invasion of their privacy. I don't know, so I wouldn't like to make any assumptions.'

Clive grinned. 'Babe, have you been living under a rock? These days everyone wants to be on TV, on YouTube for their five minutes of fame. Most people are gagging to get in front of a camera.'

Lucy knocked back the rest of her drink and put the glass down with a firm chink on the wooden table and rose to her feet. 'I can assure you, that's not the case at all. Some of us have absolutely no desire for fame or infamy. I need to say goodnight, as there are a few things I have to do. I have a hotel to run.' With that, she glided, chin up, out of the lounge passing the bar. Alex shot her a quick approving nod and the glint of admiration in his eye made her lift her chin another notch. She was definitely starting to feel more like herself these days.

Chapter 11

Thank goodness the communal staff area was a long way from the guest accommodation thought Lucy, grinning as she held out her glass towards Brynja who was standing on the coffee table in odd, thick woolly socks dispensing vodka in a high steady stream.

Arriving to a loud raucous cheer, Lucy and her bottle of cherry-flavoured duty-free vodka had been quickly absorbed into the rowdy party atmosphere which was such a relief after the sticky, dancing-around-each other meeting she'd endured with Clive.

Hekla's exuberant hug, Elin's enthusiastic wave and Brynja's shouted welcome at the top of her voice from the other side of the room made it clear there was no standing on ceremony round here and without thinking she kicked off her shoes, untucked the baggy silk blouse from the waistband of her navy pencil skirt and unwound the tidy bun at the back of her head immediately relaxing.

This was one place Clive and his access all areas could forget. The staff needed to let their hair down when they were off duty, not worry about sodding cameras.

'Don't spill it, don't spill it' shrieked Freya, holding her glass at the ready. Brynja sniffed derisively, swaying slightly on the spot.

'Nuhuh,' she said, immediately whipping up the bottle with a neat twist before starting to pour again into Freya's ready glass. It was clearly her party trick judging from the way Gunnar proudly peppered her with kisses after she'd finished. Hekla tossed over a couple of bottles of tonic with casual ease, narrowly missing Brynja's head to loud cheers from Gunnar and Dagur.

Pouring tonic into the hefty shot of vodka, Lucy sat down on one of the lumpy sofas between Elin and Hekla.

'Have you asked Eyrun about the cushions?' asked Hekla going straight in for the kill.

Wedging her glass between her knees, Lucy held both hands up in mock surrender. 'She wasn't there, yesterday. Honest.'

Hekla narrowed her eyes, her thick blonde eyebrows almost meeting in the middle, looking comically suspicious as Elin interjected laughing, 'It was Eyrun's day off yesterday.'

Lucy nudged Elin and whispered loud enough for Hekla to hear, 'Phew, thank you. I'm not sure Hekla wanted to believe me and this vodka's already about to take off my head. I'm not sure I could do shots as well.'

'Don't you worry, Hekla's really scared of Eyrun.' Elin teased. 'And the shots are to come. We've got games coming.'

'No, I'm not,' said Hekla, her pink cheeks rosier than ever. 'OK, maybe a little bit but so is Lucy.'

'You are both crazy,' said Brynja joining in the conversation. 'You are in charge.'

'And you would tell Eyrun what to do?' asked Hekla.

Brynja laughed. 'Of course not, I'd run the other way very fast but it's not my job.'

Elin joined in. 'That's why you two earn the big bucks and we are everyday people.'

'Everyday people?' Lucy quirked an eyebrow. 'I hear you are writing a novel.' That sounded big and creative, not everyday at all. She'd never met anyone who was writing a book before. It certainly wasn't the sort of thing she or her parents would ever have considered in their neat tidy, terraced house in Portsmouth. Working in a hospital or a hotel was an everyday job.

'Ja,' said Elin, brightening. 'I am.'

'You'll be a famous author one day,' said Brynja lifting her glass in toast. 'And too important to drink with us.'

'Never, I will always speak to you,' replied Elin, chinking her glass against Brynja's. 'Hekla, maybe not,' she added with a callous shrug and a mischievous quirk of her lips.

Hekla nudged her. 'Yes, you will,' she said staunchly. 'And I will buy all your books for my family and put them under the tree.'

'You will be a bestseller then,' said Brynja.

'I wish,' sighed Elin, wilting back into her chair rear-ranging her long limbs. With legs like that, modelling seemed a viable alternative to Lucy. 'I could do with a break. Just someone to say yes.'

'Elin has written five books.' said Hekla, holding up her hand ticking off each finger and a thumb with great pride.

'In Iceland we have a fine tradition of storytelling. We tell folktales around the fire on dark cold nights.'

'Our grandparents did,' scoffed Brynja, with what Lucy recognised as one of her trademark no nonsense admonishments.

Hekla shot her a *whatever* sneer.

'Yes,' piped up Elin, going back to the original conversation, 'and they have all been rejected. I could line the road from here to Reykjavik with all the letters.'

'Five?' asked Lucy, impressed. 'You've written five whole books?' And she still kept going?'

Elin nodded, 'Yup.'

'That's amazing. I'm not sure I would have had the staying power after one, let alone, two, three, four and five.' Not anymore.

Elin let out a snorty, amused laugh. 'It's the Icelandic way. I'll get there in the end. I will keep going or I will kill my way to the top, murdering one publisher at a time.'

'Sounds a bit extreme,' said Lucy her eyes widening at the thought of battered bodies in pools of blood.

'She writes Icelandic noir,' explained Brynja, 'and they're very good. I've read them all. But every time she gets a rejection, she names the next person she murders after them.'

'That's one way of dealing with rejection.' Lucy giggled, the vodka was having an effect. Wasn't that better than curling up in a ball and weeping on your best friend's sofa for a month?

Elin pursed her lips. 'Don't worry, I cry the first time,

when I open the email. Then an hour later, I think I will show you.' Her face narrowed with fierce determination. 'We Icelanders are used to adversity, we thrive on it.'

Her words and the way her elegant profile resonated with resolve, chin lifted, lips tightened, brought a flicker of recognition. Once upon a time Lucy had been known for her bloody-mindedness, for pushing up her sleeves and getting the job done. For her can-do attitude.

'I think I need to be an Icelander,' volunteered Lucy in a wistful voice, wishing she didn't have to deal with Clive and his cameras. She rested her elbows on her knees, sinking her chin into her hands.

'Hey, Lucy.' Hekla put an arm round her, patting her on the back. 'You've already made a difference.' Her blue eyes twinkled. 'The new coffee machine is ace.'

Brynja gave Hekla a reproving poke before saying, 'She means the hotel is looking much better. The paintings have been getting lots of interest. And the elves have been behaving.' She gave Lucy a surreptitious wink before looking over at the unicorn necklace that was hanging from one of the light fittings on the wall. 'And Hekla hasn't had to clean a bedroom for at least three days.'

'And the phone app for our shifts is good,' said Gunnar, waving his mobile enthusiastically at her. Lucy nodded at him. Being utterly sexist but it was something she could base on fact, men always loved the technology. Introducing the phone app, *Sortmyshift*, had been an easy win. Alex had been really helpful uploading the information onto the system for the waiting and bar staff. Hopefully he would be willing to teach Elin which would save her another job.

'I'm not so worried about the hotel. It's the film crew,' she replied, the vodka loosening her tongue. 'I've seen these fly on the wall series, looking for sensational stories behind the scenes. Any staff scandal.' Like managers misbehaving in hotel suites. That would make a great story. One she was keen should never see the light of day again but, unfortunately, with social media, once that genie was out of the bottle it was there for ever.

Elin, Hekla and Brynja looked blank until Freya in a torrent of Icelandic explained, which made Hekla nod, the graveness of her expression at odds with her usual sunny countenance. 'We won't let them find bad things. Don't worry Lucy. Everything in the hotel will be perfect.'

'We're on your side,' pronounced Brynja in her usual solemn, serious way and the others all nodded in unison as if making a pledge.

With a sudden lift of her heart, Lucy looked at each of them. Despite her brief tenure, she already knew that Hekla was a hundred percent loyal and reliable. Brynja, the straight arrow, could always be relied on to offer matter of fact, common sense advice and absolute honesty. Elin, while appearing on the flighty side was actually organised and a very hard worker. Freya, she was still working out, but so far she seemed down to earth and supportive. Dagur appeared to be Brynja's twin soulmate and Gunnar, goofy and diligent with a sweet unassuming air.

'Thank you,' she said, straightening up. They were a

good team and with all of them pulling together, things would run smoothly while the film crew were here. And – under her thighs she crossed her fingers – perhaps the new owners would be impressed enough to let her keep the job.

'And now it's time to play,' announced Elin producing a pack of cards and Lucy was quickly roped into an unruly game of spoons. Losers had to drink one of the shots of the local brew, Brennivin, which Elin had lined up along the hearth over the wood burner which was pumping out plenty of heat.

Luckily Lucy, who'd sipped slowly at her vodka, managed to keep her wits intact and was reasonably fast otherwise she'd have been under the table when Alex and Olafur made their appearance, having finally closed up the bar for the night. Hekla and Elin were at the singing stage, arm in arm, egging each other on, Brynja was sleepily curled into Gunnar's shoulder and Dagur had his head on Freya's lap. Olafur rolled his eyes and grabbed the shot of Brennivin that Hekla offered him. He lifted it in toast and smiled as Elin repeated another rousing chorus, opening her arms, inviting him to join Hekla and her. He knocked back his drink and shook his head.

'But you're such a good singer, Olafur,' whined Hekla.

He laughed. 'And I'm ten drinks behind you. I think it is time for bed.'

'Gleispillar.' Any insult in the word was softened by Elin's fuzzy smile.

'Spoilsport,' whispered Hekla translating for Lucy's benefit.

Patting Elin on the shoulder, Olafur responded in Icelandic and with a cheery wave, left the room.

Lucy suspected that she was the only sober one, having diluted her drink with frequent top ups of tonic and Alex caught her eye as Hekla and Elin sang louder. He plopped himself down next to her.

'Good night?'

'It's definitely got better,' said Lucy, everything feeling a lot lighter. 'They're all mad, but lovely.' OK, so maybe she wasn't that sober but at this moment in time she loved them all and felt brim-full of the milk of human kindness. She could hug each and every last one of them, which was really very un-Lucy-like behaviour but the girls had made her feel like a new friend rather than a work colleague. Despite frequent texts, she really did miss Daisy. With a happy sigh, she said, 'I haven't had this much fun for a long time. Shame about the camera crew. Thanks for your help with Clive. Did they stay long in the bar?'

'Hell yeah. The camera crew can put it away,' he said. 'I thought they were never going to go to bed. It was only when I gave Clive the bar bill ... he turned a funny shade of puce and rounded them all up.'

Lucy huffed out a sigh. 'He's a weasel that one. I think he was expecting free drinks all the way but that was one thing that was made clear in the original email exchanges.'

'I have to go to bed,' said Brynja, blinking and swaying as Gunnar pulled her to her feet and then hefted her over his shoulder to her squeals. Hekla and Elin jeered, the two of them making what Lucy suspected were very bawdy comments in Icelandic and followed them out of the room. Freya and Dagur had already sloped off.

The door closed behind the noisy group and it was just the two of them suddenly wallowing in a silence punctuated by the crackle of the fire dying in the log burner.

'Are you going to be alright?' asked Alex, his words tentative. 'I can see the film crew make you uncomfortable.'

'I'll have to be. These reality TV things are anything but, we all know damn well that a lot of staging goes on. Clive's already decided what he wants.'

'I thought as much.' He pulled a sympathetic face. 'At the end of the day it's all about entertainment.'

'Yeah but if I wanted to go into the entertainment business I'd have gone on the stage.' She shuddered.

'I'm with you, my idea of hell. Perhaps you can persuade them to focus on Hekla, no disrespect but she looks the part.'

'She does,' Lucy laughed, not the least bit offended, 'our very own flaxen haired Viking Princess and she's so easy going, she probably wouldn't mind. Or there's Freya, she's the actress.'

'See, problem sorted. You can stop worrying.'

'Worrying is my middle name at the moment.'

'I know,' said Alex, with a sigh lifting a finger and touching the furrow above her nose, rubbing gently at it.

They both froze, he as if he'd suddenly realised what he'd done and her at the unexpected touch.

'Sorry, I ... you worry too much. That little line disappeared today.'

He studied her and they smiled shyly at each other. Lucy was suddenly horribly aware of his thigh resting next to hers and the fact that she was so close to him, she could see the rough stubble shadowing his jawline and a couple of tiny dark freckles to the right of his mouth. And then she realised that it looked like she was staring at his mouth. Swallowing she lifted her head quickly.

'I wanted–'

'Would you–'

'You first,' said Alex, ever the gentleman, with the faintest suspicion of amusement lurking in his eyes. Damn, he seemed to be able to read her mind at any given time.

'I do worry but today ... I should have said earlier, thank you for talking me down in the office and taking me to Gullfoss. I think I was too embarrassed to say a proper thank you. Panic attacks are not my usual MO.' She was trying to sound business like and brusque, in an attempt to overcompensate for the fact that the booze had softened her and she was doing stupid things like looking at his lips and letting those eye meets extend by several seconds too many. And she was doing it again, letting her thoughts drift off. She pulled herself back. 'In fact, I don't think I've ever had one before. You'd talked me down before I'd even had a chance to call it anything.'

'All part of the service.' The quick warm smile he added to his words, made her heart bump a little in her chest.

'What – first aid and mixology comes standard with bar

staff training?' she asked quickly. Keep it business like, Lucy.

'Something like that,' said Alex. 'You need to be ready for anything and,' he looked at her with another one of those quiet smiles before pushing a strand of hair from her face, 'you know what they say about barman. We're everyone's confidant. Are you feeling better now?'

'Much,' she said trying to ignore the buzz, that fleeting touch on her cheek had left, 'I think it did me good to get out of the hotel for a while. And now I've been out I've got the bug. You were right. There is so much to see and do here.'

'It's better with two. Fancy coming out with me again?'

'That would be...' OK how did she handle this? Was this the convenience of being two aliens abroad, which made them automatic tourist companions? And Alex was just a nice, friendly guy? Or was it what her wayward pulse was suggesting? 'That would be nice,' she said crisply, trying to appear nonchalant, tipping up her glass, even though there were only dregs in the bottom.

'Nice?' Alex pulled a face. 'I can do better than nice. Remember I sparkle!' He added jazz hands which immediately made her start to laugh and the last pickings of vodka went down the wrong way, bringing tears to her eyes and a choky wheeze as she bent double coughing and spluttering.

Alex patted her back, until she coughed her way back to normality and the pats became soothing rubs, that made her want to stretch and curl like a cat.

'Better?' he asked, all of his attention focused on her.

She nodded, hoarsely whispering, 'Yes.'

'For a minute there, I thought I was going to have break out my Heimlich manoeuvre. I was...' His voice died away when their eyes met in one of those 'the world has stopped spinning' moments. Neither of them seemed to be able to stop looking at each other. Bump by bump, his hand traced the indents of her spine, a slow inexorable climb, savouring each vertebrae before he cupped the back of her neck. All her nerve endings fizzed with sudden pleasure as his fingers brushed her bare skin, teasing her hairline.

Then his lips were brushing hers with a whisper of a touch.

It was temptation and danger. She shouldn't be doing this. Her mouth lifted up to his, relishing the delicious sensation, the tender touch of skin on skin. He worked for her. She'd been burned before. His mouth moulded over hers. This was bad. But, oh so lovely. Her heart pitter-pattered in her chest. She sighed into his mouth, on the brink of surrender. His lips still skirted hers and then with another sigh, she pulled back.

'I'm not sure we should be doing this.'

With a rueful twist to his mouth, he nodded. 'You're right.' He stroked her cheek. 'I want to but it's late and,' his eyebrow quirked as he looked at the coffee table laden with empty bottles, 'I suspect you may have shipped a ton of vodka.'

Lucy blinked. That wasn't what she'd meant at all and stupidly, she liked him all the more for it.

Chapter 12

'Lucy! Lucy!' Her face fell as she saw Olafur coming towards her down the steps from reception, his lumbering form as morose as a bear.

'We have a problem.'

Lucy's shoulders tensed, as she grasped one of the four new paintings she and Alex had just picked up. All the good feelings, engendered by coffee in Hvolsvöllur and too many warm-eyed smiles from Alex, took flight like butterflies released from jam jars. She hadn't planned on going with Alex this afternoon. After last night she'd rather hoped to keep her distance from him but Hekla had had other ideas and asked him to take Lucy to collect the paintings because no one else was available – or so she said.

'What?' she asked with foreboding. When she shot a quick, longing look at the car, she felt Alex's reassuring hand come to rest in the small of her back. The small unobtrusive gesture made her lean back slightly, grateful for the silent show of solidarity. She wasn't alone anymore.

Olafur shook his head sorrowfully. 'The jeeps have

the...' he made a cutting gesture with both hands, 'sprungio dekk.'

She frowned. He pointed to the tyres on Alex's car and then did a squashing motion with his hands.

'Flat tyre?'

He nodded, vigorously.

'You said jeeps ... you mean both cars?' Alex spoke before Lucy could frame the words but she'd been wondering exactly the same thing. Both cars sounded far too unlikely but Olafur's decisive nod, his bushy beard hitting his chest, confirmed it.

'So, no tour tonight,' he said with bleak disgust. 'And the forecast is very, very good.'

Of course it was. Lucy refrained from rolling her eyes, instead asking, 'Don't you have spares?' as if she knew all about such things. Come to think of it, did cars even have spares these days?

'Ja,' replied Olafur, his eyes glowing with sudden anger. 'And both ... gone.' He made a 'poof' sort of gesture. 'Two vehicles.'

'Hell,' said Lucy. 'How does that happen? Have they been stolen?'

Olafur shrugged. 'The film crew is expecting to go out tonight. The conditions are good.'

Sod's law, they would be.

'How come both are flat?'

Olafur shook his head. 'It's a mystery. Maybe there was broken glass.'

'No,' said Alex. 'The chances of a piece of glass piercing

132

the outer tube of the tyre is unlikely. For it to happen to two, that's not an accident.'

'Thanks, Sherlock,' said Lucy, having already come to the same conclusion.

'Which means it's the...' Olafur paused.

Lucy narrowed her eyes and glared at him. If he so much as uttered the word huldufólk, she would strangle him with her bare hands.

'Deliberate,' said Alex.

'Hmph!' said Lucy, she had her suspicions. She looked at the time quickly. Four fifteen. The blue sky was deepening and a scattering of pink edged clouds glowed from the low sun which dipped towards the horizon and would drop below in the next fifteen minutes. It promised to be a clear night, tonight. Perfect conditions.

'What time were you supposed to be headed out?'

'Nine o'clock. After dinner.'

'Does the film crew know yet? The guests?'

Olafur shook his head. 'I haven't spoken to anyone, except Hekla.'

'Good, don't say a word, yet. Come with me.' She stalked into the lodge. Clive would bloody love a crisis. That would play out well on television.

As soon as she walked through the lodge doors, a camera swivelled round from where it had been focused on a couple checking in at reception with Brynja and panned to her.

Balls, just what she did not need.

Behind the camera, Clive waved and motioned for her

to stop and pointed with frantic hand gestures towards the man and woman at the front desk.

There was no way she could ignore him. Instead she shook her head and waved her hands in a scissor movement, as if that would ward him off. Besides surely he wouldn't want to film her looking like this, her off duty look had more in common with a bag lady than professional manager. Her hair was flattened on top from the beanie hat and the blonde hair below the hat line was a halo of frizz from the damp afternoon air. It was a very small comfort that, devoid of party-girl make-up, marabou trimmed lingerie and drunken lash fluttering, no one would ever recognise her.

Clive took no notice and the camera panned her way. She froze. Every muscle tensing. Oh God, she was going to throw up. Her jaw had locked with that horrible, I will-be-sick-at-any-moment sensation. Clive's pointing and head nodding became more enthusiastic. All she could think of was the cold malevolent gaze of the camera focused on her like a waiting monster, ready to swallow her up.

Forcing herself, she took a couple of steps forward, every line of her body stiff and unyielding. Surely the cameraman could see her jerky movements and frozen face. Clive beamed still miming and dancing around the cameraman. Cold sweat gripped her. Memories of her stupid smiley face in the camera lens, licking her horribly over-glossed red lips in a ridiculously over the top suggestive manner, filled her head and along with them, the cold-water douse of shame.

Close to tears, she forced herself to keep her face impassive as she took a step forward.

'G-goo ... ev ... hello. I'm Lu ... the General Manager. At The Northern Lights Lodge.'

The black-clad cameraman circled her and she felt like prey being herded into a corner.

She swallowed and tried to ignore the hand-held camera which had taken up residence in her peripheral vision. There was no escaping it.

'I-I'd like to ... erm welcome you.' The woman looked a little nervous and Lucy realised she was the cause. Pasting on a brittle plastic smile, she dredged up the right words. 'Is this your first visit to Iceland?'

Relief brightened the woman's face, 'Yes,' she gushed, her dark brown eyes bird-bright with sudden eagerness. 'It's been on my bucket list forever. Peter,' she nudged her husband, 'prefers the heat. But he booked it as a surprise for my fiftieth.' She beamed up at him with such a happy twinkle, that Lucy felt something shift inside her, especially when Peter rolled his eyes and kissed the tip of her nose.

'That's lovely. I hope you enjoy your stay and if you need anything, please let me or any of the staff know.' She shot a quick look at Alex, who to her surprise looked horrified and had circled around the back of Clive, hunching his shoulders and ducking his head almost as if he were hiding. 'Be sure to ask any of us for any suggestions of places to visit. I would recommend the Gullfoss waterfall and Thingvellir National Park.'

'Don't worry,' said Peter with a long-suffering grin. 'Jane's been researching this trip ever since I gave her the plane tickets. How many guide books have you bought, hon?'

'Oh you,' she nudged him. 'We don't want to miss anything.'

'Well, I'll leave Brynja, here, to get you all checked in and I hope you have a very pleasant stay.'

'Cut!' cried Clive. 'Great. Thanks Peter and Jane. You were awesome. Good job Lucy. We'll get you to do that again so we can do some cutaways. Iron out those stutters, ums and ers. You guys were naturals. Lucy, I think nerves got the better of you. Stand right there and say what you said earlier.'

Olafur and Alex waited, heightening her self-consciousness, as she had to film the excruciating segment again and again. Her stomach wound tighter and tighter, wishing they weren't watching.

'You'll get used to the camera,' said Clive. 'Lots of people are uptight to start with.'

'I'm not uptight,' Lucy bit out with a glare, her words rasping with grim fury hearing Chris's words again. And even if she were uptight, what did it have to do with anyone else, but even so, how dare he make assumptions? He didn't know her.

'Right, Bob. I think we've got that in the can. It would be good to get some general day to day working shots before we go grab some dinner and then head out on the hunt for the aurora borealis.' He said the Latin words with great relish. 'That's going to be epic. But for now, Lucy, if you, Alex and Olafur go into the office, and talk about whatever you were talking about when you came in, that would be great.'

Jane's head whipped around and she nudged Peter, who was busy helping Dagur gather up their luggage and looked as if she were about to say something but Dagur was already leading her husband away to their room.

'I'd rather not,' said Lucy, trying to be brisk and business-like, when inside she wanted to scream at them to leave her alone. 'We're a bit busy at the minute. I've got things I need to do.' Alex, damn him, had already darted into the office as if his heels were on fire. She could have done with his support in pushing back at the enthusiastic director.

'Lucy, Lucy, Lucy. Don't worry, you're going to look great on camera.'

Her eyes narrowed. She couldn't give two farts what she looked like on camera, she already knew what she looked like on camera and she didn't want to be on camera, full bloody stop.

'Don't mind us. And even better if you've got things to do, it will look more natural. Just carry on as normal.' He gave his watch a quick glance. 'Remind me, what time are we headed out tonight Olafur?'

Olafur shot Lucy a panicked look and opened his mouth and closed it with cartoon fish-like terror.

'Fuck. Fuck. Fuck,' Lucy whispered to herself as she led the way into the office. How the hell was she going to solve this while that sodding camera was breathing down her neck?

* * *

In the nice warm office, she sat down at her desk and peeled off her fleece, relieved to give her shaking legs a rest and Olafur leaned against the wall looking as stiff as a scarecrow. Alex had already started making coffee and had a worried frown on his face, as if something else was bothering him. She was confused by his behaviour, a minute ago he'd looked as if he wanted to avoid being seen and the next he was diving into the office at Clive's request.

Clive spent five minutes arranging them to look 'natural' which was difficult with seven people in a space meant for four at the most.

'So,' said Lucy doing her best to sound bright and normal, desperately trying not to look at the big light reflector the grip held just to her left. 'If we need to get the jeeps serviced, where's the nearest garage?' Her eyes bored into Olafur hoping he'd get the message.

Bob zoomed in on her, the camera right in her face and she flexed her fist under the desk finding it hard to resist the urge to push it away.

'There's one in Hvolsvöllur ... but it will be closed now.'

Lucy closed her eyes and pinched the bridge of her nose. If the film crew found out that their trip, when the weather conditions were perfect, was cancelled, it would not look good.

'And what other vehicles are available to the lodge, that might need servicing? Do staff have cars that...' Oh God she was drowning here and sounded as wooden as a wardrobe. Please don't let them make her do it again.

Olafur shook his head, his expression confused.

'And other hotels in the area. They use the same garage. For their vehicles that go on the tours.'

Olafur frowned.

Lucy tried again. 'You know I'm sure other places need suitable vehicles to take guests out on tours. Perhaps we could double up with them, if our jeeps were being serviced.'

'Yes,' piped up Alex. 'There must be other local hotels we could work with. Do you know any, Olafur?'

Olafur blinked slowly signalling that he understood and then rubbed at his beard, not looking the least bit impressed by the idea. 'The nearest is the Skelland Guest house.'

'OK, do we have a number for them, maybe we could sound them out. You know for the next time we have a service.'

He shook his head. 'It's no good.'

Clive held up his hand, rolling his eyes. 'Cut. You people. It's been a long day. I need something a bit more ... I don't know ... an issue. Servicing cars is ... fucking dull, if you get my drift.'

Good, hopefully they would bugger off and leave her in peace to sort the cars out.

'It is what it is,' said Lucy. 'Some jobs are like that. The day to day minutiae is a bit dull because we have to pay attention to detail.'

'Right,' Clive sighed heavily as if they were a terrible disappointment to them, 'well we'll just get a couple of general shots before we'll call it a wrap for now. Let's hope the lights give us a good show.'

'Bob, give us some office, worky shots.'

Bob put down his camera and looked around the office and then back at Lucy.

'Push yourself away from the desk but stay in the chair. John, bring the reflector this way.' Bob grinned like a fox about to eat a chicken. 'So we get a nice silhouette.' Something laced his words that made Lucy's skin crawl.

'Now, give us a smile Lucy,' he called from behind the camera and he peered out. 'And sit up a bit straighter.' Lucy frowned and then realised the camera was panning from her legs up her body.

She flushed, nausea poking at her stomach.

'You're a nice-looking girl, come on smile.'

He shot a deliberate look at her chest, where the swell of her breasts strained against the tight polo neck she'd worn under her fleece. Horrified, she folded her arms over her chest and pulled her chair into the desk where she leaned forward to look at her computer screen.

They spent another excruciating twenty minutes filming Lucy working at her desk, making a 'phone call' and having a pretend conversation with Alex.

At last Clive, the grip and Bob the cameraman headed for the door. Just as they were about to leave, Bob swung round and narrowed his gaze on Lucy's face, a sly thoughtful look in his eyes.

'I know you from somewhere.'

'I don't think so.'

'Yeah, you look familiar. Have you been in an ad or something?'

She stared back at him, her back straight and her chin

lifted with a pretended bravery that belied the recoil in her stomach.

Scrunching up her mouth in nonchalant denial, she shook her head. 'Not me.'

When he'd gone, she got up and closed the door behind them, leaning against it heavily, wanting nothing more but to go and have a hot shower and lock herself away for the rest of the night. Sadly, it wasn't an option. She still had this mess to sort out, but as soon as she had ... she was done.

'Olafur, can you call the guest house?'

'They won't help.'

'I don't understand.'

'I should say, Jan Leifsen can't help.'

'Why not?'

'His wife is pregnant and went into labour this afternoon. All their guests have been taken to other guest houses.'

'Oh shit.' Lucy dropped her head in her hands and rubbed her eyes. 'Does everyone round here know each other?' she asked, her teeth straying to her lip. Alex shot her a gentle concerned look. She narrowed her eyes at him but left her lip alone.

The unhelpful tick, tick, tick of the clock reminded her that there were a few hours for her to find a solution before she had to break the news to Clive.

Olafur nodded, slow to respond. 'Pretty much, or we know someone who knows someone.'

Lucy closed her eyes momentarily and then snapped them open. 'Where's Hekla?'

Confusion clouded the Icelander's eyes, while Alex's looked shrewd.

'She's finished for the day.'

Of course, she had, she'd been covering Lucy this afternoon. She wrinkled her nose, she really didn't want to disturb her, but ... it was sort of an emergency.

'Do you think you could find her for me? And do you know what sort of tyres we need?'

He nodded, wrote the information down on a piece of paper and hurried out as if relieved to get away.

'Here you go.' Alex slid a cup of coffee towards her. 'What are you thinking?' Warm and conspiratorial, his voice made Lucy pause, her misbehaving pulse hitching at the deep timbre in his words as she remembered the soft touch of his lips last night.

She narrowed her eyes. Keep your distance, Lucy. Keep your distance.

'I'm just wondering if the huldufólk might oblige and take a large hammer to that camera in the middle of the night. I'm sure they must hate modern technology,' she said briskly, avoiding looking at him and picking up a piece of paper on her desk and giving it serious attention.

Alex gave her a sympathetic smile. 'Clive is pretty single minded. I'm not sure he does empathy. You really didn't like being on camera, did you?'

'No.' Lucy bit the word out, still not looking at him. She wasn't about to elaborate. Suddenly all the memories of Chris's betrayal came flooding back. Alex seemed so kind and helpful but she'd been burnt before. She remembered catching him in the laundry room. She should keep up her guard.

'When are you going to break the news to him that there'll be no tour tonight?'

She snapped her head up and said with a determined glint and deliberate coolness, 'When I've exhausted every other avenue.'

Alex's eyebrows rose and she could see him take a metaphorical step back. Good. This afternoon, all that twinkly, smiley stuff had made her forget that trusting someone was dangerous. Being on camera had brought all the agony and bitterness back.

No matter how well you thought you knew someone, they could still let you down.

Hekla came tumbling through the door. 'Did you get the paintings? How was Hvolsvöllur?' She flashed a wide smile at Alex.

'Good,' said Lucy, brusquely. 'Have you heard about the flat tyres and missing spares?'

'Ja,' She frowned. 'Who would do this?'

Lucy frowned. 'I don't know but it must be someone with a bit of grudge towards the hotel. I'm at a loss. But we need to sort it out before the camera crew get wind. This is the sort of angle they'd love.'

Alex frowned in agreement.

'Really?' asked Hekla. 'But why?'

'Hekla, you know lots of people in Hvolsvöllur,' said Lucy, avoiding looking at Alex, not even prepared to try to explain the vagaries of the English tabloid media.

She nodded. 'Ja.'

'Do you know anyone who runs the garage?'

Hekla screwed up her eyes. 'Elin's brother went to school with Viktor whose younger brother works there, or maybe it was his older brother. Or they both might–'

'Do you think you could get a number for him, and find out if there's any way he would open the garage up for us to collect some spare tyres? These are the ones Olafur says we need. We can drive over to collect them.' With her head held high, Lucy gave a hopeful look at Alex, even though minutes ago she'd been trying to put a barrier between them.

Surprisingly he looked amused, a half-smile playing around his lips as he nodded in agreement.

'OK,' said Hekla, pulling out her phone and immediately dialling. In seconds she was clearly relaying the tale to someone in her pretty singsong voice. She grabbed a pen, scribbled down a number and made a second call.

Lucy kept her eyes focused on her computer screen ignoring Alex, even though she was dying to sneak looks at him, as Hekla made her way through five phone calls before finally hanging up with a beam. 'Aron, who owns the garage, says he doesn't have these in stock but he has some that will work. And he will go there now.'

'Are you sure you don't mind driving back to Hvolsvöllur again?' Lucy asked Alex after Hekla had given them instructions for finding the garage. With a heavy sigh she shook her head. 'I feel like I'm imposing on you.' And it felt like she was relying on him too much.

A flash of something filled his eyes, almost as if he understood. She swallowed. He was a touch too perceptive sometimes as borne out by the look he gave her full of quiet sympathy and that signature gentle kindness. 'Mind?' he asked, his voice teasing, 'I feel like I'm some kind of superhero dashing to the rescue. This is the most excitement I've had in ages.'

Immediately he made her feel better and that she wasn't putting him out at all.

'Apart from standing in what felt like the jaws of a waterfall,' said Lucy surprising herself once again at her own fancifulness.

Alex shot her an equally surprised look, and for a brief moment, they shared a private smile, hers apologetic, his knowing, as if he could see inside her turmoil and understood. 'Yeah, that was pretty exciting.' His low voice set off a tingle low in her stomach.

Turning quickly, she said to Hekla. 'You're a star, thank you. Alex and I will go and get them. Can I ask for one more favour?'

'Sure,' she gave Lucy her golden sunny smile.

'Can you let Olafur know we've got replacements and ask him to be ready to put them on as soon as we get back?'

Chapter 13

Lucy was dealing with a stack of invoices when she heard raised voices coming from reception. She rubbed a weary hand across her forehead, despite several days at it, she still didn't seem to have been able to conquer the mountain of paperwork in the office, although it was a very good place to hide away from the film crew and now she was horribly conscious that she'd been neglecting the rest of the hotel.

The crew were on the prowl, like caged tigers. Despite getting the jeeps on the road the other night and driving out for several hours, Olafur and the film crew failed to track the elusive northern lights. Three more nightly trips had brought further disappointment and Clive was definitely tired and tetchy. Lucy felt a tiny bit smug that she'd seen the amazing light show on her very first night. Although she felt bad for the lovely couple Jane and Peter who'd also been out each night on the trail of the aurora borealis and had yet to strike lucky.

The voices were getting more heated and she went out to find Hekla smiling grimly at an American couple who were checking out.

'I refuse to pay for a room when there was no view. This was supposed to be the best room in the house. I never saw a thing.'

Hekla's sunny face had more of a Norse warrior expression today, fixed with a stern glare.

There was no sign of her usual friendly warmth. With her feet planted squarely she was giving off more of a 'mightily pissed off Viking' vibe, only the axe and horned helmet were missing.

'It is our best room, Mr Wainwright and I'm–'

'Shall I deal with this?' interjected Lucy smoothly, pasting a smile on her face and stepping in front of Hekla, determined to defuse the situation while praying the film crew weren't about. She'd met this type of guest a thousand times over. Determined to find fault and get a discount. Threaten social media exposure, awful TripAdvisor reviews.

Hekla shot her a startled, angry look. 'I was–'

'Good afternoon, I'm the General Manager. Can I help here?' Lucy cut across her with a professional smile anxious to calm everyone down. She could see that Hekla was furious and allowing tempers on either side to fray further wasn't something she was about to risk.

'Yes, you can young lady.' The man slammed his hands on the desk. 'I paid extra for a deluxe room with views of both the mountains and the sea. I didn't get either. I'm not paying the full amount.'

'I'm sorry to hear you've been disappointed. Which room were you in?'

'I was in the deluxe with mountain and sea view.'

'Room number?'

'Four, nine,' snarled Hekla at her side, bristling with unhelpful indignation.

Lucy frowned trying to remember all the deluxe suites.

Hekla hissed. 'All our suites have views both front and back.'

Lucy shot her a quick look of gratitude but was surprised by the glower directed her way.

'I'm sorry sir but I don't understand. There are windows facing both the sea and the mountainside.'

Over the man's shoulder she saw Alex appear. Great, because she really needed an audience right now.

Oh, marvellous, right behind him came the film crew.

'Yes, but it's not acceptable to advertise a room with a view, when you can't see the view.' Mr Wainwright's carrying voice had Clive's eyes lighting up in gleeful anticipation. The camera swung her way.

Lucy focused on her irate customer, schooling her features into a sympathetic smile, still not understanding. Suddenly the vertebrae in her neck seemed to have fused, her movements as stilted as if she were wearing a neck brace.

He turned and pointed out of the reception windows. 'Can you see anything?'

The camera followed his gesture. Although yesterday had started with bright sunshine, at lunchtime the weather had closed in and ever since, the lodge had been shrouded in murky grey mist with light rain spattering the windows. There was a saying that Hekla had told her, if you don't like the weather, wait for fifteen minutes and it will change.

Seriously, he was complaining because the weather had obscured the view.

The camera made her tongue-tied, stupid and frozen. What she should have said was, was there anything wrong with your room? Instead she opened her mouth and said, with the most ridiculously apologetic smile, 'I can only apologise for the weather.'

Hekla snarled under her breath.

Lucy cringed inside, desperately trying to think of some way to salvage the situation. Why was she apologising for the weather? It was completely outside her control. What a stupid thing to have said, even the man's wife looked faintly embarrassed. The camera was capturing all of this. Lucy's smiled solidified on her face. She could do this. She was a professional. She'd dealt with people like him before. Sometimes people were impossible and you had to smile your way through it and hope that reason might magically reassert itself. On this occasion under the baleful lens of that sodding camera, she couldn't think of a single other strategy. 'It is rather changeable I'm afraid.'

She paused and looked at the man, wondering whether he might realise how ridiculous he was being or whether his wife might slap him round the head and knock some sense into him.

He stroked the side of the credit card he was holding in his hand, before tapping it on the desk. Catching sight of the camera, he puffed up, ready and willing for a fight, the faintest touch of a cocky smile on his face as if to say, now what are you going to do?

'I'm not paying for a room with a view, when I didn't have a view,' he blustered, playing to the camera. For good effect he glared at Lucy and slapped a meaty hand down on the reception desk. Lucy caught sight of Clive waving to Bob to make sure he caught all of this. Tension pinched at her shoulders, her neck stiffer than ever as she turned woodenly to look at the print out on the desk below, a plastic smile glued to her lips. Beneath her rib cage her heart banged so hard the bones almost rattled. The camera in her peripheral vision was like a black crow, perched on Bob's shoulder, watching and waiting to swoop in on her slipping up.

Lucy looked at the bill again, registering the man's address as she did a quick calculation. Perhaps she could offer him a discount on one of the nights and then she caught herself. What was wrong with her?

Breathe Lucy. Breathe. She remembered Alex's hand pressing her diaphragm. Looking up she caught his eye. She pressed her hand on the same spot. Breathe. Breathe.

'I-I do ... er ... um ... understand, Mr...' Managing conflict. Remember the training. Empathise. Listen Actively. Neutral language. It was no good, she couldn't think straight.

'Wainwright. John Wainwright the Third,' he replied sticking out his stocky chest like a self-important pigeon flashing a self-congratulatory smile towards the film crew.

The competitive spirit that had propelled her throughout most of her career suddenly fired up, rockets blazing. With a tilt of her chin, she smiled at John Wainwright the Third.

The smile took all of her acting ability and then some. She dialled it up a notch. Thought she was giving in without a fight, did he?

'American?' asked Lucy. Her sudden confidence and jolly smile making him wary. 'Now I understand.' Her eyes sparkled and she turned up the charm, injecting warmth into her voice. Not an Oscar winning performance but she wasn't doing badly. 'You're used to very high standards in the US. I'm guessing convenient weather comes as standard there?' She asked, as if she were being completely reasonable, keeping her face sympathetic. 'I see you come from Seattle.'

Behind the couple she heard Alex cough. Clive snorted. The man's wife pressed her lips firmly together holding back either a laugh or a smile.

'Well ... not ... well...' The barrel chest began to collapse in front of her.

'John,' the woman next to him drawled, digging an elbow in his ribs. 'Honey, it's not the young lady's fault that it was too darned misty to see anything. I told you we shoulda come in the summer.'

'Hmph,' said Mr Wainwright. Without another word he handed over his credit card.

As Hekla took the credit card with a gracious incline of her head to Mr Wainwright, she shot Lucy a rather ferocious glare and took the payment before handing over his receipt.

Hekla's unexpected animosity didn't alter Lucy's fixed smile, although she was having to work really hard to keep it on her face, no thanks to Alex who behind the couple's

151

back was bent double with silent laughter, along with Clive who was sticking his thumbs up at her and grinning. If the camera still hadn't been trained on her, she would have shot them both a glare. They had no shame. She was trying to be professional. Both he and the camera crew hung around until the American pair finally left reception, pulling their cases out to the front steps.

As soon as they'd gone, Hekla cast Lucy another furious look, stomped into the office and slammed the door with an almighty crash.

Lucy straightened and was about to follow her, only too happy to escape the camera, but was diverted by Alex, who let out the gale of laughter that he'd been holding onto. 'Priceless Lucy Smart. Priceless.'

Her lips twitched as she shot him a reproving look before adding a snooty tone, 'The customer is always right.'

Oh Lord this was going to be all over the TV, she could see it now. She was desperate to follow Hekla into the office.

Alex raised an eyebrow. 'Except when he's an arse and he's wrong.'

'I couldn't possibly comment,' said Lucy, serene and still now. Alex's dark eyes were dancing with amusement and something that made her feel warm inside. Unable to help herself, she flashed him a brilliant smile and then she heard Clive say 'cut' and realised the damned camera was still running.

'Well, well, well. Lucy Smart. I knew I knew that name.'

Lucy froze. Bob the cameraman filled the exit of the little

storeroom down along the corridor from the laundry, his saggy grey eyes filled with sly delight.

'What are you doing down here?' she asked, annoyed by the tremor in her voice. She'd left the crew in reception with Brynja planning a trip out to the lighthouse at Arkranes a good two hours away. She'd assumed they'd have the rest of the day in peace.

'Just checking possible locations for more fly on the wall scenes. Access...' his gaze crawled down her body, 'all areas.' Nausea rose in her throat as he stared at her right there. She felt horribly naked, wanting to cross her legs and cover her pubic bone with her hands. With an insolent raise of his eyebrow, he looked up at her face.

'I don't think this is particularly interesting.' Lucy ground the words out, forcing her teeth not to chatter in fear.

'Oh, I don't know. Furtive trysts in the depths of the building. What really goes on below stairs.'

'It's a hotel not *Downton Abbey*,' she snapped.

'Doesn't matter.' His smug smile was triumphant, a spider moving in on the prey trapped within its web. She was caught fast and she knew it. 'There's always a bit of how's your father in places with servants and staff.' He paused pudgy hands on broad soft hips before adding in a gravelly, mocking voice, 'You must know that better than anyone.'

Go straight to jail. Do not pass go. Lucy's heart turned to lead.

With a feral smile he stepped closer, his dirty trainers making no sound on the stone floor.

'Lucy Smart,' he said, clearly super pleased with himself

for figuring it out. 'Formerly Assistant Manager of the Forum Group's Manchester flagship, The Citadel.' He looked around the tiny storeroom. 'This is a long way down from a five star, five-hundred-bedroom hotel. I looked you up. Good CV on LinkedIn. A private Facebook account. Locked Instagram Account. But then, YouTube,' he grinned, 'bingo.'

Lucy closed her eyes, her skin prickling. When she opened them in exasperation and building anger, like a weeping angel, Bob had inched closer again, his eyes smug and triumphant. She could smell cigarette smoke and a cheap, cloying aftershave.

'The camera loves you.' He smirked and dropped his eyes to her chest. She wanted to fold her hands over her boobs but that would let him win. 'You've got the goods.'

'I need to go,' she tried to push past him.

He put his arm across the door frame, blocking her path. 'Not so fast, young lady. I've got a proposition to make.'

'Not interested.'

Bob's smile held a tinge of cruelty. 'Not sure you're in any position to be calling the shots, sweetheart.'

'Please let me pass.' Her level tone hid her desperation. Surely if she were firm with him, he'd leave her alone.

'I hear the hotel's up for sale. Can't be easy getting a job with a video like that out in the ether.'

She felt the hot prick of tears, her fingers clenching into impotent fists.

'Can't imagine your new bosses would be too impressed or even your colleagues. That Alex seems quite keen on you.'

'He's just a colleague,' said Lucy a tad too quickly and Bob caught the flicker of uncertainty on her face.

'You've got a lot to hide Lucy Smart ... and a lot to give. Advertising pays well on YouTube channels.'

Lucy shifted to hide the trembling in her legs.

'With your ... attributes and my camera skills, I'm sure we could come up with a mutually beneficial arrangement.'

'I'm not interested,' said Lucy, sick to her stomach at what he was proposing.

'Shy?' Bob laughed. 'Your first effort wasn't that bad, with a bit of editing, it could have been really quite something. We can make you look a lot better this time round.'

'I'm not interested,' she ground out again.

'Why don't you have a think about it? About what's at stake? I'm sure you'll come round.' He stepped aside to let her march past him, her head held high, flinching as she felt the fleeting touch of his hand on her bottom.

Chapter 14

'Erik's broken his leg,' said Hekla, skidding breathlessly into the office like a cartoon character. Lucy almost expected to see skid marks burnt into the wooden floor, Brynja following her like an anxious guard dog.

Even though she was bearing bad news, it was a relief that Hekla was actually addressing her. For the last couple of days, she'd been doing a Macavity act, disappearing the minute Lucy walked into a room and avoiding her at every opportunity.

'What! How did that happen?'

Hekla cleared her throat.

'There was an accident. The broom had fallen over, the handle was between two cupboards...' Hekla's voice faltered. Lucy glared at her. After the tyre incident, she'd made it quite clear that if anyone so much as uttered the word huldufólk, they'd get the arse-end of shifts for the next month.

Lucy looked at her watch. It was already four o'clock. 'What about Kristjan?' Erik's number two who looked about twelve, at a pinch.

'It's his day off and I already tried him. He's not answering his phone. He likes to fish, I guess he's out on a boat some-where,' said Brynja.

Lucy did a few quick calculations in her head. Darn it. None of her other options were going to work. 'And how many have we got for dinner this evening?' she asked wearily, wanting to lay her head down on the desk. No sooner had she sorted one problem, another one arose. No wonder there'd been ten managers in twelve months. It was a wonder there hadn't been forty-eight.

'We're quiet today. It's only twenty-three.'

'Shit,' said Lucy, standing up. The problem with being in the middle of nowhere was that you couldn't even send the would-be diners elsewhere.

'Brynja, you stay here and keep trying Kristjan.'

With Hekla following she headed for the kitchen because at least that felt as if she were doing something but one look at this evening's menu, printed out the day before and presented on the wooden lectern outside the dining room, had her hopes of saving the day taking flight and heading for the hills.

Grilled Halibut Steak with buckthorn, mini carrots and glaze.

Langoustine salad and shellfish sauce

Gilled fillet of lamb, caramelised sunchoke puree, sauer-kraut and mushroom glaze

Vegan peanut steak.

'I don't even know what buckthorn or sunchoke is, let alone how to bloody cook the things and as for peanut steak, I've never even heard of such a thing before,' sighed Lucy looking around as if inspiration might jump out and strike her. Fat chance.

'Lucy!' Clive's voice hailed her and she turned to see him and the crew trotting up the corridor. She deliberately avoided looking at Bob but her crawling skin told her he was there.

'Hear there's a problem. Your chef air-lifted to hospital this morning.'

How the bloody hell had he heard that? Lucy and Hekla exchanged a quick wide-eyed look.

'Yes, but it's not a problem,' said Lucy, her voice smooth and reassuring as if it was all in a day's work and she wasn't bricking it inside or feeling sick under Bob's creepy gaze. 'We have back up. Kristjan, our sous chef.' Behind her back she crossed her fingers and hoped Clive hadn't heard Hekla's quick in-drawn breath at the outrageous lie.

'Great, the sous chef to the rescue,' Clive said the words with relish, actually slapping his hands together and rubbing them with Fagin like glee. 'Perfect story. Bob, can you get set up in the kitchen. We can film Crispin arriving and being told he's got to swing right into action. Cut to his horror-struck face. Then to Luce, telling him he can do it.' He swung his arm from the elbow in a by Jove we'll save the empire style mannerism. 'And then we'll film him having disaster after disaster. I can see it now. Then it all comes good at the end.' Clive's face shone with ebullient eye-popping animation, putting Lucy in mind of an enthusiastic bullfrog. He should have been the one in front of the camera.

Over his shoulder Lucy spotted Alex coming their way, almost as if he'd known she needed reinforcements. Just the sight of him had her lifting her chin and adopting a pseudo-sympathetic but firm smile. 'I'm afraid that won't be possible. We can't have the cameras or the crew in the kitchen during service. Environmental health would shut us down.'

'Lucy, Lucy, babe, we're miles from anywhere. What are the chances? You think those little health inspectors are going to come all this way to make a surprise visit. And,' Clive's eyes gleamed, his head bobbing and weaving like a bonkers cobra, 'let's live a little dangerously. Dance in the face of rules.' Lucy's eyes darted to Bob's, worried that Clive might be in on the act, and was grateful to see Bob's eyes slide away in denial.

'I'm not worried about an inspection.' It hadn't even made it onto the list of things she had to worry about. 'I'm concerned that one of you could get hurt. Step back into the stove and knock over a pan of boiling oil. Be at the wrong end of a sharp knife.' Her saccharine smile had Alex and Hekla pinching their lips. 'Or a piece of your equipment could get damaged. The floors get very slippery in there, condensation, grease. And during service you'll find it difficult to keep out of the way. I'd hate for a frying pan to inadvertently smash the lens,' she lied. Actually, maybe that was a good idea.

Clive's eyebrows drew together and he nodded sagely. 'Hmm.' He turned to Bob, stroking his pretentious wispy goatee. 'What do you think?'

Bob shot her a considering look, before shaking his head. 'We bugger up the kit out here and we're stuffed.'

With a wince Clive agreed.

'Let's hope the aurora borealis play ball tonight. Last night was another complete bust. Although that Jane woman is quite a character. If only she had a life-threatening disease, she'd be pure primetime gold.'

'What wankers,' spat Lucy under her breath to Alex's amusement, as Clive and Bob scuttled off. Quite how Lucy managed to keep the shocked disapproval from her face, Alex had no idea, he was in complete agreement with her assessment of Clive's character, but he had his own problem to deal with.

When Clive had mentioned the guest, Jane, again, the penny had dropped, sending his stomach into freefall. Paris. That's where he knew them from. In fact that's where he'd met them. They'd helped Nina in the patisserie. They were at the official opening. Complete bollocking hell. What were the chances?

He'd had quite a long chat with her and Peter, her newish husband, at the patisserie as they ate Nina's amazing Anglo-French patisseries. It all came back to him. Nina adored them both and, even over-cautious, grump Sebastian seemed very fond of Jane. They could easily reveal who he really was – not a barman that's for sure.

Grimacing he followed Lucy into the kitchen where several industrial fridges hummed quietly in the brightly lit space along with spotless stainless-steel shelves and surfaces.

He was going to have to keep a low profile over the next few days and keep out of their way and, he glanced at Lucy, out of hers too. Guilt twinged low in his stomach. He had to remember that he was working for Quentin and his boss had good reasons for him being incognito. And as Quentin had so pointedly reminded him, *nice guys finish last*. This was business after all.

Without missing a beat, Lucy had opened up the walk-in larder and peered in before slamming the door shut. 'I don't suppose we can convince anyone that beans on toast is an Icelandic delicacy.'

Hekla looked at her blankly but Alex, following her into the room, forced a laugh he was far from feeling.

'Nice idea. But I don't think that's going to work. Shame as I love them.'

'You do?'

'Especially with haggis.'

'I'll take your word for it. I don't suppose you know how to cook?'

Alex pulled a face at her words. He'd spent most of his life working in hotels and kitchens where there was always food on tap. He knew the basics and when it came to flavours and combinations, he knew plenty but cooking was not something he'd done much of. 'Sorry, no. I've never really needed to cook.'

'What about you?' asked Lucy as they both turned to Hekla who held up both hands in horrified surrender. 'Nrr.'

'That'll be a no then,' sighed Lucy, turning her back on them. Alex watched her as her shoulders drooped and she opened a couple of cupboards before pulling out a large bag of pasta.

Where were they going to get another chef at such short

notice, he thought to himself. He'd have been on the phone to Reykjavik by now, trying to find agency staff to fill in. He looked at his watch.

Lucy caught him. 'Reykjavik is an hour and a half away even if they could find us a chef at this short notice. I phoned two agencies.'

'Oh!' Was she some kind of mind reader?

'You had that less than impressed look on your face,' she said, making him even more convinced that she must have a touch of clairvoyance. 'You reminded me of an old boss. Always waiting to catch me out.'

Her words were the perfect reminder that this was exactly the sort of scenario that Alex should be reporting back on; how she handled things, how she responded to a crisis and how she managed her staff.

He had to look away and he opened the fridge, which was fully stocked. Sometimes she was scarily perceptive. His stomach turned over, tightening in a hard knot of unease. Just because he hadn't outright lied to her, didn't make his deception any better. But Quentin was his boss and he was adamant he didn't want any of the staff here to know who Alex really was. One wrong word from Jane or Peter and the game would be up.

'Surely you're not going to try and cook,' he said, raising a curt eyebrow. That was an insane idea.

'What do you suggest?' she asked sweetly.

'Bar snacks. Sandwiches. Grills. Pizza.'

Lucy gave him a disdainful look. 'People are on holiday. They're expecting a proper meal. Not pub grub.'

'You *are* going to cook?' He asked trying to keep the incredulity out of his voice. She was mad.

She looked at him, sudden sharp intelligence in her eyes. He watched as she slipped the band from the loose pony tail at the nape of her neck and gathered her hair up again, tilting her chin. For a moment he was struck again by the smooth white skin of her long neck. Unable to stop himself he watched her quick hands, as she scooped her hair into a new higher ponytail and pulled it tight with an I-mean-business-yank. The style emphasised her face in profile, the high, sharp cheekbones and the slight pout of full lips. Lips? Why was he looking at her lips? He shouldn't have kissed her the other night. Hell, he shouldn't have gone for coffee with her afterwards, but Hekla had rather forced the issue, insisting that his car was the only one free and Lucy had to pick up the paintings that day.

Dammit. Getting involved with his target was not part of the job description. And listen to him. Target? Did he think he was Jason Bourne now?

'Have you got any other suggestions?' Her crisp voice cut into his thoughts as Lucy turned to Hekla. 'Can you go and get my laptop?' She gave a grim smile. 'We need to simplify the menu. Make things that can be pre-prepared and heated on demand. I need to Google some recipe ideas.'

'Lucy, don't you think...' The sudden hint of determination in the set of her lifted chin made him pause. With a sigh, he pulled out his phone from his pocket. 'I've got something better than the Internet. I've got a Sebastian.'

'Is that like an Alexa?' asked Lucy, the teeth worrying at her lip, belying her brisk voice.

Without thinking he lifted a finger and pushed it gently against her lower lip. 'You keep doing that. You're going to make it sore again.' For some crazy reason, he couldn't have explained if he tried, he stroked her lip with the pad of his finger as if trying to soothe the pain away. She stilled, her mouth parting and as he felt the quick, hot exhalation of her breath, his groin tightened. He had to stop this inadvertent touching her. He'd done it the other night with that insistent little furrow above her nose.

'It's already sore,' she said, her eyes darting to his, widening slightly, before her teeth immediately returned to the same spot, grazing his finger. As if he'd been burnt, he withdrew his finger.

'Sorry,' she said rubbing at her mouth, ducking her head, 'bad habit. I can't seem to help it. Please tell me your Sebastian has teleporting skills and can be here in five minutes.'

Alex laughed at her sudden humour, relieved the potentially awkward moment had been extinguished.

'None of the above, but he's a mate and moreover, a chef.'

'Do you still want the laptop?' asked Hekla her head turning this way and that following their conversation as if she were at a tennis match.

'Yes, that would be great as we're going to need to produce a new menu. It will have to be a set menu. Alex would you mind phoning your friend while I make a full inventory of what we've got.'

Suddenly she was all action, pushing a notepad and pen his way as he called Sebastian.

Half way through his conversation, which he was relaying to Lucy, he said, 'He thinks the langoustine salad is still a goer. He suggests making a salad including asparagus, peas, broad beans with some croutons. And do we have any pea shoots?'

Lucy let out a pfft. 'He has to be joking. Does he know we're in Iceland? The nearest big supermarket is over an hour's drive away and I'd be amazed if you'd get a pea shoot without forty-eight hours' notice.'

He was surprised when Lucy came to stand in front of him.

'May I?'

Without waiting for his answer, she took the phone from him. 'Sebastian, hi. This is Lucy Smart.'

As he listened to the conversation between her and Sebastian, he realised that Lucy obviously knew a little bit more about cooking than he'd first guessed. Even so, he'd seen enough episodes of *Masterchef* to know that cooking in a professional kitchen was a long way away from catering at home.

After she'd finished her call with Sebastian, abruptly thrusting the phone back at him, she began to scribble copious notes, muttering to herself with the odd aside to him and Hekla who'd returned with the laptop. 'Alex, please can you count how many langoustines there are?' 'Hekla can you weigh the lamb?' 'Can someone count the carrots?' 'Is there more than one bag of rice?' 'Can someone start gathering up all the onions?'

'Right,' she said, standing up with a military air about her as if she were a general going into battle. 'Got it. We're going to offer people a choice of starter. Traditional Icelandic fish soup with rye bread or toasted sheep's cheese rolled in walnuts with a bilberry coulis. Then a hearty lamb stew or a fish stew with baked carrots and turnip and potato dauphinoise. And for dessert it's Skyr with fruit or cheese and biscuits.

'With the exception of the toasted sheep's cheese, everything can be prepared ahead of time. We'll do waiter service on the starters, if you can manage that between the two of you. And I'll man the kitchen.' Lucy gave a quick grimace. 'I think that'll work.' And then she added more firmly. 'It's going to have to.'

The next two hours were a blur of chopping, frying and washing up as Lucy directed him, Hekla and Dagur, who'd been rounded up to help. Alex never wanted to see another one of the spiky langoustines again, which were absolute pigs to peel, but he had to admit the broth cooking on the stove smelled delicious. Lucy had focused on getting her lamb stew in the oven first and focused she was, it was as if she was another person. Organised, methodical and constantly checking on his and Hekla's progress, tasting and stirring like a professional.

'No, chop the onions a little smaller.' 'Slice the potatoes thinner than that.' 'More lemon juice.'

At last, the lamb was baking in the oven and the ingredients for the fish stew which wouldn't take anywhere near as long were all chopped and prepped.

'Phew,' said Lucy wiping at the damp strands of hair around her face. 'We're just about there. Do you two want to take a quick break and put on your waiting kit?'

'What about you?' he asked, she had to be knackered. They hadn't stopped and she'd worked with single minded dedication that had him in awe.

'Can't. I need a dry run at the starters, see if I can make them look presentable. Besides no one's going to see me,' she gave the sweat circles under her arms a quick uncertain glance and then, with a worried look, said, 'and you'll have to put up with the pong. If I have time I'll nip and put on a clean t-shirt.'

Even with lank limp hair, sweat glistening on her forehead and the baggy blouse now sticking to her, outlining a slight frame and clinging to her boobs, she crackled with energy that made him suddenly feel a bit restless and antsy, as if he wanted to kick something. He grabbed a tea-towel and wiped up a slick of water, turning his back on her, quashing the sudden urge to sweep her off to bed and kiss the living daylights out of her. Where the hell had that come from? Surely just some kind of Stockholm syndrome; they'd survived a crisis together and it was that psychological alliance post trauma thing.

Lucy let rip with a string of curses and pressed her hand to her forehead. This was never going to work. The coulis was an absolute disaster, her second lot of bilberries was on the stove, and it had taken forever to chop this small batch of walnuts for her dummy run.

Served her right for being so stubborn. Who knew toasting the sheep's cheese rounds would be so damn difficult? She couldn't even cut them evenly and as for getting the walnuts to stick, forget it. The third lot she'd pulled from the oven had dissolved into puddles of what now looked like baby sick. There was no way she could serve that.

Slumping against the stainless-steel counter, she took a couple of deep breaths and looked around the kitchen desperate for inspiration. Dear God, what had she been thinking? Alex was right, just like he always bloody was. She should have stuck to beans on toast. She wasn't a chef.

'Can I help?'

She whirled around to find Kristjan, the sous chef, in the doorway, his baby face alight with amusement as he scanned the scene of devastation. Piles of washing up were waiting by the sink, wayward walnut pieces were strewn across the floor and the smell of burning filled the air.

'Oh shit.' She made a grab for the forgotten pan of congealing bilberries which had darkened to almost black instead of deep purple.

'I got Brynja's messages and came straight back.'

'Oh, Kristjan, it's good to see you. Erik's had an accident and...' She waved at the plates of goat's cheese.

'You're cooking them for too long and too high, and the slices need to be thicker,' he said, immediately crossing to the oven and turning the temperature down. 'And you should roll the whole cheese in the nuts before slicing. It's quicker,' he flashed her a quick smile, 'and more practical.'

Within minutes he had taken over, chopping walnuts with a blur of motion, rolling the cheese in them before slicing the rounds of cheese into neat, even proportions, leaving her to stand watch over the bilberries. He made it all look effortless, which after all was why he was the chef.

In just half an hour, once she'd explained the proposed menu, he'd talked her through making the coulis while filling several trays with perfectly even slices of walnut coated cheese. She'd also had chance to catch up on the washing up and tidy up the kitchen while he tasted her lamb stew and, with a quick frown, added more seasoning, sprinkling in a generous handful of rosemary and bay leaves.

Seamlessly he took over, slicing potatoes into fine pieces, altering the suggested fish stew to a pan-fried fish with scallops which he'd dug out of the freezer.

'OK, what about the dessert?' asked Kristjan.

'We were going to offer Skyr and cheese and biscuits,' replied Lucy diffidently.

At his pained wince, she laughed. 'I'll take anything you can suggest.'

He shot a quick glance at his watch. 'I can make some meringues and with the egg yolks, some vanilla custard tarts.' He grinned. 'You have to give your permission. Erik has been hoarding his special Madagascan vanilla pods.'

'You have my full permission to do anything you like.'

'I have lots of ideas ... Erik,' his face held a trace of frustration, 'he doesn't like to experiment. The menu hasn't changed in five years.'

'Feel free, as long as the guests are fed. Today you have free rein.'

He beamed at her and rubbed his hands together with evident glee.

'Then tonight, The Northern Lights Lodge's guests will eat the best desserts this side of Reykjavik.'

Lucy raised an eyebrow. Despite his arrogant claim he looked quite modest.

'Trust me.'

Alex brought the last plate through at the end of the night, reflecting it had been one of the best evening's service he'd had since he'd arrived at the lodge, bearing in mind he was supposed to be running the bar and not waiting tables. He ought to be heading through to the bar right now. Lucy, to his surprise, was whizzing around the kitchen stacking plates in the dishwasher with a broad grin on her face, teasing a red-faced but happy Kristjan. As soon as he put the plates down she held up a hand for a high-five.

'We did it. I think the punters loved it.' She sighed and bent double. 'And I never want to have to do that again. Talk about crazy.'

'But you were brilliant.'

'No, Kristjan was brilliant. Amazing. Incredible. Although, I never want to see a round of sheep's cheese again.'

Kristjan laughed. 'Another few hours and I think you would have been fine.' He winked at her. 'Although we might have run out of bilberries if you kept on burning them.'

'Don't remind me. But thank you for cutting your day off short. We couldn't have done it without you.'

'So, I am promoted?' asked Kristjan, his face suddenly deadpan.

Suddenly everyone was looking at Lucy.

She opened her mouth and stopped, not liking the feeling of being backed in a corner but what choice did she have? Erik was going to be off for at least six weeks. They needed a chef.

'Well ... we got away with it tonight but I need to...' He was so young and she'd already realised he was keen to experiment and had lots of ideas. What experience had he had?

'It was really good out there, wasn't it, Alex?' chipped in Hekla, with an uncharacteristically shy glance at Kristjan.

'It was. The food went down really well. There were lots of complimentary comments.' Alex nodded with enthusiasm.

A knot wound tighter in her stomach. One night's service didn't mean he could run a kitchen and manage a whole week's menus. There was a lot more to being a chef in charge than the cooking and she didn't have the time to oversee him. She sighed, she'd have to make the time.

'In the interim, yes,' she said reluctantly, 'but we'll keep the menus the same for the time being.'

Kristjan's mouth twisted with the briefest flash of disappointment at her lacklustre response.

'I'm good.' He planted his feet in a stubborn gesture.

He was brilliant and it wasn't his fault that she found

171

trusting people hard these days. Maybe it was time she took a risk.

'OK Kristjan,' she smiled, 'Let's get together tomorrow morning and you can talk me through what you'd like to do.'

Chapter 15

'Are you OK? You seem to be a little...' asked Alex walking into the office where he found Hekla studying her coffee with a brooding stare.

'I'm cross,' said the girl with a rueful smile. 'It takes me a lot to get cross and then...' she laughed, 'I go boom!'

'Really?' Alex raised a disbelieving eyebrow.

'Ja. You can ask my parents. Why do think I'm called Hekla?'

He shook his head.

She laughed again. 'I'm named after a volcano. Hekla, it's not far from here. It erupts every ten years. When I was a baby I was very good for the first few weeks, then I had a big crying, angry time, and then I was good again for another few weeks, so they named me after the volcano.'

'What they waited two months to name you?'

'Ja, that is very common in Iceland. Parents wait until they get to know their children before they name them.'

Alex nodded, 'That makes a lot of sense, I guess.' His mother had his name picked out as soon as he was conceived and he'd have been Alexandra if he'd been a girl. There'd been Alexander McLaughlin's in his family for the last two hundred years and they'd owned the family hotel, McLaughlin's, which his mother currently ran, for over fifty.

'Give it up, what's made you so cross?' Alex asked as he perched on the edge of Hekla's desk. She was the sort of employee you listened carefully to, the sort of person who whether they knew it or not, intuitively had their finger on the pulse. Hekla was the backbone of the lodge.

'Lucy.'

'Lucy? I thought you two got on well.' He was genuinely surprised. Of all the people at the lodge, Lucy had managed to upset Hekla? That didn't stack up.

'How's she upset you?'

Hekla's open face suddenly closed down and her mouth flattened in a mutinous line. 'She never trusts me. She checks everything. It's so control freaky,' she pinched her lips, 'I was dealing with that American Wainwright man and she took over. Stepped right in front of me. Made me look like I am no good in front of the camera.'

Alex patted her on the arm. 'Have you considered that she was trying to help, that she thought she was the one that should take the flak not you? It is a manager's job to protect their staff, to support them with any unpleasantness. Maybe Lucy was doing her job.'

Hekla gave him a considering look. 'You see too much, like you're the manager.'

Alex stilled.

'You would make a very bad spy.' The girl smiled, tossing

her plaits over her shoulder. 'I've seen you in places you shouldn't. Looking at things.'

'Incurable nosiness, I like to know how everything works.'

Hekla looked as if she didn't believe a word of what he'd said. Just as he'd known he would be, he was rubbish at this subterfuge stuff and inwardly cursed Quentin, who had suddenly disappeared off the planet now Alex wanted to update him on Lucy's progress and the gradual turna-round of the hotel.

'Smoked lamb?'

Kristjan nodded, his baby face very serious and sombre, and pushed a plate towards Lucy along with a tiny steaming jug which smelled heavenly. She'd certainly give him marks for presentation and enterprise. She'd been worried he might get experimental, especially when he'd told her that the original Icelandic staple diet included rotted fish and boiled sheep's heads. Imagine what the guests would think of that?

Two rounds of tender pink lamb sat on one side of the plate, with a comma shape smear of potato mash, a tiny Jenga stack of carrots and parsnip julienne and a smattering of carefully placed what could have been kale or seaweed. It really did look very impressive and very *Masterchef*. In fact, sitting there with Kristjan's hungry eyes watching her every move, she felt like one of the food critic judges they wheeled in every now and then, especially as she was sitting at the one table in the dining room which had been beau-tifully laid out with smart cutlery and long-stemmed crystal glasses, which she'd never seen before.

She poured the tiny pot of jus over the lamb and feeling a little self-conscious under Kristjan's intense gaze, cut herself a tiny bite of the meat and scooped up some of the vegetables.

The sharp, sweet richness of the jus caught her first, followed by the subtle smokiness of the tender, fragrant flavoured lamb and the delicate, unadulterated taste of the vegetables. Simple and elegant, was her first thought and she nearly spluttered out loud in sudden awareness of her John Torode description.

Kristjan's face contorted in anxiety.

'No, no, it's fabulous. Sorry I was...' it would take far too long to explain. She took another mouthful and sighed, closing her eyes to show him how blissful his food was.

It really was... 'Absolutely bloody amazing.' Her eyes started open. Surprisingly good. Brilliant.

'I can put this on the menu?' asked Kristjan.

Lucy fired a slew of questions at him. She was impressed but her natural caution made her want to check he was up to the task.

'Lucy,' he pointed to his face, 'I look young but I know my job.'

She could see a hint of frustration on his face.

'Yes, you can put it on the menu,' she said quickly before she could change her mind.

Kristjan jumped up and grabbed her hand, pumping it up and down, beaming from ear to ear, uttering bold promises. 'I'm going to put The Northern Lights Lodge on the map. This is going to be the restaurant to come to. I will make you proud. Now you must try my cinnamon rolls.'

One bite had her groaning with pleasure. 'These are yum.' She sat up. 'I know, this would be perfect. Afternoon tea and morning coffee.' Her mind was off and running.

'We could put a board at the end of the road. I was thinking about ways to draw in non-residents to the restaurant. We could offer really nice tea, speciality stuff, served in lovely thin china cups, with some cakes and biscuits. In the morning we could do flavoured coffees with pastries. And hot chocolate,' she broke off to grin at Kristjan who was nodding with excitement. 'I love hot chocolate.'

'Me too, with lots of marshmallows and cream.'

'Oh, yes and served in big earthenware mugs that you need two hands to hold.' Lucy held her hands up in demonstration and laughed. 'And I have no idea where any of that came from, but I think we should do it. What do you think?'

'My aunt makes,' he held up his hands mimicking her, 'pottery.'

'Excellent, can you get some samples?'

He nodded.

'I'm also thinking ... we could hold a themed meal, an Icelandic banquet. A sort of promotional evening.' She tipped her head to one side. 'I think you must have put something in that jus.' Her brain really was on fire this morning. 'There aren't many restaurants around here, it would be good for people to recommend us. I thought we could invite local VIPs.'

Kristjan immediately began making suggestions and

within five minutes, they'd come up with a complete menu plan.

'Where did you learn to cook like this?' asked Lucy as she finished the last mouthful of her cinnamon roll.

'My dad has worked in London before he came to Iceland. He worked at the Hotel Rangi near here. They are known for good food. I worked there for a few summers but I always cooked with my mother.'

'Are you from round here?'

Kristjan laughed. 'My family lived on the other side of the hill. In the summer I would come and help Olafur, he's my cousin, on the farm before it was sold to Tomas.'

'Tomas?'

'Tomas Pederson. You know him.'

She lifted her shoulders, knowing him was pushing it a bit. 'I've never met him but I spoke to his PA via Skype. So what sort of farm was this before it became a hotel.'

Kristjan laughed. 'What do you think?' He pointed out of the window to the white dots on the hillside beyond.

'Sheep.'

'Very good. We'll make an Icelander of you yet. Lucy … what is your father's name?'

'My father's name?'

He nodded, a smile playing around his lips.

'Bryn'

'We'll make an Icelander of you, Lucy Brynsdóttir.'

Lucy was surprised at the sudden heat in her cheeks and the need to blink quickly. She found she couldn't speak for a minute. When at last she found her voice, she felt rather touched. 'That's ... that's ... I like Brynsdóttir.' It made her feel like she was someone, part of something that was bigger than she was. Even though her father was hundreds of miles away, she felt connected. Grounded in some way. Straightening up, she realised that Lucy Brynsdóttir was someone, someone who had some pride, who could start afresh. With a firming of her jaw, she lifted her chin. Someone who had to find a way of standing up to that weasel Bob. She wasn't going to let someone like that ruin her chance of starting over.

Chapter 16

Alex cornered Lucy in the dining room when she was leaving the kitchen, looking a little guilty, her fingers hidden under a cloth over the top of the small plate she carried.

'Sampling the wares are you?

'No, just checking in with Kristjan,' she said airily.

He gave her a teasing grin and leaned forward to swipe away the white icing sugar dusting her upper lip. As soon as his finger brushed her skin – he had to stop doing that – her startled eyes met his and a dart of lust tripped his pulse. And now she was staring back at him with wary silence as if she might spring back into the safety of the forest like a shy deer.

'You ... you had some...' he nodded, looking at her lips. Big mistake. A small pink tongue darted out to lick them and for a crazy minute he wanted to kiss her again.

'Cinnamon bun,' she said, her voice hoarse.

He swallowed. Hard. Her husky tones set off a shiver of awareness that twisted his gut.

'Kristjan's been experimenting. He wanted me to try one.'

She held up the plate and lifted the cloth to reveal a glistening sugary Danish pastry. 'I'm taking one to Hekla.' She frowned. 'A peace offering. She seems upset about something but ... she's avoiding me. I'm not sure what I've done.'

Alex swallowed, again, very relieved to grasp at another subject.

'I might be able to help there.'

Sharp, resigned eyes shot to his before she sighed and her mouth firmed. 'I should have known she'd talk to you.'

He stiffened at her tone. 'What's that supposed to mean?'

'For a barman, you seem to know an awful lot about what goes on.'

'Don't we always?' he lifted his shoulders.

'In the movies yes, not so much in real life. That's usually the concierge.'

'Ah well then,' he laughed, spreading his hands wide.

'Yeah, I forgot you occasionally double up as luggage boy.'

'I think its bell boy ... luggage boy sounds like a really duff superhero.'

Unexpected laughter pealed out and Lucy's eyes danced with humour, her mouth curving into a slow smile. 'You could have a very cute uniform, with a cape.'

'There's no way I'm wearing tights. And definitely not shiny lycra leggings.' He shuddered.

She gave his legs a considering look and then, as if burnt, jerked her eyes back up, a slight tinge of blush lining her cheekbones.

'So,' she said decisively. 'Hekla. You know what's wrong with her?'

Alex nodded. 'You want to hear it?'

'Of course, I do. Oh,' she paused. 'I have done something wrong. I was kind of hoping that it was something else as I've racked my brains.' She took in a deep breath and pushed out her chest. 'Go on then, tell me.'

'She thinks you think she's no good at her job.'

Lucy let out an unamused laugh. 'You've got to be kidding me. She's brilliant, although at which job you mean I don't know. It seems like she's been keeping this place going. She does reception, she works in the office, she waits tables, she ... well, she even fixed a faulty toilet the other day. I think she's amazing. I'm not sure what I'd have done without her.' Her teeth began to worry at the familiar spot on her lip.

'Don't.'

She patted her mouth. 'Sorry.' She took in another long breath. 'I really don't understand.'

'Hekla feels you don't trust her.'

'Of course, I trust her. There's lots of money in the safe in the office. Plenty of stock around the building. I trust her.'

'I don't think it's that sort of thing she's upset about. It's you, trusting her to do her job properly.'

He saw Lucy stiffen.

'I don't know what you mean ... or what it's got to do with you.' He almost laughed at the way she stuck her chin out, suddenly belligerent, except that it drew attention to the slight pout of her plump bottom lip.

'You remember when the American complained.'

'Yes.' Her brow furrowed in concentration.

'Hekla was handling it and you...'

'Shit,' Lucy slapped her forehead with the heal of her hand. 'I do remember. I waltzed right in between her and John Wainwright the Third. Took over.'

He nodded.

'I do that a lot.' She held up a horrified hand to her mouth. 'It didn't mean I didn't trust her ... it was a problem and I wanted it sorted. I should have left her to deal with it.'

He could almost see her mentally flicking through recent events, as she winced and screwed up her face periodically.

'Oh shit. And I'm doing the same with Kristjan, except he's not experienced enough yet to get pissed off with me.' She pulled another disgruntled face.

'You really do beat yourself up, don't you?'

She turned big, serious eyes his way. 'Unlike you, I need to make this job work. You can move on anytime you like. I *have* to convince the new owners to let me stay on. I need to be here for at least a year.'

Alex's mouth dried. Shit. It was slightly worrying that Quentin hadn't responded to any of his recent emails, not since he'd reported back more favourably on the progress at the hotel. What if Quentin decided to bring in a whole new team? It was what he normally did.

Hekla rose as soon as she walked in the room but Lucy put a hand on her shoulder and pressed her back into her seat, placing the cinnamon bun in front of her. 'Coffee?'

Bemused, Hekla looked at her warily, nodding.

Moving to the coffee machine in the office which was permanently on, Lucy poured two quick cups, black for herself and strong and milky for Hekla.

'I owe you an apology,' said Lucy perching on the edge of her desk facing Hekla.

The other girl took a quick sip of her drink looking everywhere but at Lucy. With a sense of shame, it dawned on her that she'd really hurt the other girl's feelings.

She reached forward and touched Hekla's arm, suddenly aware that it was the first time she'd voluntarily touched her. The realisation made her feel shoddy and inadequate. Hekla was always touching her, hugs, pats, reassuring nudges, including Lucy in her unconditional warmth from day one. She'd been nothing but generous, kind and supportive.

She deserved a proper explanation, or as much of one as Lucy could share.

'Hekla, I really am sorry.' She gave a half-laugh. 'I'm going to use the old it's not you, it's me line.'

Hekla lifted her head, already her blue eyes filling with compassion.

Lucy leaned forward and gave her a hug. 'You have helped me so much. I was in... Before I came here I was...'

With a shake of her head, the other girl started to say something.

'No, it's OK,' said Lucy. 'I want to tell you.

'Before I came here I had a big job, the assistant manager of a five star, five hundred room hotel in the centre of a big city in England.'

Hekla's eyes widened.

'Yup. Posh suits, lots of staff, a big office. The whole shebang. I was sacked.'

'You. Sacked?'

'Yeah,' Lucy lifted her shoulders to her ears, wincing. 'I did something stupid.' She shook her head. Hekla's lovely innocent face looking at her made her pause and she couldn't risk the disappointment she'd see there if she told her the truth. 'I made a mistake.' She rushed the words so that Hekla couldn't interrupt her. 'I was sacked. I came here because I can't get another job anywhere else ... and I need to make this work. After what's happened to me, I'm short on trust and long on fear. I'm frightened of making a mess and not being kept on after my two-month trial. When I came, I had no idea that the hotel was up for sale. So now I'm even more frightened. They might not take me on. And then where does that leave me? I'm trying to make sure everything is perfect, so that they have to keep me on.'

'Oh Lucy.' With a sympathetic smile, Hekla stood up and threw her arms around Lucy to give her a big hug. 'They made a very big mistake. You are a good manager. Already things are better. And you are a good person. I don't believe you did anything bad.'

'It wasn't bad, just really stupid.' Some days Lucy couldn't believe she'd really done it. 'Being sacked was the biggest shock of my life. I never thought that would happen to me. I was always good at my job. Always the best. So now ... I'm ... scared, careful. I'm sorry if I haven't trusted you. I should have done. You are amazing. You're the one that has kept this place going through all the staff changes. And you've been so kind to me. It would have been so easy to dismiss me as yet another manager and go through the motions but you never did.'

Hekla shrugged. 'You were different. I knew you wanted to stay.'

'That was desperation.' Lucy's cynical laugh prefaced her quick admission. 'But … you and your *petta reddast*, Elin, Brynja and Freya, you've made me feel part of something. In my last job, the hotel was a building, I was its custodian. Here, it's different.' She linked her arm through Hekla's. 'I'm, no, *we* are going to make this hotel the best in Iceland and those new owners are going to keep all the staff on, including me.'

'But of course,' said Hekla, the twinkle back in her blue eyes.

'And in future, if I piss you off, you tell me instead of doing the disappearing act.'

Hekla squeezed her arm. 'It's a deal.'

'We're a team and I couldn't do this job without you.'

Her modest head shake made Lucy smile. 'Although you might regret it as I'm going to start doing a lot more delegating and consulting you. How do you feel about us throwing a special Icelandic banquet?'

Hekla's eyes widened with sudden interest and her usual glow of enthusiasm.

Lucy explained her thinking. That it would be an event celebrating Icelandic food, where local dignitaries as well as hotel guests would be invited.

'It would be a good spectacle for the film crew,' observed Hekla.

'True,' said Lucy pulling a face. 'It would get them out of our hair for a change.' She turned to survey the office. 'And I'm getting rid of all this bloody paperwork...' Lucy rolled her eyes at the piles of paper that didn't seem to have diminished since she'd started. 'As of now, it's all going in the bin.'

The two of them filled four black bin bags of paper, which Dagur and Olafur took out to the recycling centre at the back of the hotel, after which Lucy turned her attention to another problem that had been bothering her. 'Can you take a look at this?' She beckoned Hekla over to look at her computer screen, bringing up a webpage. 'Look, all these pictures, on TripAdvisor. See all the cushions, throws, ornaments. Do you have any idea what happened to them?'

Hekla twisted her mouth. 'It's very odd. I was thinking about it. And then I remembered. One day everything was here, the next day it was gone. I remember Eyrun said something about the manager wanted to put them away. And the manager left around that time ... and we were too busy trying to sort everything out to look for them again.'

The little dark woman flapped her hands at Lucy as she entered the steamy laundry room and Hekla tried to hide behind her, which was laughable as the girl with her Viking genes towered over Lucy.

'Hi Eyrun. I wonder if you can help me?' Lucy started with a big pleasant smile, even though the woman was glaring at her with enough malice to frighten off a small army.

Eyrun shook her head as if she couldn't understand and let rip a flood of Icelandic.

Hekla's alarm showed in her widened eyes and her nervous translation. 'She'd ... er erm ... like us to leave.'

'Tough,' said Lucy, adopting her pleasant smile again, feeling that it might be wearing a touch thin. 'Eyrun, would you be able to tell us what happened to the cushions and throws?'

Hekla translated, although Lucy was pretty sure the woman understood every word.

'Nrr,' said Eyrun, with a discontented snarl as she continued to fold towels, not making any eye contact. Lucy did catch the sly dart of her eyes to the long tall cupboard in the other room, which was just visible through the open door.

After a fruitless five minutes of questioning, Lucy admitted defeat. Even if the woman knew what had happened to the soft furnishings. There was no way she was going to admit a thing, least of all help them by having a look anywhere for them.

'Is there anywhere else they could be?' asked Lucy as she and Hekla made their way back to the office.

'No,' said Hekla.

Lucy grinned at her. 'Well then, we're going to have to go on a midnight Ninja raid.'

'A midnight raid?' repeated Hekla, looking confused.

'I have a good idea where we might find some of the

things.' Lucy patted her on the hand. 'Don't you worry. All you need to do is find me some tools.' At Hekla's perplexed frown, Lucy said, 'You know,' and mimed a hammer and a screwdriver. Unfortunately lock picking was a skill set she'd yet to pick up. It was too much to hope there'd be a handy set of keys lying in a drawer in the laundry and she'd get that lucky.

'Come to my room, and when it's quiet we'll get to work. I still have some cherry flavoured vodka left.'

'For vodka, I will come,' said Hekla.

Chapter 17

'What are you two up to?' asked Alex as he caught them slightly giggly trying to conceal several screw drivers under their coats.

Where the heck had he appeared from? Lucy could have sworn he'd tidied up the bar and shut up shop at least half an hour ago.

'Nothing,' said Hekla in such a dead pan serious way that immediately gave the game away.

Lucy rolled her eyes as Hekla's face creased into a mischievous grin. 'We're breaking and entering,' Lucy said carefully enunciating the words, which seemed a bit tricky all of a sudden. Her tongue seemed a bit wayward and loose, as if it wanted to go one way and she wanted it to go another.

Alex's brow furrowed into delightfully perplexed lines, that for some reason Lucy had an urge to smooth away. He really was rather cute especially with the scruffy beard which had thickened up over the last couple of days. 'In your own hotel?'

'We're on the case of the missing accoutrements.' Lucy

said with an airy wave of her hands, feeling herself wobble slightly.

'Missing accoutrements, that sounds like some crime, Detective Smart.' Alex's mouth quivered.

'Want to join us?' asked Lucy raising both her eyebrows in invitation, rather liking the sound of Detective Smart. 'That's a really good crime solving name, don't you think?'

'Have you two been drinking?' he asked.

Lucy's eyes widened so far that she was worried she might give herself eye strain.

'Just a wee snifter, for Russian courage,' she said, pronouncing each consonant with great care, making it clear that she was completely sober.

'Russian courage? Isn't it supposed to be Dutch courage?'

'Have you ever heard of Dutch vodka?' asked Lucy with a superior sniff. 'I think not.'

Alex's mouth twitched. *Don't look at his mouth. Don't look at his mouth.*

It was impossible, she looked at his mouth, twitching away with suppressed laughter.

'Are you coming with us or are you going to stand there, smirkling at us?' she asked with great dignity, wondering if smirkling was even a word.

'I shall stop smirkling with immediate effect Detective Smart and join your elite band of Ninja detectives. Nice outfits by the way.'

Lucy narrowed his eyes. Was he mocking the black sock tied around her head?

'We're blending in,' whispered Hekla, holding a finger

up to her lips. 'Sh.' She started to tiptoe down the corridor. Lucy shot Alex a reproving look. 'Are you coming?'

'Wouldn't miss it for the world,' said Alex cheerfully, falling in behind them.

What did he have to be so cheerful about?

The laundry was pitch black but Hekla had procured them each a torch and the beams wavered as they walked through the first room, reflecting on the glass of the huge dryers which looked like black holes waiting to suck them in. Lucy picked up her pace and scooted past them.

They moved through into the other room, silent and still without the usual whooshing of water in the washing machines. Lucy inhaled the comforting clean smell of washing powder and fabric softener. The big white appliances sat like squat watchful sentries on the far side of the room and Lucy imagined the glass fronts like bespectacled eyes observing them, reporting back to Eyrun. Oh shit, she wished she hadn't drunk quite so much vodka. Hekla could certainly put it away. Lucy hadn't come anywhere near matching her, in fact, she really hadn't had that much but on an empty stomach it had gone straight to her head.

'That one,' Lucy pointed with her torch to the tall cupboard with its double doors in the corner of the room. She fumbled with the set of keys she'd taken from the office, shining her torch on the bunch as Hekla held the beam of light steady on the lock. It was tricky juggling the torch, the keys and trying to work through them. Nothing looked vaguely like the right sort of key.

The room was suddenly flooded with light. Both Hekla and Lucy whirled round and pointed their torches at Alex who stood by the light switch.

'What are you doing?' Lucy screeched as quietly as she could.

'Seriously?' He tilted his head, amusement bubbling in his voice. 'Did you forget who's in charge here?'

Lucy drew herself up with an attempt at dignity which was a bit difficult when Alex was starting to sway a little, or maybe it was the room. 'Well of course not ... it's just...'

'She's scared of Eyrun,' piped up Hekla helpfully, which wasn't helpful at all.

'Scared is a bit strong,' protested Lucy. 'Sensibly wary would be a better way of putting it.' Saying sensibly was quite tricky. 'Sensibly,' she repeated, feeling her lips stick together on the final syllable.

'Right,' nodded Alex.

She wished he'd keep still, it was so difficult to focus at the moment.

'Yes, so cupboard.' She turned to look at the tall white cupboard. 'I don't think any of these keys are going to fit. Bugger.' She looked at Hekla. 'Now what?'

'We could force it open with the screwdrivers,' said Hekla, leaning back against the wall and starting to slide down it.

Lucy nodded, her head drooping as she followed Hekla's progress. 'We could but then what if there's nothing in there. How do we explain it to Eyrun?'

'We had an ... an mergency,' suggested Hekla hitting the

floor with a sudden thump, her legs shooting out in front of her, stiff and stilt-like, reminiscent of an old-fashioned wooden doll.

'What sort of … mergency?' Lucy asked, frowning. Speech was getting harder.

'Washing emergency, loss of spillages on tablecloths.'

'Yes, thas good.' Lucy nodded wisely. 'We needed stain remover. Lookin' for stain remover, thas right and we couldn't find it in the other cupboards on account of I can't read Icelandic. You were never here. She likes you. We don't wanna spoil your cover. So, ish was me. I wash looking for stain remover to do a big load of washing, lots of washing, very quickly, and we wash looking for stain remover.'

'Oh, dear God,' muttered Alex, rather rudely to Lucy's mind. It wasn't as if he was invited on this mission.

He stepped in front of her to take a good look at the cupboard. 'Give me the screwdriver,' he said gently wresting it from her hand.

'You going to jemmy it?' asked Lucy. 'Our hero,' she grinned up at him. Gosh he was lovely looking. That dark slightly too long hair and the dark chin, he hadn't shaved in a few days and she rather liked it. It made him look like a dangerous pirate who could carry her off any time he liked.

Oh God, he was saying something to her. She blinked at him, smiling with a dopey sigh.

'No,' he rolled his eyes. 'I'm going take the hinges off one of the doors.' He pointed to the shiny brass hinges top and bottom of the doors. 'And remove the door.'

'Thas so clever,' said Hekla admiringly, tilting her head up, still propped up by the wall. 'Isn't that clever, Lucy?'

'Genius, I'd never have thought of that in a million Sundays. Why do they say that? Why not million Mondays. Would be aliter ... aliter ... aliterthingummy.' Lucy gave up.

'You really are plastered, the pair of you.' Alex shook his head, amusement dancing in his eyes. They were very nice eyes. 'Hand over a screwdriver, I don't think either of you are capable.'

'Yes I ... ackshully, no I'm not.' Lucy handed over her screwdriver and leaned back against the wall waiting for the room to stop moving.

Taking the screws out of the door wasn't difficult at all, but it was going to take some care and he was worried about whether the hinges on the opposite side would be strong enough to take the weight of both doors and whether the lock in the middle would be strong enough to hold the two doors together.

He glanced back at the two girls. Hekla's head now drooped, nodding as if she were falling asleep. She wasn't going to be any help at all. He glanced at Lucy who was gazing at him with big owlish eyes and a silly smile on her face. Drunk as a skunk and rather cute with it. It was nice to see her smiling properly. She didn't do it often enough. It opened up the possibility of a very different Lucy Smart and brought back a golden memory of the day at Gullfoss. When she smiled her whole face brightened.

'Lucy, do you think you could give me a hand?' This

could all end in disaster he realised and relying on her probably wasn't the wisest choice but it was all he had. 'Once I've got these screws out, I'm going to need your help. You need to hold the doors in place and take the weight here where they join at the lock.'

'OK, you're the boss.' She rolled up her sleeves, bouncing on her toes like a perky boxer ready to go into the ring. 'Let's go.' With a half-crouch, sticking her bottom out, she took a couple of steps forward, almost dancing around him to reach the spot he indicated.

'What are you doing?' he asked.

She straightened and gave him that haughty stare he'd seen a couple of times which now he found amusing. 'Are you dissing my finest ninja moves?'

'Oh, that's what they were. Sorry.' He pressed his lips together to stop himself laughing at the serious, semi-outraged look on her face.

'I'll have you know I've done karate,' she said sticking her chin up in the air at him.

'You have, have you?' He grinned at her and something in his chest tightened as she looked up at him slightly glassy-eyed but so serious and determined. For all her bravado, there was a vulnerability about her. Since she'd arrived, she'd never asked for help. That initial lethargy and slowness to act had been replaced by a decisive and almost stubborn determination to get the job done.

'You've got dimples.' She lifted her hand and stroked his cheek. 'They're nice,' she breathed, her face softening, her eyes suddenly warm.

Warmth bloomed as the unexpected touch floored him, sparking a desire to scoop her up into his arms and kiss the mouth mere inches from his curving upwards in a secretive feminine smile.

'Yeah,' he said brusquely, 'I was a really cute baby. Now are you going to help me or not?'

His heart thudded. What the hell was he doing here? In a parallel universe in Paris he would have asked Gustave the head of maintenance to go and get the cupboard door opened and he wouldn't be reporting back to Quentin on Lucy Smart's performance.

She moved around him and stood as he carefully started to undo the screws on the top left hinge, relying on Lucy to keep the doors in place.

'You'll need to slide your foot underneath that little gap to stop the door on the left dropping and twisting the hinges on the right,' he said. It took a good twenty minutes to take out all of the screws and pull the doors away from the door frame, but it had worked a treat.

'You take that side,' he nodded to the right-hand edge of the two doors, 'and I'll take this and we'll shuffle forward.'

'That what you were looking for?' he asked as the gap widened to reveal a walk-in room filled with shelves packed with a bright array of cushions, neatly folded throws and boxes of wooden birds, their beaks and feet poking up over the top of the cardboard like bizarre jackstraws.

'Bingo!' said Lucy peering around the door. 'Exactly what we were looking for. Hekla! Hekla. Oh.' Lucy turned to look at the sleeping Hekla on the floor. 'That's sobered me up fast.' She blinked at him. 'I thought we might find a couple of things but not the whole damn shooting match.'

'What do you want to do now?' asked Alex.

'What would you do?'

Alex winced. He was here to judge her. That was why he was here. He knew exactly what he'd do. How Lucy would tackle it? As a good manager she had to be able to handle this sort of thing. 'I've no idea.'

'Well I do,' she said, her mouth firming as she looked up at him. 'I shouldn't have to resort to this ridiculous behaviour.' Her imperious manner was slightly at odds with the wobble to her head as she tried to indicate the cupboard doors. 'I want to get everything out and dress the lounge and library the way they should be. I'm really cross that these have all been locked away. What was Eyrun thinking?'

'OK, but we'll need to prop the doors up over there while you get everything out. Do you want to do it all now? And after that? Do you want to leave the doors off or put the door back on?'

Lucy thought for a moment and then she shot a calculating look, his way.

'I don't have to explain myself to Eyrun. If she has a problem with it, she can come and see me tomorrow. I asked her about these things and she denied all knowledge. I'm on the warpath now.'

Alex smiled and felt a sense of relief.

'But,' said Lucy with a wicked grin, 'it would be quite funny if we put the door back on.'

'It would?'

'Oh yes.' Now she looked positively Machiavellian. 'If she goes inside the cupboard and finds it empty, she can't say anything, can she? Because then she'd have to admit that the items were all here in the first place.'

He held out a fist and Lucy bumped hers against him. 'I think I'll call you evil genius from now on.'

'Evil genius Ninja Queen, please,' said Lucy with a regal nod.

Together they worked as a team to get the cupboard door off and once it was removed and propped against the wall, Lucy bent to nudge Hekla. 'Wake up.'

She started and looked blearily up at Lucy and then beyond her at the packed shelves.

Hekla slowly got to her feet, her hand holding onto the wall to steady herself. 'Fokk,' she breathed, her eyes so wide at the sight of the hidden booty that it was almost comical. 'You found them.'

'We did. Now we need to liberate them. Why don't you go to bed? Alex will help me load everything up into a couple of the laundry trolleys and we'll put them in the office overnight.'

She also muttered something after it, which was unintelligible apart from the word Eyrun, which Alex took to mean *Holy shit Eyrun is going to have a cow* or something in that vein.

'Go on, go,' said Lucy.

'Are you sure?' asked Hekla looking a little confused.

'Yes, then you're not involved. You weren't here.'

'But I was,' replied Hekla looking even more confused.

'You didn't see what we did. You didn't touch anything. If Eyrun asks, *you know nothing.*' Lucy lapsed into a familiar Spanish accent.

Alex burst out laughing and she shot him a reproving glance. It really did feel like a scene out of *Fawlty Towers*.

'Go to bed Hekla. Then you can plead innocence with Eyrun. This way you can blame everything on me.'

A flash of understanding finally registered and Hekla nodded solemnly. 'OK. If you are sure.'

Lucy gave her a little push towards the door.

'But you're quite happy to throw me to the lions,' teased Alex as the door closed behind her.

'Even if she suspected you were involved, with those good looks and dimples you could easily charm the socks off her,' she said patting his cheek, which rather took the wind out of his sails.

Chapter 18

'It's Alex, isn't it?'

Damn. This was his first breakfast shift for a while as Olafur and Dagur were off today and in the rush to get up and get into the dining room, he'd completely forgotten the risk of bumping into Jane and Peter.

'Hi. Nice to see you,' he said smoothly, hiding the fact adrenaline had kick started his heart rate into warp speed. 'Jane and Peter. What a small world, what brings you to Iceland?'

'We came because of you, actually. Nina mentioned you'd been posted to Iceland.'

Alex shot a cautious look over his shoulder, grateful that no one was in earshot.

'And I've always fancied coming here. So, Peter decided to surprise me. I spotted you the other day but you disappeared before we could speak to you. We've been looking out for you and I was going to ask in reception when you worked. I'm sure being manager you're very busy all the time.'

Alex's skin goose bumped. Could this get any worse?

How did he explain that he wasn't actually in charge here without blowing his cover?

'Well, nice seeing you. I need to...' He angled his head towards the coffee pot in his hand and a table on the other side of the dining room.

Jane gave him a sympathetic smile. 'I love that you still help out even though you're the boss.'

'We do what we have to,' he said, wiping at the cold sweat that had broken out on his forehead.

As soon as he delivered the coffee, he shot into the kitchen and sagged against a table, rubbing his forehead.

'You OK?' asked Gunnar, coming in with an armful of dirty crockery.

'Yeah, fine.' Alex smiled weakly and straightened as his mind raced. What were the chances of Jane and Peter mentioning to Lucy that they'd met him? Had Nina told them why he was here? He was pretty sure they knew he was the manager of the hotel in Paris. He remembered Nina mentioning that he'd allowed Sebastian to stay in one of his suites. Would they mention that?

How would he explain it to Lucy? What would she say when she found out that he'd been lying to her all this time? If it were him, he'd be furious. But he couldn't tell her. Not yet. The sale was still going through and although the staff all knew the lodge was being sold, no one knew who the buyer was. Quentin didn't want anyone to know he was involved until the deal had been done. It wasn't Alex's secret to share.

'Alex, table five are waiting for service,' said one of the other waiters.

'Thanks.' Forcing himself to push it to the back of his mind, he went back to the restaurant.

'Morning,' he said to Clive, the director, who was unfortunately at his table.

'Oh, it's you. Waiter?'

'Barman. Waiter. Wherever they need me.' He kept his smile pleasant, even though Clive's false bonhomie and pseudo trendiness pissed him off and he didn't like the way he'd insisted Lucy took part in the filming even though she was so clearly uncomfortable with it.

'Can you get us coffee?' Clive wasn't even bothering to look at him, he and Bob had their heads together setting up a laptop on the table.

When Alex returned with two coffee pots, they were looking at the coverage they'd shot on the laptop. He was about to leave when he saw the footage from the other evening. The sight of Lucy's obviously tense face stopped him in his tracks. The small line furrowing one cheek bothered him.

As he stared at the screen, the scene changed, the shot pulling out and away before the camera panned up Lucy's body, zooming in on the swell of her breasts constrained by the tight top. It lingered there ... Alex counted the seconds – one, two, three, four, five, six – before moving up to her pale, strained face.

The utter cockwomble. Alex clenched his fists, a hot rush

flooding him. He shot a look of dislike at the dumpy, squat cameraman, who had a smirk Alex longed to wipe off his face.

Clive, sensing him, turned around and perceptibly shifted in his seat at the expression on Alex's face. Good.

'Alex! Didn't see you there.'

Bob's smirk widened. A pulse pounded in Alex's temple. He slowly leaned towards the cameraman, making the other man aware of his height as he towered over him.

'I'm assuming you were about to cut that scene,' he hissed, almost touching noses with the little prick.

Bob swallowed, trying to lean away and his shark-like eyes slid towards Clive.

'Hey man, stay cool,' said Clive, putting a jolly hand on his arm as if they were all mates together. Alex shook it off, his lip curling.

'As I said cutting that scene would be beneficial to your health and the wellbeing of your equipment.'

'Piss off,' said Bob, suddenly finding his balls and thrusting his chin up at Alex. 'We've got releases. We can film what we damn well like. And a jumped-up waiter isn't going to stop us.'

Alex raised a single eyebrow and stared unblinking at him. The restaurant had hushed and everyone was looking their way even though there'd been no raised voices. It was as if the incipient menace had snaked across the room in silent waves, upsetting the balance.

Bob swallowed.

'Do you want to put that to the test?' asked Alex in a low voice infused with threat and barely contained rage.

Clive tried to smile but his voice had a very slight tremor to it. 'Like he said, we have releases and we have the management's permission to film.'

'The management being the person you are sexually harassing in that video?' Alex's voice radiated disgust.

The production assistant opposite winced and shot a look of dislike towards Bob.

'I would think very carefully about how much you want to remain in this hotel and remember there is another level of management both above that and above you.' He clenched his jaw. 'Delete it now.' Staring the two of them down wasn't difficult. Alex had been dealing with arsewipes, awkward customers and arrogant dipshits for the last decade, these two were small fry in comparison.

Clive rolled his eyes. 'OK, keep your knickers on. I'm sure we can–'

'You married? Got a girlfriend,' snapped Alex.

Clive sank into his seat slightly and nodded with tiny movements. The production assistant, tossed her pony tail over her shoulder and folded her arms, watching with predatory interest. Alex almost smiled, he wouldn't like to be in Clive's shoes.

'And you'd be happy if some piece of shit focused on her chest for national TV?'

And yes, the girls' eyes narrowed as she leaned forward very slightly.

Clive had the grace to look shamefaced for all of ten seconds. 'Bob, would you ... delete the *offensive* footage for Mr Sensitive here.'

Bob radiating resentment started pulling up files on the laptop and jabbed at the keys with furious displeasure.

'And shall we make sure there's no repeat of that sort of thing?' Alex's voice might have sounded full of reason but it was clear exactly what he meant.

Clive's mouth sneered. 'And you watch yourself waiter-boy. You might find you just got too big for your boots.' His girlfriend rolled her eyes at the pathetic display.

Alex gave him a humourless smile. 'I wouldn't bet the bank on it.' As soon as he got out of here, he'd be straight on the phone to Quentin and the head honcho of the production company as well as checking whether Lucy had signed the release form. He didn't trust Clive or Bob as far as he could kick them.

'Bloody flaming marvellous!' He heard Lucy's shout as he walked into the office. Maybe now wasn't a good time.

'Morning,' he said, coming in to find her clutching her head and Brynja standing wringing her hands.

'I don't bloody believe it.' Lucy turned to him. 'There's a sheep in the hot tub.'

'What now?'

'Yes, now. I haven't got the first clue as to the procedure for this one but I do know someone is going to have to go in and get it.' She pulled an eugh face. 'And of course, Magnus isn't around today. Olafur has gone into Hvolsvöllur to get the spare tyres sorted. It couldn't come at a worse time. And if the bloody film crew get wind of it...' she shuddered. 'I can imagine what wonderful TV that would make. Honestly I think we're jinxed.' She was already grabbing a coat and pulling on a pair of wellies from under her desk.

Alex thought it was a bit more than that and he suspected so did she. Lucy Smart's name suited her to a 'T'. She was no fool.

'Or maybe the huldufólk really do exist.' She shot a quick look at Brynja. 'Sorry.'

'That's what happens,' said Brynja. 'You think that it is a fairy tale but then...' She shrugged, her eyes wide moving from Lucy to him, like a friendly owl. 'You don't want to believe.'

'One thing I do know is that I need to get it out of there pronto and then find out if the maintenance guys can get over here to do what's necessary.'

'Not got volunteers lining up then?' he observed.

'I haven't asked anyone yet. Why? Are you volunteering?'

'It's not top of my list of fun things to do today but if all else fails, I'll pitch in. Do you want a hand?'

'Seriously?' she looked at him, her face softening. 'I was hoping to help it scramble out. I really do not want to get in the pool with it and I have no idea how heavy a sheep is.'

The sheep was bobbing up and down in the pool bleating piteously.

'At least it's not cold,' said Lucy.

'And appears to be able to swim,' added Alex.

'Or float.'

'How the hell did it get in here though?' She narrowed

her eyes and scanned the fencing around the property. 'Seems far too much of a coincidence.'

'So you do think it's deliberate?' asked Alex. 'I wondered.'

'Give me some credit. Sheep are valuable around here, it's well fenced in to prevent this sort of thing. There's no way it could have wandered up here and fallen in. Someone helped poor Dolly.'

'They're making quite a statement.'

'Yes, but who and why?' She shot him a shrewd look holding his gaze.

He had nothing to feel guilty about … yes he did. He absolutely did, but not this.

'I'm a waiter. I've got no reason to go around coercing sheep into hot tubs.'

A slight smile played around her lips and he realised that perhaps he'd been a tad defensive when he hadn't really needed to be.

'I've been wondering,' she said, her attention going back to the sheep bobbing in the water, 'if it's an ex-employee or someone with a grudge. The only way I'm going to find out is by doing some questioning. Hekla seems to know everything but if I start asking her questions, she might think I don't trust her again. I upset her enough before, I don't want to do it again.'

'Would you like me to sound her out?' he asked. 'It would be easy to make small talk about the events and ask her opinion.'

'That would be great,' said Lucy so quickly he realised that she'd manoeuvred him right into it.

He laughed. 'Nicely delegated.'

'Sorry, was it that obvious?' Her conspiratorial smile lightened her face, her sharp, bright eyes filled with intelligence. His eyes lingered on her face. Smart cookie. And yet there was a vulnerability about her, that she kept well hidden. It made him doubly pleased he'd sorted Clive and Bob out this morning. She didn't deserve that crap.

He winked at her. 'Only because it's exactly what I'd have done in your place.'

'You're wasted as a waiter.' As soon as she said it, she clapped her hand over her mouth. 'Sorry that was rude. I didn't mean that … there's nothing wrong with being a waiter, it's just that…' She pulled an agonised face and part of him was dying to put her out of her misery, but what to say? Lying already was bad enough, embellishing it would make him feel far worse. Although another part of him was rather enjoying seeing her disconcerted and the pink tinge to her cheeks.

'Anyway,' she said, her eyes drawn back to sound of the bleats, all business again. 'We need to get Dolly out. I think we need to try and entice her to the side, although I'm not sure if she's swimming or floating?'

'You know it's a ewe?' He was impressed.

'No idea!' She shook her head. 'But she needs our help and it seems kinder to refer to her as a she rather than an it,' said Lucy sticking her chin up in the air as if daring him to disagree with her.

Something dislodged inside him at the sight of that defiant chin and her soft-hearted defence of the sheep, making him think that perhaps Lucy was the one in need of help and kindness for a change. She seemed to feel she had to do everything on her own.

Lucy bent down on one knee at the side of the pool. 'I don't know whether she'll come to us. What do sheep eat apart from grass? And how do we get her out?'

With visions of her holding out handfuls of grass, he shrugged. 'What about the hot tub equipment? You know the big sieves that pool maintenance guys use in swimming pools, maybe we could use something like that to push her to the side and we can haul her out.'

'That's a great idea. Let's check out the shed, see what there is.' She motioned to the outhouses on the slight incline behind them on the boundary of the grounds. 'Do you think one of us should stay with her?'

Alex eyed the sheep, which apart from the bleating, didn't seem to be too distressed. It wasn't thrashing about and didn't appear to be panicking. Not that he was any expert. 'Well she doesn't seem to be in danger of drowning, I think we'll be alright to leave her for a few minutes.'

'I'm more worried about a guest or the film crew coming by.' Her teeth gnawed at her lip and looked back at the big windows reflecting the morning's blue sky and the hills opposite. It was impossible to tell if anyone was looking out their way.

He nudged her with his elbow. 'The guests are all busy heading out for the day and the film crew are reviewing the footage they've got. Come on. If we're quick, we should be able to get her out before anyone spots us. And I don't think they can see her from the hotel.'

Lucy half walked and half ran up to the outhouse and wrenching open the door she went inside first to switch on some lights to help them find their way in the gloomy exterior which held lots of grounds maintenance tools and equipment.

'Perfect,' said Lucy crossing to the far wall and grabbing a long-handled, triangular shaped net and holding it up in triumph like a warrior princess with a spear. He smiled at the image she made, the net held aloft, her mouth firming in a determined line. 'We can scoop her to the side with this.'

'Ever caught a sheep before?' he teased.

'No, there's a first time for everything.' Her sudden unexpected light-hearted grin, dazzled him and for some reason his breath caught in his throat.

'Honestly this job can be so bizarre, but that's why I love...' she paused and tilted her head as if some amazing revelation had struck her. 'That's why I love it. I do love my job. I'd just forgotten.' She was already turning towards the door.

Sucking in a quick breath he turned to give himself some equilibrium, something about her bright smile made him feel off balance. He had the urge to hug her and tell her she was doing OK but she was all bustle and business this morning and it felt like it might be a distraction for both of them. Disconcerted by the conflicting emotions, he glanced away. What the! He let out a long low whistle.

'What?' Lucy turned around and looked the way he was pointing.

'Well look at that. By the generator. I guess they need one out here, the weather can get pretty severe and we're quite isolated.' He knew he was gabbling but the stark confirmation of their fledgling suspicions along with the need to fight his natural inclination to comfort Lucy had scrambled his brain.

Her gaze followed the direction of his finger. Two large tyres were propped up against a large electricity generator.

'Bloody hell,' muttered Lucy, the brightness doused immediately as she stomped over and gave them a light disgusted kick. 'How do you think they got here? Those huldufólk are mighty strong and clever.' Her mouth twisted with sarcasm before she added with a scowl, 'Houston we have a problem.'

Still clasping the net, she put her hands on her hips and let out a heavy sigh. 'Damn. I was hoping it was all coincidence. Stupid huh.'

He winced and shook his head.

She threw her head back in disgust, before lifting her chin again with that resolute thrust, he just had to admire. 'In the meantime, we have a sheep to rescue.'

'Oh bum,' said Lucy when Alex leaned forward as far as he dared trying to scoop Dolly towards the edge so that she could grab the sheep. It was worse than bobbing for apples. No sooner did he try to reach the animal's back end, the stupid creature dipped and swung out of reach floating towards the other side of the long rectangular hot tub. But he refused to be beaten. Stupid bloody animal. Didn't it realise he was trying to help it? And why was he doing this?

For what felt like the umpteenth time, he stalked around the end of the hot tub to the other side with Lucy following him. It was ridiculous. They both must look ridiculous. But he wasn't giving in. Not when Lucy was looking at him like he was some kind of hero. Now, the sheep was bobbing right in the centre of the pool just out of reach. If he could stretch that extra inch. For a moment he floundered on the edge, a rush of adrenaline pumping when he almost fell in.

What was he trying to prove?

'Let me have a go,' said Lucy, with another glance over her shoulder. He could tell she was anxious that someone might spot their antics. They'd been at this for twenty minutes.

'What? You think you can do better?' he said a touch grouchily. OK, he was being childish, but it was bloody annoying. How hard could it be to round the damn thing up? The sheep's glassy eyes seemed to be sharp with malevolent glee as if it were enjoying the chase. He narrowed his eyes and glared back at it. Lucky sheep was toasty in there while he was starting to get seriously cold where the splashes of water had soaked his clothes. He jabbed the net into the water, trying to make waves to get the sheep to drift back to the other side.

'No,' she pursed her lips as if trying to hold back laughter.

'Are you laughing at me?' he asked rounding on her.

Immediately her eyes widened in a guileless expression that wouldn't fool anyone. She pressed her lips tighter. 'Not laughing. No. N-not...' Her eyes twinkled a little. 'But it,' she sniggered, 'it's a bit like man versus beast. You are determined not to be beaten.'

Straightening up, he glared at the sheep and then her. He was about to throw the net at her with a childish, 'well, you try then,' when he realised how ridiculous the whole situation was.

'You should see me playing Fifa on the Xbox,' he said with a sudden grin.

'Competitive, much?' she asked, a giggle escaping as she looked up at him.

'Hell, yes. And, I am determined to get this sheep out.' With another push he reached out towards the sheep aware of the small smile playing at her lips. The net swished through the water and he leaned further forward. Steady Alex, he told himself. He didn't want to fall in, in front of her but it felt as if Lucy had challenged him and he wasn't about to concede defeat. The sheep was bobbing towards the far side now. If he made a quick dash around there he could pull the sheep to the side and fish it out.

Slipping on the wet deck, he made a quick clumsy circuit, barely staying upright on his feet like some cartoon klutz, narrowly missing falling in. When he reached the side where the sheep now knocked against the side, he ducked down on his knees to grab it, but the creature bleated and with its legs going like the clappers under the water, it swam away.

'Bugger!' said Alex as Lucy burst out laughing.

He glared at her, unable to see the funny side of things. Instead he gripped the net tighter and reached for the sheep again, managing to hook the net over its head. The animal's shrill indignant bleats filled the air.

'Come here you stupid thing, I'm trying to help you,' he ground out through gritted teeth, hanging onto the net and trying to coax the sheep towards him.

Lucy laughed again, the usual strained lines on her face lifting as if she hadn't laughed quite so openly and easily for a while. He paused, his cold fingers clenched around the handle of the pole, realising the absurdity of the tableau. If his Paris staff could see him now. He couldn't help but smile. They were used to seeing him in an expensive, well-cut suit, calm and in control of the busy hotel, like a captain at the helm.

'Glad you're finding the funny side of this, but any suggestions?' he asked with a crooked smile.

She pressed her lips together, her eyes dancing and looked at the water.

'And no, I'm not going in.'

'I didn't expect you to,' she said blithely, her mouth twitching. 'This is my problem.' She tossed her hair over her shoulder. With a sudden movement, she wriggled out of her coat, dropping it to the floor.

Not quite believing it, he watched as she yanked her jumper and t-shirt over her head in one smooth move.

'Lucy?' but before he could say anything more, she was kicking off her boots and shimmying out of her skirt and tights.

Like a stupid dolt, he gaped at the sight of her in bra and pants. Speechless. Wow, she was gorgeous. Eyes down, Alex. Eyes down. But he couldn't seem to help himself and he sneaked a peek at the high well-rounded breasts peeping over a lacy white bra and the creamy white skin cinched in at a narrow waist. Then, with a quick shudder as if steeling herself she jumped into the water

Striking out with a determined front crawl she swam toward the sheep.

'What are you doing?' he asked stupidly.

She cast him an unnecessary *what the hell do you think* look. The sheep like a spectator on centre court, thrashed its head from side to side with a loud baa, but Lucy went straight up to its side, standing up and pushing it towards Alex. It took less than a minute for her to manoeuvre it his way and for him to crouch down and channel his inner Australian sheep wrangler to grasp the soggy mass of wet wool and yank it out. The damn thing was heavier than he'd thought but with Lucy grinning up at him, ten degrees of smugness glimmering in her eyes, there was no way he was letting go. As soon as the sheep landed dockside the ungrateful creature skittered off the decking, hooves clicking on the wood, without so much as a look back, and scampered off down the field towards the fence, baaing as it went.

'Bloody typical,' he snarled as Lucy laughed again, her eyes sparkling with suppressed glee.

'It's kind of funny,' she snorted, her shoulders shaking, making the water swirl and lap across her breasts.

He narrowed his eyes and then unable to help himself laughed back at her. 'That's one way of doing it. Want a hand?' Still on one knee, he leaned forward and extended a hand, half wondering if she might pull him in. Being a gentleman he tried not to take in the sight of her cleavage. She pulled her hair out of her face, the movement pushing her firm breasts upwards.

Her eyes caught his and he realised despite his good intentions, he'd been staring and that all the blood in his body had gone someplace it shouldn't and his jeans felt uncomfortably tight. Worse still her eye level was right on the same place.

With a nonchalant hand he brushed down his jeans. When he looked at Lucy a fierce pink tinge ran along her cheekbones and she was studying the floor with great diligence. There was an uncharacteristic vulnerability about her that brought out the quick, sharp desire to pull her close and wrap his arms around her.

She peeped up at him, uncertain and shy. His heart stuttered in his chest, the next beat misfiring completely.

'Let's get you out of there.' He held out a hand and hauled her up on to the side. Hitting the cold air, she immediately tensed, folding into herself and crossing her arms over her chest. Without thinking he unzipped his coat and wrapped it around her, pulling her towards him. As soon as he pressed her wet soft body up against his all he could think about was wanting to kiss her. Right there on her pale pink lips. She lifted her head, wary eyes zeroing on his own lips. It was the shyness that did it, so unlike her normal practical, decisive attitude. He ducked his head and grazed her lips very gently, hearing her startled, quick indrawn breath. Alarm bells were ringing in his head – proceed with caution – but she tilted her head up like a sunflower and a tremulous smile filled her eyes, so he kissed her again, pulling her closer into the shelter of his coat. Her lips met his in cautious exploration and despite wanting to deepen the kiss he held back, sensing a fragility about her.

When they pulled back looking at each other, her eyes were dazed and wary again, and he drew her into a swift instinctive hug, holding her against him. She hugged him back, standing in the circle of his arms for a minute.

'We need to get you inside and warmed up. It's not really the weather for swimming.'

She sighed and he felt her small frame shudder. 'Thanks Alex.'

He wasn't sure what she was thanking him for but he felt like a conquering hero and he grinned like an idiot at her. What was wrong with him? This was standard nice guy behaviour, what had happened to being business-like? He was supposed to be evaluating her and the hotel. Although, what was the corporate line on fishing a sheep out of a hot tub? Or falling for someone your boss might fire in a couple of weeks...

Chapter 19

Hekla blew. And boy did she blow – a stream of curses erupted from the office as Lucy stood talking to Brynja and Kristjan at the front desk. Despite the language difference, the vehemence of her tone made it quite clear she wasn't being particularly complimentary.

There was a shocked silence and then the three of them peered around the office door.

'Ónytjungur,' snarled Hekla, ripping a sheet of already mangled paper out of the printer.

'Roughly translated as?' Lucy asked Brynja who was trying to contain her laughter. It was pretty comical, tall blonde Viking goddess versus squat black plastic box, the former circling the latter as if she might finish it off at any second. All she needed was a large dagger covered in runes.

Brynja pulled a face and whispered. 'Useless sack of shit.'

To be fair, the printer had become increasingly temperamental over the last few days, although it had always been Hekla's sworn enemy. Now it was causing too many problems as they relied on it to print out guest receipts at the end of their stay. As it had taken to chewing up every other sheet of paper, it did hold people up when they were trying to check out and were already antsy about catching a flight.

'Hey Hekla,' Kristjan tossed her a heavy book. 'Why don't you beat it to death?'

She caught it, slicing it out of the air and Lucy thought she was going to throw it right back at his head.

He ducked his shoulders and beat a hasty retreat back to his kitchen, as Hekla let rip with another stream of angry invective and stomped back to her desk where she started hammering at the keyboard of her laptop.

'Hey,' Lucy said. 'Time out. What's the problem?'

'I'm trying to print off the itinerary for the golden circle tour for the party that arrived yesterday. They're being picked up at ten o'clock by the tour company. And the –' she used a word that Lucy could have guessed at the translation, 'printer won't work. They will be here in a minute.'

'OK.' Lucy looked at the pile of churned up paper, making a quick decision. In a move she'd never have done at her last hotel, she put an arm around Hekla and gave her shoulders a squeeze. 'Why don't we use the manual feed for now? Get it done and then let's take a trip to Reykjavik and buy a new one. Brynja, we don't have many bookings for tonight, you can hold the fort. We'll have our phones on.'

'But...' Hekla's lower lip trembled.

Lucy gave her another squeeze. 'Come on. You haven't had a day out for a couple of days. I bet you could do with a change of scene. We can go and have lunch. You can show me a bit of the city and we can pick up a new printer.'

'New printer.' Hekla shot the current one a triumphant sneer. 'Ha! Yes. A new printer.' She was already reaching for the down coat hung on the back of her chair. 'I'll ask Olafur for the keys to the jeep. He won't mind as long as we're back in time for him to take the crew out tonight.'

'Right. Give me ten minutes. I need to ... er...' Lucy gave her watch a surreptitious look and then wrinkled her nose, feeling the tiny bite of disappointment. Breakfast service had finished half an hour ago. The serving staff would be long gone. Alex had been on duty this morning. She gave Hekla a catch-all sort of nod and slipped out into reception. She hadn't seen him since yesterday morning although he seemed to have taken up most of her thoughts. That kiss. Holy heck that kiss. His first kiss that night in the staff room had made her heart race, the one by the hot tub had been off the scale. Her cheeks heated at the memory. And what had she been thinking stripping off like that? God, hadn't she learned her bloody lesson? She was his boss for crying out loud.

And then as if she'd conjured him up, there he was, crossing the lobby coming straight towards her, still wearing his waiter's uniform, looking ridiculously handsome in smart black trousers and a white shirt which was unbuttoned to half way down his chest, as if he'd been changing and had remembered something. He just needed a loose bow tie dangling from his hand and he'd be sexy tuxedo man after a night on the town. Lucy's mouth went dry.

'Hey Alex,' her voice came out unnaturally high.

'Hi Lucy,' he grinned at her. 'No sheep crises today?'

221

'No, thank goodness. And thank you so much for helping yesterday.' Keep it professional, she told herself.

'No problem.' His eyes twinkled and held hers. She swallowed, being professional going straight out the window. A hot flush raced over her skin as she remembered, for what felt like the thousandth time in the last twenty-four hours, his gentle kisses. It had taken all her will power not to pop into the kitchen this morning during service to see him. Ever since yesterday, she'd been trying to persuade herself that he'd just been offering comfort during a stressful situation. She was his boss. Kissing him was wrong. Wanting to kiss him again was wronger ... was that even a word. It showed how discombobulated her brain was around him.

'Kristjan hasn't collected the print copy of today's menu.' Alex's voice interrupted her thoughts. 'I thought I'd pop by and get it for him.'

She frowned. 'But Kristjan just left,' she said looking back at the office, puzzled. The young chef knew the printer was out of action.

'Oh, I-I er,' stammered Alex.

Lucy pressed her lips together intrigued by his very un-Alex-like discomfit, although he recovered quickly, those amber flecked warm brown eyes holding hers with a steady gaze.

'Well, now I'm here.' And normal, in control, Alex was back. 'I'm planning a glacier walk and I know how much you enjoyed the trip to Gullfoss. Fancy tagging along?'

Lucy's heart did a quick flip. 'That would be great,' she said trying to emulate his matter of fact tone, despite her excitement at the thought of spending time with him. Her pulse was rocketing at a ridiculous pace completely ignoring the stern voice in her head, reminding her of boring things like boundaries and employee rights.

The drive to Reykjavik followed virtually the same route as the trip Lucy had had with Alex, although with Hekla driving it was somewhat different. Where he'd been cautious and careful on the road, Hekla didn't know the meaning of the word caution. She raced around corners, hit the gravelled edges frequently and turned her head when she spoke to Lucy, taking her eyes off the road constantly.

Gripping the seat and keeping an eye on the road certainly took Lucy's mind away from brooding about Alex and her contrary reaction to him, and she was grateful to see the environs of the city.

'We'll park down by the harbour, you can see the Harpa Concert Hall from there and the Sun Voyager, a beautiful sculpture. One of my favourite things to see here, although I don't like the city so much,' said Hekla as she drove through the centre.

Lucy realised that although she hadn't missed city life before, now she was here, her senses had come alive. Although it felt more like a small town than city, with its wide-open streets and the so, so pretty houses, white with brightly coloured rooves, and then as they moved through another part of the city, the houses themselves were bright red, green, a gorgeous blue, orange and even lime green.

The sky had brightened since this morning and now

light clouds were strewn across a blue sky, which was reflected in the huge glass frontage of the rather impressive Harpa, the concert hall and conference centre, which Hekla had explained was home to the Iceland Symphony Orchestra and Icelandic Opera. It looked incredibly modern, perched like a jagged hunk of ice on the edge of the old harbour, with its unusual glass tessellations reminding Lucy of a giant frozen honeycomb.

'As we haven't got much time, I'll take you Hallgrímskirkja, the biggest church in Iceland. It is very beautiful, well I think so. It was built like a volcano is formed.' She grinned, her good-natured face sunny and happy now as if her earlier explosion had never happened. 'And you know I like volcanoes.'

'I'd say you have a certain affinity with them,' said Lucy with a wry grin.

Hekla hooked her arm through Lucy's and led her down a few streets until they hit a long street, Skólavörðustígur. The street was wide and clean with lots of interesting craft and gift shops and cafés. Lucy insisted that they stop at one called The Puffin, she was so charmed by the iconic looking birds.

'You know that we eat them,' said Hekla, her big blue eyes mournful.

'Noo!' said Lucy. 'That's awful.'

'Actually, it's more the tourists than locals.'

'Well I can tell you now, we are never having puffin on the menu at The Northern Lights Lodge,' declared Lucy.

* * *

Window shopping in Reykjavik was such fun. Of course, in some ways it was very touristy but at the same time, it was clear that people here had a real eye for design and comfort. For someone used to the same endless chain stores, it was a revelation. They stopped outside one particularly striking display in the window of a jewellery designer store, Lucy's eye caught by a simple gold ring with a large uneven shaped pale blue-green stone.

'You know how well the pictures have gone down?' They'd sold three to guests in the last week. 'What do you think about us showcasing more local art and design at the Lodge?' she asked Hekla.

'Ja. That is a good plan. In reception. We could put some shelves in the corner and pictures in the bar.'

'Exactly my thinking. Come on.' She nodded her head towards the entrance of the jewellery shop and without waiting, pushed her way inside.

The owner, who was thrilled with the idea of a display at the Lodge, chatted details to Hekla as Lucy prowled around the displays, drawn back several times to the same ring in the window. It was horribly expensive, but then she hadn't touched her salary since she'd been here. And just six weeks ago she hadn't even dare buy herself a coffee at Costa. How things had changed? She glanced at Hekla. She'd made new friends, started to fall in love with the landscape and The Northern Lights Lodge was beginning to come into its own. Even the TripAdvisor reviews had improved and, dammit, there was still so much more she could do. She wasn't ready to leave the Lodge.

'It's amazonite,' said Hekla, coming to stand next to her as she looked once more at the ring. 'You should buy it. A celebration.'

Lucy caught her eye. 'That's exactly what I was thinking.'

As they left the shop, a deal done to set up a display in the next week and a little white box nestled in Lucy's pocket, she asked, 'Hekla do you know anything more about the lodge being sold?'

She always seemed to know everything before anyone else. 'No, it is strange. There's been no news. Maybe it might not happen now? The reviews are getting so good. Maybe Mr Pedersen will change his mind.'

Lucy crossed her fingers in her pocket. Unfortunately, they might make potential buyers keener still.

Hallgrímskirkja was perhaps the most striking building Lucy had ever seen, a modern gothic tower made of concrete that put her in mind of the white tower in *Lord of the Rings*. She couldn't decide whether she liked it or not. Part of her liked the simplicity and elegance of the lines but then she found it stark and cold.

'The view from the top is fantastic,' said Hekla. 'There's a lift if you'd like to go up.'

'Sold.' Lucy grinned at her. 'I'd like to see the view and then how about some lunch and then we'd better get to the electrical shop.'

'Perhaps you could buy another coffee machine for the staff lounge,' suggested Hekla. 'Then we might get some work done.'

The office had become a lot more sociable since the arrival of the coffee machine, which reminded Lucy that she needed to stock up on more pods, especially the hot chocolate ones which had proved very popular.

Lucy shook her head. 'I like everyone coming to the office for their coffee fix, it means we all see each other.' She shot Hekla a knowing grin. 'And it gives Kristjan a good excuse to come and see you.'

Hekla's face glowed with a sheepish smile. 'He likes coffee.'

'He likes Hekla.'

She began fiddling with the zip on her thick red, padded coat.

Sparing her blushes, Lucy added, 'And having it in the office is a good way of knowing what's going on. For example, Elin moaning that the towel rail had broken again in one of the rooms and that Magnus had fixed it for the third time.'

'How does that help?'

'Because I realised that the towel rail isn't fit for purpose. If Magnus has to keep fixing them, we need to get some different ones.'

'That is good. I never would have thought of that,' said Hekla in admiration. 'I learn so much. You are very good at your job. I think they made a mistake. But,' her face dimpled and that sunshine smile burst out lighting up her face which immediately made Lucy laugh. 'It is good for us because you are here making the lodge much better. And why are you laughing?'

'Because you ... you're smiling now and I can't believe you were so cross earlier.'

Hekla's eyes twinkled. 'I told you, I was named for the volcano.'

The view from the top of the church was stunning and Lucy took lots of photos on her phone, while Hekla humoured her and pointed out the landmarks. Mount Esja, overlooking the city, the harbour and the domed top of Perlan, a shopping and entertainment centre which apparently used to be water towers serving the city. After they left the magnificent church, taking a quick look at the statue of Leif Eriksson, a rather imposing looking Viking, Hekla led the way to Café Loki, her favourite place in the city.

'They serve traditional Icelandic food and a really cool rye bread ice cream, which is delicious.'

Lucy kept her thoughts to her herself but clearly her face told a different story. Hekla laughed. 'It is, trust me...' her voice petered out.

Lucy put a hand on her arm, 'I trust you.'

'But someone is not...' her English deserted her, and worry creased her face. 'I talked to Alex. He thinks we have a ... a bad person. I don't like to think that someone is doing these things on purpose.'

'They are. Alex and I found the spare tyres, you know. Someone put them there.'

'No!' With her widened eyes Hekla looked like a surprised bush baby.

'The mice. The slashed tyres. I'm guessing the sheep in the hot tub. The phone call saying I'd changed my plans. The locked hotel door.' Lucy didn't want to think it was personal but it was looking that way. 'Someone doesn't like me.'

'No,' said Hekla urgently, laying a hand on her arm. 'Before you came there were things happening. Small things. There was a problem with the taxi company taking someone to the airport. They didn't turn up. Gunnar had to drive the people. The taxi company ... they were very upset and said the ride had been cancelled by telephone.'

'You think that was deliberate.'

'I know it was,' said Hekla fiercely, 'the taxi driver is my brother-in-law. My sister makes all the bookings.'

'Well, that makes me feel better,' said Lucy. 'Marginally.'

It was when they were half way through lunch, Lucy having the Freya Icelandic plate with an amazing trout tarte, salad, and the famous ice cream, when a sudden thought occurred to her.

She waved her fork at Hekla. 'Can you think of other things that went wrong that might have been deliberate?'

Hekla thought for a minute before finally shaking her head. 'No, the cancellation of the taxi booking just came to me.'

Chewing slowly, Lucy thought some more, going over it in her head before saying, 'So that was the first thing. Can you remember when it happened?'

Hekla who was having a hearty-looking meat soup, which smelled rich and smoky, with a side dish of bread and the traditional dried salted fish, which she'd insisted

Lucy try. It was not an experience Lucy planned on repeating any time soon.

'About three weeks before you arrived.'

Lucy had been racking her brains to think why someone might want to harm the lodge and she kept circling back to the same thing.

'Was that before or after Pedersen started talking about selling the lodge.'

'Just after. Oh!' Hekla slapped her hand on the table making the cutlery rattle.

'I'm no detective but I'm guessing someone doesn't want the lodge sold or not to the person who's put a bid in.'

'I think that's right.'

'Do you know if anyone else was interested in buying the lodge?'

'Mr Pedersen never discussed it, so I don't know.'

Lucy tilted her head, 'As soon as we get back, I'm going to send him an email.'

'We might solve the mystery.' Hekla looked excited. 'We're like Miss Marple.'

Lucy rolled her eyes. 'I'd rather be Charlie's Angels. Miss Marple was ancient.' She took a swallow of the lager she'd had ordered.

'Yes, one of us would have to change our hair, as there's only one blonde one and Brynja is the other one and Alex is Charlie.'

Lucy almost spat her lager out. 'I'm sure Alex will love that.' Alex was about as far from a middle-aged, avuncular uncle figure as was possible.

'He likes you,' said Hekla, with a mischievous lift of her fair eyebrows.

Lucy tried to shrug but the other girl laughed.

'He does. Do you like him? He's fiiiine,' she said with distinct appreciation.

'He's very nice.' Lucy winced, she sounded like an elderly aunt.

'I wouldn't kick him out of bed on a cold night.' Hekla waggled her eyebrows. 'He's a grade A hottie.'

Heat burned in Lucy's cheeks.

'I-I hadn't noticed.'

Hekla hooted with laughter drawing the gaze of other diners.

'Liar liar pants on fire.'

Lucy narrowed her eyes, unable to stop herself smirking. 'You know your English is far too good.'

Across from the table, Hekla beamed at her. 'What are you going to do?'

'Nothing,' said Lucy. 'I'm his boss.' Under the table she crossed her legs, straightening in her chair, as if that would stop the memory of the deliciously soft kiss on the deck. The tender way he'd swept the hair from her face.

'So,' said Hekla.

'I'm his boss.'

Hekla shrugged. 'And?'

Lucy thought of all the things that could go wrong.

'You're a good person Lucy.' Hekla's face creased in sudden amusement. 'You are worried that you will take advantage of Alex.'

Lucy sniggered and then both burst into laughter at the thought.

'No. More that other staff might feel uncomfortable.'

'Brynja is with Gunnar, Freya sleeps with Dagur. We're miles from anywhere. Who else are you going to sleep with?'

'Well...' Lucy was a little taken aback at her blunt approach, 'I don't have to sleep with anyone.'

With a wrinkle of her nose, Hekla waved a dismissive hand. 'That is no fun.'

'And I've got baggage. My last relationship didn't turn out too well.'

'Best way to get over someone is to get back on the horse,' drawled Hekla.

Lucy raised her eyebrows in response to the very good American accent.

'Lived in Washington DC for a year.'

'Given the last horse bucked me off good and proper. I'm being more careful.' She should keep her distance. Alex's dark eyes saw too much and she liked them too much, especially the way they'd softened before he kissed her. If she avoided him perhaps he'd forget about going to the glacier. She could always tell him she was too busy to go. She was half way through her contract and she really wanted to make a good impression so that hopefully the new owners would extend it.

Chapter 20

'You've been avoiding me.'

Bugger, he made her jump. He must have been waiting for her to come out of her weekly meeting with Elin. It had been a week since the episode at the hot tub, which had had to be drained and cleaned.

'I've been busy.' And avoiding him had taken considerable work, making sure she went back to her staff accommodation before he closed the bar in the evenings, checking which shifts he was doing in the mornings and spending a lot of time closeted in the account's office rather than in the general office, claiming she needed peace and quiet to go over some figures.

'And I'm still busy now,' she added as she walked down towards the glass corridor to inspect the hotel rooms. It was an extra job she had to do each day, but she had no one else to do it. It was important that the rooms were inspected properly but despite pinning the list up for Eyrun, the housekeeper insisted she was too busy in the laundry to do it daily. Lucy foresaw things slipping if she didn't take charge. Elin was doing a great job, scheduling the other girls as well as cleaning all the communal areas, but she had enough to do.

'You chickening out of the glacier walk?' Alex's question cloaked a double meaning as he fell into step alongside her.

She swallowed, her stomach churning and stopped, turning to face him. No one accused her of being a chicken.

'When are you thinking about going?' she tipped her head up in response to the challenge.

His eyes twinkled and she wondered if she'd been had. 'Tomorrow, or the day after. You haven't had a day off since you went to Reykjavik.'

'You're counting?' A little hit of warmth coiled in her chest. He didn't answer. It was a good technique because now she felt duty bound to fill the silence. Nerves prickled her skin.

'I could go the day after tomorrow,' she offered, before adding so that they both knew exactly where things stood, 'I could do with the fresh air and a change of scene.'

If Alex picked up on her pointed words, he gave no sign, instead with a business-like nod, he said, 'Excellent, I'll book the tour. I'll let you know what time.'

He sauntered off and she watched him go. 'I hope you know what you're doing, Lucy Smart,' she muttered to herself wishing he wasn't quite so good looking and that the flipping silly bunny hops in her chest, every time he gave her that warm, intimate smile, would stop.

Clive and the crew were filming an interview with two guests in the glass corridor, as she cut through the hotel to head towards the laundry. Lucy's heart sank and she prayed they wouldn't take it upon themselves to decide to shadow her for the morning as they'd been threatening for the last few days. She really didn't want an audience while she met with Eyrun.

'Lucy, just the lady,' trilled Clive as they wrapped up the interview. 'We're struggling here to get some decent fly on the wall stuff. No sign of the elusive lights and well to be honest, you guys are all a bit tame. I was expecting a few ructions, rows, you know, new manager throwing her weight around. You gotta give us something.'

She tensed. 'Well, we're planning a traditional Icelandic banquet. That might be of interest.'

Clive beamed. 'Yes! Now you've got me thinking. I can see it, *Game of Thrones*, flaming torches, open fires, fur capes.' As he turned and began enthusiastically babbling to the crew, Lucy ducked out of sight and scurried away to find Eyrun.

Bearing the clipboard like a shield, Lucy went into the laundry, which as always was like slipping into a warm cocoon. Eyrun who was pulling a pile of fluffy white towels out of the big dryer paused and glared at Lucy as she came in and then carried on, putting them on the side. When she started to fold them, Lucy put her clipboard down.

'Let me help you with that.'

Eyrun stared but didn't say anything and carried on. Lucy picked up a warm towel almost tempted to bury her face in it. Instead she watched Eyrun fold the towel in half on the longer length and then fold into equal thirds. Copying her she folded her first towel and then another.

They fell into a smooth rhythm and Eyrun's face lost some of its taut suspicion.

'Eyrun, you're still not doing the inspections,' said Lucy not looking at the housekeeper. 'Is there any reason why not?'

Eyrun refused to meet her eyes.

Lucy sighed.

'And you had all the throws and cushions in the cupboard, even though I asked about them.'

'I was told to put them away until the lodge was sold.' Eyrun's jaw was tight with mutiny, her grey hair picked out by the stark overhead light under which she stood.

Despite rehearsing the formal warning speech in her head in readiness for this, the words upped and left her. The delaying tactic of looking around the room didn't help. Like before, something nudged at her. What wasn't right in here? The noticeboard was still empty apart from the solitary check list she'd pinned up before. Funny, given Eyrun's antipathy, she'd expected it to have been torn down. The sight of it, lonely on the board, jarred. In her office she had all sorts of things pinned up, relied on them to remind her of things. Then something clicked. She remembered the first hotel she'd ever worked in and the housekeeper there.

'You can't read, can you?'

The other woman's head shot up, her eyes fearful. Damn, Lucy hadn't meant to blurt it out but it had popped into her head so suddenly. It all made sense, the lack of any kind of memos or information pinned up and Eyrun not even looking at the paperwork she'd tried to give her.

To Lucy's horror tears began to well up in Eyrun's eyes.

'Is that why you wouldn't do the inspections? Because you couldn't read the checklist?'

Eyrun's jaw tightened and she gave an almost impercep-tible nod, as a tear rolled down her cheek.

'Oh, no,' said Lucy, feeling the other woman's distress. 'I wish you'd said, we could have...'

Eyrun sniffed and blinked. 'I didn't go to school much. The letters move. I have dyslexia. I don't read anything. But I can do my job.'

'I know you can,' said Lucy, catching the other woman's hands as she reached for another towel.

'And you're really good at it.' Everyone knew the laundry ran like clockwork.

'Every manager, they give me papers. It's on the paper. You have the lists.' She drew in a shuddery breath and put both hands up to wipe her eyes. 'I can do my job,' she said fiercely again, but Lucy caught the rigid set of her jaw.

'Yes, you can. And now I know,' Lucy put her hand on her hips, 'it will work out OK.' She was thinking of Hekla's *petta reddast*.

Eyrun lifted up a tear stained face to look at her. Lucy recognised that wary, suspicious expression only too well, she'd seen it in the mirror.

'Come,' she beckoned Eyrun into the other room. 'I have some ideas. Perhaps we can use pictures instead of words. Photographs?'

When she'd left the laundry, half an hour later, to her utter amazement, Eyrun had given her a big hug and patted her on the head, the latter of which was a tad embarrassing but Lucy was confident it was well-meant. She was delighted to have got to the bottom of Eyrun's problem and got her onside. No wonder she'd been so angry and uncooperative. For the first time in ages, Lucy let herself enjoy a moment of self-congratulation. Good managers looked after their people. This morning she felt she'd made a difference.

Chapter 21

As she crossed the car park towards Alex's car, Lucy tugged down her hat and tucked the scarf tighter around her neck, grateful for the gloves she'd remembered to grab as they were leaving. It was a miracle she'd remembered anything when she'd spotted him waiting for her in reception, casually propping up the desk chatting to Brynja, enthusing about the northern lights which thankfully had made an appearance last night. The film crew had been full of it at breakfast.

When he'd unfolded himself, his mouth curving and eyes crinkling, to fall into step beside her, a warm glow had lit inside her, gentling the butterflies that had been leaping about like lunatics in her stomach since she'd woken up this morning.

This was not a date, she reminded herself as she did up her seat belt. Fresh air and a change of scene. A day off. With a colleague. No matter how many times she reiterated this in her head, those bloody butterflies ignored her.

'So where are we going?' she asked, trying to keep her words light and nonchalant after they'd been driving for ten minutes. 'And thank you for taking me on your day off. It's good to get out. Get some fresh air. Change of scene.' The sentences trotted out, clipped and sharp.

'We're headed to Sólheimajökull.' Alex turned his face towards her as he drove, giving her a long, level look which punched straight to her chest. This morning he was clean shaven and looked more gorgeous than ever. 'And I wanted you to come, not because I'm worried about your health and well-being but because I enjoy spending time with you.'

The damn butterflies were all agitated again.

'Thank you,' she said and, realising it was an olive branch to her earlier churlishness, she reached for the guide book and leaflets in her daypack. 'So, what you do you want to know about Sólheimajökull?'

He laughed. 'Sock it to me Tour Guide Lucy.'

She tested her new footwear, feeling a little unsteady with the unfamiliar weight of the crampons attached to her walking boots. Now that they were well into November, there was a sub-zero chill in the bright clean air making her skin tingle and her breath came out in plumes of white steam. She hefted the ice axe in her right hand and pulled a face at it, still not sure what the hell she was supposed to do with it, despite the lengthy and rather intense safety talk.

Alex grinned at her, having teased her nonstop in the car as she relayed numerous facts about the glacier en route.

'Feels like we're about to go into battle,' he said, holding an axe up mirroring her move.

'As long as we come back victorious,' said Lucy, immediately relaxing and smiling back at him encouraged by his blithe confidence. He didn't seem the least bit nervous.

'You OK?' he asked.

'I was but that safety talk put the fear of God into me.' She pulled a face, looking up at the glacier peeling down the mountainside. The guide had impressed upon them, the importance of following him and not diverting from his track as there were deep fissures and crevices in the ice. He didn't need to worry, Lucy would be following his instructions to the letter.

'That's so you follow their instructions. They wouldn't do this if it weren't safe.'

'You're right. I think the footwear is freaking me out slightly. I feel like I'm wearing the equivalent of Megatron, evil Transformer, shoes.' She held up the sharp metal-toothed crampon encasing her walking boot. 'I'm worried I might lose control and they'll take a chunk out of someone.'

Alex laughed. 'Don't worry, I'm pretty sure Optimus Prime will be lurking nearby.' They both looked out over the ice. It was easy to imagine they were in another world or on a far distant planet. Ahead of them peaks of striated ice rose like an alpine range, the mysterious milky aqua blue tipped in some places with black ash from the not so long-ago volcanic eruption of Eyjafjallajökull, famous for bringing most of European air traffic to a standstill for several weeks in 2010. That bit had been part of Sven, the guide's, talk.

'It's so weirdly beautiful,' sighed Lucy. 'I've never seen blue like it.' She took in a deep breath, her nose tingling. 'And the air is so fresh.'

Cricking her neck, she looked up at the sky. Puffed up, white clouds scudded quickly across, playing hide and seek with the patches of blue. Difficult to believe that snow was forecast for later. A rueful smile curved her lips. One thing you learned quickly in Iceland was how changeable the weather could be. For someone who'd been such a slave to routine in Manchester, it was funny to realise that she now rather liked the fickleness of the weather. Embraced it. She liked not knowing what the conditions would be the next time she looked out of one of the big plate glass windows of the Lodge. She liked seeing the different seascapes each morning, diamond days where the sun sparkled on the skipping waves or emerald days when heavy rain filled clouds turned the rolling heavy swell a deep green. And then, there was the opposite horizon, where the difference in the light wrought a dramatic change in the appearance of the craggy outline; soft sunsets turned them into pink tipped, snow topped fairy lands while dark cloudy days revealed the brooding mountains of Mordor.

A frisson of excitement whispered through the group as the tour guide set off. Alex knocked his axe against Lucy's.

'Here we go.'

His boyish enthusiasm was contagious and she smiled again, lengthening her stride to keep up with him as they walked to reach the glacier.

Tentatively she took her first step on the ice, anticipating the glass-like, slippery surface of an ice-skating rink but when the crampons bit into the ice with a satisfying crunch, she turned her feet out to walk like a penguin as they'd been instructed to do.

'OK,' she said with a sudden light-hearted laugh, 'I've changed my mind, I think these might be my new best friends.' Taking another couple of sure-footed steps, she turned out her hands in flipper-like motions as she exaggerated her penguin waddle. 'They're kind of cool.'

Alex laughed at her. 'So we've gone from *Transformers* to *Happy Feet?*'

'Oh, yeah.' Lucy waddled a bit more, beaming at him as he shook his head in amusement.

Following the guide in strict single file, the group walked a little way across the ice.

'You look like a natural,' said Alex from behind her.

'I'm concentrating really hard,' she said loudly, wishing he was in front of her instead of getting an eyeful of her backside in baggy black waterproofs.

They stopped after twenty minutes to catch their breath and take in the amazing view of the ice spread before them, its surface like a huge uneven slab of marble, veined with black.

'Amazing isn't it?' Alex crunched his way to her side, putting an easy hand on her shoulder.

'Yes, it's so quiet.' There was a stillness to the air which emphasised the sensation of isolation and of being a very long way away from anywhere.

'Makes you think. Other people right at this minute are

standing on the Champs Elysée, or on Broadway or Oxford Street and we're here. It's hard to imagine cars and people, noise, traffic.'

Lucy let out a quiet laugh of agreement. 'Especially when it's so peaceful. It is beautiful but also quite intimidating, which is part of the thrill. You almost feel as if nature could turn on you in a minute. That ash is a telling reminder. Those volcanoes erupt with a certain frequency.'

'You've said it well.' Alex gave her a long look, his mouth lifting at one side. 'I feel like it's a place to reset. Work out what is what. What really counts.'

Lucy nodded, a quick ping of agreement resonating. 'Reset is the perfect word. The size of all this puts everything into perspective. Makes you realise what's important ... or rather, what's not important.'

She turned at the same moment he did, her eyes zeroing in on the flat indent of his lower lip, before they flicked up to his brown eyes. Her heart stalled at the expression in them, the dancing amusement replaced by a steady warm gaze, serious and full of intent. She heard the crackle of his coat as he manoeuvred closer and felt the quick hot stamp of warmth as he cupped the icy skin on her jaw to lift her face before lowering his mouth to kiss her.

Cold lips, hot breath, icy noses, warm air, the rustle of waterproofs, the thudding of her heart and the slow slide of skin on skin as his mouth moulded over hers in a gentle, leisurely exploration. She wasn't sure who pulled back first, possibly her, because she needed to catch her breath but his was coming in little steamy puffs on the air too. As if reluctant to sever the contact, his hand came up to stroke her face. The kiss had lasted mere seconds but energy and excitement buzzed low in her belly.

'We shouldn't...' she whispered, giving into the little nugget of anxiety that had niggled its way into her head. None of the other tourists seemed to even be looking their way or remotely interested in them. He touched the furrowed line on her face.

'You're thinking too hard.'

Huffing out a sigh, she gave him a careful, direct look. 'I'm your boss. We shouldn't...'

'Or,' he paused, his hand sliding to cup her jaw, a finger skimming across her lip, 'we could forget about the lodge. Just be Lucy and Alex? For today? Enjoy all this.' With a wave of his arm he encompassed the vast landscape with its raw nature. 'A reset?'

'OK,' she said and suddenly life seemed so simple.

Alex's mouth quirked and that elusive dimple appeared.

'Selfie,' asked Alex holding up his phone.

'Go on then,' she said. He looped his arm around her shoulder pulling her close, the soft cold skin of his cheek touching hers, as he held the mobile up. 'Smile.'

Together they stood looking up at the little round eye, Alex squeezing her as he pressed the button on the side of his phone with a long elegant finger which made her think of the times he'd touched her.

'You have to airdrop that selfie to me.' Lucy tried her best to sound normal to get them back on to safe territory but her words came out breathy and sultry which made

Alex smile and drop another quick kiss on the corner of her mouth.

'Sure. I–' He was interrupted by Sven who began to talk about the glacier, which apparently was the spur of a much larger glacier, one of the biggest in Europe. He spoke with that engaging confidence that tourist guides so often had.

They walked, climbing upwards for another twenty minutes until Sven stopped on a smooth topped plateau which stretched as far as the eye could see up towards the snow-covered peaks on the horizon.

'And now I will show you one of the crevasses. Two at a time. The rest of you stay here. Do not wander off. If you want to take photos, I will guide you to safe places.'

Lucy listened to the multi-lingual chatter around them, the quiet respectful tones of a group of quite elderly Japanese people, whose age certainly didn't hold them up, the brash loudness of a rather unpleasant man who dominated his group of four, the guttural consonants of four enthusiastic German photographers who were keen to go first and the slower drawl of some mid-twenty something Canadians.

When it was their turn, Sven led them to the edge of the metre-wide crevasse, like a sharp cut in ice with sheer sides of deep aqua blue.

'I will hold you, if you want to look or take pictures,' he said, grasping Alex's coat to let him edge forward and peer over the side.

'Wow,' Alex said impressed, 'how deep is it?'

'It is difficult to tell, the glacier is in a constant state of flux. It is moving every day, a tiny amount but new cracks can open up. That is why it is important to have a guide.'

Then it was Lucy's turn. She peeped over the edge to see the incredible blue of ancient ice almost glowing. It was both terrifying and mesmerising. Pulling back, Lucy gave a little shiver.

Alex smiled at her. 'Makes you think doesn't it.'

'It does. I can't believe people would be crazy enough to come out here on their own and try and walk without a guide.' Hekla had told them about the lengthy search and subsequent discovery of a body after a young tourist had gone missing on the glacier a few years previously.

Sven shook his head, the dancing light in his blue eyes snuffing out with sudden seriousness. 'It can be very dangerous up here. I've studied hard and done lots of training to be safe up here. We don't want any other fatalities. If the weather gets worse, we will go back. The risks are too great.'

Sven rounded everyone up and they set off again, leaning into the wind which had picked up, making the going a bit harder. Puffs of steam punctuated Lucy's heavier breathing.

They stopped a couple of times more, for which she was thankful for as she caught her breath and rubbed at her aching thighs while one of the little Japanese ladies, twice her age, beamed sympathetically at her.

That changeable weather caught up with them, thick clouds closing in bringing the promise of snow and Lucy caught Sven the guide checking his watch a couple of times and

247

speaking to the ground crew back in the car park. Rounding the corner of a wall of ice, he signalled for everyone to stop. The sudden change in the landscape from open wide space to enclosed ice caves and tunnels, made Lucy imagine she was in a computer game and had reached new level. They were in a small enclosed area with a large wall of ice ahead of them, sloping away to the right with a small ice shelf off to the left which dropped less than six feet to a lower level below, the edge of which Sven urged them to stay away from.

'This is where we will do some ice climbing. We will not have much time because the weather is moving in. Who would like to try?'

There were several enthusiastic yeses, including Alex, and Lucy was about to say no when it occurred to her that that word had become her automatic default.

When had she stopped trying new things? That first year in Manchester, she'd travelled the city, walking, cycling, exploring. Then she'd met Chris and he, she acknowledged with a regretful downturn of her mouth, hadn't been one for stepping out of his comfort zone. More of a pub or a night in with Netflix man.

Sven gave them good, clear instructions, handing out helmets and ropes and they crowded round watching as he demonstrated, hefting his axe with an impressive sweeping he-man strike into the ice before grinning back at his eager audience.

Alex caught her eye and winked. He was the first to climb, moving up the wall of ice with an easy natural gait, placing his feet quickly and confidently and striking hard at the ice with the axe as Sven had shown them all. The Canadians all looked like pros too, one of the German photographers was enthusiastic but clumsy, the others hopelessly uncoordinated, which Lucy suspected she would be too.

And then it was her turn. Sven was very thorough, checking her helmet, tugging at the strap and lacing her into a harness. From the bottom of the sheer wall of ice, climbing up looked like an impossible task but when she nervously looked over her shoulder, Alex gave her a warm smile and the thumbs up.

Swinging the axe to get purchase was much harder than it looked, but the crampons were her new best friends and slowly she inched her way up, enjoying the sense of satisfaction of stretched muscles and hard work with every piece of ice covered.

By the time she reached the top she was breathing hard but she waved her axe in the air down at Alex. Abseiling down was, she decided, a lot more fun. Lucy was unhooking her harness when Sven said, 'Sorry folks, this will be the last one of the day, we need to turn back and cut short the tour.'

'What, I'm not going to get my ice climb?' protested Brad, a strapping six-foot four man. From his slight European accent tinged with strong American overtones it was difficult to determine his nationality, but one thing was for sure, he was certainly full of himself. For most of the trip, his loud carrying voice had provided a non-stop commentary on his brilliance as a sports coach and how to manage a sports team. Knowledge that Lucy could quite happily live without.

'But that's why I came on this tour. And we're here now. Come on man, give us another couple of lousy minutes.'

'I'm very sorry, but the weather is closing in earlier than was forecast. We must turn back.'

The man looked at the sky. 'Looks OK to me. Those clouds are miles away.'

Sven gave him a tight-lipped polite smile. 'We must leave now. Base has said the weather is moving fast. The winds are picking up and bringing snow with them.'

Folding his arms, Brad shook his head. 'I'm not budging. I paid for a tour and an ice climb. I'm an experienced climber.' He looked around at the rest of the tour group.

Lucy sighed, wrestling with the chin strap of her helmet, trying to undo the plastic clip.

'Don't be crazy man,' said a Finnish girl, while a Canadian muttered 'Asshole,' and the four photographers lapsed into German, but it was obvious from their body language they were saying, 'Who is this dickhead?'

'Seriously folks. This is shit. We paid for a walking tour and an ice climb.' He looked around hoping to recruit supporters.

Alex stepped forward from the circle of hikers. 'He's the expert, you should be listening to him. He's responsible for all our safety.'

'Yeah,' drawled Brad, 'you know these places are always over cautious. Another twenty minutes isn't going to kill anyone.'

He crossed to the wall and swung his axe in a wide angry arc. Startled, Lucy reared back, ducking away from the blade in a Matrix like swerve which probably worked if you were an Olympic gymnast but not if you were ordinary out of shape Lucy Smart. Off balance, her feet anchored by the stupid crampons, she flailed like some windmill-armed cartoon character before gravity took the victory and she toppled backwards in what felt like a perfect slow-motion comedy bronze moment, straight over the edge of the small shelf of ice that Sven had warned them to stay away from.

Although it wasn't a big drop, no more than six feet, she felt every one of them. Once she'd gone over, there was no way she could gain purchase on the ice and she slid down, limbs flapping and her head still in the helmet, thunk, thunk, thunking all the way down until she slithered to an ungainly halt with an end of the road thud and one last bang to the head. Everything went black.

When Lucy came to, she could feel someone gingerly checking her limbs. Opening her eyes, she winced as light stabbed into her head. A ghostly, twin edged image of Alex hovered above her.

'Lucy! Lucy.' He gently tapped her face with two fingers.

'You've been on the same first aid course as me,' she said, except it came out as *youbeonnnsamfirsacrseasme*. Her head was blurry with a fuzzy memory of a trainer doing that tap, tap on a colleague playing the unresponsive body. Were they on a training course? Was that why she was lying on the floor? It was cold down here.

Alex frowned and leaned back on his heels as Sven loomed into view. She struggled to sit up, got halfway and promptly felt sick. With a groan she slumped, her shoulders barely able to hold up her head which was about to explode.

'Can you move your legs?' asked the guide urgently, looking at his watch.

What? Did he have a train to catch? Were there trains back down the glacier? Maybe she could hail a cab. She closed her eyes and was about to sink back down when she felt her shoulders grasped.

'Lucy.'

Blearily she opened her eyes to find the identical concerned faces of Alex one and Alex two peering at her.

'Hello. Hello,' she said to both of them, her voice sounding foghorn loud in her head. 'Hello, hello,' she whispered but that still hurt her head and then nausea punched into her throat.

'ThinkI'mgoingtobesick,' she mumbled, rolling away to the side. Everything hurt but she could move. As she stared down at the crystal packed surface, a vision of tumbling and nose planting the ice came back to her and she remembered falling.

Forcing herself to sit up, she wriggled her legs.

'Nothing broken,' she said, everything coming back to her like the slam of a door. She was conscious of the audience of horrified faces peering over the ledge a few feet above. It was embarrassing. She hadn't fallen that far at all.

Anxious to reassure Alex and Sven that she hadn't broken

anything, she lumbered to her feet and swayed on the spot, the world whirling around her. Yikes it was worse than being on the Waltzers at the fair. They were both looking so worried, she didn't dare tell them about the double vision or the mother of all headaches threatening to split her skull in two. The wind had already picked up and the tiny ice pricks foretelling of snow bit into her skin.

'I'm fine. Bit bruised.'

Relieved, Sven took her at her word, with unsympathetic alacrity, picking up her ice axe and pointing out a route that would take them along a parallel path with the others before convening a few yards ahead. He picked up his walkie talkie and held an anxious conversation with the base in the car park.

'Are you sure you're OK?' asked Alex one and two, their heads dipping to one side as if trying to see into hers.

She failed in her nod, it was too painful. Instead she bit her lip. Both Alexes took her hands, all of them, enfolding them within his with a reassuring squeeze as if to say I'm right here.

Then Sven's voice was beside her. 'We need to start down the glacier.'

Lucy could sense some kind of exchange between Alex and Sven in the heavy silence that followed her statement.

'Do you think you can walk down?' asked Alex.

'Yes. I'm having a bit of trouble ... I'll be fine. Just bruised,' she lied. She could tell the men flanking her were still holding some unspoken conversation.

'I need to lead everyone down, and we need to go quickly

because the weather is closing in. The wind is getting stronger.' Sven's easy-going face was now lined with worry.

'I'll be fine,' she reiterated, conscious that she was already holding things up.

'It's OK, I'll look after her.' Alex's words resonated with firm resolve.

Sven climbed up the slope using his axe, with the renewed stern warning that everyone must stay on the path, while Lucy and Alex walked in a parallel path until they joined the main party.

The group stepped out of the lee of a field of ice peaks, to find the wind hitting them full in the face, blustering around like a playground bully, pushing and pulling at them as they formed a two by two line.

She stumbled and immediately Alex's voice was at her shoulder, he took her arm.

'Remember what Sven said when we set out. Trust your feet. You're going to be fine.' His voice rang with conviction that she knew he couldn't possibly be feeling but she was grateful for him trying to reassure her.

Nodding she tried to calm herself. Suddenly getting down the glacier seemed a huge task. Nerves jangled as the muted voices floated back along the line. She could do this. Not that she had any choice. She had to. Around her the blur of figures moved slowly, carefully picking their way in rank and file formation. And then it began to snow, swirling flakes gathering momentum above them, coming down with the driving wind.

Pinching her lips tight so that she didn't start to cry, she shuffled along beside Alex, their arms still linked, his body slightly sheltering her from some of the wind and the bite of the snow. She didn't like having to rely on other people. She focused on the sounds around her. The crunch of the crampons, one foot after the other, in a steady tramp as they trekked back across the glacier, the buffeting sound of the wind and the eerie echo of silence.

She gripped her ice axe and doggedly put one foot in front of the other, fighting against the double vision. One. Two. One. Two.

After what felt like hours, but was probably mere minutes, they came to the bit where they needed to stay in single file and follow Sven. Alex reluctantly relinquished her arm. She remembered the wicked looking creases in the ice running parallel to their path on the way up and Sven's warnings.

She froze. Her legs refusing to move. Feet too heavy to lift.

'Lucy. Come on, we've got to keep moving.' The others were already marching off in a blurry single file, the heavy snow further distorting her vision. Two Svens turned back and gestured fiercely at them. His hoarse impatient shout was tossed away in the strengthening wind.

'I ... I can't.' Her vision faded in and out, one minute double, the next merely fuzzy. Both made her feel very sick.

'Of course you can, it's not much further. You've come this far. Put your hand on my shoulder and follow me.'

'Which shoulder?' she asked, swaying, a little

disorientated by the stop. She'd become used to the rhythmic routine of one foot after another other. Starting over confused her. With her gloved hand she reached for his shoulder but missed.

Alex's frown jumped in parallel across his faces. He peered into hers, staring right into her eye with impersonal determination. 'Lucy, can you see properly.'

'Sort of,' she said, with a wince. 'There are a couple of you. I'm not sure if I tried to kiss you right now, I'd hit the target.' Her attempt at levity hit the deck. Alex's frown turned into a fully-fledged glower.

'Why the hell didn't you say anything before?' he asked, with the snap of an angry crocodile.

'Because it wouldn't have made any difference. We needed to get down and I ... didn't think it would be this hard.' Her head drooped and tears pricked at her eyes. Tiredness, or maybe it was fear, threatened to hijack the muscles in her legs which protested at the weight of her limbs refusing to cooperate.

Then she was encircled in a reassuring hug, the brief touch of an icy kiss on her already cold, forehead. Snow had collected in clumps, dappling the fringe escaping from her woolly bobble hat.

'Unfortunately luggage boy isn't on a par with Superman, so I can't offer to carry you.' He squeezed her. 'But we'll get down together. Trust me.'

Trust. Oh shit. Everything inside her rebelled. Trust him. Could she?

It must have shown on her face.

He gripped both her hands. 'I'll look after you Lucy, I promise. We'll get down together.'

'You ... you promise?' she asked in the most pathetic little voice, both the words and her wimpy tone embarrassing her already. Tomorrow she'd probably die of shame.

'I'll get you down.' The low timbre of his voice, redolent with certainty poured over her like molten treacle. It was a promise.

And she knew, with bone deep certainty, one that he would honour. For a dizzying moment, she wavered. To trust or not.

'OK,' she sighed heavily. 'Let's go.'

'Take the other end of my ice axe and give me one end of yours. Trust your feet and take it one step at a time.'

It was a brilliantly practical and an eminently Alex solution.

Crunch. Crunch. Crunch. Like an army of ants, footsteps marched across the frozen glacier and Lucy listened hard trying to match Alex's steps in front, but the outlying silence of the air which seemed oppressive was also disorientating. Trying to rely on her hearing was more tiring than she could ever have imagined.

At last they came to what she knew was the penultimate leg. While they didn't need to walk in single file, it was still quite a challenging section made worse by the diminishing visibility thanks to the thickening snow. Alex gathered up both ice axes in one hand and took her hand with his other.

'Well done, Lucy. Not far to go now. How's your vision?'

'I can see better now, there's only one of you but it's easier to close my eyes and open them every now and then,' she said. 'I've got such a headache. The white hurts.'

'OK, well I can guide you. You're doing great. I'll hold your hands and talk you through everything. You just open them when you need to. OK?'

She gripped his hand. 'OK. Lead on. I'm in your hands.'

Warm breath fanned her forehead. A tantalising brush of his lips danced across her skin.

'Right, we're going down a small slope and twisting to the left. Plant your feet really carefully. Put your hand on my shoulder.' Stiff with tension, she followed his instructions, feeling the pull on her calves as they carefully inched down.

'Only five more steps and then this bit is over.'

One. Two. Three. Four. Five. She let out the breath she'd been holding for all five steps. Her headache was making it difficult to concentrate.

'Great. Now it's a slight incline. Hold my hand and I'll help pull you up. It's probably about ten, twelve big steps. It's steep.'

Counting made it easier and Alex counted with her. His voice became a beacon, her personal lighthouse, never faltering in the clear concise instructions he relayed.

Gradually her muscles began to relax. Following Alex's low-voiced instructions became as natural as breathing. It was easier to stay silent so that she could concentrate and not miss anything he said.

'We can walk two abreast here.'

'Ok, the ice is slushy here, remember the stream, where we stopped to drink the water, we're coming up to that. When I say you'll need a big step to cross.'

The final leg was the part she was dreading. The open ice field sloping downwards with nothing to shelter them from the driving wind and the increasingly heavy snow and nothing to stop them tumbling down if they fell. As they left the lee of the mountain, the wind funnelled down the glacier, blasting at them so hard, Lucy thought she might be blown off her feet, but Alex was there grabbing her arm and wedging himself up against her to take her weight as she stumbled down the slope.

The last part of the walk was only twenty minutes, although it was miserable with the wind tugging and screaming at them, driving the icy snow like needles into their faces.

When they staggered onto the rough pebbled path from the glacier, Lucy heaved a huge sigh of relief. Around her she could hear the others scrambling to remove the crampons, which at the start of the trip had been welcomed with a sense of adventure and were now being discarded in haste, an irritant rather than an exciting novelty.

Crouching, she fumbled with the fastenings.

'Here, let me,' said Alex. 'You don't want to cut your fingers.'

'No more *Happy Feet*,' she mumbled, too weary to protest and past the point of putting up any resistance.

Chapter 22

Ten past three in the morning. Lucy shifted her head gently on the pillow, turning away from the digital numbers glowing on the bedside clock.

Her head felt a lot better, clearer and less muddled, compared to when Alex had led her back in to the lodge. He'd phoned Hekla from the car asking for the nearest doctor and they'd called in on one in Hvolsvöllur on their way home. The doctor, Hekla's uncle's best friend, had shone a too bright light in her eyes, declared she had mild concussion and wasn't to be left on her own for the next forty-eight hours. News that Hekla received with grave concern when they'd arrived back at the lodge.

'Lucy, Lucy...' she'd lapsed into sorrowful Icelandic, before wrapping her arms around her with a big hug.

'Hey, Hekla, I'm OK,' Lucy had said when she felt the other girl's tears on her cheek, touched by her worried concern.

Now Lucy smiled as she recalled the scene in the guest lounge, the fire crackling and spitting in the big hearth as Hekla had insisted on taking her to the nearest sofa.

'Come. Come. Sit.' Hekla had tugged off Lucy's coat,

handing it to Elin lurking behind her. Beyond her, Brynja and Olafur hovered. Brynja clasping her hands while Olafur looked tense and unhappy.

Freya had run forward, dropping to her knees to tug off Lucy's dirty, wet walking boots.

Now in bed, Lucy's eyes filled with sudden tears at the memory of them fussing over her.

'Sit. Sit,' Hekla had said, insistent on guiding her onto the sofa, ignoring Lucy's feeble attempts to say she was fine. All she'd really wanted to do was go straight to bed, but with all of them looking so worried, she didn't have the heart, especially not when Hekla had said, 'We'll look after you,' and firmly pushed her down onto the sofa and tucked one of the soft throws around her, enveloping her in a soft hug of cashmere.

'Would you like something to drink?' Elin had immediately asked, plumping up a cushion and handing it to Hekla who put it behind Lucy's head.

Lucy rolled her head from side to side as gently as she could, mimicking the attempt she'd made to say no, back in the lounge. It didn't hurt as much as it had done then. Not that it had done any good, Hekla ignored her anyway.

She and Brynja had had a brief argument as to the merits of proper hot chocolate, which would be delayed by a trip to the kitchen, or the office machine hot chocolate which was more immediate. Hekla won the argument but it was Elin who'd volunteered to go the kitchen. Lucy's attempt to protest that office chocolate was fine was met with Elin's raised finger, which brought a smile to Lucy's face. Elin was far too ethereal and willowy to threaten anyone. Elin and Hekla had headed off to the kitchen, bickering gently.

Minutes later, Kristjan had appeared with a plate of brownies followed by Hekla and Elin with a tray of steaming hot chocolates in the pretty blue glazed earthenware mugs that Kristjan's aunt had started making for the lodge.

'I brought these for you. Chocolate is good, ja? What happened? Did you fall?'

'Yes, how did this happen?' asked Brynja, perching on the edge of the nearest chair, flanked by Freya and Olafur. Hekla and Elin snuggled on the sofa on either side of Lucy and Kristjan plonked himself down at her feet leaning against Hekla's legs.

Lucy closed her eyes remembering how as she'd slowly retold the whole sorry tale with regular interjections from Alex, they'd all listened with the rapt Icelandic attention to storytelling. When she reached the end, there'd been a satisfied silence punctuated by the fire crackling merrily in the grate until Olafur had piped up. 'Yes, you were very lucky. Remember that guest who broke her ankle, last year. And the Swedish guy who died up there. There was also—'

She had been lucky. No bones broken, although with the bruises starting to make themselves felt, she didn't feel quite so lucky. The thumping against her skull had eased but turning over was difficult. For a few seconds she struggled, unable to understand why her legs were pinned by the duvet. It took a while for her brain to catch up and realise why.

Next to her, fully dressed, slept Alex, his legs crossed at the ankles and arms folded at his chest, propped up on a pile of pillows. Feeling slightly guilty at spying on him while sleeping, she turned and raised herself on one elbow. It felt good to be at an advantage for once, instead of mid throe of a crisis.

His formal, quiet pose reminded her of one of those stone carved mediaeval knights she'd seen in Winchester Cathedral, like Chaucer's *veray parfit gentil knight*. His still-ness fascinated her and a breath caught in her throat, stuck fast as she studied his handsome face, trying to break it down into component parts.

Was it the whole that made him handsome or the sum of individual parts? Her vote went to those melted choco-late eyes that seemed to see everything with unnerving accuracy but then there was the mobile mouth with the fuller lower lip with that central indent that shouted sexy. There was also the tiny smattering of dark freckles on one side of his mouth that marred the overall perfection but made his face interesting. Her breath stuttered out as she watched the gentle rise and fall of his ribcage, moving in tandem with the light shallow breaths she could hear over the crackle of the fire on the other side of the room.

Savouring the luxury of being able to study him, she took her time, continuing her slow inventory. Wide shoul-ders, slim build but toned. There was a pleasing firmness to the biceps filling out the sleeves of his faded blue t-shirt. He'd changed into faded, well-worn jeans, a rip at the thigh exposing a tantalising glimpse of tanned skin and dark hair which made her pause to wonder what the hair would feel like under her lips and how he would feel if he woke to find her kissing that tiny patch of skin.

Jerking her gaze away from the ridiculously tempting oasis in the worn denim, a little pocket of warmth spread through her chest at the thought of him being here all night. He'd woken her two or maybe it was three times in the last few hours and she barely remembered what she'd said to him, just that he was here, smelling lightly of wood smoke and hot chocolate. She leaned forward, checking she hadn't imagined the scent.

'Feeling any better?' His eyes flicked open.

'You're awake.' She squeaked, her limbs stiffening like a spooked, spiky cartoon cat.

'Dozing.' Amusement danced in his dark eyes. 'How's your head?'

'Better.' Her voice rasped, her throat dry. 'I don't feel as if Erik the Red has attempted to halve it with a dull axe.' Just the rest of her then, that felt as if she'd done a few rounds with an unforgiving ice surface. Wriggling her shoulders, she groaned, pulling a face. 'Everything else hurts.'

'You took quite a tumble,' he winced. 'You were lucky you didn't break anything.'

'Just my skull.'

'The doc doesn't think so but we need to keep an eye on you. How are you feeling? Nausea? Double vision?'

'Both of those have worn off, I have a headache, although nothing like earlier.'

'You can have another painkiller if you'd like or you could have a nice hot shower.'

Eek, now she remembered, stripping off in front of him down to her pants and t-shirt, too exhausted to worry about things like modesty.

With another groan, she swung her legs from under the duvet to sit on the edge of the bed. 'A hot shower.' Now he'd put the thought to her head, she couldn't imagine anything better. She turned to him and he hastily averted his eyes from her legs. The quick flush on his cheekbones made her pull the duvet over the top of her thighs ignoring an internal ping of feminine vanity.

'Would you like anything to drink? I could go and raid the kitchen while you shower?'

'Yes,' she said, without even considering whether she was thirsty or not.

Alex smiled at her alacrity. He never missed a thing. 'Fancy anything particular or shall I surprise you?' asked Alex.

'Anything is fine,' she said now desperate for him to go, so that she could shower and get back into bed before he returned.

'Let me bank up the fire.' He pulled a couple of logs from the metal basket and put them into the fireplace.

As soon as he'd left the room, Lucy lumbered to her feet with another heavy groan. Standing beneath the warm welcome flow of water, she examined her bruises. Her inventory read; one bluish one on each knee; a dark purple one, right elbow; a violet and ochre monster bigger than her hand on her shoulder blade; a series of almost-black conker-sized ones dotting along the right edge of her spine and an angry red mark ink blotted across three of her ribs. Ouch, now she felt worse, the collection an unwelcome reminder of her vulnerability and frailty.

Reluctantly she left the shower, the anxiety to be dried and in a clean t-shirt and pants before Alex came back, outweighing the longing to stand longer under the hot stream of water soothing her battered body.

'Hot chocolate,' announced Alex, pushing through the door with a tray and a large gift bag. 'And more of Kristjan's secret stash of brownies and a goodie bag, courtesy of Hekla.'

Lucy pushed herself higher on the pile of pillows, wincing at the heavy dull ache of pain in her shoulder as Alex handed her a steaming mug. 'Oh, marshmallows as well.'

He sat down on the edge of the bed, putting the goodie bag beside her.

With a smile she rubbed at the blue glaze, cupping her hands around the chunky pottery. She really did love these mugs.

'Please tell me Hekla isn't still up at this time?'

'No, she brought it earlier, you were out for the count.' Alex frowned. 'You ok?'

'Yeah,' she pulled a face. 'As long as I don't move.' Since she'd got back into bed it was as if someone had sucked all the energy out of her, but now snuggled back under the duvet with the delicious hot chocolate, she felt cosy and well looked after.

'I bet...' he pulled a pained expression, 'you've got some bruises.'

'Just a few,' she pinched her lips. Now he'd said that, it was as if all the points of pain had woken up and were vying for her attention.

'I can't believe you didn't...' He shut his eyes and shuddered. 'When you went over that edge ... I'm sorry I took you ... I...'

'Hey Alex.' She put down her drink, leaning over to pat his knee. 'Don't be silly. It was a freak accident and ... without you I'd never have got down.'

He shrugged. 'Hekla's worried about you. She says you have to put Viking Balm on your bruises, it will make you feel better.' He nudged the goodie bag towards her.

Despite his unsubtle change of subject, he seemed subdued and almost guilty.

'Viking balm? Please tell me that's a real thing,' she said trying to lighten the atmosphere.

She dug into the bag and brought out a small round jar.

'Oh it is as well. And...' She delved in again to pull out a crime novel and a pair of heavy-duty woollen socks. 'I love Hekla,' she said taking the socks and rubbing the soft – was it cashmere? – wool up against her face.

'So, you'd better do as she says.' Alex unscrewed the lid of the jar, releasing a delicate perfume of almonds and lavender and offered it to her.

It did smell good and she dipped a hand into the balm. With a smear on the tips of her fingers, she turned her other arm attempting to reach her throbbing elbow but let out an involuntarily yelp as she twisted her shoulder.

'Careful,' said Alex, sitting down on the edge of the bed at her hip. 'What hurts?'

'What doesn't?' she moaned, flopping back into the pile of pillows, before adding under his stern gaze, 'mainly my shoulder blade.' She gestured to her right shoulder.

'Turn over on your side.'

Her eyes lifted to his but his face was impassive and steady as if he expected to be obeyed and there was no big deal about it. The quiet authority made it a simple decision and she turned away from him.

Gentle fingers skirted the neckline of her night shirt, tugging it away trying to get a better look. Cool fingers probing at her still damp skin.

'Lie on your front, I'm going to lift your top up.'

Silence. Her jaw clenched. She was being ridiculous. He was trying to help.

Stiffly she moved onto her front. Making sure the duvet stayed at waist height, he eased her t-shirt up exposing her back. *Exposed.* She clenched her jaw.

Tension curled up in every muscle making her bones stand to attention, nerves twitching ready to buck his hands off at any second. She heard him suck in a tiny breath and waited, the silence between them stretching out as the fire popped and crackled. Then the sheets rustled as Alex's weight shifted. Her stomach turned over as the seconds ticked by.

His first touch was tentative, a whisper of fingers testing the way as if he wasn't sure where to start. Another indrawn breath and an almost inaudible murmur of 'Oh Lucy'. With his anguished words, came a rush of warmth. This was the man she'd trusted to bring her down the glacier. The man who'd stayed with her every step of the way in blizzard conditions, talking her through with gentle support and encouragement, never once impatient or exasperated.

She felt him hesitate as his fingers traced a loop around her shoulder blade. A slow glide, gently easing the balm into her skin. It warmed under the pads of his fingers as he rubbed in a smooth circular motion, gradually increasing the size of the circles and flattening his palm to massage the taut muscle under her shoulder blade. An involuntary sigh escaped from her lips as her body finally relaxed into the mattress. She was safe with him.

Alex's careful touch continued as he traced the bruises dotting her spine. Then his hands stilled. She closed her eyes, feeling him lean forward. Warm breath and then a whisper of a kiss on her back, then another and another as he kissed each one. She stiffened. Then with careful hands he eased her t-shirt down, gently securing the duvet back around her as if determined to make her feel safe. Tears pricked her eyes at the subtle gesture. This man saw so much. Slowly she rolled over to look up at him.

His eyes were soft with concern but also dark with something else. Neither of them said a word.

Picking up his hot chocolate he walked around to the other side of the bed and lay on the top of the duvet again, propped up against the pillows. They drank their drinks in silence.

Lucy kept thinking about those gentle kisses on her back. His gentle handling of her as if he knew she was a skittish horse.

'Alex?' her voice broke the quiet dark stillness as she nursed the heavy mug in both her hands, clutching it to her like a talisman.

'Yes.' As if knowing she needed comfort to get through this, because she had resolved to tell him the whole sordid Lucy Smart story, his hand crept behind her neck and around her shoulders. Even though she probably didn't deserve it, she allowed herself to relax within the crook of his arm, her head nestled into his neck.

She swallowed, pausing, the weight of everything so heavy, she felt almost a physical need to lift it from her chest. Closing her eyes, she took a deep breath, and without lifting her head, plunged in. 'You know I told you I'd been sacked.'

'Yes,' said Alex, the hand on the top of her shoulder flattening and the warm palm encircling the top of the bone under the fabric of her t-shirt.

'I messed up ... big time.' She dared herself to lift her head and look at him.

Eyes full of nothing but kind encouragement looked back her. His clear steady gaze held hers before he asked, 'Did anyone die?'

'No!' she said quickly half-shocked at his matter of fact question.

'You didn't kill anyone?' He asked.

'No!'

'OK, did you cheat on someone?' The corner of his mouth lifted.

She shook her head.

'Did you sleep with someone else's partner?'

Again, she shook her head. He put down his drink on the side and took hers from her hands.

'Did you steal something?'

'No.'

'Did you betray someone's confidence, steal their job, fire someone deliberately and unfairly?'

'No.'

'OK.' He laced his fingers through hers. 'I'm running out of the really bad stuff. I'm pretty sure that's most of the commandments taken care of, at least the ones I think are important.' He pulled her closer to him, his breath warm on the side of her cheek. 'Thou shalt not kill, steal or commit adultery. I'm not particularly religious, although don't mention that to my mother, she's Scottish Presbyterian, but those are the key ones in my book. So, whatever you've done can't be that bad.'

Lucy gnawed at her lip.

Alex's fingers touched her mouth. 'Don't.' They slipped from her lips sliding up to cup her cheek as patience and understanding warmed his chocolate eyes.

She cleared her throat, desperate to sound unemotional. 'Without sounding ridiculously egotistical, I don't suppose you've ever googled Lucy Smart, hotel manager.'

'Funnily enough, I haven't.'

'Just as well.' Lucy's mouth twisted bitterly. 'You'd get quite an eyeful.'

Alex's brows drew together. 'Now I'm intrigued.'

'Yes, most people are, when they hear. Can't resist taking a look.'

'Lucy.' His gentle tone almost felled her. 'You've lost me. Why don't you start at the beginning?'

Lucy focused on the fire, watching the embers glow and wane in a dragon's pulse of red, orange and black.

'Once upon a time, there was a hotel manager. Her name was Lucy Smart, and she was quite smart. Got a first in Hospitality Management, worked her way up to Assistant Manager with the Forum Group. And then she was fired for gross professional misconduct, bringing the company into disrepute.'

Alex's expression was a picture of calm, equanimity. Did nothing faze him?

'I had a boyfriend Chris. We went out for four years. Lived together in a flat in Manchester. He worked for the same hotel chain, in a hotel on the other side of the city. We were both Assistant Managers.' She recited the key milestones in her life in a dull monotone reducing them to mere facts.

'You don't have to tell me,' he said softly, stroking his thumb over hers

Lucy grimaced. 'I've started, so I'll finish.'

'Whatever you tell me, it can't be that bad.'

Lucy stomach knotted. This was harder than she'd thought, but she had to tell him.

'I'm a bit uptight.' She blurted the words out. Alex's eyes widened in surprise. 'Not really very ... adventurous. Chris ... he bought me this sexy Santa two piece. You know the type: cheap red satin and white fluff. Went on and on about me wearing it for him. Teased me about being a prude.' She pinched her lips together. 'I'm a "lights off" sort of a girl, if you know what I mean.' Easy tears welled up. 'And a late starter. Chris was my first serious boyfriend. I wasn't very good at ... at sex.'

Alex didn't say anything but his jaw tensed and his face had a curious expressionless set to it.

'Oh God, this is ... embarrassing.' Lucy steeled herself. Go in, get the job done. Closing both eyes, she carried on. 'It was our anniversary. Things had got stale ... his words, although he was probably right. Working ridiculous hours does that to a relationship. I got drunk.' She could hardly bear to say the words. 'Put the Santa outfit on. Did an awful Marilyn Monroe pastiche complete with breathy singing. You know, *Santa Baby.*'

Alex lifted a hand to her lower lip where her teeth were homing in on the scarred tissue on the inside of her lip.

It made her pause, a lump sticking hard in her throat. 'You keep doing that.'

'Because I don't want you to hurt yourself. You seem to have suffered enough.' The soft words struck her, making her tighten her jaw.

'Don't be nice to me. I don't deserve it. It was all self-inflicted,' she scowled. 'I should have known better. Chris filmed me. It seemed a laugh at the time, although things

273

do when you've knocked back a third of a bottle of vodka. Dutch courage—'

'Not Russian this time?'

'Any kind of vodka induced courage is a dangerous thing.' She winced and shuddered. 'God, it was excruciating.'

'Can't sing?'

'Pardon?' Of all the things he could say that was the last thing she expected.

'Don't worry I sing like a strangled cat too. It's nothing to be ashamed of.'

Lucy almost laughed.

'We should do karaoke together, *Islands in the Stream* or something.'

The reluctant half-laugh did escape this time. 'It wasn't so much the singing. It was the stripping.' She risked a look at him. Please don't be too disgusted or repulsed.

'Stripping? Ah, I don't have much experience of that. I've seen pole dancing once. Standard stag night, but not really my idea of fun. If I want to see a woman naked, I'd rather it was just for me and a certain level of intimacy is involved.' His eyes met her dark with meaning. 'So, I'm probably not one to judge. Amateur was it?' His flippant, matter of fact tone almost made her giggle. He was supposed to be taking this seriously. Not see the funny side of it. There was a funny side? That hadn't occurred to her before. The thought took up residence in a small back room in her head.

'Very,' said Lucy, nudging him with her elbow, before he started to smile. 'I'm not very good at stripping. Trying to get your knickers off sexily and twirl them around your head when you're as pissed as a newt is not as seductive as it was in my mind.'

'That would be the vodka goggles,' said Alex, putting his hand over the lower part of his face, as if trying to physically school his features into a semblance of equanimity.

Lucy let out a reluctant laugh. His light-hearted quips had diluted the humiliation. It was the first time she'd been able to find any humour in the whole miserable episode.

'Yes, they have a lot to be responsible for. I'd never done it without forty percent proof alcohol running through my veins. Burlesque is so not my thing.'

'So, you're an excruciating singer and stripper. Anything else I need to know?'

'Is that it?' she asked.

He frowned. 'Isn't that my question?'

'What? You think it's nothing?'

'It's what you let it be.'

She lowered her voice to a whisper. 'People saw me naked.'

Alex didn't say anything. No funny comeback this time.

'Chis ... h-he,' she closed her eyes in utter shame. 'He shared the clip with a few friends at work, who shared it with a few more and so on and so on.' She swallowed. 'I became an overnight sensation on the company's intranet.'

'Oh Lucy,' he sighed into her hair as he pulled her close.

'Five thousand hits on YouTube,' she muttered bitterly, the churning in her stomach horribly familiar.

'I'm so sorry. That's shit, but it's not your fault.' He traced her cheekbone with a finger, anger flashing in his eyes, warming a tiny part of Lucy's heart that she thought had been irrevocably shattered. 'I can't believe anyone would do that.'

She blinked back tears. 'That was j-just the s-start of it.'

He held her tight as they slid down her face. 'People ... they...' she shuddered. 'Complete strangers said horrible things. Men I barely knew suggesting ... some touching me as if they had every right. My boobs. My bum. And then getting arsey when I told them to get lost as if I had no right to say no to them.' She hauled a breath into her lungs, the tightness in her chest painful with the memories. 'Even women. Calling me slut, slapper, tart. Sometimes under their breath as I walked by. People I worked with. Someone was always quick to tell me what so and so was saying. Even supposedly good friends of mine were suddenly much cooler with me, as if they didn't want to get tarred by the same brush. And then...' she paused, still able to see the dispassionate expression of the woman from HR, 'the icing on the cake.' She pulled a bitter face. 'I was sacked.'

Alex stiffened, his hand on her shoulder tightening. 'On what grounds? They can't fire you for something that happens out of work. And if it was put on the company intranet, they had a duty of care to you. They should have removed it immediately.'

'You would think. Even the directors shared the damn thing. No, I got sacked because it was clearly filmed in one of our hotel rooms. It's an instant disciplinary if an employee uses a guest room without paying for it. Goes back to one of the concierge staff many years ago, running an escort service in the empty rooms. That night, it was our four-year anniversary,' she swallowed remembering the conversation vividly. 'I told Chris that I had something special for him. Emailed him a picture of a Santa hat and told him Santa Baby was coming to call.' She cringed. 'What an idiot. I'd caved in to his constant nagging and decided I'd ... well you know the rest. Chris said in honour of the night and my promise, he'd booked a suite through the company's friends and family site, so it was all above board.' She rubbed at her forehead. 'Turned out he'd *borrowed*,' she put the words in exaggerated speech marks with her fingers, 'a keycard. There was no official audit trail of payment. The video clearly showed me in one of our rooms ... not just a room but the flipping Presidential Suite. I was fired for gross misconduct.'

'And him?' asked Alex.

'Huh! You're joking aren't you. My word against his. While they took a dim view of the video and me being in a position of responsibility, bringing the company into disrepute, it wasn't a sackable offence. What was a disciplinary offence was that a hotel room was used. I was in the video, he wasn't. The weasel rat bastard claimed it was nothing to do with him and that he hadn't been there.'

'You're kidding?'

'I wish I was. His argument was that it wasn't worth us both losing our jobs as we still needed to pay the mortgage.'

Alex sucked in a breath, his eyes wide with disgust. 'What an absolute tosser. I hope you punched his lights out.'

'No,' she wrinkled her mouth, slightly ashamed now of her lack of backbone at the time. 'I slunk away tail between my legs. Tried to get another job. Without references. And word spread. Quickly. I couldn't get another job anywhere.'

'Except in Iceland.'

'Except in Iceland.'

Alex sighed in sudden comprehension. 'Now I understand why you're so wary of the TV crew.'

'Oh God, can you imagine. I'm desperate to keep a low profile, because I know what the word viral really means. We're talking deadly contagion. Stuff on the Internet spreads so quickly. And then a bloody film crew rocks up, hell bent on putting my face on TV.'

Alex's eyes suddenly sharpened. 'Bob knows.'

She nodded and slumped tiredly against him. 'Yeah, Bob knows.'

'Has he been threatening you?'

How did Alex get to the point so quickly, every time? 'Just making lewd suggestions about going into business together.'

She felt his tendons snap into attention, his muscles flexing as his whole body went on angry alert. 'I'm going to kill that piece of shit.'

'Alex!' she sat up in surprise at the unexpected violence vibrating from him.

'I knew he was a dick, but this...'

'Please don't say anything to him. He'll say something to Clive. They'll tell the hotel owners. The new owners might find out. I really need this job.' She turned pleading eyes up to him.

'But Lucy, you can't let him get away with this.'

'He's not getting away with anything. I avoid him. Make sure I'm never on my own. Please don't say anything to him.'

Alex settled back, a furious cast to his face.

'As soon as I know what's happening about my job, I'll tackle it.'

'We'll...' A strange expression crossed Alex's face. 'We'll tackle it.'

Chapter 23

'Morning.' Hekla pushed into the room bringing with her the delicious smell of bacon. 'I've brought breakfast.'

Lucy pushed her aching body up, her shoulder protesting as she twisted to pull up her pillows.

'How are you feeling?'

'Squished. Like a truck ran over me and then reversed again to finish the job properly,' she groaned.

'Ouch.' Hekla put the tray down and perched on the bed, in the same place as Alex had last night. Lucy hadn't heard him leave this morning.

'Alex says you are to stay in bed today.' Hekla's eyes gleamed speculatively and slid to the Alex shaped dents in the pillows and duvet next to Lucy.

'He did, did he?'

'He's very worried.' Hekla teased with a knowing look.

Lucy rolled her eyes. 'He's very bossy too.'

'So am I and you should stay in bed today.'

'To be honest I'm feeling much better. My head doesn't

hurt at all. My mum always said I had a thick skull. I think she might be right.'

'It's still good to rest.'

Lucy winced. 'But there's so much to do. We've got the banquet to arrange. Honestly I wish I'd never said anything. Clive's got the bit between his teeth and is expecting a scene out of *Vikings*. Thank God he's got his precious northern lights footage. I thought that might calm him down, but no, he's like an excitable toddler about this. I was just planning an Icelandic themed menu.' She gave Hekla a speculative look of her own. 'I don't suppose you'd bring me my notebook and a pen from the office.'

'Lucy.'

'No stress the doctor said. I'll get stressed if I don't start planning.'

Hekla narrowed her eyes and made a noise like a small pony but quarter of an hour later she returned with Brynja who immediately offered to dress the dining room.

'I can use the theme of nature for the tables. Bring the beach inside,' she suggested. 'I promise you will love it.'

'That sounds great,' said Lucy, who wasn't very good at that sort of thing at all. 'Storytelling,' suggested Hekla, as they brainstormed ideas to jazz up the evening, without the blood and gore of a certain TV series. 'Icelandic folk tales. Freya would do it. She's the actress. She could tell stories about the huldufólk.' She gave Lucy a sly wink.

'I think we've enough stories of our own,' said Lucy. Things had been quiet of late. No more disasters. She was hoping that whoever was behind the mischief had given up. She exchanged a look with Brynja who looked more like a wise old owl, with her mouth scrunched in a line of disquiet.

'Do you have any ideas who it could be?' the other woman asked quietly.

Lucy winced, loathe to voice her suspicions.

'It's got to be someone here, hasn't it?' Brynja answered her own question with bitterness.

With a sad nod, Lucy said "Fraid so.'

'It makes me so mad.' Brynja spat. 'Why would anyone do this thing?'

'If I knew that, we could stop them,' said Lucy.

'It's so unfair,' she burst out. 'We've worked really hard. The hotel has never looked so good, run so well and always ... in my head I'm waiting for the next bad thing. And the horrible Bob. He is waiting too. I see him watching you.'

Touched by her outburst, Lucy leaned over and squeezed her hand. 'And we'll keep on working hard, as a team. I couldn't do it without you guys. We're going to make this banquet our crowning glory.'

'Yes,' said Hekla fiercely, Viking battle light in her eyes. 'Let's make Clive pee his pants.'

Lucy and Brynja burst out laughing. 'Oh Hekla, I do love you. Your English is brilliant. But I get what you mean.'

By the time the two of them left, Lucy's notebook was full of ideas. Clive and his crew's last night was going to be spectacular, if it was the last thing she ever did, which she reflected it might well be. Time was running out on her contract, three more weeks, and there was still no word about whether the sale had gone through and whether there'd be new owners.

She dozed until lunchtime when Alex appeared with a bowl of soup, his dark eyes glimmering with approval when he advanced across the room.

'Well someone looks a lot better.'

Feeling lighter than she had done in a very long time, she turned and looked around the room. 'Who?'

Alex laughed. 'I brought soup for the invalid.'

'Apart from the bruises, I feel fine. A bit of a fraud, sleeping away while everyone else is working.' She gave the dark shadows under his eyes an anxious look. He hadn't had much sleep last night.

'Make the most of it, we've had a flood of bookings for next week and umpteen enquiries. There have been a slew of TripAdvisor reviews about what a great place it is to come for coffee. And a rave review on some travel blog. They loved the food, the friendly welcoming staff and the huggulegt ... whatever that may be.'

'It's the Icelandic version of hygge,' said Lucy, squirming her toasty toes in the lovely socks Hekla had given her.

'Of what?'

'Hygge,' repeated Lucy, pronouncing it hooga.

'Never heard of it,' said Alex. 'Am I missing something?'

'If you're planning to stay in Northern climes, I'd say yes. There are different versions of the word all over Scandinavia, it means to be cosy but there's more to it than that. To be huggulegt is to savour being cosy, taking time to enjoy the simple things in life to engender feelings of warmth and well-being.'

Alex wrinkled his nose. 'Sounds a bit ... new agey, bollocks to me.'

With a sputtered laugh, she rolled her eyes. 'I have to admit, I was in that camp at first, but do you know what, having been here a while and spent time with Hekla and the others, I understand it now. The weather can be a bit grim.'

'That's an understatement,' said Alex looking outside at the grey clouds and sleety rain sliding down the windows.

'Yes, but that's the thing, look how cosy it is in here.' She waved her hand at the log burner merrily blazing away, the soft light of the lamps and the blanket across her knees. She pointed to the steaming bowl of soup on the tray on her lap.

'People need to find a way through the long winter, so making things cosy and indulging in small celebratory rituals is one way of doing it. And we are talking small, but it's about making the time to do them. For example, making a conscious effort to sit, enjoy a log fire, setting the room with the soothing light of nice candles, lamps and reading a good book with a really lovely cup of tea, not any old stuff but a special one served in a beautiful china cup with a delicious chocolate or biscuit treat.' Her voice warmed as she described the scene.

She gave Alex a nudge at his raised eyebrow.

'It's a thing. I promise. You should try it some time.'

'Hmm.'

'Well the guests like it. The morning coffee and afternoon tea sessions have been booked out.'

'Must be the beautiful china cups.' He winked at her.

'Don't mock. It makes a difference.'

'Well I'm sorry the soup is in an ordinary bowl but you should eat up, while it's still hot.'

'Have you eaten?' She said picking up her spoon and taking a welcome, warming mouthful of mutton broth.

Alex smiled. 'Who do you think made the bacon butties earlier? It's impossible to cook bacon for someone else and not have it yourself. And I'll grab some soup later.'

'How's the book?' he asked picking up her discarded paperback, reading the blurb quickly and then opening up the book to read the first page as she carried on eating her soup.

It felt oddly companionable, him reading, her eating.

'Mm, that was delicious, thank you.' She'd scraped every last mouthful out of the bowl.

'No lasting damage to your appetite,' said Alex laying the book aside taking the tray from her lap. 'How's your shoulder?'

'Sore,' said Lucy.

'Let's have a look.'

Without thinking she rolled onto her front, awkwardly trying to lift her t-shirt.

'Let me.' Without fuss or awkwardness, he took over. 'Ouch. Those bruises look worse today.' He reached for the pot of balm and unscrewed the lid. 'Do you think this helps?'

'I...' She had no idea, but, 'it ... smells nice,' she substituted the words at the last minute, wondering what he'd say if she'd said it felt nice.

Not nice, delicious, she decided as his fingers moved across her skin, working the balm with infinite gentleness into her shoulder blade. Closing her eyes with a sigh, she savoured the pull and tug of skin over bone, the heated friction of the warming balm and Alex's careful, unhurried thoroughness. Magic hands chased down every bump and bruise, tender on the hurt spots, firmer on the bunched aching muscle. Her heated skin tingled and she squirmed into the mattress, aware that her nipples had peaked.

'Mmm,' she gave into the long low groan, when he hit a knot, kneading with a rocking motion that chafed her nipples against her bunched-up t-shirt. She softened her spine in pure appreciation, losing track of time as his hands mapped every inch of her back, paying slow careful attention to the landmarks of her accident. Finally, he reached the dip of her spine where the duvet covered her hips and for a few delicious seconds his fingers stroked the hard valley of bone, toying with the smooth skin. Anticipation balled in her stomach, a primeval longing for his hands to dip lower, to stroke down her bottom, find her thighs. Involuntary, she shifted, widening her legs.

She felt the loss when his hands lifted and she wriggled her hips in complaint.

'No kisses today,' she said dreamily, and then froze when she realised what she'd said. Her fingers dug into the feather down of the pillow.

Alex didn't say anything.

She bit her lip, fighting the urge to bury her head under the pillow.

Then one by one, he carefully brushed over the bruises, gently circling each one. An open-mouthed kiss and her skin quivered under each gentle silken stroke.

'Sorry, the balm doesn't taste that great.'

She gulped, her face suddenly a fiery red, wanting to die of embarrassment.

Alex chuckled and pulled her t-shirt back into place and then dropped a kiss at the nape of her neck, his breath hot over her ear as he whispered. 'Maybe next time. I need to get back to work.'

In the event, she didn't see Alex again that evening. Hekla dashed in with a meal at six o'clock, looking harried.

Lucy who'd spent the afternoon in unwelcome solitude with the company of too many brooding, regretful thoughts, was desperate for someone to talk to, to take her mind away from Alex and her unsubtle, slappery, blurted out invitation. She wasn't sure which was worse, the fact that she'd uttered the words or the fact that he'd turned her down.

'Can you stay for a while?' she asked rather pathetically.

Hekla's blue eyes looked haunted.

'Is everything alright?' asked Lucy immediately suspicious.

'Ja. Fine. Fine.'

'Which means it isn't,' said Lucy pinning her down with a piercing look.

Hekla lifted her hands in frustrated surrender.

'Alex said not to bother you.'

'He did, did he?'

'And it's fine ... he's taken boss, I mean he's in charge. With everything under charge, I mean control.'

'Hekla,' Lucy's warning note made the blonde girl look even more flustered.

'A coachload of forty people arrived half an hour ago. For dinner. The driver says there was a booking. I don't...' her brow creased in consternation. 'I don't remember.'

Lucy threw back the bedclothes, swinging her legs.

'No, no. It's fine. Now it is. Honest Lucy. Brynja and I are helping Alex in the dining room. Kristjan has already come up with a plan. There is nothing you can do. But I can't stay too long.'

'Are you sure?'

Hekla nodded. 'Alex is on it. Like he's the manager.'

'Yeah, he is good.'

Hekla grinned, raising cheeky eyebrows.

'At managing things,' said Lucy sharply, blushing but unable to keep her mouth from tilting into a reluctant smile. 'We ought to think about promoting him. It would cut your workload.'

'Ja, that would be good. He would be in the office with us more. A nice view,' teased Hekla.

'I don't know what you mean,' Lucy said primly, pursing her lips.

'You do.'

Lucy sighed and sat back against her pillows.

'If you're feeling better, I have a plan,' said Hekla suddenly.

'I'm feeling better,' said Lucy, sitting straighter.

'I need to make some arrangements.' Hekla looked rather pleased with herself. 'It will be a surprise,' she said as, with a skip in her step, she headed for the door.

'I don't like surprises,' called Lucy but it was too late, Hekla had gone.

Chapter 24

'You're going to love this,' said Hekla paying the entrance fee to go into the Fontana Geothermal Springs, grinning happily as she looked up at the tiny flakes of snow which had started and stopped several times throughout their journey here from the Lodge.

'Girl time,' added Elin with a happy sigh. 'This is perfect relaxation. There is nothing like a day at the hot springs.' She gave Lucy a wink, spotting her curious looks up at the heavy grey sky. The imminent snow forecast for today didn't seem to have deterred any of them from making the trip.

Lucy didn't mind this surprise. It turned out that Hekla had done some complicated rota jigging to release everyone for today. Alex and Dagur were on reception duty, despite the fact Alex had had virtually no sleep for the last few nights, and Gunnar was helping Freya to change beds and clean bathrooms, so that Elin, and Brynja were free to come.

'I'm looking forward to it,' said Lucy meaning it. After a full day in bed, she felt so much better, although ... weirdly she already missed Alex. She hadn't seen him properly since lunchtime yesterday but had been dozily aware of him popping in to check on her throughout the night. Laying a finger on her cheek. Brushing her hair from her face. A whispered, '*Good night, sleep tight.*'

When Hekla had suggested the trip out, Lucy's aching body had welcomed the idea and Alex, who had brought her breakfast, had cautiously approved once Hekla had promised there would be nothing more strenuous about the day than relaxing.

She tucked the bag containing her towel under her good shoulder and along with the others followed the signs to the changing rooms. So many of the guests spoke about their visits to the various hot springs and pools around Iceland, she'd been dying to try one and this place looked super smart and a little bit trendy.

'The tourist people all know about the famous Blue Lagoon,' explained Elin, 'but this is my favourite. Quieter and less money.'

'Especially now, before the bus tours arrive,' chipped in Hekla, with a slightly superior air that made both Lucy and Brynja burst out laughing.

'Even though we had to drag you out of bed at a ridiculous hour,' Brynja teased. She was the one that had insisted they set off early.

Hekla lifted her shoulders in a good-natured shrug and then smiled. 'Laugh but I have these...' From her bag she produced a bundle of the lodge's fluffy white towelling robes that were kept for the deluxe guest suites. 'I borrowed them for today.'

'Good thinking,' said Elin.

'I'll pretend I haven't seen them,' said Lucy, with a deadpan face, happily accepting one.

The changing rooms were sparse and there were a couple of other people in there and to Lucy's horror one big communal shower. Before she had time to ask about other shower facilities, it was too late. Hekla, Brynja and Elin were gaily stripping off, without any sense of modesty whatsoever. Lucy gulped. This was way outside the pay grade of her comfort zone! For a minute she dithered. But the others were so unconcernedly peeling off their clothes and trotting over to the shower, that she couldn't not join them.

'Have you seen this mole?' Hekla pointed to one south of her nipple, as she raised one arm under the flow of water, to soap her armpits.

'Wow, is that for real? It looks like mount Hekla,' said Brynja with an amazed face. 'What are you, some elf child?'

'I know, how cool is that? Who needs a tattoo when you can have your own personal mark?'

'I want a tattoo,' said Brynja. 'That one's cool.' She pointed to the butterfly dancing above Elin's belly button.

'Yeah,' Elin grinned, 'Especially when my boyfriend Roger kisses it and works his way down. Oh yeah, baby.'

'Go Elin,' said Brynja with a shake of her dark head, the water sluicing down her broad shoulders. 'Gunnar is a bit shy in that department.'

'Try honey, show him a trail,' said Elin. 'Works every time.' She gave an outrageous wink.

Lucy stripped to her knickers. Took a silent deep breath, forcing her shoulders away from her ears and with her back to the other girls, slid them down. She could do this. Pasting a ridiculous smile on her face, she lifted her chin and strolled, nonchalantly into the showers. Yeah right, she felt about as un-nonchalant as was humanly possible.

'Hey Lucy.' Brynja shunted up to make space as she lathered her dark pubes, turning back to Elin. 'Do you think Brennivin or vodka would work instead of honey?'

'Or you could draw an arrow and write this way to the honey pot,' suggested Hekla.

'Hey, you could have a tattoo with the instruction,' said Elin with a wicked smile.

They burst out laughing and Lucy took a handful of liquid soap and lifted her arm.

'I need to find someone to check out my honey pot,' said Hekla with a mournful frown, now working soap down her long lean legs. 'It's been too long.'

'What happened with that really hot guy, the Danish one?' asked Elin, throwing her head back and letting the water run through her short cropped blonde hair.

'He went back to Denmark. He was here on holiday.'

'That's a shame,' said Lucy trying to join in the conversation, trying to look blasé as she soaped under her arms. From the posters depicting what you had to do before you went into the hot springs, she had to get pretty thorough elsewhere.

Hekla laughed. 'No, you can do a lot in two days. He was ... how do you say it ... good in the sack.'

'Two days?' Lucy tried not to let her surprise show.

'Don't worry he wasn't a guest. I met him in Reykjavik.' Hekla smiled.

'Have you seen that new bar in Reykjavik?' piped up Elin, one hand between her legs, soaping herself. 'The one with the blue lights. It's so cool. We should go there one night after payday.'

'Remember that night at the...' Brynja said some Icelandic name which sounded like a bunch of letters, Lucy couldn't even begin to translate. There was a chorus of ascent.

'You all speak such good English.' Their command of colloquialisms was incredible. 'I feel bad, if you want to talk in your own language...' She took a breath and began to clean herself down there. No one noticed. Of course, they didn't. This was completely normal here.

'No. It's cool,' said Brynja. 'We're all used to it. I lived in the States for a while. Elin lived in Canada for four years when she was a kid and Hekla, where haven't you lived?'

'London, Washington DC, Auckland. My dad used to be an ambassador.' Hekla shrugged. 'English is second nature to us.' She stepped out of the shower and walked over to the bench when they'd left their bags.

When Lucy stepped out of the shower, standing completely starkers in front of the other three who were chatting away as they pulled their costumes out of their bags, the water running down their bodies, she realised that no one batted an eyelid. This was completely normal.

'Here you go Lucy, this will fit you.' Elin handed over the smallest bikini she'd ever seen. When she pulled it on, she tugged at the tiny triangles trying to stretch the fabric to cover a little bit more, which given she'd just been in the buff with them all was totally silly.

'Hey,' said Elin. 'Stop girl. You've got a gorgeous figure. You should be showing it off.'

'Yeah,' said Brynja. 'You've been hiding that.'

'Yeah,' said Hekla, 'she loves a baggy jumper. I noticed you, Lucy Smart. Why do you do that?'

Lucy shrugged, embarrassed now, as they all looked at her.

'I'm ... shy I guess.'

'Well you shouldn't be. You're freaking gorgeous.' Hekla grinned at her. 'Although I guess Alex already knows that.'

They headed out to the pool area with Lucy blushing furiously. 'Er, no. He ... erm ... stayed the night.' Aw, heck that sounded something it wasn't.

'When a man that fine is spending the night with you babe, we all want to know the deets,' said Elin, slapping at Lucy's hand which was still toying with the triangle just about covering her left nipple.

Lucy hoped the quick discussion as to whether they would go to the sauna, the hot tub, the steam room or one of the pools would be a useful diversion but no such luck. As soon as they settled into one of the pools, Hekla went in for the kill.

'Come on then. Tell us. What's going on? Is he looking after you?' Hekla next to her, stroked her arm. 'Because you need looking after.' She pushed Lucy forward and outlined the large bruise on her shoulder blade.

'It's feeling much better. Thanks to your Viking balm.' Not Alex's tender ministrations.

'I didn't mean that,' said Hekla giving her a meaningful look. 'You. When you came here. You were damaged and a bit broken.'

The other two girls nodded in unison.

Lucy groaned, sinking her shoulders below the water level. If she could have, she'd have completely submerged herself. 'Oh God, was it that obvious?'

'Only to us, because you've got better,' said Elin, stretching her long elegant arms out on either side of her. 'But you looked so bruised and frightened of everything, when you didn't think we were looking. We kind of decided to look out for you, except you kicked ass that night in the kitchen when Erik had broken his leg. Hekla said you were super organised and,' she grinned at Lucy across the pool, 'super bossy. Then we realised that maybe you didn't need it.'

Lucy's heart tripped a little. 'Well, I'll be honest. I had a few issues.' Under the water she pedalled her feet for a moment or two before taking a breath and plunging into the whole story.

Having told Alex so recently, and actually managing to find some humour in it, suddenly it didn't seem so bad and the story didn't sound quite so sordid anymore, until Hekla got out of the pool and fetched her phone to search YouTube for Lucy.

Sitting, watching herself cavorting about half pissed, while in a hot tub with the snow coming down felt slightly surreal, especially compared to the one and only time she'd watched the video, huddled in her office with the lights out and the door locked.

'You really can't sing, can you?' said Brynja, half way through starting to giggle. 'My cat sounds better than that.'

Elin began to giggle too. 'It's really bad. I'm worried you're going to fall over at any minute.'

'I think I did at one point,' said Lucy.

'Oh there look,' Elin laughed again pointing to the screen as Lucy faceplanted, her bottom filling the screen. 'Good job you've got a nice ass.'

Lucy blinked. The three of them seemed to find the video hilarious rather than embarrassing.

'That's an awesome move, Lucy. Rewind Brynja,' Hekla, laughing, tried to snatch the phone. 'I want to see how she got her panties off.'

There were plenty more laughs and jokes but not one of the three looked the least bit censorious, shocked or disgusted. When the video finished, Hekla looked her up and down and said, 'I want to borrow that outfit.'

Lucy let out a half snort half giggle at the thought of the strapping Hekla in the tiny red and white outfit. 'You'd look amazing,' she said pinching her lips together. Hekla would have been able to carry it off easily, in fact with their unabashed attitude to nudity any of the three girls probably would have done.

'What a dirt bag though,' said Elin. 'It was a private thing. I can see why you would be upset. What did you do to him? I would have threatened to chop his penis off with a pair of blunt scissors and cooked it as sausage meat.' She sliced her hand into the water with a splash that made them all laugh.

'Me, I would have killed his car. Sugar in the tank. Olive oil on the windows – that is a bitch to clean off and a fish in the engine,' said Brynja.

'I'd have got him very drunk, waited until he was asleep and written kúkulabbi in permanent pen on his forehead,' said Hekla with enthusiasm, demonstrating on her forehead, as the other two girls roared with laughter.

'When we say kúkulabbi, we mean scumbag,' explained Brynja seeing Lucy's reticent smile, 'but the literal translation is poo on two legs.'

'Please tell me you didn't do that,' said Elin, suddenly turning to Hekla who was sniggering to herself, the water rippling out around her chest.

'Who me?' Hekla's innocent wide-eyed expression wouldn't have fooled anyone.

'I'll remember not to get on the wrong side of any of you,' Lucy said with a mock shudder.

'What did you do?' asked Hekla. 'Please tell me you did something.'

With a twitch of her mouth, she nodded. 'Although, nothing quite that brutal.'

'But you did do something.'

Lucy nodded, worrying at her lip. She hadn't even told Daisy about her petty revenge. 'The day before I came here, he went away and I went to collect some of my things. I had the keys to the flat we shared, so...' she smiled at the thought, 'I sewed fresh prawns into the hems of the curtains in our flat.'

'Excellent,' said Brynja.

'And very smelly,' said Elin, wrinkling her nose.

'That is a good revenge, I think,' said Hekla with an enormous smile. 'Subtle and very long lasting.'

Lucy pictured Chris trying to identify the smell and where it was coming from. She began to giggle. She hadn't allowed herself to think about what might have happened to him since then.

Hekla held up a hand and they all high-fived Lucy in turn.

'Don't mess with Lucy.' Elin nodded.

'Armed and dangerous with a sewing needle.' Lucy grinned.

'And you still didn't tell us about Alex,' said Hekla a few minutes later, sitting up straighter, her shoulders rising up out of the water.

Darn it. Lucy thought she'd got away with it.

'There's nothing to tell,' she said. 'He stayed the night, but it was...' she thought of the kisses on her back. 'It's too soon.'

'Ah, but your head is OK now,' said Brynja, deliberately misunderstanding.

'I'm ... I'm seeing him tonight.'

Butterflies' wings beat against the inside of her stomach, anticipation wheeling with excitement, at the memory of the brief exchange when Hekla having secured permission for the trip had dashed off to get ready.

'You're looking better,' he'd said. 'Let's have dinner together here tonight when you get back. You don't want to overdo it. I'll get Kristjan to make us up a tray.' Weirdly, for someone who was used to making all the decisions, she rather liked him taking charge. When she'd been going out with Chris, he'd been so ambivalent about so many things; where they ate, what film they saw, that it had become wearing, always having to make the decision, especially as he'd often sulk if it turned out to be a film or meal he didn't like that much.

'You're seeing him tonight.' Hekla rubbed her hands together.

'And which bit of him are you seeing tonight?' asked Elin, splashing water towards her.

'Yeah, that's one fine man,' drawled Hekla. 'I know which bit I'd want to get my hands on.'

Elin nudged her. 'You need to get laid and soon.'

'I know. Toys just aren't quite the same as the feel of man. And I love watching a man get naked.' Hekla let out a low moan. 'I miss that. Especially when I can hear Miss B here going at it with her man.'

'I'll get you some earplugs,' said Brynja seeming completely unconcerned.

'We're not going to…' protested Lucy, grateful that the warm water had already made her look quite pink.

'Why the hell not?' asked Hekla. 'He's hot. He's gorgeous and he's a really good guy. I bet he's considerate in bed. Not a selfish, take it all for himself.' She smirked and flashed a grin at Elin. 'Bet he knows his way to the honey pot.'

Lucy gulped. OK, since that kiss, when she'd inadvertently opened her legs, she'd played a few private fantasies about Alex's magic hands, but they were very private and certainly not that graphic. She lowered herself into the water as if it might hide the inadequacy she felt next to their enthusiastic inhibitions.

To her mortification, Elin and Hekla began to elaborate further with tales of the best techniques they'd encountered.

Lucy knew she was blushing furiously.

'They're showing off,' said Brynja, in a low tone, spotting her discomfort. 'Hekla would love a steady boyfriend, she's desperate for Kristjan to notice her and Elin adores Roger. But we are much more open about talking about sex in Iceland.'

'I wish. Maybe if I could have talked ... after Chris ... I don't think I'm very good at sex.'

Brynja laughed softly. 'No one is very good at sex on their own. It takes two and both of you need to care enough to make it right. This Chris, I don't think he cared. He pressured you to do things that didn't make you feel right. Be gentle with yourself. If Alex is right, you won't have to do anything you don't want to. We're all different. Hekla is proud and confident enough to share her body with anyone she chooses. No one makes her feel bad about it. It's a great attitude to have ... if you can carry it off. Women shouldn't be ashamed of enjoying sex ... that's something that we grow up with.' She smiled.

'It's not like that at home. I guess I grew up with the negative language, all female of course, slut, tart, slapper.

And my parents never ever talked about sex.' Lucy winced. 'I can't imagine how I was conceived. I don't think I've ever seen my dad kiss my mum.'

'That is a good thing,' said Brynja with a quick beam and roll of her eyes. 'Over demonstrative parents are so embarrassing. I promise you.'

Together they laughed as Hekla jumped up. 'Come on, let's hit the sauna.'

During the rest of the morning, the snow began to come down more heavily. It was the weirdest sensation, thought Lucy, lifting her face to the icy kiss of snow flakes, while the rest of her was toasty warm beneath the water. Barefoot, their hot skin in contrast with the ice-cold wood, they flitted from the sauna and from pool to pool before visiting the steam room. Lucy was slightly disconcerted by the latter which had a vented floor over a bubbling hot spring, through which could be heard the boiling and hissing below. At lunchtime they donned their robes and went to the bright airy restaurant to have lunch. Rye bread baked in the nearby hot lava along with delicious melt in the mouth smoked salmon, which was the best Lucy had ever tasted, washed down with a glass of red wine.

She felt pleasantly weary and oh so relaxed. A day to remember. She would definitely do this again.

'This was a good thing to do, thanks so much for inviting me,' Lucy smiled at Hekla. 'I should make more time for this sort of thing. I ought to have my nails done, get a haircut.'

Hekla whipped out her phone. 'My sister's best friend is a hairdresser in Hvolsvöllur.' She was already busy texting. 'We can call in on the way back this afternoon.'

Before Lucy could change her mind, it seemed she had an appointment arranged.

'Thanks,' she said, leaning back in her chair. 'And for today. I feel so relaxed and my bruises don't hurt as much. My shoulders were so knotted.' A fact she knew thanks to Alex's careful kneading of the tense muscles there. 'That water fountain thing has done them wonders.' She'd spent ages under the torrent of water that poured into one of the pools. 'They were killing me.'

'Because you've been spending too much time at the computer.'

Lucy shrugged. 'There's always so much to do.'

'And it's a good place to hide from the film crew.' Hekla's stock in trade amused eyebrow shot up again.

'There is that.' Lucy tried to be deadpan and failed, as she added, 'I can't wait for them to leave.'

'Not long now. They leave the day after the Icelandic evening.' Hekla grinned, 'Which is going to be a huge success. Half of Hvolsvöllur is coming, since you invited the Mayor. Everyone wants to come to the hot ticket. It's going to be a very busy night and a good evening. You have Freya telling the folklore tales.'

'Yes, hopefully the camera will be focused on her and not me running around like a lunatic.'

Another frown from Hekla.

'Crazy person,' explained Lucy.

'Ah, yes. That man Bob does seem to like filming you,' said Hekla thoughtfully.

'Yes,' added Elin. 'He's always watching you. And the Clive man is so irritating. Always talking with too much enthusiasm. He's such a phony.'

'But not creepy like Bob.' Brynja wrinkled her nose. 'Has he been bothering you?' she asked with sharp-eyed insight.

Lucy was about to shrug it away but instead nodded grimly, 'Yes. He knows about the film. He's been threatening to tell the new owners. He wants me to film a video with him.'

'Gross,' said Elin, indignant fury dancing in her eyes.

Hekla mimed being sick.

'I've managed to stay out of his way and they'll be gone soon. Now who wants coffee?' Lucy folded her arms over her chest making it clear the subject was closed.

Bob the cameraman was lurking in the corridor when they returned, heading towards the laundry, in a flurry of conversation, snow dusting their hair, carrying bags bulging with their wet costumes and soggy towelling robes.

'I'll put them in the wash,' volunteered Lucy pulling her robe out of her tote bag and steadfastly ignoring Bob. 'Thanks so much for organising today, Hekla. It was brilliant.'

'Been somewhere nice ladies?' he asked.

'The hot springs at Fontana,' said Elin, with the sort of polite smile that was reserved for difficult guests.

'Nice.' He grinned. 'All the single ladies.' He did a brief

imitation of Beyoncé sticking her bottom out in a misguided twerking move.

'Oh Bob,' Elin lowered her voice in a breathy voice, before saying 'you bad bad boy,' and promptly slapping the builders bottom hanging out of the back of his jeans, so hard, a resounding clap echoed down the corridor. Bob's head shot up, his eyebrows dancing like caterpillars on speed. Startled and unsure, he shot her a wary look realising that the two other girls had circled him, like a pair of worrying hyenas and somehow he was bundled through the door into the laundry.

Now Elin was doing a sultry exaggerated walk round him, feet crossing her legs with that model walking a tight-rope gait, stripping off her coat and dropping it to the floor.

'What do you think girls? Do you think we should take this pony out and ride him hard?'

Bob's eyes bulged, Lucy swallowed back a giggle realising that Brynja had her phone out and was filming the whole scene.

Elin, standing a good few inches taller than him, pressed up against his side, pushing her breasts forward as she ran her fingers over his pudgy face before pinching his ear lobe hard between her fingers as she whispered something in his ear. One hand dropped to below his waistband to cup himself protectively as he turned white.

'I hear you want to make a video,' she said loudly.

Bob swallowed, his eyes darting around the room as if looking for an escape.

With one smooth move, Elin pulled off her top.

'Now you Bob.'

Glassy-eyed and sweaty, he stared at her.

'Come on, join in the fun,' said Elin tweaking the bottom of his t-shirt. Slowly he pulled it over his head.

Then Hekla stepped forward and pulled off her top, shameless and statuesque in her balcony bra.

Bob didn't know where to look, his head bounced back and forth between Hekla and Elin.

'Your turn again Bob.' Elin nodded towards his belt buckle.

'Do you want a hand?' she asked, making an obscene gesture with her own hand.

Lucy pressed her lips hard together. Elin was ruthless, ignoring the terror beading sweat onto his brow. Already she was tugging at his belt.

'I can...' Bob batted her hands away.

'What are you waiting for?' She'd undone the buckle and was pulling at his zip.

She and Hekla were crowding him now.

'I ... I ... I don't think this is ... is a good idea.' He wriggled out of reach, hands clutching at his trousers, darting a miserable look at Brynja who was holding up her phone, as if realising with his camera man's inner vision how ridiculous the tableau must look. Two gorgeous blonde beauties with a short, tubby little man.

'The thing is Bob,' said Elin. 'We think it is.' She put a hand on her hip and thrust her breasts under his nose.

'I don't think I want to,' he sounded whiny.

'You don't want to.' Elin swung her head around to look

at the others, like a tribal leader about to demand a sacrifice.

'No, I don't,' he went to grab at his t-shirt, the flabby folds of flesh concertinaing over his waistband. Like a matador with a cape, Elin swiped it out of reach. 'Give me that back.'

Lucy felt a touch uncomfortable as Elin baited him.

'That's enough.' She looked at Brynja and nodded.

'So Bob,' Lucy stepped forward. 'Perhaps you know how it feels now, to be at someone else's mercy. Not very nice is it. It's not just a bit of fun is it?'

He turned bright red, scrabbling his way into his t-shirt.

'I didn't … I was … I was joking about making a video. You must have … you must have misunderstood.'

Hekla, Elin and Brynja had lined up, their arms folded looking at him with icy disdain.

'Ah, right. I misunderstood. Well that's fine then,' said Lucy. 'I think we understand each other now. But just to be sure, perhaps we can agree that if you show my video, I'll show yours.'

Bob swallowed hard, nodding vehemently as he backed away towards the door, his eyes shifting every now and then to Elin as if she were a cobra that might strike at any second.

When he reached the door, Elin gave him a feral smile and a cheeky wave and wink.

Depending on how fast he shot down the corridor in his escape, Bob may or may not have heard the shout of laughter that went up exactly five seconds after he'd departed.

Chapter 25

Feeling relaxed, loose and just a little triumphant after the run in with Bob, Lucy pottered around her room, lighting candles with a big smile on her face. Spa days should be compulsory she decided or at least hot tubs, no, make that hot tubs in the snow.

She glanced outside, fat flakes were tumbling down in a whirlwind of white, bright against the dark night sky, remembering with a quick shiver their icy touch on her skin in the spa pools. Touching the cold glass, she looked up at the blur of feathery snow falling thick and fast, almost mesmerised as they landed in silent defeat, melding seamlessly into the blanket already covering the wooden decking. Her reflection looked ghostly as it hovered against the snowy backdrop but she knew she looked so much better than when she arrived, despite the fine collection of bruises she was sporting.

Dressed in a comfy sweatshirt, leggings and Hekla's cashmere socks, she'd abandoned the idea of make-up. If she didn't treat this like a date, then she couldn't possibly feel disappointed if it didn't turn out like one. 'Let's have dinner tonight,' wasn't like a date, was it? A date was going out. Doing something. Alex was looking after her because he felt responsible for her accident and because that was the sort of thing Alex did. Or so she told herself...

But if you were organised, you'd put a bottle of wine in the fridge just in case and nick a couple of nice glasses from the dining room because you never knew when you might need those. And you had a fire because on a night like this, with a snow storm raging outside, it was the obvious thing to do and not necessarily romantic. She eyed the flames dancing like fierce devils in the wood burner and the healthy stack of logs which would last the rest of the evening and forced herself to sit down with a book, not that she read much. With the fire and the snow to look at, she was quite content curled up on the sofa watching the fascinating juxtaposition of fire and ice, her left foot tapping a little every now and then.

'Dinner is served,' said Alex, whirling in with a tray when she opened the door to his knock. 'Wow, this looks nice. That snow is really coming down. I'm glad I don't have to go anywhere tonight. Clive and co are not happy. They were hoping for more northern lights footage but they're not likely to see them in this.'

Lucy stepped back surprised by his unexpected info dump. Nervous Alex was kind of cute.

'Something smells good,' she said, touching his arm, wanting to put him at ease.

'Phew, I wasn't sure what you liked.' He gave her a

sheepish smile, and deposited the tray covered in small covered dishes on the coffee table in front of the sofa. 'So Kristjan has given us little taster dishes of everything on tonight's menu.'

'A carpet picnic,' said Lucy, clapping her hands. 'And I have wine.'

'Perfect.' They exchanged identical grins.

It was easy then; for them to fuss with plates and cutlery, for Alex to open the wine and to sit on the floor facing each other across the coffee table. Easy to make small talk about the food, and not at all cheesy when they fed each other mouthfuls of the different dishes, a salty, fish chowder, sweet, marinated pork, slivers of rare steak, twice cooked chips, roasted tomatoes in balsamic and rosemary, greens tossed in butter and glazed carrots with cumin seeds. OK, it might have been a tiny bit cheesy with the twinkly eye meets and exaggerated care with which they held out their forks.

'How were the hot springs?' asked Alex as they took their wine to sit in front of the fire on the sheepskin rug.

'Hot and cold. A bit weird in the snow but the place was fab. Quite smart and trendy. And the girls were on great form.' Her eyes suddenly twinkled. 'We had some very interesting conversations.'

He chinked her glass. 'I don't think I want to know. Cheers.'

'Cheers.' She paused. 'I told them about the video.'

Alex watched her carefully. 'And.'

'They wanted to see it.'

He winced.

She laughed. 'No, do you know what, it was the best thing. I should have done it a long time ago. It wasn't anywhere near as bad as I've built it up in my head. They all thought it was bloody hilarious. They don't have the same hang ups about nudity and sex as we do.'

'Speak for yourself,' teased Alex. 'I'm a proud kilt-wearing Scot.'

She raised both eyebrows hinting at what he might wear beneath his kilt ... if anything.

'And I'm no telling you, Sassenach,' he said broadening his accent, his eyes darkening with mischief.

'It's like a massive load has been lifted. And I didn't appear as naked on camera as I thought. Chris had some decency. My memory of the night got muddled with the actual footage.' Although the girl's complete unabashed approached to nudity today had made her think. There was no way she was never going to be as uninhibited as them, but there was a case for challenging that internal censor, the one suggesting her body was something to be ashamed of. Something that should be covered up and kept in the dark.

'Ah, well he must be alright then.' Alex's words were edged with the sharp touch of what might have been jealousy.

'I didn't say I'd forgiven him,' said Lucy, her cheeks dimpling at him. 'I feel so much better. One day I might even show it to you.'

'Only if you want to,' said Alex, his voice quiet, 'but I promise you I won't go searching for it.'

'I know,' said Lucy. He didn't need to tell her that.

'So now you can tell weasel man, Bob, to take a running jump and impale himself on the nearest iron railing.'

'That's a bit bloodthirsty,' said Lucy. 'The girls had a much more satisfying solution,' and she told him what they'd done.

'Serves him right,' said Alex when she confessed she felt a little bit sorry for him. 'He doesn't deserve your sympathy.' He pulled her to him and put his arm around her waist easing both of them back against the front of the retro padded leather armchair.

'Perhaps not but two wrongs don't make a right. I didn't take any pleasure in humiliating him. Maybe because it was too close to home, I know how it feels. That awful sense of powerlessness. Knowing that someone else has done something, other people know and you have absolutely no control over the situation. I never want to feel like that again.'

Alex squeezed her waist and dropped a kiss on her cheek. 'I hope you don't have to.'

Sitting next to him in the golden glow of the fire, comfortably full with food and sipping at her wine, she closed her eyes, feeling the solid warmth of him next to her. Contentment settled and she laid her head on his shoulder, happy to gaze at the somnolent effect of the flames ebbing and flowing around the burning logs hissing and popping in the burner.

She shifted and winced at the twinge in her back.

'You OK?' asked Alex. 'How's that shoulder?'

'Just starting to stiffen up again.' With a wriggle, she

twisted left and right, sucking in a sharp breath as her body protested. 'My muscles hurt more now than they did the first day, but the bruises are starting to ease.'

'Want me to put some balm on?'

Despite his matter of fact tone, Lucy's mouth went dry.

'That would be good.' As he stood up to retrieve the jar, she turned her back to him.

When he returned, dropping to the floor to sit behind her, she heard the squeak of the thread of the lid on the jar, and smelled the lavender.

She crossed her arms in front of her, pausing. With a deep now or never breath, in one determined fluid move, she pulled her sweatshirt and bra vest top over her head. There was a sharp inhalation behind her as she exposed her bare back. Portentous silence held them in its grip, punctured by the dragon's hiss of the fire.

Alex's fingers, butterfly wing soft, skimmed the top of her shoulder blade. She held her breath as he explored every inch of skin with painstaking thoroughness. Her heart hummed when his palm flattened to stroke down her back in a slow, smooth possessive sweep. A pause. His hands slid down her sides, feeling their way, finger to rib, finger to rib, finger to rib, before coming to rest on the soft curve of her waist. Holding her with the delicacy reserved for precious china, she felt him lean forward. She stiffened in anticipation, aware of pinpoints of warmth of the fire on her upper back, the outline of his shadow blocking the heat. Then the touch of his lips, the brush of his hair flopping forward against her back. His mouth moved over her shoulder blade.

Soft lips and the tiny tingling abrasive prick of stubble. Mmm, she writhed flexing her shoulders. In response Alex trailed his mouth down, peppering her bruise with tiny fluttery kisses before moving with languid ease across to her spine. Time melted away.

The touch of his tongue. She arched her back in sinuous response. Her skin tingled as, with his mouth on her, he traced his way down.

Fingers tightened on her waist, a subtle pressure that relaxed as soon as his mouth resumed its deliberate exploration of her spine, lips working slowly, slowly down, exploring and tasting every indentation of her spine. She purred, arching her back in a supple curve, inviting Alex to follow. He licked her skin. It jolted her. The warm liquid honey of lust pooled between her legs. She groaned as he slid his hands up her sides, skirting her breasts, running over her shoulders to lift her hair where he pressed a long gentle kiss on the nape of her neck.

She lifted her arms and bundled the hair up on top of her head leaving her hands there. Against the snow and the dark, she could see herself in the glass, breasts proud and pert, the nipples pebbled and almost painful with want. Lifting her chin, her eyes met Alex's in the reflection shimmering in the window. They stared at each other, his eyes dark and focused, hers womanly and proud, the erotic image imbuing a curious combination of feeling sensual and safe at the same time.

She watched in the reflection as he began to unbutton his white shirt, their eyes never leaving each other's. With a swallow, she gazed at his broad shoulders and the hair-dusted, brawnier than she'd expected, chest. Everything about Alex on the outside always seemed so smooth and urbane, but this contrast as he shimmied the shirt down his arms made her heart beat a little faster. Oh boy, kill her now. When he pulled her back against his warm, firm chest, his arms wrapping around her, she sighed, all her muscles relaxing. For once she felt feminine, fragile and deliciously protected and she didn't care one bit. If this was heaven, she was taking it. Bound against him, the hair of one arm teasing the underswell of her breast and the other clasping her possessively around the waist, she felt safe to let go, relinquish all the control for a change.

When Alex dropped his gaze and kissed the side of her neck, she shivered and let out the tiny moan bubbling in her throat. His tongue touched the vibrating sensitive skin and she moaned again. Then his head lifted and he watched her again in the reflection, watching her reaction as he moved one arm, his hand palming one breast in warm sensual massage, his thumb lazily rubbing over one nipple as the other held her fast across the waist against him.

Her mouth opened with a sharp gasp of pleasure, her eyes closing but he squeezed her nipple in tiny warning. She opened them again and in their shared reflection, she saw a satisfied smile curve his lips. His eyes never left her face as he stroked and massaged her breasts in small gentle rolls, tormenting her with lazy arrogance that had her whimpering. Then cupping one breast, his arm a band around her chest, the other hand began to skim across the surface of her stomach, his fingers dipping and circling the belly button in slow tantalising circles.

His hand dipped lower, sliding over the fabric of her leggings, lower again, skimming over her pubic bone. She held her breath in tell-tale silent anticipation. Nerve endings, warm and desperate for his touch, budded between her legs making her blink furiously as she tried to fight the urge to roll her hips forward. Alex smiled as if he knew exactly what she was thinking. What she was hoping for. Nipping at her neck, he watched her as he slipped his hand to cup the warmth between her legs, pulling her back against him. The image in the glass of him clasping her to him, the possessive hold and the steady look in his eyes brought another moan and helplessly she gave into the fire burning beneath his fingers and ground against his hand, unable to stop the tortured, 'Oh, Alex,' escaping.

His hand rocked against her, fingers at her nipples, his lips nipping at her neck. She felt consumed, sensation on all sides and all the while he watched in the glass.

Pressure, pleasure, pressure, pleasure. It was building, building, building.

'Alex,' she whispered, her eyes closing, unable to hold on. His hand kept up the stroking, pulling, teasing rhythm, her hips pushing into his movements, mindless and desperate. It was there, she could feel it, the sensation building, the need to crest the wave, she pushed for it and then she tumbled over the edge, riding out the delicious shuddery spasms vibrating through her, crying out his name in a breathless litany. Alexalexalexalex.

Limp and dazed she collapsed back and he caught her in his arms dragging her down to the floor, turning her so that they faced each other. Wide eyed she stared at him, before reaching for his jeans' zip and sliding it down.

'You don't...' Alex's breathe wheezed out as she eased her hand below the waistband of jeans and jersey boxer shorts, her fingers touching the hard length of him. 'God,' he moaned and she smiled to herself as she leant forward and kissed his chest, the smattering of hairs tickling her nose.

'Luc ... ahh ... you ... d ... mmm.'

Licking and nipping at his chest, she drew her hand up and down the satin skin cupping his balls, gently working him, rolling the head between her fingers, taking her cues from his hoarse breaths and drawn out moans.

Her own breath was becoming raspy and short as she could feel the velvet heat building again.

Then Alex pulled away, his forehead resting against hers. 'We shouldn't be doing this.'

Lucy ignored him and gave him an open-mouthed kiss, her tongue dipping along the edge of his mouth. It took a second or two before he crumbled, giving into the kiss, deepening it, his mouth roving over hers. The heat of the kiss began to rise, their tongues in an increasingly aggressive duel. Their hips drawn together in a determined dance, rolling and grinding against each other.

'I want you,' breathed Lucy desperately. 'I've never been so turned on in my life.'

Alex swallowed and kissed her hard. 'I'm supposed to ... you had concussion ... you're supposed to ... mmm, stop

... you're supposed to rest,' he made an inarticulate noise when she encircled his hard length again, 'reeeelaaax.'

Lucy laying back on the velvet embrace of the sheepskin gave him a slow smile. 'I'm relaxed, don't you worry.'

'Lucy,' he tried again, his eyes drawn down to her bare breasts as her eyes widened in seductive invitation.

'Alex, shh,' she said and kissed him hard. 'If you say we shouldn't be doing this again, I might just have to kill you.'

He laughed. 'It's because I don't have anything with me and ... I so want to be inside you.'

Lucy's stomach flipped, her core contracting at the very thought. 'Mmmm,' she nuzzled his neck. 'Good job I have a friend who insisted I shouldn't become a dried-up old stick and packed me off with a supply of condoms.' She started to rise as Alex fell back onto the rug with a heart-felt, 'Thank fuck for that.'

The unexpected swear word made her laugh, startling her. Sex with Chris had always been a serious get down to business affair, the stupid video had been her one attempt at being the sexy seductress he wanted her to be. This was hot, erotic, fun and she'd already had her first ever non-self-induced orgasm with, judging by the promise in Alex's amber-flecked, desire-filled eyes, more to come.

Chapter 26

'Have a good day,' said Alex, dropping a kiss on her temple, drawing the duvet up over her shoulders. 'I'll see you at four. Dress for outdoors.'

'Sounds like a hot date,' said Lucy with a grumble. 'Hiking in the dark?'

'If I told you, it wouldn't be a surprise, would it?'

'Who said I like surprises?' She pouted, sexy and sleep ruffled. He traced her pouty mouth with a finger, amused at the contrast he'd uncovered. He liked this bedroom version of her, but then he also liked the capable, take no prisoners, bossy hotel manager. Knowing that she didn't need him to, made the desire to protect her from all the bad things that had happened, even stronger. At the moment he couldn't decide who topped his hit list, Bob or that miserable dickweasel ex, Chris, who sounded like the ultimate piece of slime.

'Trust me.'

She paused and something in her eyes shimmered, making him feel like he'd conquered Everest.

'I do,' she said, then gave him a sultry look that made

him regret being fully dressed and expected in the dining room in the next fifteen minutes.

'You're definitely feeling better,' he said, regretfully pulling away.

'It's all that balm you've been rubbing into my back.' She rolled her shoulders but under the sheets she shifted her legs, a dreamy smile crossing her face. Damn, she was waking parts of him that by now should be exhausted after the last two long and pleasurable nights, and a brief lunch time break yesterday, when they'd nearly be caught by Hekla coming for a meeting with Lucy. As if reading his mind, Lucy lifted her face to his, mischief burning bright in her eyes.

'Hekla tells me the same company make something called Fire of Love.'

'They do, do they?' Alex's mouth twisted in a crooked smile as he shifted his legs, needing to accommodate the growing bulge in his trousers. 'That sounds like fun.'

'Not that I've been ... you know, talking to Hekla about ... you know. She knew you'd spent the night and...'

He laughed at her contrary shyness. 'Don't worry. I've already been given the third degree about not being a dick, making sure I treat you properly and where to get something called Fire of Love.'

'Oh no, she didn't.' Lucy put her hand over her mouth and giggled, looking gorgeous and good enough to nibble on.

'She's certainly not shy about these things.' His finger stroked her collarbone, watching as her eyes darkened and she gave a little shiver and a sharp indrawn breath. 'I was tempted to tell her we didn't need any help burning up the sheets.'

Lucy giggled again. 'You can't say that to her. I'm her boss.'

'I've got to go. I'll see you at four.' It would be good to get away from the hotel for a few hours and thanks to Hekla's help he'd made plans for a secluded and, he hoped, romantic date. Although he was slightly worried that part of Hekla's idea was a bit ambitious.

He also had a call to make.

Walking out to the hot tub and standing on the decking by the rising steam, he pulled out his phone with a sense of disquiet. Quentin hadn't responded to any of his recent email reports about what a great job Lucy was doing. After her early shaky start, she'd more than proved herself. The problem was that now he couldn't out and out recommend her to be the new manager. What would that look like, now that he was sleeping with her? It was important that, after all she'd been through, Lucy's merits were recognised in their own right. He didn't want anyone to ever say or intimate that she'd got the job for any other reason but that she was absolutely the best person, which he knew she was.

'Ah, young McLaughlin. I have good news,' said Quentin without preamble as soon as he picked up the call. 'Your timing is impeccable. The purchase is being signed off with my legal team five-thirty, Paris time, I believe an hour ahead of you.'

'Well that's good news. You're buying a gem. This place is a real treat and with more investment, it could be even better.'

'Yeah, you've been very thorough and it sounds like the place is being run much more efficiently. I liked that app to manage staff rotas, *Sortmyshift*. We should roll that out.'

'Yes, what about the staff,' Alex paused gripping his phone tighter, 'You should–'

'Yeah, yeah, yeah. I got your reports. I get the message. I'll accommodate everyone. But we're not going public with the news until the PR people make the official announcement next week because we've put in a bid for another place. Like the lodge. I've got to tell you about this great idea, well your mother's really, she's really into this higgy stuff.'

'Hygge,' corrected Alex, easing out a sigh of relief. He'd been worried about Lucy's job as Quentin's standard operating procedure was to put his own management team in as soon as he took over a hotel.

'Yeah that's the baby. You've heard of it then.' Alex tuned out as Quentin began to talk about plans to launch a new chain of smaller, cosier hotels. He was looking forward to seeing Lucy's face this afternoon when the surprise turned up. Hekla had promised him it would be the most romantic thing ever.

Once Alex had gone, Lucy dressed, looking over her shoulder in the mirror, giving her fading bruises a quick inspection. They were now dark smudges of green and grey.

She glanced up at her face. The afterglow of morning sex lit her skin and her eyes had lost their purple shadows. Even her hair looked so much better, thanks in part to the haircut and because it seemed to have thickened up. It wasn't coming out in handfuls any more and her lip had healed.

Eagle-eyed Hekla missed nothing and as soon as she walked into the office, she grinned at Lucy. 'Good night. Good morning.'

Lucy rolled her eyes. 'I'm your boss. You're not supposed to say things like that.'

'Pfft,' said Hekla waving her hands. 'Would you like an update on the guest list?'

For the rest of the morning they talked banquet plans, although Lucy was easily distracted. The minute anyone came into the office, her head bobbed up, her heart leaping in hopeful anticipation.

'You've got it bad,' Hekla teased.

Lucy blushed. 'I'm his boss. This is bad. Does everyone know?'

'No, just me.' She wrinkled her nose. 'Elin. Brynja. Dagur.'

Lucy groaned and dropped her face into her hands.

'It's not very professional. What if the new owners find out?'

'How are they going to do that?' Hekla put her hands on her hips. 'This is Iceland. There are only 340,000. When we find someone, we ... take them.'

Lucy snorted. 'Sounds very Viking.'

'Ja,' Hekla stuck out her chest in a proud pose. 'When

323

you are snowed in somewhere, in a remote place, you find the right chemistry then it is good. I think you and Alex, there's chemistry.'

'Mm,' she said trying to sound non-committal as the blush raced up her throat from the heated skin of her chest. She exhaled loudly. 'I still don't even know if I've got a job in two weeks' time. There's been no news about the sale. Mr Pedersen hasn't responded to any of my emails.' With a stab to her heart, she thought about having to leave. Surely Mr Pedersen would have been in touch if he wasn't happy. The reviews were improving daily, sales had started to pick up and the camera crew were stoked about the banquet.

And what about Alex? The thought of having to say goodbye to him pinched painfully at her heart. Finding him was so new and shiny. Perhaps, she let out a sudden laugh that had Hekla shooting a suspicious glance her way, if they didn't renew her contract, she could stay on as a chambermaid or a waitress. Swap her luxurious room for Alex's single staff bedroom. With a delicious shiver she decided it would be worth it.

Over the last few weeks Elin's team had done a fantastic job on sprucing up the library, the tables had all been buffed to a gleaming polish and the newly liberated cushions were tucked into the armchairs, arranged in convivial groupings. Lucy breezed through doing one of her daily inspections and made a mental note to congratulate Elin on the improvements that had been made to the communal guest areas. The lodge looked a very different place compared to when Lucy arrived.

So much had changed in such a short space of time. It had become her habit to pause in the guest lounge to stand at one of the big glass windows to see what the sky and the sea were doing today. A thick blanket of snow, courtesy of the last two day's solid snowfall, lay on the ground, softening the harsh contours of the land, glistening in this morning's bright, clear sunshine, although the sun had barely risen above the horizon. The clouds had rolled back to reveal a brilliant sapphire sky of endless blue that was reflected in the almost indigo tones of the sea. The waves raced with golden backs, tinted by the hovering pink gold sun which would vanish in a few short hours. Lucy smiled, entranced by the colours, the contrast of the white and blue, the long shadows and the warm light. She could stand here every day and never grow tired of this view.

'Luce.'

Reluctantly she turned away from the view, her heart sinking at the Essex accent.

'Clive.'

'Olafur says we've got another chance of seeing the lights tonight. We got enough in the can the other night but I still want that human interest angle. Got any new guests who can give us a banging story?'

'Actually yes,' Lucy heaved a sigh of relief. She had no qualms about pointing out the querulous, loud Irish woman, who'd arrived yesterday, telling anyone who would listen it was a feckin' miracle she was alive and she was on her way out, so *jest* had to see the lights. 'Moira Flaherty. She's your woman.'

'Sick, and any more news on the banquet? Do you think you could get Björk to come or the dentist football manager?'

'Sorry?'

'We were thinking, a couple of celebrities would spice things up a bit. They were my first thoughts. Or maybe a Viking re-enactment. A bit of pillaging and running amok.'

'I'm not too sure about the Viking bit, but I'll definitely ask Hekla about celebrities, she seems to know most people,' said Lucy with equanimity as if being asked to drum up a couple of national treasures was all in a day's work. 'The Mayor's coming.'

'Hardly set your knickers on fire material. Do you think he might wear a helmet and carry an axe? Add a little local colour?'

Lucy opened her mouth, too bemused to express her doubt that helmets and axes were part of the mayoral regalia. 'I'll ... I'll see what I can do.'

'Excellent.' Clive scratched at his puny little goatee. 'Because even if we see the lights tonight, the banquet is all that's stopping this being another crapsville tourist board promo.' Disgruntlement soured his features. 'There's not been an ounce of drama in this place. No disrespect but this place is as dull as shite.'

Lucy bit back a wry smile thinking of the sheep in the hot tub, the sabotaged tyres, the unexpected coach trip and her wan-faced return after the glacier walk. She for one was delighted to hear that he thought the place was dull.

Four o'clock and it was dark and she was dressed in several layers, supervised by Hekla, who was jumping about on the reception steps in the freezing weather with no coat but bags of barely restrained enthusiasm. She reminded Lucy of a toddler held captive desperate to make a run for it.

'You have gloves. Hat. Scarf.'

'Yes Hekla. All I'm missing is a St Bernard with a brandy flask.'

Luckily Hekla didn't hear her because she'd pricked up her ears to a sound out on the drive and was busy scanning the darkness.

'They're coming. They're coming,' she cried in glee. 'Oh this will be so much fun.'

Outside, with the glow of the snow under a full moon, it was as bright as day, and Lucy saw two Icelandic ponies trotting up the drive, their hooves clitter-clattering on the stony surface, shaggy manes shaking and hot steam puffing from their noses.

'Oh my goodness, they are gorgeous,' said Lucy.

Between them a man held the reins in each hand, with a pair of black helmets hanging from one arm.

'Hello.'

'Anders,' called Hekla, jumping down the last few steps to meet him, giving his leathery cheeks a big kiss.

'And Toto and Ilsa.' She put her hand out to each of the horses, holding a carrot that had appeared from nowhere, in each palm.

The satisfying crunch of carrot filled the air as the man and Hekla exchanged rapid conversation.

'Hello,' said Lucy, rubbing the velvety nose of the pure grey horse nearest her, breathing in the familiar sweet scent of horse. 'Aren't you gorgeous?' She stroked the thick shaggy coat.

'That's Ilsa,' said Hekla. 'Isn't she beautiful?'

'She is,' said Lucy, letting the horse nuzzle her empty hand. 'Got any more of those carrots?'

With a quick delighted grin, Hekla handed over a handful.

'You're used to horses? We must go riding together. In the Spring there is a good trail to Seljalandsfoss.'

As a child she'd ridden for years in the nearby New Forest. 'It's been a while, but yes.' Excitement spiked, making her blood fizz. 'Alex and I are going horse riding?'

'Ja.' Hekla grinned. 'And here is Alex.'

Without any subtlety she handed him a key and murmured something to him.

Ilsa nudged at her looking for more carrots and Lucy laughed patting her nose. 'No more I'm afraid.' She turned to Hekla. 'They're so friendly.'

Hekla patted the little horse on the nose. 'Icelandic horses are very friendly. They have been pure bred for a thousand years and are known for their easy-going temperament. Perfect for beginners.' She winked at Alex.

Alex wrinkled his nose. 'So you promised. And if Lucy can ride, she can look after me.'

'You don't need looking after, these horses are bomb proof,' said Hekla proudly. 'Small, strong and very hard workers. They are the best horses in the world, aren't they Anders?'

He responded in gruff Icelandic before handing over the helmets.

'Are you going to tell me where we're going?' asked Lucy as they set off, slowly across the snow, side by side on horseback.

'Up there,' he pointed to a distant light shining from the hillside about a mile away.

The wide broad saddle, set further back than she was used to, felt unfamiliar at first but she quickly settled into Ilsa's rolling gait, sitting loose and letting her hips rock forward with the motion. Gradually she relaxed, leaving the little horse on a loose rein. Despite his comments, Alex had clearly ridden a time or two before and when she asked him, he admitted his uncle had had a farm where he'd learned to ride with his cousins.

The night air was silent and still apart from the steady crunch of the horses' hooves on the virgin snow. They could have been the only people in the world as they crossed the wide, white covered expanse, the moonlight dancing on the surface turning ice crystals into glistening diamonds. Lucy threw back her head and exhaled heavily watching the plume of steam rise up into the star filled night sky.

'I've never seen so many stars,' she sighed. Without the light pollution she was so used to, the brilliance and sheer number of the thousand upon thousands of stars was spectacular. The dark sky looked as if it had been draped with a distant tracery of lace.

Alex pointed. 'You can see the Milky Way.'

'It makes everything seem so small and insignificant.'

They both lapsed into thoughtful silence as the horses plodded carefully across the snow-covered meadow.

'Want to pick it up a bit?' asked Alex after a few minutes. The cold was starting to seep through her layers.

'Yes.'

With very little urging, they pushed their mounts on to a canter, hooves churning up the snow as the game little horses charged up the hill, their manes rippling in the wind. The cold air whistled in her face and she tipped her face up, her skin tingling. Alex looked back over his shoulder at her, a broad grin on his face. Exhilaration fired through her, pure joy fizzing in her veins. She couldn't remember the last time she'd felt so unequivocally happy and worry-free. For the rest of her life she would remember this moment in time. The scene would be imprinted on her brain, Alex's face silhouetted against the snow, the horses flying manes, the star filled universe and the wonderful sense of being close to nature.

'Look,' called Lucy when they reigned in a little while later on the crest of the hill. The horses' breaths puffed out in clouds of steamy white air, while the metal of their bridles jingled as they shifted on the spot. Across the sky delicate fingers of green crept above the horizon, fine threads of colour, undulating in serene, soundless waves.

'I don't think I'll ever get used to seeing it,' she said, gazing up at the night sky. 'The northern lights. They are truly amazing.'

Alex leaned over and took her hand. 'They certainly are.'

As they neared the wooden cabin perched on top of the hill, Lucy could smell the smoke streaming out of the tall metal chimney and see the steam rising from a hot tub perched right on the edge of the cabin's deck.

There was a small shelter for the horses, complete with waiting haynets.

With barely disguised impatience, Alex dragged her from the stable up the stone stairs to the door, pulling out the key that Hekla had given him.

They pushed open the door and Lucy's mouth dropped open in an 'o' of pleasure. She glanced at Alex.

'Wow, look at this, I think the huldufólk are back in business.'

'Pesky huldufólk eh?' he grinned at her.

'Who knew they were such a dab hand with a box of matches and a ton of candles.' She paused and looked around at the cabin which smelled of woodsmoke and … chocolate. 'This is very…'

'Huggulegt?'

'Yes,' she said simply gazing around at the fairyland of tiny tealights in various coloured glass votives flickering on every surface. Hurricane lanterns with large church candles flanked the open fireplace where a roaring fire dominated. In front of it were large floor cushions and on the hearth a flask and two of her favourite earthenware mugs, along with a bowl of marshmallows and a jar of metal skewers.

'It's magical,' she said, crossing to the big picture window. 'Oh,' she said when she saw the steaming hot tub below the window, strategically placed on the edge of the hill to take in the magnificent view out across the valley down to the sea.

Alex came to stand beside her. 'This is amazing. Thank you.'

'I had a bit of help. Hekla, Elin and Brynja were desperate to get involved when I said I wanted to do something ... nice for you.'

'Nice,' she teased.

'OK, romantic.' He lifted a finger to her cheek and stroked her face.

They unwrapped their layers, nestling into the cushions on the floor in front of the fire. Lucy pulled her knees up to her chin as Alex busied himself toasting a marshmallow and handing it to her.

She smiled, her eyes serious.

'You OK?'

She nodded. 'The ride up here ... it puts everything into perspective. Makes you brave.'

'You don't need to be brave, just be yourself.'

She gazed into the fire, the shadows flickering over her face as she twisted on her cushion as if literally screwing up the courage to bring up the words.

'This is ... fast. We sort of tumbled over a ledge. It's all ... new to me. I don't know the rules. Before the video,' she rubbed at the back of her neck. 'Maybe I should divide my life into BV and AV. Before the video, I had everything under control. I knew what was what. I went out with Chris for months before we...' she lifted her shoulders, her face turning up to his, full of questions. 'Do you think that maybe we didn't sleep together for ages because ... we didn't feel enough for each other? But you and me ... the feelings, it was as if I'd burst if I didn't have you. But is it ... what is it? I don't know where I am? I only ever slept with him. This has happened so quickly. Like I said, I don't know the rules.'

He laughed softly and brushed her mouth with his, laying a soft kiss on her lips. 'Lucy,' he made the solemn declaration, brushing a stray strand of hair behind her ear, his fingers lingering on her cheek wanting to maintain the contact. 'This is all new to me too. I don't know about rules but I know this is more than I've felt with anyone else.'

'Really?' She looked so disbelieving that it tugged at his heart. 'I was such a mess when I arrived.' She touched her hair self-consciously. 'What on earth must you have thought, me clambering out the hot tub sopping wet?'

'You weren't a mess. Just a bit translucent.' He pulled her to him and put his arm around her as they snuggled back against the cushions.

'What, like a ghost?'

'Yes,' he stroked her jawline. 'Exactly that. Like you were

there but you weren't really. I didn't quite realise it at the time. But you were so sad and defeated. I wanted to put a smile back on your face. Except...' Shit, he needed to tell her who he really was and why he was here. It had been playing on his mind. 'There's something I need to tell you.'

'Alex, I know.' She put a hand over his.

'You do.'

'Yes. You should never play poker. I could tell from your face. You thought I was completely rubbish and useless at my job.'

'Well ... I didn't–'

'Yes, you did,' she poked him in the thigh with her finger.

'OK, I wasn't...'

'And you were right. It took me ages to get my act together. No wonder you thought I was rubbish. Not that you'd have said anything. You're far too nice.' Alex scowled. Nice. And nice guys finished last. He didn't want to be nice.

'And kind,' she said with a trace of belligerence, as if she dared anyone to challenge her on that one. 'You are one of the kindest people I've ever met.'

'I'm not, honestly.' What would she say when he finally confessed that he wasn't a barman at all? And that he was due back in Paris at some point, although that still hadn't been determined.

'Yes, you are. You helped me all the time and never once said what you thought, even though it was obvious on your face, most of the time. Seriously you would lose a fortune at cards. That first morning with the huldufólk business, I knew you thought I should tell them to put a sock in it and get back to work. And yet when I came up with the crazy unicorn solution, you backed me up.'

'It was such crazy idea, how could I not?'

'I could tell you thought I was taking too long to get my act together, but all the stuffing had been knocked out of me. I was so scared of making the wrong decision, it was easier in those first few days to hide in the office and not make any decisions at all.'

'Knowing what you've been through, I completely understand.' He didn't add the *now*, it would underscore the fact that he had taken a dim view of her abilities at first. He wished he'd known back then, before he'd spoken to Quentin the first time.

'Admit it, you thought you could do a lot better. You should be running a place like this. You're so ... you'd make a brilliant manager. If I stay, depending on what happens with the new owners, perhaps you could...'

He tensed. Shit. She was worrying that he might be insulted at the idea he should aim higher than being a waiter.

'I've never asked what your long-term plans are,' said Lucy worrying at her lip with her teeth. 'I assumed you'd stay but ... I guess you'd like to travel and move on.'

Alex frowned. Paris to Iceland, it was a three- and half-hour flight. With jobs like theirs, a long-distance relationship was often inevitable. His assistant manager in Paris had been successfully travelling back and forth to Austria to see her boyfriend for the last year. It was doable.

'Leave your lip alone,' he growled, 'It's healed and you won't be able to kiss me properly if you make it sore again.'

'Does that mean you want to keep on kissing me?'

'Fishing for compliments?'

Her smile turned shy.

'On the kissing front, you really don't need to worry.' Heat curled low in his belly. 'You're pretty good at kissing.' Damn he still needed to tell her. 'But–'

'I definitely can't put that on my CV. Not after what's happened.'

'Lucy there's–'

'Do you know I've been thinking about it ... I'm wondering if I should have fought back a bit.' He recognised the pugnacious tilt to her chin as she sat up spearing a marshmallow and poking it towards the fire.

'Lucy I need to–'

'I told you that the video wasn't as bad as I remember. And I've been thinking. My boss did nothing to stop it spreading across the company's intranet. He was a board director. He knew about it straight away because the day after Chris posted it, he made a comment. In front of a regional manager and my immediate boss, both men. He said, "Maybe we should get you to provide room service. We could include the video as part of our next marketing campaign."'

'He said what?' Everything else went out of his head blasted away by the white heat of anger at her words. Alex couldn't comprehend anyone being that crass. He'd have sacked the bastard immediately. 'What did you do?'

'I left the room and went to the ladies and burst into tears. In hindsight I should have gone straight to personnel and made a complaint but I was in such a state about the whole thing I wasn't thinking straight.'

'Too bloody right. How dare he? You should still make a complaint. A, he was being totally inappropriate and B, if he was a board director and knew about the video, he had the power to get someone to take it down. He had a duty of care to you as an employee.' Alex would have fired Chris's sorry arse straight away and he'd have had stern words with all members of staff about it. 'I've got a couple of friends in HR who I could ask.'

'Is there any point?'

'It might get you a reference, which would be fair.'

'True. I was hoping for one from here, but I'm not sure how that's going to work. I've still heard nothing from Mr Pedersen. I keep emailing and his PA says she'll let me know. I don't even know if the sale of the hotel is going through or whether the new owners might keep me on.'

Alex ignored the temptation to look at his watch, at the date inscribed in the little box on the right.

'I can't see why they wouldn't,' he said quietly.

'They might want to put their own people in.'

'Not when they've seen what a great job you've been doing,' said Alex with a smile, relieved that he'd been able to speak to Quentin this afternoon. 'I bet you anything they keep you on as manager.'

Chapter 27

For the last week, she and Alex had made the most of every spare minute off duty, either holed up in her room or exploring the amazing sights on their days off. Neither of them talking about the imminent deadline of Lucy's contract drawing closer. There was only a week before it was up and the last email she'd had from Mr Pedersen was that the sale had gone through and the new owner would be in touch about her contract.

'I think waterfalls are my favourite,' said Lucy as they drove back from their trip to Seljalandsfoss and the less well known Gljúfrabúi.

'Do you think we should try and visit them all?' Alex drove with one hand on the wheel, the other resting lightly on her leg.

Lucy laughed and waved her guide book at him. 'There are over ten thousand.'

'Ah, maybe not. I was wondering if you fancied an overnight trip to visit a couple of places up in the north of Iceland.'

Now that they were almost in mid-December, the sun was even lower and the daylight hours were shortening.

'Alex ... you know I might not be here.' They'd been skirting around this ever since the night at the cabin.

'Of course, you will.' His hands tightened on the steering wheel. 'After tonight, the new owners would be insane not to take you on. The film crew will capture your fantastic organisational skills, the huge success of the banquet and they'll be falling over themselves to keep you.'

'They're cutting things a bit fine but I don't mind, you know.'

'What?' Alex's head whipped round.

'If my contract is made permanent, that would be amazing. I love it here. But if it isn't ... there's nothing I can do about it.'

Alex made a small distressed sound in his throat.

'But it doesn't mean I have to leave.'

'What do you mean?'

'I've been thinking. I could stay in Iceland. I know I don't want to go back into a big corporate hotel. I'd be happy in the short term, if you were staying, to work alongside Elin and Hekla.' After all the years of striving and pushing for promotion, suddenly it didn't seem quite so important. Admittedly she might find it difficult working for someone who had her job but she wasn't too proud to wait tables or work as a chambermaid. Jobs she knew the hotel always needed to fill.

'You would?' Alex sounded a little worried.

'Yes. Being a manager isn't the be all and end all. With live in accommodation, I could stay here ... if you wanted me too.' Her voice trailed off. He didn't look that keen, in fact he looked a little panicked.

'You're not going to have to do that, I can guarantee it,' he said and when she glanced at his profile, his chin was set and he was gripping the steering wheel with purpose.

She turned and looked out of the window. Things had moved quite fast between them, maybe she was scaring him off with her offer to downgrade and be with him. They'd never really talked about what he wanted in life, he seemed happy with his lot, but then he hadn't been here that long, perhaps he had plans to move on. Had he thought about including her in those plans? And would she want that sort of nomadic, follow the work sort of lifestyle?

Distant lights followed them up the road as they turned off the main road up the track towards the lodge and Lucy glanced over her shoulder.

'Taxi. Must be guests arriving,' she said with a sigh. 'And back to work. Thanks for this afternoon. It was good to get out and take a break before tonight. It really cleared my head.'

'My pleasure,' said Alex shooting her a warm smile that made her feel a bit antsy and edgy.

She leaned forward and kissed his cheek as he was driving. 'I wish we didn't have to go straight back to work.'

'Me too. Shall I pull over and we can make out in the car for five minutes.'

340

'Don't tempt me. But tonight's a big deal. I need to get back.'

'It's all going to be fine. You've got this and it should all be straight forward. You've got enough tealights to fill an Ikea warehouse. Kristjan's got a kick ass menu, Freya is word perfect and she's got the sexy story telling siren act off pat.'

'Hasn't she just?' said Lucy, gathering up her bag and coat as they wound round the last corner towards the lodge.

'Yes, and it's an inspired idea. I told you that before.'

'You did,' she grinned happily at him.

'I'm going to start calling you Lucy Smug, if you're not careful.'

'Well, everything should go to plan as long as all the VIP guests turn up. I can't believe the Mayor said yes at such short notice. In Manchester you had to book the Mayor's diary six months in advance, although I guess that's the power of TV cameras for you.'

'And they leave tomorrow. Hurrah!'

'Hurrah in ... that's odd. The lodge looks very dark.'

As they drove nearer, a sense of foreboding settled on them both.

'I don't like the look of this,' said Lucy, as Alex speeded up. As soon as he stopped the car, she threw open the door and hurried up the path to the steps to the reception doors, with Alex close behind.

Inside there was a dull glow as a few tealights fought valiantly to light up the reception area. Hekla, Brynja,

Olafur and Dagur were gathered by the desk along with a short bald man with a huge handlebar moustache

'Hi Lucy,' said Hekla with a weak smile. 'I was going to call you...'

'Wait!' Clive appeared, the area suddenly lighting up with the light on Bob's camera and a spotlight from the grip, Tony. 'I want to capture this.'

Lucy shot him a filthy look but she didn't have time to mess about. The great and the good of Hvolsvöllur would be arriving in a few hours' time for a grand banquet. She ignored him and turned to the small crowd gathered in waiting.

'What's happened?'

'The electricity went out. I called the electrician.' She pointed to the bald man who nodded and spoke quickly in Icelandic shaking his head and looking quite put out.

'He says it's very strange.' Hekla had that familiar child-like expression of wonder on her face.

'Please don't tell me it's the huldufólk again.'

'Well...' Hekla began.

Brynja spoke up. 'It's strange because he can't figure out what's wrong.' She shot a quelling look at Hekla who pouted a little. 'The electricity company says there is no power cut, but Henrik has just arrived. He's checking all the distribution boards to see if it's a fuse somewhere.'

'And is everything out or just the lights?' asked Lucy.
'Everything.'

Of course, it was. 'Right,' she looked at her watch and then remembered. 'But we have a generator on site.'

Hekla nodded glumly as Olafur shook his head. 'It's not working,' he said with a mournful droop to his mouth.

Why didn't that surprise her?

She looked at Henrik. 'Do you have any other ideas?'

'I can keep looking but ... without knowing the building it's ... it's very difficult.'

Lucy turned to Hekla. 'Do you know if there are any drawings? Site plans with the circuits drawn on?'

Hekla widened her eyes and shrugged. 'I have never seen anything like that.'

Alex added, 'There should be some sort of plan somewhere.'

Lucy looked at him and the familiar flash of warmth shot through her. 'Would you mind going through the office with Hekla looking in all the files, trying to see if you can find anything like that?

'Brynja, there are plenty of tealights for this evening but we're going to get through them too quickly. Can you round up all the candles you can find? I know there's an excellent stock of them in housekeeping. Dagur can you make sure there's a good fire in the bar and lounge area and then if the two of you can put candles in there, we'll invite all the guests to come to the bar for complimentary ... damn no coffee. We'll have to offer them *a* complimentary drink. I'll go and see Kristjan in the kitchen and find out what the food situation is with regard to tonight.'

'Cut,' called Clive. Lucy glared at him.

'This is dynamite. Great job, people. Go Lucy. I like this ball, busting, bossy broad.'

Lucy rolled her eyes and gritted her teeth.

'Now Lucy, if we could get a quick close up and we'll follow you to the kitchen.' Clive was already directing Bob and his camera towards her. Lucy glanced towards Alex and stopped.

He looked as if a lightning bolt had hit him, his eyes filled with horror.

'Alex! Darling.' An immaculate red head, in a white down jacket and emerald green trousers which shouted expensive, designer and look at my perfect bum, appeared from nowhere and crossing the lobby in rapid strides, threw her arms around him. 'How wonderful to see you.'

'Gretchen,' he extracted himself from her enthusiastic hug, his body so stiff it could have doubled as an ironing board. 'What are you doing here?'

'Quentin sent me. I'm the new general manager.'

Silence fell with the swift, efficiency of a guillotine.

Lucy felt her heart whoosh into the bottom of her stomach as a dozen heads whipped her way.

Clive quivered with excitement, brushing his hand through his blonde hair whipping it up in a peak, gesticulating with his other hand for Bob to pull back so that he could film the whole frozen tableau.

There was a rushing in Lucy's ears and leaden disappointment made her limbs heavy as she stood glued to the spot.

'B-but,' spluttered Alex, glancing with horror at Lucy and shaking his head. He looked as devastated as Lucy felt.

'Quentin says to tell you The Metropole is about ready

and he expects you to get your arse back to Paris by the end of this week. You lucky bugger. GM of Paris's newest, flashiest hotel.'

GM! Her brain took a moment to compute the facts. General Manager. Lucy thought she was going to be sick. A range of conflicting emotions rushed across Alex's face, guilt, surprise, embarrassment before terminating in regret. She shot him a look of dismay. What the hell?

'So, nice to meet you all.' Gretchen's words trailed lamely as she shifted on the spot, finally realising that she was in hostile territory as all of the staff glared at her.

Lucy lifted her chin, blinking hard. 'Welcome to The Northern Lights Lodge, Gretchen,' she ground out with a forced smile, before adding, 'As far as I'm aware, I'm still the General Manager until Friday and I've got a job to do. We have a banquet to host, electricity to come up with and a thousand other things. I'm rather busy at the moment. Alex, please could you show Gretchen to the staff quarters?' With a regal tilt to her head, she nodded towards the doorway, she was rather proud that she managed to sound so calm and level. 'She'll have to share with Elin and Freya for the next few days.

'Dagur, the candles. Brynja, please can you keep showing Henrik round and check every nook and cranny to see if there's a distribution board we don't know about. Hekla see if you can find the plans. If you do, give them to Henrik. Olafur you can help Hekla, as...' By some miracle she kept her voice even. 'Alex will now be otherwise engaged.' She deliberately didn't bother looking at him. 'I'm going to see

Kristjan.' With that, head held high, she swept out of the reception horribly aware of the camera following her every move and the pin-drop silence left in her wake before there was a collective, horrified sigh.

Stalking along the corridor, with the bloody film crew tracing her every move, she kept her head up and her face impassive, despite a gazillion furious thoughts racing through her head. Quentin. The Metropole. And Alex a GM!

'Oh, for fuck's sake!' she burst out.

God he must have been laughing his socks and flaming hiking boots off. The Metropole. She shook her head, scowled and groaned out loud before realising that the crew were loving this.

There was a thumbs up from Clive trotting along behind Bob who was unfortunately keeping pace.

With gritted teeth she ignored the camera, focusing on the end of the corridor.

The Metropole. Only set to be smartest, chicest, every-thing-iest hotel in the whole of sodding, flaming, flipping Europe. And if you worked in hospitality and hadn't heard of Quentin Oliver, then you'd been living under a rock since pre-history. Smart, influential and apparently Alex's boss. Alex. Fuck. No. She WAS NOT going to think about Alex. Not think about that last kiss in the car. Not think about him kissing the nape of her neck, which he'd declared his favourite place. Not think about ... bastard. Barman! The lying... What the hell was wrong with her? Of course, he wasn't a barman. It was so obvious. How many times had she considered that he seemed too over qualified, too experienced? She was so bloody stupid.

She wrenched open the door leading down to the kitchen, letting it slam between her and the crew.

And as for super svelte Gretchen swanning in, she could sodding well wait in the wings. Lucy was not giving up this job until the absolute last minute of her contract and today she had a banquet to rescue.

'Hold up, Lucy.' Clive called as they came through the door, grinning from ear to ear. 'This is dynamite. Can we catch that again? Film you from this side, barrelling through the door.'

'What!' She whirled round, her eyes narrowed to vicious points.

At the expression on her face, he and Bob backed up a step.

'Maybe Lucy would like some peace,' said Bob, his face sober. 'A bit of space.'

'Don't be ridiculous,' said Clive, 'This is action woman, kicking ass. We want to see this.' He mimed a kung fu kick. Clive's sound man rolled his eyes.

Hmph. With a snarl she turned around and marched into the kitchen.

Damn it. The camera had caught everything and now Clive was proverbially rubbing his hands in glee. This was exactly the sort of story he'd been looking for. She could almost hear the voice over, '*With the clock ticking will Lucy, the manager, be able to save the day. Will the banquet go ahead? Will the hotel guests go hungry? Will the Icelandic*

Julie Caplin

banquet in Hvolsvöllur go down as the biggest non-event in the town's history? And what will she do now she has no job and no home to go to? She grimaced, imagining thousands of people waiting through the ad break to find out if she'd gone down with the sinking ship or managed to emerge victorious from a potential disaster.

Kristjan was loping backwards and forwards in the dimly lit kitchen, like a hungry lion. A camping lamp was suspended from the rack above one of the counters where there was a chopping board full of diced onions and a discarded knife. As soon as she walked in, he threw up his head and his hands.

'Lucy. We have no electricity.'

She glanced at the gas burners on the big ranges as Kristjan shook his head. 'The ovens won't work without the fans or the ignition, which are all electric.'

Bob carrying the camera let out a little snigger. Lucy shot him a quelling glare.

'I know.' The poor boy looked ready to cry. She patted him on the arm. 'But the electrician is here and I'm sure he'll find the problem. We've got some time.'

Kristjan's eyes widened. 'But what if the electricity doesn't come back?'

'Then we'll come up with plan B.'

'You have a plan B?'

Lucy gave him a grim determined smile. 'Always,' she said, lying through her teeth. 'So, tell me what still needs to be done and the critical timings. When is the absolute last minute you need to have the electricity back?'

Kristjan frowned in thought and picked a knife, poking at the pile of onions. 'I've done most of the preparation, the fish is filleted, the smoked hogget is browned but I can't heat anything and keep it hot or cook the starters. The night will be a ruin. My food.'

He'd put so much effort into devising the menu; langoustine risotto with fennel salad or a caramelised potato salad to start with followed by Icelandic smoked hogget or baked Icelandic cod accompanied by a choice of vegetables including diced potatoes with rosemary and garlic, slow baked carrots and kale. Lucy couldn't count the hours he'd spent perfecting the beloved brownie recipe he'd come up with for the dessert and had in his enthusiasm, even added a second option of lemon Skyr cheesecake.

Lucy ignored the twist in her stomach. She had to remain calm. 'Now Kristjan, you are a brilliant chef. I'm sure we can come up with a solution. Let's not get carried away. We still have plenty of time. First of all, what's the absolute latest you can start cooking?'

He studied her face and brightened a little. 'Another half hour would be the best. The lamb needs to cook for at least two and half hours, but I've just started preparing it. Maybe I could do it in an hour and half but the meat might be a little tough. Then the fish doesn't need to go in the oven until half an hour before service. The risotto I would do an hour before. The potatoes, I was going to boil first, before they are caramelised and they were going to be served warm. But I could do them in an hour. So,' he screwed up his face, 'the latest I could start cooking would be in another hour.'

'OK. We'll go with the hope that the electrician can get the power back on. But in the event he can't, where's the nearest commercial kitchen? Could we see if we can cook the food there and transport it here?'

'Too far away, we couldn't get there, make the food and come back or keep the food warm enough.'

'OK. So, the menu. What could we do cold? With the ingredients we have. Talk me through what we can do.'

'I could make a langoustine salad instead, the ingredients will be fine as long as we keep the fridge doors closed.'

Lucy worried at her lip. 'Any other ideas for cold dishes that you have enough ingredients to serve sixty?'

Kristjan frowned and took down a notepad. 'Possibly I can make a big prawn salad. I have frozen cooked prawns. And I could make a ceviche with the cod. But I would need to start soon, it takes time.' Crossing his fingers, he looked up at the clock on the kitchen wall.

'That's fresh raw fish picked in lemon juice, right?' Didn't sound a bestseller to her but she wasn't a big fish fan.

'Yes, the acid cooks the fish but ... I'll need some help chopping the fish to get it done in time. Anna, the kitchen helper is coming in an hour. I could ask her to come earlier.'

'OK, that's a start. Keep thinking. See if you can come up with a menu and I'll come back in half an hour. If we can make it work, we will.' She looked at her watch again, even though she knew exactly what the time was. 'If not, we'll have to cancel.' And that would happen over her dead body.

'Cut,' yelled Clive. 'This is bloody great.'

'I'm glad you think so,' said Lucy. 'Now if you don't mind I have a lot to do.'

'No problem. We'll do a piece in here with Kristjan.' Clive turned to the young chef. 'Now you keep pacing and maybe you could throw a pan in the sink. You know, show us your frustration at the situation.'

Lucy rolled her eyes and walked out of the kitchen.

She passed Brynja and Henrik in the corridor, peering into a cupboard with a large flashlight. It was one of many that she'd walked past a dozen times and never even opened. The place was full of them.

'Any luck?'

Henrik shook his head, his mouth pursed tight. 'It is most odd.'

She and Brynja exchanged a quick look. Lucy checked over her shoulder. There was no one else around. 'Hypothetically. If you wanted to switch the electricity off deliberately, what would you do?'

From the confused look on his face Henrik clearly didn't understand, so Brynja translated quickly.

He responded in Icelandic which she then relayed to Lucy.

'He says he would take out a fuse in the main fuse box. But here because the building has been changed so many times, there is more than one box. He is worried that even if we do find the right box, the fuse could be very old and then he will have to send away for a replacement, which

351

might take some days. He says we should look at getting another generator.'

Lucy nodded. 'And get the current one fixed. I'll add it to the list.' Although it wouldn't be her list for very much longer.

'Keep looking,' she looked at her watch.

'Are you going to cancel?'

'Not if I can help it.'

Back in the office, Hekla was standing on a chair methodically taking down the ring binder files from the very top of the shelves that lined the back wall. With an armful, piled high, she looked down at the desk below her.

'Wait, let me,' said Lucy, with visions of the whole lot going flying as Hekla tried to jump down.

'Thank you.' Even as she handed over the files, they started to slip and slide. Lucy managed to grab them and dump them in an unruly pile which then spread itself across the desk.

'When this is all over, we need to do some archiving and some throwing away,' she said looked at the battered files, some of which were falling apart with yellowed handwritten pages escaping. 'We need a better...' her voice trailed away.

Hekla turned and gave her a sympathetic look.

'Except when this is over, I won't be here.'

'That's so unfair, Lucy.'

Lucy shrugged. 'Looks like the sale went through and looks like the new owner is Quentin Oliver and you have a new general manager'

'And Alex?' asked Hekla unhappily.

'It seems he works for the new owner, Quentin Oliver.' The bastard. He'd been lying to her all this time.

Hekla frowned.

'He's not a barman?'

'He's definitely not a barman.' Lucy almost spat the words out.

'Who is this Quentin Oliver person?'

'Famous hotelier. Owns some fantastic hotels in Europe and is about to open a new one.'

'And Alex works for him?' Worry lined her face.

'From what the lovely Gretchen said, Alex, appears to be one of his right-hand men. A manager of a big five-star hotel in Paris.'

'So why was he here?'

Lucy raised an eyebrow at the question. 'Probably inspecting everything for his boss.'

'Oh,' said Hekla. 'But he's so nice.' She frowned looking unhappy and confused. 'You did not know?' She pulled an ancient folder down from the top shelf which she was now working her way through.

'I most certainly did not know,' said Lucy, her face grim. How stupid was she but it made sense now? He'd been doing exactly what she would have done if she was taking over an unknown quantity, checking out the lie of the land. Reviewing the current staff and assessing their performance.

'That is ... not very fair. This new lady. She is taking over from you. No one told you?'

Lucy shook her head, her throat suddenly too tight to speak.

'What are you going to do?'

Lucy lifted her chin, swallowing hard before she was able to speak. 'Carry on working until Friday. And make tonight's banquet happen. And where's Olafur? I asked him to help you.'

'He said he would help the electrician instead.'

'But I've just seen the electrician with Brynja.' Lucy frowned as a few bits of jigsaw slotted together in her head. 'Do you have a number for Eyrun?'

'Ja.' Hekla nodded, her brow creasing in a frown.

Lucy dialled Eyrun's number, apologising for calling her at home when she answered.

'Remember you told me that you'd had an email from the previous manager ordering you to put all the throws and cushions away.'

'Ja.' Eyrun laced the word with caution.

'You can't read. Someone must have read the email to you.'

'Olafur. He read it to me,' said Eyrun, suddenly more succinct.

'I don't suppose you kept the email,' asked Lucy.

'No, I never saw it. Olafur came to the laundry. He spoke to me. The next day the manager,' she made a sound like pfft and then said, 'he had left.'

'Thanks, Eyrun. See you tomorrow.'

Lucy frowned, rubbing at the bridge of her nose. The call confirmed her unwanted suspicions.

The door opened. She and Hekla both whipped around to find Alex in the doorway.

'What can I do to help?' he asked, with his usual quiet sincerity.

'I think you've probably done enough, thanks Alex.' Lucy's frosty dismissive tone brought a tiny smile to Hekla's face.

He rubbed at his forehead, with a wince. 'I don't suppose *I can explain everything* is going to cut it?'

Why did he have to look so damn regretful? Why did he look as if he really cared?

Half of Lucy wanted to hear him out, the other was too damn crushed.

Caught in the middle, she lashed out, spitting, 'What do you think?'

And typical Alex he took it right on the chin. No ducking or denying.

'I owe you an explanation and I made a mistake not telling you before.' He stood in front of her not making any excuses or trying to deny it. Bastard. Being grown up and reasonable and honest about things. 'But it was business. I couldn't tell you.'

Lucy wavered, looking at his earnest face, trying to ignore the hollowness in her chest. It was her own bloody fault. Hadn't she learned her lesson? She should never have trusted him with her heart.

Her phone pinged. The text was from Kristjan with an update. He didn't have enough prawns to make a seafood salad.

She glared at Alex. He knew how important it was for her to make tonight work, especially now flaming glamorous Gretchen was on the scene and the bloody film crew were lapping up the drama.

'I don't have time for this right now,' said Lucy, pushing her shoulders back, swallowing back the huge lump in her throat. She was on her own. No one rescued her last time and no one would this time. She didn't need anyone else. If it was the last thing she did, tonight would be a success.

'You're right,' said Alex, 'we need to sort out a rescue plan.'

Hekla did the tennis match thing, her head swivelling from Alex to Lucy.

'We?' Lucy mustered as much disdain as was humanly possible. Lady Bracknell and her famous 'handbag' line couldn't have done it better. 'If I recall you are the barman. I am the manager. This is my problem. Not yours.'

Alex swallowed and moved to stand right in front of her, putting a hand on her forearm.

She felt the warmth of his skin with a pang.

Those warm brown eyes met hers, sincere and direct. 'I understand that you're mad with me. I don't blame you. You have every right.' His hand squeezed her arm. 'I should have told you–'

'Yes, you should,' snapped Lucy, straightening and pulling away from him. She looked at her watch lifting her wrist right up in front of her face. 'But as of right now I don't care. I am still the manager and I have a banquet to organise.'

Alex smiled, a touch of pride and admiration sweeping across his face.

'Don't you dare!' she growled at him. Hekla's saucer eyes widened even more.

His eyes softened, the smile remaining in place which infuriated the hell out of her. 'I know you can do it. You can do pretty much anything you set your mind to. Smart by name, smart by nature.'

He didn't get to be proud of her. Not when he'd gone behind her back. Not when he'd lied to her.

'And keep that Gretchen bitch out of my hair.' Ouch, had she really said that. 'And stop bloody smirkling like an idiot.' Damn why had she said that. It brought back the memory of the night in the laundry with a painful pang.

'Yes boss. What do you want me to do?'

'Grrr.' Oh God, she was doing it again, it reminded of her when she'd growled at the recruitment consultant. Except this time, she wasn't going down without a fight.

There was a startled silence. Hekla seemed to be finding her feet incredibly interesting all of a sudden and Alex was still sodding smiling at her. His gorgeous face sympathetic and supportive. Damn it. This was worse than before. It had all been a lie. Why hadn't he told her who he was? Because he'd been spying on her all along. Playing a part.

'I trusted you,' she said in a low voice.

At last his smile slipped. 'I know. I'm sorry. I wanted to tell you but...'

She swallowed. Shit. No. She. Was. Not. Going. To. Cry. Not in front of him.

The precarious pile of files on the desk suddenly shifted and like an avalanche gathering speed, the ring binders tipped off the edge clattering to the floor. Ducking to her knees, Lucy along with Hekla started gathering them up.

'Make yourself useful. Help Hekla go through these and see if you can find any drawings.'

Thrusting a ring binder hard into his chest, deriving considerable satisfaction from his strangled, 'oof', she escaped from the office, pulling the door firmly shut behind her.

Out in the reception area on her own, she blew out a breath, reached up and tightened her pony tail. This girl meant business. She looked at her watch. Time was still ticking.

She was going to have to make a decision very quickly. Even if Henrik found the fault, it didn't sound as if he were completely confident that he could get the electricity back on. Shame about the generator.

She frowned. Someone had made sure they'd fixed both the electricity and the generator. Someone who had a good reason to want to cause problems for the hotel. She walked into the bar, where there were already a few guests who'd returned from their day's excursion. Thank goodness there was plenty of hot water, at least that wasn't affected by the electricity. Those sitting in the lounge didn't seemed remotely bothered by the gentle light radiating from the motley collection of votives and the fierce glow of the fire, which had been banked right up so that it was throwing out plenty of heat.

Dagur was busy distributing more tealights around the room filling every surface with votives, little dishes and sauces. He grinned at her.

'By the time we've got all these little guys lit, it's going to look cool in here. And I've got a ton of firewood ready, so it's going to be cosy, cosy.' He lowered his voice. 'And the guests all seem to be mighty happy. Everyone loves a free drink.'

'Mm, they do,' said Lucy dryly, looking around with a quick burst of pride. They'd manage and somehow tonight would work out because she had a wonderful, supportive team on board, with one or two exceptions. 'It looks great in here. Now all I have to worry about is the food.'

Dagur shrugged. 'Can't help with that I'm afraid,' he said before adding with a wink, 'but if we get everyone drunk, maybe they won't care.'

'That's plan C,' said Lucy. Giving the room a last quick once over, she turned on her heel and headed to the kitchen to get an update from Kristjan.

Thankfully she passed the film crew heading back up to the bar to 'catch some atmosphere' and when she arrived in the kitchen, Kristjan was poking at a piece of lamb with a scowl on his face.

'How are you doing?' asked Lucy.

He let out a mournful sigh. 'There isn't enough. I don't have enough seafood to make the salad stretch to sixty people,' he said with an agitated shake of his head.

'OK.' She tilted her head. 'What do you know about generators?'

With a frown he put down his knife and turned to her. 'How much do you want me to know?'

'Do you know how to start one? How they work?'

'Sure. I have worked in a place before where we had one for when the weather was bad. As long as you've got enough fuel to keep them going, there's not too much that can go wrong.'

'Excellent. Leave that and come with me. And bring the lamp. My phone is about to die.' She'd been using the torch function to get around.

He peeled off his apron and unhooked the lamp before grabbing his black fleece from a hook on the back of the little office. 'Here, take this spare. It's cold out there.' He handed her an outsized ugly beige jacket

When they reached the outhouse, it was in complete darkness. The last time she'd been here was with Alex ... and she wasn't going to think about him.

To her immediate right, there were a couple of large petrol cans lined up in one corner of the room and she picked one up to check its weight and felt the liquid inside it sloshing about.

'We have fuel.' She lifted a couple more. 'Plenty of it.'

'That would last the night,' said Kristjan knowledgeably as he moved towards the generator which sat in the centre of the room like a small tractor, holding the camping lantern high above it. Lucy moved behind him.

'Do you know how to work it?'

'I'm a farm boy, hell yes. We need to connect it to the supply here.' He plugged something in, and Lucy was grateful that he knew what he was doing, then he turned a big black knob and flicked a switch, beaming at her as he then grasped a black handle and pulled hard. There was a whirring, rattling sound and then the generator flared into life, chugging away with a contented hum like some bovine electrical creature.

Through the window, Lucy saw all the lights in the lodge blink into life.

'Well, there's a surprise,' she said with her hands on her hips. 'Doesn't seem too broken to me.'

'Who said it was?' asked Kristjan flicking on the light in the shed and looking over the generator. 'It works like a dream. And with that amount of fuel it will keep turning for a long time.'

'Excellent,' she said avoiding the question.

With a big grin, he turned to her. 'We're cooking! I'd better get back to the kitchen.' Kristjan almost skipped out of the shed and away back to the lodge.

Lucy leaned against the wall of the building watching the generator noisily vibrating, her legs feeling a little weak. Phew, she'd done it.

The disappointment gnawed at her. Knowing who the saboteur was brought no satisfaction, just a slightly sick feeling. It felt like a betrayal. Another one.

With a heavy sigh, she let her head fall back against the wall. Bugger, bugger, bugger. She so hadn't wanted it to be any of the staff she'd come to know over the last two months. The leaden disappointment left a sour taste in her mouth, although at least the electrical problem was well and truly solved. Now all she had to do was get through the rest of the evening without thinking about Alex or her job.

Chapter 28

She walked back into the office to a loud cheer. Hekla, Alex, Dagur, Brynja, Henrik and Olafur were all there.

'The electricity is back,' said Hekla with a beam.

'The generator,' said Lucy, shooting a glance at Olafur, who immediately coloured. 'Seems it wasn't broken after all.'

Everyone began talking with the speed and volume of excited starlings chattering and there was that post-catastrophe semi-hysterical euphoria as everyone realised how close to disaster they'd been, as if they hadn't dared think about how truly awful it would be if they hadn't got the electricity back on in time for the banquet. Only Alex noticed the brief inter-change, probably because he was keeping a careful wary eye on her. Lucy had already decided her best strategy was to treat him like any other member of staff.

Hekla clapped, 'That is good news,' while Olafur mumbled something into his beard.

'But not so good,' said Brynja with frustration, 'because Henrik still can't understand what is wrong.'

'The generator will keep us going for this evening and I think the electricity might magically fix itself in the night,' said Lucy. 'You know the huldufólk.'

'But you don't believe...' Hekla's voice trailed off as she intercepted the stern look Lucy sent Olafur's way. Alex gave the other man a thoughtful look, although the others were all busy talking and missed it. Alex caught Lucy's eye and raised a questioning eyebrow.

She ignored him.

'Right everybody, we've got a banquet to organise. It's all hands-on deck. We need to move the furniture in the dining room and get all the tables laid up. We've lost a bit of time, but we should be OK.'

Quickly she dished out a list of orders, allocating everyone but Olafur a job. For once she was going to have to leave them all to it and trust them to get the job done.

'Olafur, if you could stay a moment.'

Alex loitered at the back of the office.

'Did you want something?' Lucy asked pointedly,

'I thought maybe I should stay,' he said.

Lucy held the silence for a beat before saying. 'You thought wrong.'

It hurt to say the cold words and to push him away. Hurt more as she realised that from now on, for the next few days, she was on her own. She hadn't realised how much she'd come to rely on his quiet, steady support. Although it was no bloody wonder he had good instincts, as an experienced hotel manager, he knew the job inside out.

The quick disappointed frown on his face, hardened her resolve. Tough shit. He'd lost any right to play supportive colleague or – there was a hollowness in her stomach – any other role. 'But don't you–'

'I don't *want* or *need* anything further from you. I suggest you return to your waiting and bar duties. There's an awful lot to be done in the dining room. I assure you, as the manager, I can handle this thank you,' she said, rocking the snow queen impersonation even though the acid words gave her no pleasure, they just heightened her sense of misery. Lashing out at him underlined the anger bubbling inside and gave it fuel, making her even more mixed up and furious.

She almost caved in when she saw the resigned, guilty look on his face as he realised she meant it. With great reluctance he trudged out of the room, casting one last regretful look over his shoulder.

She swallowed hard, her muscles stiffening. Confrontation was her least favourite thing.

Waiting until he'd shut the door, she leaned against her desk, her arms folded and her legs crossed.

'Well Olafur?'

He shrugged, fiddling with the waistband of his jeans, tugging at the loops that held up his heavy leather belt. 'The generator must be faulty.'

'Did you really try it?' asked Lucy very quietly, her demeanour calm although inside her stomach was churning over and over.

Olafur stood in hesitant silence, his eyes not quite

meeting hers as he carried on fidgeting with his clothes, his hand had graduated to pulling at the seam of his flannel shirt sleeve.

'I think it would be really helpful if you fixed the electricity so that it's back on this evening.'

He shot her an uncertain look as if confused by her quiet, calm approach. She could almost see the mental perambulations of his mind, the torpid calculation of whether to lie or to come clean. Lucy had absolutely no doubt in her mind that Olafur was behind all the petty sabotage but she had absolutely no proof. In HR terms, she didn't have a leg to stand on.

'I know that this farm belonged to your family. You must have spent a lot of time here growing up.'

The gentle observation drew a fleeting flicker of surprise, his eyes widening briefly.

'I'm pretty sure someone with a thorough knowledge of this building, like you, will know where the source of the problem is,' she said wishing he'd make life easier and help himself by admitting it and agreeing to put things right.

Olafur stared at her, his lips moving as if he wanted to speak but couldn't quite bring himself to.

'Come on Olafur. I know it was you.' She leaned forward fixing her gaze on him, speaking with more confidence than she felt. Know was putting it a little bit strongly but Sherlock Holmes had never got very far by pussyfooting around. 'At the moment, no one else has worked it out ... yet. When they do...' She left a helpful pause, not letting up on her direct scrutiny of him. 'Don't you think everyone is going to be disappointed when they find out it was you? And how are you going to cope when it gets out? Everyone knows everyone. The story will spread. It will be hard to get another job. And there'll be whispers. Always. Behind your back. To your face. This is a small community.' She gave a small mirthless smile. 'I promise you, I know how awful it is, everyone talking behind your back, sniggering on your account.' Her bitterness coloured the words with added vehemence.

His bushy eyebrows drew together and he winced, screwing up his eyes in regret.

'I ... I...'

She gave him an encouraging nod.

'The farm...' he spread out a hand. 'It belonged to the family.' He covered his face with his hands. 'I'm ... I didn't ... I wanted...' He lifted his shoulders as the words deserted him.

Lucy realised he was crying.

'It was wrong. I know ... I'm so ... this was our home. Until I was fourteen. Pedersen bought it, for nothing. My Dad, he drank, kept losing his job, then he lost the farm. We had nothing and Pedersen knew.' Olafur sniffed and shook his head. 'Now he's going to make a big profit. On the back of my family. After he sold ... the money, it soon went. We had to go live with my aunt in Reykjavik, mum's sister. They split up.' His moustache quivered. 'I wanted to make it too hard for Pedersen to sell. I didn't want him to profit. Not to make so much money.'

'I'm sorry,' she said tilting her head to one side, feeling

desperately sad for him. She knew what it was like to hit rock bottom but it was hard to forgive him when he hadn't thought about how it would impact on other people. 'That sucks. But what about Hekla, Brynja, Gunnar? What if the hotel had to close? If no one came to stay here anymore? What would happen if they lost their jobs?'

The stricken look on his face suggested that he hadn't thought that far ahead.

'Do you think the electricity will be turned back on this evening?' Her pointed question had him nodding furiously. 'And we'll have the end of all further mishaps from now on?'

Another nod.

'Then I think we'll say no more about it. We all make mistakes.' Lord knew she had. 'I believe everyone deserves a second chance,' saying that made her pause for thought and Alex's stricken face came to mind, 'but if you do anything like this again, you will be out on your ear. No warning.' She looked at her watch. 'Can you get the electricity back on? Or will you need Henrik's help?'

'I can do it,' mumbled Olafur from underneath his beard. 'Thank you.' He shambled to the doorway like a big shaggy defeated bear and then paused in the doorway. 'I ... I'm sorry. Thank you for not...'

Lucy pursed her mouth and gave him a curt nod praying she wasn't going to live to regret this. 'Officially I won't be in charge in another couple of days. I won't say anything. You got lucky, this time. Not everyone would be as forgiving. Now go get that electricity back on.'

* * *

When he'd gone she sank into the chair at her desk, putting her head and arms on the flat surface. She closed her eyes feeling all her energy suddenly desert her, leaving her as limp as a deflated balloon. Back to square one again. Sitting up slowly she stared out of the window, it was dark outside but the landscape was lit up by the brightness of the snow. Out of habit she went to worry at her lip. It had healed. She straightened. And she'd healed too. Forget walking away with her tail between her legs. Gretchen might have the job but she was the one that turned The Northern Lights Lodge into a cosy haven, offering its guests a warm and homely welcome. If Quentin Oliver's reputation was anything to go by, Lucy was passing the Lodge into good hands, not that she was about to forgive the other woman's tactless announcement in any kind of a hurry.

This was the sort of hotel she wanted to run from now on, not some big branded multi-bedroomed place with no personality or warmth and she was going to make sure that she got a reference out of Mr Pedersen or Quentin Oliver if it was the last thing she ever did. With a sad smile on her face, she looked out at the snowy landscape. She'd come away with plenty of good memories of Iceland and the sad ones ... well, time would tell.

Lucy let out a delighted gasp as she walked into the dining room, taking in the sight of dozens of tealights flickering creating a golden aura like a halo embracing the room. Above her, strung along the wooden beams, lots of tiny, golden fairy lights glowed creating a charming, welcoming atmosphere. She crossed to the centre of the room where the big rustic table had been moved to take pride of place. Charmed, she did a quick three sixty to take in the cosier arrangement of the dining tables which had been moved to circle the main table.

Wow, they all looked fabulous. Brynja had worked her magic, spending ages creating whimsical centrepieces of pebbles and driftwood to make it look as if a little piece of the beach had been brought to each table. On the larger pebbles, words of welcome in several different languages were handwritten in some sort of white pen, and they were interspersed between the cutlery and glassware. Finishing off each place setting, Brynja had placed napkins bound with a strand of straw-coloured raffia double wrapped around the white linen with little sprigs of heather and bilberry tucked into the raffia.

'Oh my, it's gorgeous,' she said, as Brynja walked in. 'And wow look at you.' Around her shoulders was a dark green cloak fastened at the neck with a silver brooch, which looked rather familiar.

'Elin's done a good job, don't you think?'

'She has,' said Lucy with a grin. 'I love this.' She pointed to the brooch.

'It's borrowed. Elin said it would be good advertising for the jeweller. The one who is going to sell jewellery in reception.'

'Good idea.' Lucy glanced down at her ring which still gave her huge pleasure every time she looked at it. 'And you've done a wonderful job on the table decorations. I'm so impressed.'

Brynja beamed at her as Kristjan, in his chef's whites, came through the kitchen door.

'We're all set. Come taste the langoustine risotto.'

Lucy followed him into the kitchen and tasted the risotto, the lamb and potato salad under Kristjan's watchful gaze, aware that he was holding his breath. This was his big moment too. The flavours danced over her tongue. He'd done an amazing job.

'They're all divine,' she said putting down her spoon. 'You've excelled yourself.'

He gave her a big hug and twirled her around the kitchen, before putting her down and giving her a high five.

'And you didn't even check the costings!'

'Shh,' she grinned at him. 'Don't tell everyone, they'll think I've gone soft.' With a wink over her shoulder, she walked out of the kitchen back through the dining room and up to reception. The VIP guests were due any moment and she wanted to be there to greet them.

Hekla was waiting in reception for her, she too clad in a cloak with a brooch, although it was a little skewwhiff and her hair was in an intricate braid.

'Ready?' asked Lucy.

Hekla nodded. 'Yes, the Mayor is on his way. His taxi left five minutes ago.'

Lucy raised an enquiring eyebrow and Hekla gave her a mischievous grin.

'My cousin's brother is the driver tonight. His wife phoned me.'

'Where would I be without you and your network?' asked Lucy, straightening the other girl's cloak.

'We couldn't do it without you Lucy. Don't forget this was your idea.'

'Let's hope it was a good one but thank goodness the electricity is back on.'

Hekla frowned, her fair brows drawing together in thought. 'It's very odd, don't you think, how it just came back on?'

Lucy laughed. 'On this occasion, I think the huldufólk might have been involved.'

Hekla beamed. 'I think so too.'

In the bar Alex, Dagur and Gunnar were lined up, they too had been cloaked up and looked rather fetching. She swallowed as Alex gave her a dashing bow, sweeping his cloak out to greet her.

What was it about a man in costume? She scowled at him to hide the traitorous leap of her heart.

'You've done well, Lucy. Tonight's going to be a huge success. The dining room looks amazing and Kristjan's menu sounds like a real gourmet treat. I think people are going to be talking about this for a long time. And congratulations on sorting out the electricity. Huldufólk again was it?'

'You can't help yourself, can you?' she swallowed, hating the pettiness that dogged her tone.

'Lucy, we're on the same side.'

'Yes, we are … a fact you failed to mention … on so many occasions.'

'Lucy, think about it, there was never the right time. At first I was doing my job. Then … well I started to like you and there was that spark. Being completely selfish, I was worried it would make you back off. And if you had known … it … it could be construed that I was taking advantage, especially when I knew how much you needed this job. Or people might think you were sleeping with me to get the job. I didn't want to put you in that position.'

The quiet truth of his words echoed in the pleading expression in his eyes.

'I had no idea he was sending Gretchen. He told me … he gave me the impression he would keep you. I don't understand but I'll talk to him in the morning. We can sort this out. Get your job back.'

Lucy looked at him. 'You don't get it. I don't care about that. I trusted you.'

His eyes fell and he couldn't look at her.

'Yeah, those three little words,' she said with sorrow, her heart shrivelling in her chest, leaving pain and emptiness.

With eyes filled full of anguish and regret, he shook his head. 'Three more, I messed up.'

'Yeah, you did.'

A buzz in the doorway announced the arrival of a group of people.

'Showtime.' She turned and smoothly went to greet the Mayor and his party which included the head of the tourist board from Reykjavik, the local tourist officer and someone else, who Hekla in a whispered exchange later, told her was from a government department. They all seemed to know each other, of course they did, this was Iceland, and she was quite relieved that she'd decided to keep things informal and not join them for dinner.

For once Clive and his crew kept a discreet distance, filming the VIP party in the bar as Alex and Gunnar served drinks. It had been agreed that they could conduct a couple of interviews after dinner. Hopefully all the visitors would have nice things to say. Lucy crossed her fingers behind her back as she escorted the party down to the dining room, which was filling up already from the resident guests who were all oohing and ahhing over the transformation.

The waiters began bringing out the first course and the room filled with the aroma of langoustine, the sweet honeyed smell of caramelised potatoes and the hum of contented customers, and Lucy allowed herself to relax. As she surveyed the room, taking in all the details, checking that everyone was being looked after and that they all looked happy, she felt that familiar thrill. Looking after customers and making them happy, that was why she did this job. Out of the corner of her eyes, she caught sight of Bob, his camera trained on her. Turning to face the camera lens, she paused. The camera closed in on her and she gave it a big full-on smile, letting her happiness shine through without feeling the least bit shy or self-conscious.

* * *

'Freya, you were amazing,' said Lucy plumping down into one of the chairs in front of the fire where the embers still glowed.

All the guests had departed and only the staff remained in the bar, the tealights gently popping out every now and then around the room.

A sense of euphoria and job well done fizzed in the air.

From the dining room the guests had been ushered into the bar and given a shot of Brennivin and once they were settled in the comfy chairs arranged around the fire, Freya had picked her way through to settle on a cushion by the floor. There'd been an audible sigh as she appeared dressed for the occasion in a long flowing green dress with her hair braided into a thick plait, at least twelve inches longer than it had been this morning, which hung down over one shoulder. Like the others she also wore a woollen cape, except this one was floor length and fastened with an even bigger gold brooch. On her lap she'd held a heavy book, which looked as if it might be a family grimoire full of spells, from which she read a series of traditional folk stories, her soft lilting voice filling the room with tales of princes and forests, witches and sea monsters.

'The guests were completely mesmerised,' said Lucy, remembering the hushed spellbound atmosphere. 'I think the head of the tourist board wants to offer you a job. And as for the Mayor...'

Hekla giggled. They'd had to virtually pour him into his official car, almost tearful in his appreciation of the best night ever.

375

'Everyone loved it,' said Hekla giving Freya's plait an affectionate tug. 'Viking girl.'

Freya grinned. 'The extensions were a good idea.'

'The story telling was a wonderful idea,' said Brynja, leaning forward and patting Lucy's shoulder.

'Elin made the costumes.'

Elin grinned. 'Shh don't tell Lucy, but I used a throw to make Freya's cloak.'

Lucy laughed, taking a sip of her spirit. 'I thought it looked familiar.' She looked around at all of them, a hitch in her chest. She raised her glass.

'Thank you everyone. I'm so proud of you all. Tonight was a real team effort. You all did your bit.' She deliberately avoided looking at Alex. 'I couldn't have done it without you.'

Olafur ducked his head, when she tried to catch his eye.

'It was very successful. We took a lot of money behind the bar,' said Dagur, with an avaricious grin. 'The Mayor was very generous with his expense account. He bought drinks for lots of people.'

'Good because Lucy didn't check my budget on the food,' said Kristjan with a teasing smile.

'I didn't need to,' she said. 'You did a fab job. And I know that I can trust you.' She gave him a smile as he blushed and toasted her with his glass. 'All of you were brilliant.' She lifted her chin away from Alex, so that he'd know he was not included in that comment.

'That's because you let us,' teased Hekla.

Lucy wrinkle her nose at her. It was true. She'd delegated

the tasks and then let them get on with their jobs. And boy had they done her proud and it was all caught on camera. Only the film crew were a little disappointed that near disaster had been averted without going down to the wire but as Clive glibly announced, with a huge grin waving a large glass of whisky about, they could edit the final footage to make it look far worse. Thankfully they'd all disappeared to bed once the Mayor had left, as they had to pack for their departure the following day. Not a moment too soon as far as Lucy was concerned.

'Oh yes,' said Hekla. 'We all did good.' She curled her feet underneath in one of the chairs and snagged a cushion for behind her head. 'Agneta from the tourist board was very impressed. She wanted to know who the chef was, she thinks you're a genius.'

Kristjan preened in the red glow of the fire, stretching his feet out in front of him and putting his hands behind his head with a cocky grin.

'Don't tell him that,' said Alex at exactly the same moment as Lucy said, 'Don't tell him that.'

Her lip curled, furious with herself. They were so bloody similar and she wondered if it had been the other way around, would she have told him who she was?

'He'll want a pay rise,' finished Alex with a wry smile at Lucy. Clenching her jaw, she ignored him and turned to Hekla, realising that she was holding the young chef's hand and said, 'You don't want him turning into a prima donna.'

'Someone has to be on reception in the morning,' said Hekla heaving herself out of her chair, tugging at Kristjan's hand. 'And I'm sure you want to check the kitchen is all finished.'

Kristjan turned bright pink, nodding and gave a tongue-tied response half in English and half in Icelandic.

'And you're on breakfast too,' said Brynja dragging Gunnar up out of his chair.

Oh no, they weren't doing that to her. She stood up with them, ignoring Alex who also stood, trying to catch her eye. He could forget it. He'd had plenty of time before to explain things and he hadn't chosen to. She didn't want to hear any more now.

Chapter 29

Gretchen was sitting in *her* chair at *her* desk when Lucy walked into the office. So that was the way it was going to be, was it? Ignoring Gretchen, Lucy went straight to the coffee machine and made herself a black coffee without saying a word to her. Hekla sauntered in, widened her eyes and like a trapped moth stopped in the doorway unsure whether to come in or leave.

'Morning Hekla,' said Lucy as if she didn't have a care in the world. 'Sleep well after the excitement of the banquet?'

'Ja,' said Hekla her usual enthusiastic smile reasserting itself. 'It was one of our best nights.'

Then she pulled a horrified expression as if realising that perhaps she'd said the wrong thing.

'It was an excellent night for the lodge,' Lucy reassured her, with a weak smile. A professional triumph, even if it had been a personal disaster. But only if she let it.

She'd lain awake for most of the night thinking about Alex. Yes, he'd let her down by not telling her the truth about who he really was but she owed it to herself and to him to talk to him properly today. She'd given Olafur a

379

second chance last night, maybe Alex deserved one too. In hindsight, he'd seemed as shocked as she was to see Gretchen and just as horrified to hear that she'd been given the job. In fact, over the last couple of weeks, he'd been so adamant that Lucy would be kept on, almost as if he knew something and then he'd said last night that Quentin had given him the impression he would.

Lucy sighed and rubbed her tight forehead, as if to ease the nagging headache that had dogged her since she'd woken this morning.

She hadn't put up a fight when she lost her job last time. She'd walked away and accepted the situation. This time she wasn't giving up on Alex or the job.

Lucy turned to Gretchen and smiled sweetly. 'May I have my desk back? I have quite a lot to do today.'

Gretchen's mouth firmed. 'I thought I might as well take over now.'

'And why would you think that? I still have a contract until Friday.'

The dark-haired woman gave a sour laugh. 'On paper, yes but let's face it, if you were any good, Quentin would have offered you the job instead of me.'

Lucy felt herself turn bright red.

'Alex certainly didn't rate you.'

'What do you mean?' asked Lucy, her words sharp in response to the sudden pain in her chest. That wasn't true. He'd been full of praise in the last few weeks. *The new owners would be insane not to take you on.' 'What a great job you're doing.' 'Your fantastic organisational skills.'* Last night, in the dark hours of the early morning, she'd picked over his words with the intensity of a miser focused on a shiny new penny. Alex had worked in some seriously big and prestigious hotels, he knew what he was talking about.

'I don't believe that,' she said, remembering her promise to herself, this time she would fight.

'Here,' Gretchen shook out a sheet of paper with an impatient hand. It was an email from Alex or at least from an email address alex.mclaughin@theolivergroup.com. Lucy's eyes raked over the words *'lack of initiative', 'failed', 'lack of', 'poor leadership'*.

No. This couldn't be true. Alex couldn't have said this. He couldn't have been so two-faced. She almost laughed out loud, when she thought of the time she'd told him he shouldn't play poker. Alex's face was far too expressive. There were so many times when she'd been able to read him. Surely she couldn't have got it so wrong. Pain twinged in her heart.

But there it was in black and white. Alex.

Her lungs constricted. Swallowing hard, she forced herself to remain impassive. Everything had been a lie.

'I'm sure you can see why Quentin is keen for me to take the reins as soon as possible.' Gretchen flicked through another couple of pages and scowled. 'Although to be fair, from what I can gather you've not had much experience. At least this will look good on your CV.'

Lucy clenched her fists. This was so unfair.

'Lucy's a very good manager,' said Hekla. 'She's the best

one we've ever had. The lodge is so much better now that she's here.'

'I admit, it looks in much better shape than I expected...' she gave a snarky laugh, 'although that's probably down to Alex being here and now he's gone, I'll take over.'

'He's gone?' Lucy swallowed. The bottom dropped out of her stomach and she thought she might black out. Gone?

'Back to Paris. Flew out this morning,' said Gretchen briskly, already picking up a sheet of paper that had come off the printer. The room swam and Lucy took in a sharp breath. Alex had gone without saying a word to her. Just like Chris, he'd abandoned her without a word when he'd got found out. Goosebumps pricked at her arms as a chill swept over her, she felt cold to the very bone.

'Now, as you're here perhaps you can explain to me why the housekeeper isn't managing room service.'

Lucy took a moment to process the words.

'As you're now in charge, why don't you ask her yourself?' As soon as she said it, she regretted her moment of spite. It was unlikely the fearsome Gretchen would be sympathetic to Eyrun's inability to read and it wasn't Eyrun's fault that once again she'd trusted the wrong man. And she wasn't going to let history repeat itself. This time she wasn't going to be cowed into submission. This time she was fighting back. 'Sorry, I should have explained. Eyrun and I agreed to hand the job over to Elin who wanted more responsibility.'

Gretchen did a double take. 'Oh. I can see why you would do that. That sounds like a good staff retention policy. I guess its difficult recruiting staff around here.'

Hekla nodded joining in the conversation. 'Ja, especially with the huldufólk.'

'Sorry?'

'The hidden folk,' said Lucy. 'Like elves, only more troublesome. You get used to them.' She smiled at Gretchen. 'You're not in Kansas anymore.' With that she turned around and walked out of the office.

Hekla came running after her as she strode down the corridor.

'Alex wouldn't have said those bad things about you. He wouldn't,' she said desperately, her pretty face crumpling which almost broke Lucy's heart. 'And I can't believe he would leave without saying goodbye. To you. To me. To everyone.'

Lucy pinched her lips hard, holding back sudden tears She couldn't believe it either. All the fight she'd promised herself, vanished with a punch of pain. Alex had gone. The words echoed in her head, a fierce, heavy ache filled her chest. It hurt to breathe. He hadn't even tried to fight for her, hadn't waited to talk to her. Her plan to talk to him had been pulled out from under her. Alex had gone.

Chapter 30

Lucy waited at the luggage conveyor belt watching as the cases lumbered around the belt with painful slowness. She wondered what would happen if she got on the belt, lay down and gave up. Just let herself go round and round. She tried to rouse herself and be positive, but it was hard. It was comforting to think that Daisy would be waiting for her through the other side, ready to mop up the tears with prosecco and gin, once again. At least this time, apart from the puffy eyes, on the outside she looked a lot healthier, her hair had all grown back and her lip had completely healed. It was a good job the inside didn't show. Inside she was a mess, a tangle of regret and sadness. It made her realise that the way she'd felt about Chris didn't even come close to how she'd felt about Alex.

With a sniff, she blinked hard. Broken hearts were fixable. Her phone beeped into action. All those irritating texts, no doubt announcing which network she was on. As if she didn't know. She pulled her phone out of her pocket to delete them and spotted several missed calls from the same unknown number. Her heart leapt. Alex? Was he trying to get hold of her? She'd never known his number, they'd never needed to use their mobiles at the lodge because the signal had been so dreadful.

Her finger hovered over the number wondering whether to call it. Why would Alex be calling?

He'd left her. Gone back to Paris. He can't have cared that much, he hadn't even put up a fight. Somehow that was the most disappointing thing. Feeling weary and now understanding the true meaning of heartsore, she focused on the bags peering at each one. They all looked so similar, if she wasn't careful she'd miss hers and end up with some stranger's dirty washing.

Just as she was grabbing her bag, her phone rang. The same number. Without hesitation she stabbed at the button to answer, adrenaline tripping through her system.

'Alex?'

'Oh, nun on a bicycle, you're as bad as he is,' growled an unfamiliar voice. 'Seriously!'

'Sorry,' disappointment had her voice stiffening and she sounded like an outraged matron from the fifties, 'who is this?'

'This is a man who can give you a job,' said the strange voice imitating her frigid tone. 'I'm Quentin Oliver.'

'Oh,' said Lucy, stopping dead on the concourse to a chorus of tuts and a near miss with a pull along cabin bag.

'And you are a difficult woman to get hold of. I've been ringing all afternoon. Don't you ever pick up?'

Lucy was tempted to point out that she had done, otherwise how would they be speaking now but decided against it. He sounded like a man short on patience and long on sarcasm.

'You still there Lucy Smart?'

'Yes.' And very confused.

'So, I was impressed with what you did at the Lodge. It's a new venture for me. Small, boutique. I don't get it personally, I want swanky, luxury and gold-plated taps. My wife, who runs her own exclusive hotel, says I'm out of date. And as I dote on her and listen to her every word, she's been on about higgy or however you say it.' Lucy frowned. For a man whose reputation for business savvy proceeded him around the world, he sounded a tad bonkers to her.

'You mean hygge,' corrected Lucy, suddenly paying attention.

'That's the bugger. Anyhow. What you did at the Lodge, I'm interested in something similar at a new property. Can you get to Edinburgh tomorrow?'

'Sorry?'

'Don't make me regret singling you out for this job. I'm told you're smart by name and nature. You heard me.'

'Are you offering me a job?' Was this really Quentin Oliver? For a man who was so successful, he sounded quite mad. She really wasn't sure what to think.

'Are you interested?'

'I-I … don't know. Why? You didn't let me keep *my* job.'

'I admit, you worked wonders but I'd already offered Gretchen the job, she's been nagging me for her own hotel. I know you should have got it, the latest TripAdvisor reviews are through the roof and Alex certainly put plenty of good words in for you. If I didn't know better, I'd say you were sleeping with him.'

Lucy winced. Hadn't Alex worried about that very thing. 'I find it difficult to believe Alex put in a good word for me. Gretchen showed me an email. I think poor choice and limited managerial skills were a few of his descriptions of me.'

Quentin laughed. 'You gotta hand it to her, she's a minx that one. That email was the first one Alex sent me. He'd only been there five minutes. You riled him good and proper the first week. I knew straight off with that email, that things weren't right. He is never that quick to judge. Christ when I've asked him before to give me an opinion, I promise you, he's slower than a tortoise. Mind you, give him his due, the tortoise always takes the race out from under the hare. That's our Alex. Deliberate, takes his time but he's always spot on the money.'

Lucy raised an eyebrow at the unflattering and somewhat surprising description of Alex as she sat down on one of the benches in the baggage reclaim hall beginning to wonder if she was in the middle of some weird dream.

'So, tomorrow. Edinburgh. Can you meet me there?'

Daisy was waiting at the barrier with an A4 piece of paper that said *Welcome home* in bright pink Sharpie surrounded by a couple of daisy doodles. The home-made sign among the more professional Mr Azia, Mr and Mrs Rhodes and The Mitchell Family notices, brought a smile to Lucy's face, or maybe it was the rather bizarre telephone conversation.

'Hey babe,' said Daisy, throwing her arms around her. 'You look amazing.'

'Thanks,' said Lucy her hand immediately straying to her hair.

'Told you it would grow back.'

'In this case I've never been happier with an "I told you so."' Lucy thought back to the panic she'd felt that first night in Iceland. Now she had money in her pocket. A reference. And a possible job offer. She ignored the 'and a broken heart' the voice in her head helpfully added.

'Bummer, you didn't get the job. The hotel sounded lush.'

'It was by the time I'd finished with it,' said Lucy, shaking her head. 'But I've had the most bizarre conversation with the man that didn't give me the job.'

'Hold that thought, until we get in the car, I've got to remember where the heck I parked,' said Daisy leading her out of the terminal. 'Then tell me all.'

As they negotiated the airport concourse, car park and initial drive out onto the A38, Lucy filled Daisy in on her conversation with Quentin Oliver. 'Well it sounds to me, like he's offering you a job,' said Daisy, pulling out at a roundabout to the blaring horn of the car that had right of way.

'I think that's pushing optimism a bit far. At most I'd say tomorrow is an interview.'

'Job,' insisted Daisy obstinately, 'no one drags you all the way to Scotland for a chat.' She turned her head to face Lucy to emphasise her point, reminding Lucy of Hekla's driving. Then she stamped on the brakes stopping the car from going into the back of the one in front of them at a roundabout. 'Maybe Alex put in a good word. Have you spoken to him?'

Lucy gnawed at her lip, careful not to break the skin. 'Believe it or not, we never gave each other our mobile numbers. I only swapped numbers with Hekla and Brynja this morning when I left.'

'So,' Daisy winced. 'Have you any idea where he's gone?'

Lucy let out a grinding laugh. 'I'm assuming he's gone back to Paris, to his fancy hotel.'

'So what are you going to do?'

'Go to Edinburgh to see what Mr Oliver has to say.'

'I bet he offers you a job,' said Daisy, with her usual loyal optimism.

'Hmm, I wouldn't bet on it. He's eccentric but very well connected and hugely influential. So I'd be mad not to at least go and meet with him.'

'Well as long as you're sure he's not going to sell you into the sex trade or anything?'

Lucy gave a brittle laugh. 'As he's paying a fortune for me to travel first class on the train tomorrow, I'm thinking he'd be making quite some investment.'

'First class. Hmm. You see to me, that sounds like a serious business proposition.'

'Hmm, but why me? We've never even met. And if he thought I was any good, he would have given me the job at the lodge.'

Chapter 31

With plenty of time and only a small overnight bag, Lucy decided it was easier to walk to the hotel even though there was a bitter wind blowing. The six and half hour journey from Bristol Temple Meads to Edinburgh Waverley had given her far too much time to think and now she needed to clear her head before meeting the bombastic Mr Oliver.

Although she'd been to the city a couple of times before, once for the Festival when she was a student and once to a conference, it had left a lasting impression of gothic splendour and magnificent historic buildings. As she left the station she could see the Castle perched up on the hillside away to her right. Battling against the wind she put her head down and walked up the steep incline of Cockburn Street to the Royal Mile. She followed the street down the hill past all the tourist shops with their tartan blankets, highland cattle stuffed toys, kilts, fudge and t-shirts, all bedecked with tinsel in a nod towards Christmas, towards the Scottish Parliament and Holyrood Palace.

She passed a few interesting looking bars, pubs and

restaurants all of which looked lively and busy, a few heads decked with paper crowns from crackers. The streets were, even in mid-December, packed with tourists, wrapped up in hats and scarves with raincoats, prepared for whatever the Scottish climate could throw at them. She wished she'd adopted Hekla's three-layer approach to the weather. During the train journey Hekla had sent her five WhatsApp messages complaining about Gretchen. Apparently Eyrun had flown into a huge rage, Kristjan was very unhappy and Brynja was threatening to leave. It gave her a grim satisfaction, although she felt sorry for Gretchen, remembering how much of a fish out of water she'd felt when she'd first arrived.

Her response had been. *Be kind to her. She's new. Remember how rubbish I was!*

Finally coming to the end of the Royal Mile, with Holyrood Palace in front of her and the rather beautiful contemporary buildings of the Scottish Parliament on her right, she crossed the road and after another five-minute walk she came to the hotel.

She nodded, her GM hat on already. The location in the shadow of Arthur's Seat was perfect. A little way out of the main city but close enough to Holyrood Palace and the Royal Mile that it would appeal to visitors. The building was one of those grand granite structures, made of large stone blocks, which looked sturdy and imposing as if built to withstand all the northern weather could throw at it.

A fizz of excitement sparked along with a sense of calm. She could live here. Live in this city. She'd fallen in love with it before.

Inside the hotel a weary looking receptionist greeted her.

'Can I help you?' she asked in a gentle Scottish accent, which immediately reminded Lucy of Alex. She tightened her fingers in a small self-defensive fist in her pocket.

'Yes. I've got a booking for one night in the name of Lucy Smart.'

The girl suddenly straightened up, her eyes darting this way and that.

'Welcome. Welcome. Yes, I have your booking right here. You're in the honeymoon suite.' She beamed. 'Our best room. Has a fine view of Arthur's Seat.'

'Well, that sounds wonderful.' Lucy gave her a gentle smile, surprised at getting the VIP treatment. 'Thank you. I'm supposed to be meeting Mr Oliver here. Has he arrived yet?'

The girl looked ready to burst. 'Oh yes. He's here. He's been here for a while.' Her big brown eyes communicated so many messages, Lucy couldn't decide if Quentin was inspiring terror, confusion or pleasure in the staff. 'He's in the Wee Tartan Room. Said to send you in as soon as you arrived.' Her voice dropped, her eyes growing wider as she said in a hushed tone, 'And to send in our best whisky.'

'I'd love a cup of tea,' said Lucy firmly.

'Right. Yes. Straight away.' The girl snapped to attention with military precision. She must have been all of eighteen.

Lucy gave her a smile. 'Do you mind if I leave my bag here and can you point me in the direction of the ladies?'

* * *

Freshened up, with a quick smear of lipstick and a swipe of mascara, tugging on her dress and donning a pair of heels to replace the flats she'd walked in, she left the ladies to face the intriguing and indomitable Mr Oliver.

The Wee Room was a tartan terror and it took all of Lucy's attention before she finally turned to greet Quentin Oliver, who was not at all what she was expecting. From his speech and gung-ho attitude, she was expecting someone quite rough and ready, well-built with a healthy paunch, certainly not this rather elegant silver fox with piercing blue eyes and a ready smile. She'd never imagined that he'd be dressed in a Noel Coward style plum velvet jacket and black polo neck, although the orange trainers were slightly incongruous.

'Hideous, isn't it?' he said, which almost made her laugh out loud, as he indicated the walls. Clearly he was oblivious to his own dress sense. She stared around the room, speechless as the sight of at least fifteen different tartan patterns covering the walls, the floor, the sofas and cushions hit her. A visual car crash of red squares, sharp black lines, yellow patches and smoky purple quarters. It was difficult to know where to look, although she could guarantee that if she had her way, those red glossed skirting boards would be the first to go.

'It's certainly colourful,' she replied, giving a scarlet and black foot stool a wide berth.

'I don't want colourful, I want tasteful. I want to be able to bring my wife here in mid-winter or in summer and for her to feel its cosy and comfortable. Your mission,' he paused

393

and grinned at her with sudden wicked charm, 'should you choose to accept, is to turn this into The Northern Holyrood Lodge.'

The young girl from reception scuttled in with a tray containing a pot of tea and cut-glass tumbler of whisky. She put it down on a glossy mahogany table which separated a sofa decked out in what Lucy recognised as Black Watch tartan and another which she would have described as punk tartan in its orange, purple, red and yellow.

'Tea?' asked Quentin with a fair amount of disdain as he sat down opposite her.

'I figured this was an interview,' said Lucy pouring herself a cup and settling back against the sofa. 'Perhaps you can tell me what you're looking for.'

She'd decided on the way up here, as the man had a fearsome reputation in the hotel world and he'd asked her here, she had absolutely nothing to lose, and, she'd decided, he was the sort of character who valued plain speaking.

'What would you change in this room?'

His blunt, unexpected question made Lucy smile. 'The red skirting board.'

'Why?'

'Because it jars and it looks a bit tacky. The over the top tartan, I would expect. We're in Scotland. It's fun. Although I would tone it down, perhaps just a couple of co-ordinating tartans. The soft heather coloured ones are a bit more soothing. And you can explain the tartans to a guest. I would look them all up so that I knew the names of all of them. The skirting board looks cheap and nasty. And not authentic. It bugs me.'

'Excellent answer. The job is yours.'

She stared at him over the rim of her tea cup.

'Seriously? On the strength of my views on tartan?'

'No, but if I don't give you the job, Alex will never come back. And if he thinks you're good enough, its good enough for me. But HR will give me a hard time if I don't pretend to interview you.'

'Sorry?' Lucy stared at him.

Quentin let out a laborious sigh. 'God give me a box of Weetabix. When was the last time you spoke to him?'

Lucy's mouth firmed in a mutinous line.

'I trusted him. He lied to me. He was spying on me.'

'You are flaming kidding me.' Quentin bashed his forehead with the heel of his hand. 'For crying out loud, the boy was doing his job. I pay his wages ... I'm also married to his mother.'

'What?' That was news. Alex had never mentioned that little nugget.

'He's my stepson. I met his mother when he was working for me. Had a devil of a job persuading her to marry me. Little sod refused to put a good word in. I had to prove myself.' Quentin's dreamy smile shocked the heck out of Lucy. The last thing she'd have thought Quentin was, was an old romantic.

'He was doing a job for me. And I prize loyalty. So does Alex. Come on love, if it were you. You strike me as a straight arrow. What would you have done?'

Bugger Quentin for reading her so damned well. In the same circumstances she probably would have done the same and once they started sleeping together, he was in a no-win situation.

His craggy face softened for a moment. 'When was the last time you saw him?'

'I haven't seen him since he went back to Paris.'

'When numbnuts resigned.'

'He did what?' Why the hell would Alex do that?

Quentin rolled his eyes. 'The grand gesture. Chuck everything away for the sake of love.'

Lucy stared at him. The man was a lunatic. Quentin held her gaze, his face hardening.

'I never had young McLaughlin down as a hot head or a fool for love. Had his knickers in a right old twist because I didn't give you the Iceland job. Resigned and flounced out.' Despite his aggrieved tone, there was a definite twinkle in Quentin's eye. 'The wife, incidentally his mother, thinks it's the most romantic thing she's ever heard.'

'Alex resigned?' Her vision blurred. Alex resigned. Because of her.

Shame washed over her. It had been easy to take the high ground that night, talking about trust, but she hadn't trusted him to do the right thing, despite the fact Alex had shown her in so many other ways that she could trust him. Perhaps, just perhaps, she'd messed up too.

'Yup. The blithering idiot didn't give me a chance to explain. He'd been emailing me glowing reports about you for the last month, telling me you were brilliant but like I said I'd already offered the job to Gretchen.' He screwed up his face. 'And I admit, I ignored his emails. I screwed up there but I was busy. For God's sake will you accept this job and tell him to stop being a big girl's blouse and come back to work for me. He's the best bloody manager I've ever had, although don't tell him that. I don't want it going to his head.'

Lucy smiled at that. Alex would never be big-headed or arrogant, he was far too kind and lovely for that. 'I don't know where he is?' she whispered, suddenly longing to see him. He resigned for her. Given up one of the best jobs in Paris, in Europe.

'We'll talk contracts later over drinks this evening...' he glanced up, his gaze shifting to a point over her left shoulder, 'but I ought to be going.'

Quentin rose and nodded at someone behind her. 'Afternoon, glad you could make it.'

'You didn't give me much choice, threatening to sue for breach of contract is a fairly brutal way of forcing someone's hand and insisting they fly all the way to Edinburgh to meet you. And Mum said she wouldn't speak to either of us until we'd sorted it out. So let's get this over with as quickly as possible because I've got someone to track down and I've wasted enough time as it is.'

At the sound of the familiar voice, a hot flush raced over Lucy's skin and she almost forgot how to breathe. Alex. She froze and closed her eyes, almost too scared to turn around in case she'd got it wrong.

'Desperate times. Desperate measures,' drawled Quentin

with an indifferent shrug. 'This is the bit where I duck out and leave you two to sort things out.' He lifted his whisky glass toasting them.

'Leave ... leave who?' Confusion filled Alex's voice and Lucy realised that he couldn't see her in the high back sofa. She rose slowly on new-born-foal, wobbly legs, her heart banging so hard she was worried it might burst out of her chest and turned to face him.

Alex's head jerked up as if he'd been shot and his eyes widened. The shock in his eyes was quickly replaced with a flash of temper. 'Where the hell have you been?'

Lucy almost smiled at his uncharacteristic grumpiness.

'I went back to Iceland and you'd gone,' he muttered.

Shifting awkwardly on the spot, she felt unaccountably nervous when he began to walk towards her with a purposeful stride and she thought he might shake her.

'I-I thought you'd left for good. You l-left without saying goodbye.' Her voice cracked. 'I assumed you'd gone back to Paris because your work was done.' The memory still hurt.

His mouth quirked and regret haunted his eyes. 'I went back to Paris because I was so furious with Quentin.'

Standing in front of her, he reached forward and took both her hands. 'I couldn't sleep. I had to see him face to face.' Alex eyes softened as his gaze roved over her face, greedily drinking in the sight of her. 'God I've missed you. I couldn't believe it when I went back to Iceland and you'd gone. Hekla was almost horrible to me.'

Lucy let out an unwilling snort. It was impossible to

imagine Hekla being horrible to anyone. She shrugged. 'There didn't seem to be much point in staying.' She swallowed, feeling the quick stab of betrayal again. 'Gretchen showed me the email you sent. The one where you said I wasn't manager material. And before I could talk to you, you'd gone without any explanation.'

'That's what I get for being impetuous.' Alex winced. 'She would. And I don't suppose she showed you the other nine that I sent to Quentin saying I'd misjudged you and that he would be mad to let you go.'

Lucy shook her head.

Alex took another step towards her, his hands framing her face, staring intently into her eyes. 'We must have literally crossed paths in the airport. I came back from Paris to tell you I'd told Quentin to stuff his job ... and you'd gone. Of course, I didn't have your phone number. Hekla said you'd gone back to England. And then Mum insisted I came to see her because she was upset that Quentin and I had fallen out ... which is why I'm here but what are you doing here?' His brow crumpled in a puzzled frown.

She gave him a tremulous smile. 'Having a job interview.'

'Really?' A smile crossed his face. 'And?'

'Quentin's offered me a job...'

He shook his head in startled disbelief. 'That's brilliant. Bloody Quentin, he's a sneaky sod. He never said a word to me.'

'I think there are conditions attached, it's on the proviso that you rip up your resignation.'

'I can do that but...' he paused and a serious expression

filled his eyes, 'can you forgive me. I'm sorry I didn't tell you who I was but ... at first I didn't feel I could and then, well it got too complicated.'

'I understand now. I couldn't swear to it, but I might have done the same. I'm sorry I didn't listen to you on the night Gretchen arrived. The next morning I woke up and wanted to speak to you, but you'd already gone. And then *she* wasted no time in stirring things up.'

'I'll forgive you, if you forgive me,' said Alex, with a delicious twinkle of mischief.

'We're negotiating are we,' teased Lucy, suddenly feeling so much lighter and happier.

'Looks that way,' he responded, looking down at her with a more serious expression.

She paused and looked up at him, wanting to get this right. 'I'm sorry that I didn't give you a chance to explain properly,' said Lucy. 'After the business with Chris, I automatically assumed the worst and that you were only looking out for yourself. It didn't occur to me that you were trying to protect me. I would have hated anyone to think that I'd got the job because we were sleeping together.'

He lifted a finger and brushed her cheekbone. 'No one who knows you would have ever thought that you'd got the job on anything but merit. You are brilliant, Lucy Smart. Can you forgive me for messing up?'

'I'll forgive you, if you forgive me,' she said with a low laugh, repeating his words back to him before standing on her tiptoes and wrapping her arms around his neck to kiss him quickly on the mouth.

Wrapping his arms around her, he pulled her back so that they were nose to nose.

'That's not quite enough,' he murmured.

In response she trailed a series of kisses along the underside of his jaw, her lips feeling the rasp of stubble and her heart pinging when she heard his indrawn breath as she worked her way to his mouth.

'Mmm,' he said with a throaty groan. 'You're getting there.'

Pressing her mouth against his, she slanted her lips over his to deepen the kiss, feeling his warm hands slide down her back to splay on her hips. Everything receded in the pleasure of the kiss and she was vaguely aware of the hiss and crackle of the open fire, the thunder of the pulse in her ears and the feel of Alex's warm, firm body against hers. When the fire popped, they both jumped, slightly breathless and smiling like idiots at each other.

'So, if I rip up my resignation?' asked Alex with a crooked grin. 'Will you accept the job?'

'I think I might.' She gave him a considering look. 'Although, it's rather dependent on how good the flight service is between Edinburgh and Paris.'

'I happen to know that there's an excellent service,' said Alex with a teasing smile. 'And it goes both ways.'

'You would come and visit me in chilly Edinburgh?'

'Try ... keeping ...me... away.' He punctuated each word with a kiss. 'Although I should warn you, you do know my mother lives near the city.' He pulled a face. 'But we could keep my visits on the down low.'

Lucy raised an eyebrow.

He looked around and put a finger over his lips. 'She's bossy, nosy and will want to get to know you.'

Lucy laughed. 'I'm sure I can cope.'

'I know you can. So, what do you think?'

'I think the case for accepting is pretty good.'

'Thank goodness for that. Although are you sure you want to work for Quentin? He can be a tricky old sod.'

'Are you kidding?' Lucy grinned. 'He's a terrible old romantic. He set us up today.'

'More like he's terrified of Mum.' He shook his head and rolled his eyes. 'She'll take all the credit for this. In fact, I wouldn't put it past her to have put Quentin up to this. She's a sucker for a love story.'

Lucy raised an eyebrow. 'This is a love story?'

Alex led her to the sofa and pulled her onto his lap. 'You bet. Beginning, middle and happy ending. I love you Lucy Smart, you're brave, loyal and gorgeous inside and out.'

'That's funny because I love you Alex McLaughlin because you're kind, gentle and look after me beautifully even when I think I don't need looking after.'

She leaned in to kiss him again.

'Dear God, are you two still making up?' Quentin stood there shading his eyes as if the view was too much for him. 'Can I just ask if I have a manager for this place and whether Alex will be getting his arse back to The Metropole any time soon?'

Lucy grinned at Alex and whispered. 'I'm booked into the honeymoon suite for the night.'

He grinned back, smoothing a strand of hair from her cheek taking his time before turning to Quentin.

'Sorry, we're still in negotiation, it's going to take some time but I think we'll have an answer for you by tomorrow morning.'

Quentin grunted and stomped back out of the Wee Room.

'Now, where were we?' asked Alex, his lips descending back down to hers.

She never answered.

Epilogue

'For the love of God, Lucy, Gretchen is chewing my ear off, can you stop poaching her staff.'

'She's still got Eyrun,' said Lucy, tracing the grain on the mahogany reception desk shooting a broad grin at Hekla who could hear every word of the telephone conversation with Quentin.

'No more, do you understand me. And when Alex gets there, have him call me. How are the plans coming along? We going to be ready for a March first opening?'

'Yes, Quentin,' she said for what felt like the fiftieth time, giving the newly decorated entrance hall with its Georgian paned windows, smartly painted plaster cornices and Wedgewood blue walls a proud new mama look. 'The bedrooms are all finished. The Wee Tartan Room has been redecorated and the chimneys have all been swept. The new sofas and armchairs were delivered yesterday and we're waiting for the electrics to be finished in the kitchen. You won't recognise the place.'

'I'd better not,' growled Quentin. She laughed, she'd learned pretty quickly that the best way to deal with his barky, overbearing exterior was to stand your ground. 'Make sure Alex calls me.'

'OK,' she said blithely, with absolutely no intention of passing the message on. She checked her watch for the thousandth time that afternoon. Alex would have left Charles De Gaulle by now and be somewhere above the Channel.

Over the last few months they'd managed to spend a couple of days together each week. Thanks to the power of Wi-Fi and excellent duty managers, Alex seemed to be able to work in Edinburgh nearly as well as in Paris.

When she put the phone down Hekla began to giggle. 'There is no one else to steal. Only Olafur,' she shot a sly look at Lucy, 'and he is too ashamed to dare ask to come.'

Lucy ignored the comment. She'd never said a word to anyone about what he'd done and if Hekla had her suspicions, they could stay that way.

'It's not as if I'm not stealing Elin,' said Lucy, 'she was mine to start with.'

As soon as the news that Lucy was going to manage The Northern Holyrood Lodge in Edinburgh broke, her phone had buzzed with texts. 'Besides, it's not as if I've had any choice in the matter.' She put her hands on her hips and rolled her eyes. 'You all told me you were coming to work for me, whether I wanted you or not.'

Hekla pulled an outraged face. 'Of course, you wanted us.'

Lucy laughed, and gave her a quick hug. 'I did. I'm thrilled that you did.'

'And me,' said Kristjan, bouncing into reception from the office, brandishing a newly printed menu on stiff cream card, which Hekla gave a narrow-eyed glare.

'Did you print that?' she asked bristling with suspicion.

'Ja,' he waved it at her in smug triumph.

Lucy laughed at the other girl. 'The printer seems to work perfectly as long as you stay away from it. It's brand new.'

'Hmph,' said Hekla, snatching the menu from Kristjan. 'What's for dinner?'

Tonight, Kristjan was trialling his menu in preparation for the official launch of the hotel the following weekend. For the last month, Lucy, Hekla and Brynja had been working non-stop managing the make-over of the hotel, setting up new systems, interviewing staff, not that Lucy needed to recruit that many, while Dagur had been helping Kristjan set up the kitchen and the bar, the two of them rapidly becoming whisky experts.

'Yes, what is for dinner?' asked Lucy leaving Hekla to peruse the menu. She had every confidence that it would be absolutely delicious. Kristjan had had a lovely few weeks visiting local suppliers and researching other restaurants and with so much to do in the hotel, she'd left him to it.

'Smoked salmon terrine, Angus beef with a potato and turnip rosti, my homage to neeps and tatties, glazed carrots, followed by a plate of local cheeses.' His eyes brightened. 'You have to try this chilli cheddar from the Isle of Mull.' He put his fingers to his mouth and mimed a chef's kiss.

'I shall be serving at seven-thirty unless Alex's plane is delayed.'

Lucy crossed her fingers and held them up. 'The last time I checked it was right on schedule. And on that note, I've got an hour to go and get ready and that nice new roll top bath in the Balmoral suite needs a road test.'

'I'm sure the mattress will be getting one later, too,' said Hekla.

Lucy blushed. Spending time with her Icelandic girl-friends had made her a little more open about sex but you didn't need to share too much information.

'Once we have paying guests, we'll all be up in the attics,' she said ignoring the ribald comment. Thankfully there was plenty of staff accommodation in the old servants' quarters at the top of the building, room enough for all the staff that had insisted on coming with her.

'Enjoy the bath,' said Hekla. 'I'm going to have a quick drink in the pub with Brynja and Dagur. We'll see you later. Don't work too hard Kristjan,' she teased patting him on the arm.

'I won't, but we don't have a bus boy yet, so you're on washing up duty.'

Hekla laughed. 'It will be worth it.'

'Where are you off to, the Kilderkin?' asked Lucy with a knowing tilt of her head.

'I might be,' said Hekla demurely. 'The beer is very good.'

'Cheap and the barman is rather handsome I recall and partial to tall, Icelandic blondes.'

Hekla allowed herself a small smug smile as Kristjan

glowered. 'I get served first.' She shot the chef a naughty smile. 'But I'm partial to Icelandic men.'

'Honey, I'm home.'

Lucy sat up quickly, drawing her knees to her chest, sloshing water over the side of the bath as she heard the thud of an overnight bag drop onto the new carpet in the other room.

'Alex?'

He peeped his head around the bathroom door. 'Expecting someone else?' He grinned at her and sauntered over, sinking beside the bath on his knees, and wrapping an arm around her to pull her in for a long, slow thoroughly satis-fying kiss.

'You're early,' she said beaming with pleasure.

'I caught the earlier plane, although I'd say I've arrived at exactly the right time. Nice bath. Room for a small one in there.'

'I'm not looking for a small one,' she quipped, her eyes dancing as she watched him strip off without any hesita-tion or modesty, her knees still clutched to her chest.

'Just as well. Scoot up.' He hopped in the bath, behind her, pulling her back as she twisted to lie on his chest. 'Now this is the perfect way to start a Friday night after a hard week in Paris. How's your week been?'

She giggled as he began to kiss her, his hands sliding down to cup her bottom.

In between kisses and caresses, they caught up with each other's news despite the fact they spoke every night on the phone. It became increasingly difficult to talk as she became more and more breathless in response to Alex's busy hands.

Finally, he sighed into her ear, his lips nuzzling her neck as his fingers took shameless advantage. 'Lovely as this bath is, it's not quite right for what I've got in mind.'

'Mmm,' was all she could say, her mind had turned into delightful mush and she knew exactly what he had in mind when he stood up, the water running down his hair slicked legs and a certain part of his anatomy primed for action.

They were only a few minutes late for dinner, although Alex's hair was still damp and Lucy had to spend quite some time teasing out the tangles in hers. Looking pink and flushed, she held Alex's hand as they walked down the rather wonderful sweeping staircase exchanging secretive smiles.

'They're going to know what we've been doing,' whispered Lucy, nibbling at her lip.

'Of course they are, and you know they're going to take the piss. We don't stand a chance. But don't forget,' he grinned at her, 'you're the boss, Lucy Smart. Threaten to dock their pay.' He winked.

She took a breath, knowing the comments would make her blush, and crossed into the dining room, rolling her eyes as a ribald cheer went up. Seated around a round table, sat Kristjan, Dagur, Brynja, Gunnar, Kristin, and Hekla and...

'Elin!' Lucy threw her arms around her. 'When did you get here?'

'I met Alex at the airport, we shared a taxi.'

She shot him a glance. 'You didn't tell me,' she pouted in a most un-Lucy like way.

'I got side-tracked.' He raised his eyebrows.

'Oh, this is lovely,' said Lucy forgiving him. 'Everyone's here.'

'Yes. Nice of you to join us at last,' said Brynja with a quick wink.

'I was checking out the new plumbing,' said Lucy, immediately regretting her choice of words. Luckily for once Hekla's colloquial command of English failed her. Alex ducked his head but she could see his shoulders shaking.

'How is the new bath?' asked Hekla.

Lucy smiled. 'Very satisfactory. How was your Scotsman?'

Hekla raised a glass. 'Very Scottish. He poured me lots of beer. I like Scotland a lot.' Everyone laughed. 'I'm so glad we came. And I still like Kristjan more.'

Kristjan smirked as he poured Lucy a glass of wine and handed it over. She took it and paused standing before the last empty chair.

'As we're all here together, I want to make a toast. To all of you, for trusting me and coming to share this new adventure. It,' she looked at each of them in turn, her gaze coming to rest on Alex's last, 'really means so much to me. This place ... it's lovely but you're the people that will make the difference. That will make it cosy and welcoming. I'm sure The Northern Holyrood Lodge is going to be a great success, because of all of you. Thanks for putting your faith in me.'

She raised her glass, as her friends all raised theirs in

tandem. She was among friends and she knew without a doubt she could trust every last one of them. Alex winked at her and mouthed. *I love you.*

Kristjan jumped to his feet and raised his glass, 'To you, Lucy Brynsdóttir,' and everyone repeated his words, which just about finished Lucy off.

Acknowledgements

This bit of writing a book is possibly my favourite, the writer's equivalent of an Oscar's speech, where you get to thank all the people who have helped whether they knew it or not.

First up, is my pal, Debi Game, who inadvertently put the idea into my head of removing things from someone who wasn't supposed to have them in the first place, resulting in the delicious consequence that they couldn't complain that they'd been removed.

Thanks to all my writerly friends who offer endless support and encouragement, both in real life and across the ether, particularly Donna Ashcroft, the lovely Darcie Boleyn and Sarah Bennett as well as my much loved agent, Broo Doherty, a saint who puts up with my author's angst with endless patience.

Gin helps enormously when you're on a deadline, and I'm fortunate that my husband is always ready to swoop to the rescue with a glass and that my children have developed the sterling ability to know when mum needs leaving be.

Julie Caplin

Last but not least, you, the readers who send me such lovely comments, leave kind reviews and keep buying my books. Thank you for enabling me to be a writer.

Fancy another escape with Julie Caplin?
For something a little bit warmer, don't miss

The Secret Cove in Croatia

Keep reading for a sneak peek at
the first two chapters...

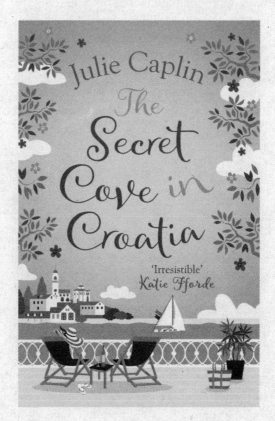

Chapter 1

Northumberland

Nick huddled into the collar of his coat, grateful for the thick tweed barrier that protected him from a brisk, northerly wind that whipped around the lea of the craggy hillside. A wry smile touched his mouth at the sight of the two models shivering together like highly strung Arabian fillies.

Today the models were dressed in vibrant — Pucci style, he'd been informed, whatever that was — wool ponchos. Although if anyone had asked his opinion, he'd have said it looked as if someone had run amok in a paint shop, but he was no fashion expert. The outfits were topped with dashing Tam O'Shanter hats, perched jauntily on their heads while striped woollen scarves, wrapped several times around their elegant long necks, flapped in the breeze like Himalayan prayer flags. The poor frozen models were as out of place as a pair tropical birds as they waited for the photographer to line up the next shot.

Normally at seven-thirty in the morning, he'd have the

417

bleak moorland to himself, although, if it weren't for the quelling looks his sister-in-laws had shot his twin brothers, Dan and Jonathon, over dinner last night, there might have been a few more people up here.

'Tara, stand on that rock in the shaft of sunshine,' directed the brusque photographer whose facial expression was well-hidden behind dark bushy eyebrows and a fearsome, glossy black beard of biblical proportions, a stark contrast to his bald head.

Nick had to give her credit, the minute Tara moved into the unforgiving eye of the lens, she stopped shivering and threw a cool indifferent pose as if the freezing temperature was nothing. Her thin, haughty face stared out over the view, dispassionate and seemingly oblivious to the valley unfolding before her; the rich green grass softening the contours of the hillside and the sunshine dancing on the distant sea at the mouth of the valley five miles in the distance. Something twisted in his stomach at the sight of her standing on the outcrop of rocks, with one knee bent, a delicate, almost fey figure with her flawless complexion and mane of golden hair burnished with red and gold threads picked out by the spring sunshine. She looked as if she might slip away into another realm at any moment. Then he told himself off for allowing the little kick of something to affect him and the odd desire to want to protect her from the cold. Compared to her, he was a steady, reliable carthorse hitched to unremitting destiny while she was like a delicate faerie creature, as unattainable and remote as the stars. She came from another world. A world a million miles away from this remote farm and the village community where he knew everyone and everyone knew him and had done since he was born. This was home. Always had been, always would be. His mouth twisted. Besides if he weren't here, what else could he do? This was all he'd ever known or was likely to know.

'Nick can you get one of the sheep into the foreground,' called a peremptory voice, waving a finger indicating where the animal was required.

'Sure,' he said, whistling to his border collie, Rex, and not bothering to correct the photographer's assistant. He'd tried to explain several times, but no one was interested in the difference between the sheep – actually ewes – and the lambs. They wanted the cute, photo friendly lambs, which were now six weeks old and more photogenic than the just about to be sheared sheep which looked scraggy and unkept with their mud encrusted, shaggy fleeces.

Since British Wool had approached him to photograph their brochure on Hadley land, offering to pay for his time, this job proved one of the most … entertaining was probably the best word. Who knew that taking a few photographs was actually a full-scale production? Two vans arrived two days ago, filled with several rails of clothes and enough photographic kit and caboodle to take pictures of the entire population of Bowden Rigg. These had been followed by three taxis from Carlisle station conveying a full entourage of four models, two stylists, two wardrobe ladies, the photographer, his assistant, a creative director, a PA and two clients from British Wool.

Rex rounded up one of the lambs, which skipped into shot baaing furiously making the model smile winsomely. 'Oh isn't he so cute.'

'He'd be a damn sight cuter if he stood still for a moment,' grumbled the photographer, peering through his lens.

Following a quick whistle and a few subtle commands, Rex nudged the skittish lamb back into place. Nick, impressed by her patience, watched as Tara tilted her head this way and that, angling her body to show off the garments. To his surprise, she turned her sleepy almond eyes his way, a sultry smile lifting the corners of her mouth as she stared rather blatantly at his.

'Yes, Tara. Yes, that look. Lovely. Lovely. Just tilt your head to the right, keep looking at Nick. Yeah, that's it. You want him bad. I'm loving it.'

A wicked glint lit the model's eyes and Nick felt himself blush to the very roots of his blonde hair and a heated flush raced up his body. With a swallow, he resisted the urge to duck his head. Instead he met her slightly mocking gaze, with a quick lift of one eyebrow and some heat of his own. Country born and bred didn't mean that he was clueless. Nick Hadley, to his mother's despair, had yet to find the right woman, but that didn't mean he hadn't played the field.

Tara smirked in retaliation and then, in accordance with the photographer's next slew of commands, put her hands on her hips and threw her head back, once again distant and unattainable. Nick suddenly felt like a third wheel, he had a ton of stuff that he should be doing this morning instead of hanging around like ... like a grubby school boy.

The photographer called out to Tara. 'OK, you're done for the moment.'

As Nick walked forward to chase the lamb back to the rest of the flock, Tara stepped forward to the edge of the rock. 'Catch me,' she said and launched herself into the air.

Surprised, Nick took a step forward and caught her easily in his arms. She weighed nothing and she crowed delightedly at his catch, as if he'd done something amazing, making him feel like every superhero rolled into one. Gently he set her down on the ground, disentangling himself from her poncho and scarf. He gave her a smile. 'There you go, safe and sound.'

'You're all man,' she breathed and, for a moment, he almost wanted to laugh it was such a clichéd line, but the knowing, suggestive look in her eyes stalled him.

'Last time I looked,' he said with easy confidence. Now it was her turn to blush. 'You're staying at The George Inn, in the village, I believe.'

She nodded. 'Quaint but I've stayed in worse on location.'

'Dinner?' asked Nick.

'Are you asking me, or telling me?' Tara replied, her eyes coy, with a gentle smirk playing around her mouth.

'There's a very good restaurant at the local manor house. I could pick you up at seven-thirty.'

'Make it eight and you have a date,' returned Tara, with the air of someone who was used to having her own way.

Damn, it was after six. It had taken longer than he'd planned to finish today. Unfortunately farming waited for no man and he had to catch up with those jobs that going out on the photo shoot had forced him to neglect.

The warm glow of the farmhouse kitchen, filled with the scent of sausages and Yorkshire pudding coming from the Aga and the comforting sound of chatter and laughter, embraced him – a hug of familiarity and simple pleasure. The huge pine table in the centre of the room was being laid by Gail, married to his eldest twin brother, Dan, and she looked up to give him a quick warm, smile. He liked both of his sisters-in-law, although had yet to fathom how on earth either of the twins, Dan and Jonathon, had persuaded them that they would make suitable husbands. But then he'd grown up with them.

'Hey Nick,' called Dan from where he stood in front of the dresser rummaging through the assorted phone chargers and cables. 'Long day.'

He nodded.

At thirty-three, like his twin brothers and their wives, he still ate in his mother's kitchen, partly through sheer laziness but also because the warm, busy kitchen had been so much part of his life for so long. However, much as he loved them all, he was thankful for his own small cottage on the edge of the farm which afforded the necessary privacy for a bachelor, especially one whose mother was keen for him to settle down.

'Hey Mum,' he turned to her. 'I'm sorry. I've only just finished work but I'm going out tonight.'

'Excellent,' said Jonathon, eying up the toad in the hole, she was in the process of removing from the Aga. 'More sausages for me.'

'Are you sure you don't have time for a quick bite to eat? I'm literally serving up now. You can eat and run,' she grinned at him. 'I don't mind.'

'Or he could sod off down the pub and leave the sausages for us,' said Jonathon, dancing past his mother and pinching a piece of crisp Yorkshire pudding.

She gave his knuckles a sharp wrap.

'Yeah, I vote for more sausages,' agreed Dan, backing up his twin. 'You can sod off to the pub.'

'There's plenty,' said Lynda Hadley, shaking her head with a tut. 'Honestly boys, you'd think you'd been starved all your life. It'll take me two minutes to serve up and your father should be here any second.'

Bugger. He'd really hoped to make his excuses and make a quick get-away.

'No, seriously Mum. I haven't got time. I haven't even washed up yet.'

'But when will you eat? You've been up since silly o'clock and I bet you only had sandwiches for lunch.'

'I'm eating out,' he said, edging towards the door.

Just then his father came in, tossing his car keys on the dresser on the side, scooping his wife up for a quick kiss.

'Evening. I've just been in the village. I hear you're eating at Bodenbroke Manor this evening, Nick.' He raised his eyebrows with a knowing twinkle in his eyes.

Nick held back the groan. *Thanks Dad, drop me in it, why don't you?*

'Bodenbroke Manor,' piped up Jonathon, settling against the back door, his arms folded and a mischievous smile playing on his face. 'Now that's posh. A date, is it? Who's the lucky girl this week?' He frowned. 'I thought you'd finished with that posh, horsey bird.'

'Her name is Henrietta,' said Nick with a frown. 'And I'm not seeing her anymore.'

'Didn't last long,' observed Gail, with a sly smile.

Nick shrugged, edging ever closer to the door, hoping that Jonathon would move sooner rather than later. 'It was mutual.'

'When did you fix this up?' asked Dan, joining in the conversation, having found a charger to fit his phone and plugged it in. His face creased in sudden interest.

'Today,' said Nick, 'Look if the inquisition can lay off, I need to shower and change.' He was so close to the door and he actually had his hand on the doorknob, when Dan suddenly crowed.

'It's one of those London photo women, isn't it? You've been up on Starbridge Fell all day. You sly devil. You asked one of them out.'

Jonathon laughed and stepped back to block the door. 'What? And they said yes?'

Nick froze. 'Why shouldn't they?' he asked, regretting the sudden stiffness in his voice.

'Punching above your weight, aren't you?' teased Dan. 'Which one is it? One of the wardrobe ladies? The blonde one. What's her name, Georgina?'

Nick shook his head.

'What the darker one?'

'Neither of them,' he said trying to keep his face pleasant.

'Well, who then?' asked Jonathon, screwing his face up in perplexed confusion. 'The stylist woman is married and so is the PA and Creative Director.

'Bloody hell, you didn't pull a model, did you?' gasped Dan, pretending to reel back bumping into a chair which screeched across the tiled floor in protest.

Gail and Cath shook their heads in mutual mock despair at Dan's theatrics and then Gail said with a naughty grin, 'And why not? Let's face it, he's the best looking one out of all of you.'

Dan clutched his chest. 'I'm hurt, dear wife. I thought I was.'

'You're the best looking of my husbands,' she teased, winking at Nick, who was grateful for the brief diversion in conversation. Sadly, Jonathon wasn't about to let go.

'Seriously? Which one?'

Nick sighed, knowing if he were going to get out of here in time to wash and change, capitulation was the only solution. 'I'm going out with Tara. We got chatting. We fancied dinner together. For God's sake, it's not as if I'm going to ask her to bloody marry me or anything. She'll be gone by the end of the week. And I'll still be here,' his voice rose. Realising that he'd made a bit of a tit of himself, he grasped the door handle and yanked it open, leaving behind a collective gasp and a telling silence.

'Gosh, this place is really rather nice,' said Tara, taking in the expensive wallpaper, which reputedly cost over two hundred pounds a roll, the stylish furniture and the retro designed lighting. 'We could almost be in London,' she added in a conspiratorial whisper behind one hand.

Nick lifted his wine glass and took a sip. 'We're not all heathens up here, you know.'

'I think I can see that,' said Tara, giving his body a rather blatant once over.

From the minute he'd picked her up from the George, she'd been flirtatious and forthright, which was a huge relief. If he were honest, as he was driving to collect her, he'd had a sudden last-minute panic. What on earth he was going to talk to her about all evening?

He needn't have worried, as he'd helped hoist her tiny frame into his truck, she murmured. 'Oh this is very masculine,' as she settled herself into the seat. 'I don't think I know anyone who drives a truck,' she'd said, drifting her hands across the dashboard as he started the engine up. Within a few miles one hand had drifted to his thigh and he drove the rest of the way trying to not to wriggle like an over-excited teenager.

She wore a chiffon, floaty pantsuit thing with tiny straps that dipped so low it made it obvious she wasn't wearing a bra. Her legs in skyscraper heels, so high you surely needed a health and safety certificate to walk in, looked endless and made his heart bump uncomfortably in his chest. She was the most gorgeous woman he'd ever laid eyes on. Her glorious hair was bundled in a big messy up do of some sort, with lots of tendrils curling around the white alabaster column of her throat.

For God's sake, get a grip man, she's a flesh and blood woman not a flaming Greek statue.

'How long have you been modelling?' he asked, forcing himself to make sensible conversation instead of staring at her like a love-sick puppy.

'For ten years,' she pulled a self-deprecating face. 'I'm old.'

'Don't be ridiculous,' he laughed. 'What, you're twenty-six, twenty-seven?'

'Twenty-seven,' she whispered, looking around the room, 'but don't tell anyone. That's quite old in this business. Although I'm ready to move on now. Do something a bit more meaningful, you know? I'd like to be an ambassador for something worthwhile. You know saving the planet. Eradicating plastic. Something like that.'

'Sounds noble,' he teased.

For a moment her nostrils flared and he saw the tendon in her neck tense.

'I'm serious. I feel very passionate about some of the issues facing our planet. The amount of plastic in the sea is a terrible thing. It's a big issue. Animals are dying.' She fixed him with a rather intense stare.

'Sorry, I didn't mean to belittle your ambition. I was teasing. I'm used to brotherly banter.'

She dipped her head with gracious acquiescence. 'We have to save our planet.'

'You're right,' he concurred realising that this was a big deal to her. 'Although I tend to get worked up about issues closer to home I guess.' He gave a self-deprecating smile. 'Bit selfish really. We're already seeing the effects of climate change on the seasons.' Last year's hot dry summer had had a major impact on the grasslands where the sheep grazed. 'So what will you do?'

She shrugged. 'I'll be an ambassador. You know, do photo shoots highlighting the issues. Be the face of a campaign. I'm just waiting for the right offer.'

Nick nodded, feeling a little out of his depth. He had no idea how these things worked. They lapsed into silence for a minute, until the waiter came to take their order.

'I'll have the Medallion of beef,' said Tara before adding to Nick's surprise, 'And can I have chips with it?'

'We do pomme frites,' said the waiter, in a slightly stuffy accent, which made Nick want to laugh. They played five a-side together on Thursdays and he was light years from stuffy.

'Perfect,' said Tara.

Nick grinned as soon as the waiter departed taking his own order for confit of duck and seasonal vegetables. 'And there you've blown the preconception that models never eat anything but salad and carrot sticks.'

Tara tossed her hair over her shoulder. 'I have a fabulous metabolism. I can eat what I like.' She almost sounded defiant. Nick smiled. 'That's good to hear as the food here is excellent.'

Tara nodded and picked at the tines of her fork, before rearranging her cutlery several times.

'So, do you have any brothers or sisters?' Nick asked to fill the silence.

She shook her head, pulling her mouth into a sad little moue. 'Just little old me. Mummy and Daddy had me very late in life. Poor Mummy nearly died, so Daddy put his foot down and said no more children. Mummy said that I was such a beautiful child, she was glad she couldn't have any more children because she could bear risking having another child in case they were a disappointment.' Tara gave a tinkling laugh and tilted her head on one side looking up at him. 'Isn't that the sweetest thing? Of course, utter nonsense. All parents think their babies are perfect.'

Nick laughed. 'You should speak to my mother. She doesn't have any illusions about her children, but then she had five of us.'

'Five! Good lord,' Tara's eyes widened dramatically and put her hand on her stomach. 'Gosh. That's a lot. Your poor mother. That must have wrecked her figure.'

Nick's mother would have laughed her head off at that comment, she adored all of her children. 'I'm not sure she sees it like that.'

'Are they all as good looking as you?' Tara slapped her hand over her mouth, as if the compliment had slipped out by accident. She lowered her eyes to the table.

Nick laughed, thinking of the conversation between his brother and sister-in-law as he'd left. 'I'm one of four brothers and one sister. I think we all agree that our little sister is the best looking.'

'Oh,' said Tara, as if this were a very strange thing to say.

'So what do you do when you're not sheep farming?' she asked.

'It's not exactly a nine to five job,' said Nick, 'but when I can, I like to get away from the farm. My sister lives in Paris—'

'Oh I adore Paris. I was there for the Paris Fashion Shows. I did a catwalk show for Dior this year. It's such a super city. When were you last there?'

They talked Paris, with Nick dredging up everything he could possibly remember of his two visits there, until dinner arrived.

Tara certainly had a healthy appetite and scoffed down her food as if she were starving.

'You were hungry,' he said, looking at her clean plate as he finished the last of his food.

'I was in the fresh air all day,' snapped Tara, again sounding defensive.

'I had no idea modelling was such hard work,' said Nick, appeasing. Clearly she wasn't used to the sort of banter he enjoyed with his family. He ought to remember she wasn't from a big family like his.

'It's not for everyone. I don't think people realise how hard it is. They just think we turn up and have our photos taken.'

The waiter appeared and took away their plates before returning with the dessert menu.

'Would you like anything else?' he asked.

'I shouldn't,' said Tara, perusing the menu, her tongue poking out rather adorably between her lips. 'Are you going to have anything?'

'I've not really got a sweet tooth.'

Her face fell.

'But we could share something perhaps?' he suggested.

'Yes, the profiteroles. I adore them.'

Nick ordered dessert with two spoons, although he needn't have bothered because although the dish was placed in front of him, as quick as a snake, Tara's hand would strike and snatch a spoonful of choux pastry and cream. She made regular moans of delight with each mouthful.

'I haven't had chocolate in ages. I'd forgotten how delicious it is. Such a sensual pleasure, don't you think.' She dipped her spoon in the last of the chocolate sauce and slowly licked the back of it, with long slow strokes, all the while her eyes intent on Nick. She let out a breathy sigh. 'That silky richness on your tongue.' She ran her tongue up and down the handle of the spoon, her eyes dark and sultry with the sort of promise that had Nick shifting in his seat, very relieved that the table cloth was covering things up.

When the waiter came to clear away the dessert dish, Nick was ready to decline coffee and take Tara straight back to the George. Given the suggestive signals she'd been sending him, he thought they were on the same page, but she rose from her seat, tossing her napkin on the table.

'Darling, could you order me an espresso. I just need to go to the ladies. Sort myself out.'

'OK,' he said, ordering himself a cappuccino and settled back in his seat, feeling his heated skin start to cool. He pulled out his phone quickly checking his Facebook feed, smiling as he saw a post from his sister, Nina.

Chocolate Heaven was the caption underneath a perfect chocolate éclair and her fingers and thumbs just beyond it, shaped in a love heart.

God, how much would Tara enjoy one of those and what sort of state would he be in watching her eat it?

Looks delish, sis, he posted quickly, scrolling through more of her pictures. Since moving to Paris to run a patisserie and moving in with her boyfriend, Sebastian, who happened to be Nick's best friend, Nina had become the queen of éclairs and all things sugar. Perhaps he could take Tara there one day. He had a sneaking suspicion she might rather like it.

He commented on a few pictures, liked a few others and then realised a full fifteen minutes had elapsed. Where was Tara? Please don't say she'd done a runner. No, surely not. Despite his pre-date qualms, it had gone pretty well. She certainly seemed interested. Without being big headed about it, he got on with women. Most dates he went on turned out well, more than well sometimes, although there had been the one time he'd been on a blind date with one of Gail's friends, who turned out to be best friends with one of his exes. That had been rather excruciating.

Just as he was seriously considering sending a search party up to the ladies, Tara reappeared, her eyes glittery and her face all smiles as she slipped back into her seat and took a sip of Espresso as if there was nothing wrong.

Perhaps she'd had some female issue and she was too embarrassed to say anything.

'Ugh, this espresso is cold,' she said, pulling a face.

'Would you like me to get another?' said Nick equably, not wanting to make her feel self-conscious by saying that she had been rather a long time.

'No, it's OK. It's quite late now and it will probably keep me awake.' She looked at her watch and then gave him a beautiful, sorrowful smile. 'You need to drop me back at the hotel. I'm afraid I need my beauty sleep. I can't turn up tomorrow with bags under my eyes.'

'Let me get the bill,' said Nick, wondering at what point the evening had suddenly petered out.

Chapter 2

London

Maddie gripped her knees together, her hands clasped over the kneecaps to stop them shaking, as Henry Compton-Barnes, complete with suede patches on the elbows of his jacket and dicky bow, stared down at her work. It seemed to take forever before he finally looked up and spoke.

'Professor Gregory is a good friend of mine and you've come highly recommended. I shall therefore be completely honest with you.' His mouth pulled into a regretful line as if someone were tugging at strings attached to each end of his lips. 'Technically you are very good. These are well executed. The detail, in fact, brilliant.'

Despite the words, she knew there was a giant sized 'but' headed her way.

'What I'm looking for in a painting ... for this gallery...' he shook his head. 'These have no originality. No flair. They're missing that *je ne sais quoi*, the indefinable, that makes a piece of art stand out. What I'm looking for is something that only the artist can conceive. When you look at their work, you know that only they could have painted it. I liken it to a singer, someone like, forgive me, I'm considerably older than you, but someone like, Carly Simon for example. You hear her voice and you know immediately it's her. Her voice, like a signature, is unique and that's what I'm looking for in a painting.

'These I'm afraid, are good, very good but I don't see your soul, or any investment from you as an individual.

'Can I give you some advice, Maddie? Go somewhere new and different. Forget everything you've ever been taught or thought you knew – break the rules – experiment but, most of all, paint from the heart.'

Paint from the heart. Maddie rolled her eyes picturing a Salvador Dali image of a red heart skewered by giant paint brush on a desert plain, with scarlet drops dripping from the brush onto the pale-yellow sand. Paint from the heart. What the hell did that mean? Had anyone told Picasso to paint form the heart? Rodin? Van Gogh? Maddie winced. Not that she was anywhere close to emulating anyone in that league.

She sipped at her coffee regretting the impulse to drown her sorrows with a ridiculously expensive cappuccino.

'Dear God,' drawled an upper-class voice as someone sat down behind her. 'What a chav. What was Henry thinking?'

'What? That girl that's just been in? I thought she was in fancy dress. You know Toulouse Lautrec.'

Maddie clutched the felt beret on her lap under the table.

'He was doing a friend a favour. He told me when he put the appointment in the diary.'

'Did he take her on? Surely not. God, the gallery would be going downhill fast.'

'Don't think so. By the look of her when she left, I think he sent her out with a flea in her ear. I could have told him when she turned up he was wasting his time. I mean, seriously, did you hear the way she spoke?'

The other girl let out a peal of laughter. 'Common as muck.'

'Sshh, you can't say things like that now. It's not PC. I'm not sure you're even allowed to say chav anymore.'

Both girls laughed with malicious superiority as Maddie flushed, feeling the heat in her cheeks. She probably looked like an overripe Christmas elf. Picking up her beret, she crammed it firmly onto her head and turned around. One of the girls looked up and at least had the grace to start, her mouth opening in a gasp.

'Thing about chavs,' said Maddie conversationally, 'is that they have no class, speak their minds and don't take crap from supercilious, stuck up bitches like you two. Not all of us were born into money and quite frankly if that's how you talk about people, you need to go back to school and learn some manners. You should be ashamed of yourself.'

Pleased with the way both girls sat there gawping like a pair of guppies, she sailed out of Costa with her head held high.

Unfortunately having the last word didn't change the fact that she had failed at her one and only shot at actually getting through the doors of a gallery in London and used up her only useful contact.

Maddie glared up at the departures board at Euston. Another two hours before her cheap fare train departed. Back to Birmingham and another conversation with her mum about another failed job interview. Maddie hadn't actually told anyone apart from Professor Gregory what she was really doing in London.

Sighing she scrolled through her WhatsApp feed.

Urgent. Urgent. Urgent. Do you still need a job?
It's temporary but it's in Europe and they're desperate. Call me. Nx

The message from her friend Nina, made her smile. They'd met in Paris while Maddie was on her year of study abroad and, with so much in common, had quickly become firm friends. Both came from big families and, like Nina, Maddie was one of five, and while they missed being part of a community, they didn't necessarily miss the demands of their families.

The key word in the brief message was Europe. A siren call. Maddie longed to get as far away from home as possible. Since her year abroad in France, last year, she just didn't feel like she fitted in anymore.

'OK, what's the deal?' she asked, as Nina picked the phone on the first ring. 'Where in Europe? And what? Grape picking?'

'Something much classier.' Nina's voice bristled with that *ta-dah excitement*. 'It's Croatia.'

'Did you just sneeze?'

'Very funny. No, seriously. Nick phoned Sebastian half an hour ago. He's going on this amazing holiday lined up with his new girlfriend, a bunch of them are chartering a yacht ... but the girl that was going to work on board as a hostess dropped out yesterday and they go in three days' time. All you have to do is a bit of cleaning and cooking. Basically looking after the guests. And there are only six of them.'

'I'm your girl,' said Maddie, without hesitation, despite the fact that she'd never been on a boat in her life, unless you counted the pedalo in Tenerife that time. Her cooking skills had come on loads, for someone who's repertoire once consisted of nothing more than shepherd's pie and Lancashire hotpot. Thanks to a bit of tuition from Nina's chef boyfriend, Sebastian, she'd learned a lot in six months. Besides didn't everyone on holiday live on salads and ice cream?

Nina squealed. 'Brilliant. You need to phone this Croatian guy. I'll WhatsApp his number. Oh, you're going to have such a great time. Three weeks in Croatia! I'm quite jealous.'

Maddie squealed back. 'That's so cool. Thanks so much, Nina. And I can't wait to meet your brother. I feel like I know him already.'

HELP US SHARE THE LOVE!

If you love this wonderful book as much as we do then please share your reviews online.

Leaving reviews makes a huge difference and helps our books reach even more readers.

So get reviewing and sharing, we want to hear what you think!

Love, HarperImpulse x

Please leave your reviews online!

amazon.co.uk   kobo   goodreads   L♥vereading   iBooks

And on social!

f/HarperImpulse   **🐦@harperimpulse**
📷@HarperImpulse

LOVE BOOKS?

So do we! And we love nothing more than chatting about our books with you lovely readers.

If you'd like to find out about our latest titles, as well as exclusive competitions, author interviews, offers and lots more, join us on our Facebook page! Why not leave a note on our wall to tell us what you thought of this book or what you'd like to see us publish more of?

/HarperImpulse